THE KILT MAKER

Kilt maker Kirsty Muir finds life hard in sixties Edinburgh where money is tight and excitement hard to find. When a charming Scottish fiddler, Jake MacIver comes into her life and introduces her to a glamorous new world, it seems she has finally found her way out. However, when one day he disappears off on tour, Kirsty is left broken hearted. Her heart is mended by Andrew Macrae, owner of the kilt shop and it seems as though Kirsty will find happiness after all. That is until the day when she finds Jake waiting outside her door, full of apologies and claims of love. Kirsty must now make a decision: follow her first love or settle for the dependability of Andrew. Or is there another way?

Anne Douglas titles available from Severn House Large Print

THE GIRL FROM WISH LANE
A SONG IN THE AIR

THE KILT MAKER

Anne Douglas

Severn House Large Print
London & New York

This first large print edition published 2011
in Great Britain and the USA by
SEVERN HOUSE PUBLISHERS LTD of
9-15 High Street, Sutton, Surrey, SM1 1DF.
First world regular print edition published 2009 by
Severn House Publishers Ltd., London and New York.

British Library Cataloguing in Publication Data

Douglas, Anne, 1930-
  The kilt maker.
  1. Women tailors--Scotland--Edinburgh--Fiction.
  2. Fiddlers--Fiction. 3. Edinburgh (Scotland)--Fiction.
  4. Love stories. 5. Large type books.
  I. Title
  823.9'14-dc22

  ISBN-13: 978-0-7278-7910-3

Severn House Publishers support The Forest Stewardship Council
[FSC], the leading international forest certification organisation. All
our titles that are printed on Greenpeace-approved FSC-certified paper
carry the FSC logo.

Printed and bound in Great Britain by the
MPG Books Group, Bodmin, Cornwall.

PART ONE

One

Kirsty Muir, key in hand, stood at the door of Macrae's kilt shop, looking out at the late January afternoon that might have been night. So dark, so bitter, yet only five o'clock. There were the Edinburgh clocks, striking the hour. Closing time!

Shivering, in spite of her thick blue sweater, she took some breaths of the sharp air, for the room where she worked as a kilt maker was stuffy, and thought how quiet the ancient High Street seemed under its mist-ringed lights. Only a few brave souls were hurrying by, well wrapped against the cold.

Kirsty liked it when it was busy. When better weather brought great tides of visitors sweeping down from old St Giles to Holyrood, soaking up all the colourful history that seemed part of the very stones of the famous Edinburgh street. Aye, and stopping sometimes to look round at tartans and sporrans in Macrae's fine old shop, even occasionally ordering kilts like local folk.

Couldn't expect such excitement in January of course, and on that evening in 1964, even the sales were over, and the shop was as quiet as the street. Which was why they were closing early.

* * *

'Hi, Kirsty!' called tall, dark Dermot Sinclair, the sales assistant, from his wide counter in the front part of the shop. 'You're letting all the cold air in! How about locking the door?'

Kirsty, twenty years old and pretty, with copper-coloured hair and velvety brown eyes, laughed and turned the key in the heavy door, half glass, half oak, that was part of the original shop opened in 1920 by Henry Macrae, the present owner's father.

The plate glass windows on either side, displaying models dressed in elegant plaids and doublets, were replacements dating from the fifties, so were still considered 'new' in 1964, but nothing else in Macrae's could be described as new. Good quality, solid oak fittings – shelves, drawers, racks – subdued carpeting, heavy bevelled mirrors, well-placed chairs – these, Kirsty knew, were what made the difference between Macrae's and newer, cheaper kilt shops, and were what the clientele expected. And as some of the clientele seemed as old as the fittings themselves, Kirsty and her colleague Lil couldn't see any changes coming. It would not be Macrae's if they did.

'Beat me to it,' Dermot told her as she came back, twirling the key, into what they called the front shop. 'You know it's my favourite job, locking the door at closing time.'

'You saying you don't love your work, Dermot?' Kirsty smiled. 'Why, selling and hiring and chatting up customers suits you to a T.'

'Aye, but I like going home, too. And going

8

out. Fancy coming to a disco tonight?'

'Sorry, Dermot, no' tonight.'

'Other plans, eh?'

'No, but look at the weather. Once I get home to Pleasant Hill, I shan't feel like turning out again.'

'Aye, it's a fair trek to Pleasant Hill. Bet you get sick of it, eh?'

'Bet I do.'

'Maybe we can go out from here some time then?'

'Maybe we can. Some time.'

Kirsty moved on into the workroom at the rear of the shop, the hub of Macrae's, where the kilts were made. Measurements worked out, tartan cut, pinned, bound, stitched, stiffened, pressed. Say it quickly and it didn't sound much. But – think of it – six thousand stitches in every kilt! No wonder it had taken Kirsty five years to learn her craft.

She loved it, too. Always had, ever since she'd left school early to work as a trainee. Loved the smell of the tartans and the leather of the strap fastenings; loved the long tables where she spread out her work, and the drawer at the side where she kept her shears, tape measure and needles. This was her own special world. Which didn't mean to say she wasn't aware of other people's worlds in the 1960s, and of how exciting they might be. And thinking sometimes that she wouldn't mind seeing something of those worlds for herself. Didn't seem likely that she ever would, of course.

Everything was tidy now in the workroom, ready for the night. Just the way Mrs MacNee, the senior kilt maker, liked it. Och, she was a fusspot, all right, but a wonderful needlewoman and teacher, who had trained both Kirsty and lively Lil Buchanan to her own exacting standards. Even if at times she could make them want to tear their hair out, they had to admire her, eh?

After all, she had devoted more than half her life to Macrae's. Could even remember old Mr Henry, long dead, who'd founded the firm, and still thought of his son and present owner as 'young Mr Andrew'.

Now, as she tied a headscarf over the greying ridges of her perm, she checked with Kirsty if she'd been sure to turn the sign round on the door so that it showed 'Closed'.

'Yes, Mrs MacNee, I turned it round.'

'That's good, dear; don't want folk thinking they can still come in.'

'Very few out in weather like this.' Lil – blonde, freckle-faced and attractive – was gasping with the effort of pulling on her wellingtons. 'Hogmanay's over, the sales are over, it's all gone quiet.'

'Still, you never know who'll be wanting a kilt or a sporran for Burns Night, or whatever,' Mrs MacNee declared. 'Just when you want to get away, in they want to come.'

Lil laughed and, having won the battle with her Wellingtons, moved closer to Kirsty.

'Dermot want you to go out again? One of these days you might really go.'

'I wouldn't mind going out somewhere, but

10

no' with Dermot.'

'He's very attractive, though.'

'He is. Just no' my type, I suppose.'

'How about going to the New Club for drinks with Mr Macrae, then? You know he pushed off early? All right for some, eh?'

'The New Club's a bit old for me,' Kirsty answered, admiring her calf-length leather boots with buckles and square toes, a Christmas present from her stepmother, Lena. As for going anywhere with Mr Macrae, she couldn't imagine it. Why, he was over thirty! And probably had some well-to-do girlfriend his mother thought suitable – if she thought anybody could be.

'Hey, I'm away!' she cried, glancing at the workroom clock. 'I'll miss my bus if I don't watch out. Goodnight, Mrs MacNee. You coming, Lil?'

'Too right, I am. I want to get home, too.'

'You folk let yourselves out, then I'll lock up again,' Mrs MacNee told them. 'Take care, now, it's a terrible night.'

'Walk you girls to Princes Street?' asked Dermot, appearing in the doorway with a raincoat over his jacket and kilt.

'If you're quick, then.'

'Better watch out. The snow's turned to slush.'

'I'm wearing my new boots, I'll be OK,' Kirsty said, buttoning her coat and turning up her collar.

But outside in the slush, with the wind tearing at them like a mad thing, she was glad to take Dermot's arm, and so was Lil. Making their way gingerly up the High Street and down the Mound

11

to Princes Street, they laughed together at nothing much and parted at Kirsty's bus stop.

'You be all right?' asked Dermot, who, with Lil, had to cross to Hanover Street to catch the number 23. 'Haven't missed your bus, have you?'

'No, I've a few minutes to spare. See you tomorrow, then?'

'Aye, tomorrow. Goodnight, Kirsty!'

'Goodnight, goodnight!'

Standing in the queue, slapping her arms with her gloved hands, Kirsty watched them run across the road, dodging traffic, not waiting for the lights. What a pair, eh? Now, was that Angie she could see, dodging traffic too, but coming her way? She hoped so. If she wasn't in one of her moods, her stepsister would be company on the long ride to Pleasant Hill.

Two

Kirsty's brother, Reid, always said that Angie Ramsay wasn't really their stepsister. Not a relative at all, as she was only their stepmother's niece. But then they'd all three been brought up by Lena, after she married Callum Muir, and that made Angie a sort of relative in Kirsty's view. Even if sometimes she got the impression that Angie herself didn't believe she 'belonged'.

Anyway, here she came now, slipping across

12

the street in the flimsiest of little shoes. Tall pale Angie, with her unfashionably long fair hair, and her sweet mouth that rarely smiled. Only seventeen, she'd already had several jobs, and would probably soon leave the hairdresser's in Frederick Street where she was working now. Shampooing, sweeping the floor – it was not for her. Too boring. But then Angie found most things boring.

'You're early, eh?' Kirsty asked, pleased that she would after all have Angie's company on the bus trip to the other end of the city. If anything was boring, that was! On winter nights like this, you couldn't even see out of the windows, and with the usual fog of cigarette smoke, couldn't see much inside either. 'How'd you get away, then?'

'Och, the weather's been that bad, there were no clients in, so Mr Logan said we might as well go.' Angie, hatless in the keen wind, did fling a thin scarf around her neck, but seemed not to mind the cold. 'Suits me, I can tell you.'

'It's time you found a proper job to train for,' Kirsty told her earnestly. Though only twenty, she sometimes felt the need to give advice to Angie – though heaven knew, she got plenty from Lena, as did Kirsty herself.

'Like you, you mean?' Angie gave a shrug. 'Stay for ever in one place? I'd never stick it.'

'If you really liked the work, you would.'

'Could never imagine liking any work as much as that.'

'I do.'

'But you're different. Seem to be. D'you never

13

want a change, then? From Macrae's?'

Kirsty kept her eyes on the buses going by.

'I'm a kilt maker, it's my job,' she answered at last. 'But sometimes – OK – I'd like to see something new. I mean, there's so much happening these days that we never get the chance to see.'

'Have to keep looking,' Angie said shortly, as her scarf fluttered at her neck and her eyes glittered in the streetlights. 'I'm always looking.'

But for different things from me, Kirsty thought, as their bus suddenly rolled up to the stop and the queue began to move.

Sitting at the back of the bus, squashed in with silent pasengers reading evening papers, Kirsty stole a glance at Angie's profile. Her fine nose, her quite noble brow, her mouth, as usual, turned down. Poor Angie. Never at rest. With no father and a mother who'd dumped her, it was no wonder she always seemed unsettled. Though given a home, was never at home, in spite of all that was done to make her feel so. What more could anyone do?

Feeling Kirsty's gaze, Angie turned her head.

'You see in the paper The Beatles are going to America next month?'

'Aye, they were saying so at the shop. Probably send all the American girls crazy, just like here.' Kirsty folded her bus ticket. 'I wouldn't mind seeing America.'

'Pretty tough place, seeing as somebody killed the President.'

14

'Terrible, eh?' Kirsty reflected for a moment on the assassination of President Kennedy only a couple of months before, but then her brow cleared. 'Shouldn't blame a whole country for something like that, though. I bet it'd be a grand place to see, with plenty going on.'

'Not much going on where we live. Or at Macrae's, either.'

'Never expect it at Macrae's,' Kirsty said, and laughed as the bus moved on, through a very different Edinburgh from Princes Street, taking the girls home.

Home to Pleasant Hill, a council estate of multi-storey flats beyond the areas of Gorgie and Sighthill. Almost, but not quite, into open country. Certainly the tenants never felt that they were in the country, even though the blocks of ten-storey flats had all been given the names of plants: Harebell, Heather, Briar and Clover. No, they didn't feel that they were in the country, or in the city, either. A sort of limbo, perhaps.

Yet the intentions had been good. Like the rest of the estates springing up around the city, Pleasant Hill had been built to rehouse people from the old tenements, providing space, fresh air and all 'mod cons'. To begin with, the tenants were thrilled.

Imagine it – bathrooms! And central heating! No more cleaning or black leading of stoves, no more trying to wash from tin basins, no more dirt! Folk couldn't believe their luck when they moved into Harebell, Heather, Briar and Clover. It was only as time went by that the snags to these homes 'in the sky' became evident and the

15

complaints began.

Why did they have to live so far out from everything? asked the tenants. Why were there so few shops near at hand? Or a medical centre, or schools? Why no places for the children to play, or things for the young people to do, except vandalize the lifts?

Much was promised for the future. One day, it would come. But on that wintry evening when Kirsty and Angie arrived at Clover, their particular block, they found the lift out of order again.

Three

'Lift's no' working,' Kirsty called, catching her breath as they reached Lena's flat on the fifth floor and found her waiting. 'Glad we're only on five, eh?'

'Think of climbing up to ten!' Angie sighed.

'They say some places in Edinburgh have over twenty storeys,' Lena remarked, taking their coats. 'But five to climb is bad enough. Is it sleeting again? I'll have to hang these coats up – they're wet through.'

'Like my feet,' said Angie, sitting down to kick off her shoes, and shrugging at the expression on her aunt's face. 'Och, it's no' the end of the world, is it?'

'I did say this morning you shouldn't wear those silly shoes,' Lena said reproachfully. 'You

16

should've let me buy you some boots like Kirsty's. I'd my overtime money, remember.'

'I don't want any boots,' Angie declared, rubbing her feet with cold fingers. 'They're – what you call it – constricting. My feet canna breathe.'

'Better than catching your death in such flimsy slippers. But come away, then – I've got the kettle on. We'll have a nice cup of tea.'

'I'll just change out of my boots and good kilt,' said Kirsty, who wore a kilt every day at the shop, one of her own making from the Muir tartan of blue, green and black with narrow red stripes. 'No need to be a walking advertisement for what I can do now I'm home.'

At forty-one, Lena Muir was an attractive woman, though time and hardship had taken their toll, and her harshly bleached hair didn't make her look any younger. Still, she had a likeness to Angie, Kirsty thought, and maybe to her wicked sister, too? Impossible to know, since there were no photographs of Beryl Ramsay in the flat. Though she'd always sent a little money towards Angie's keep at irregular intervals, there had been no letters, and never a return address. Lena said once it was best not to think too much about her, and never mentioned her name. No one did. Though who knew what Angie thought?

Both Lena and Angie had come into the Muir family long ago, when Lena had married Callum, Kirsty's father, as his second wife. She'd been a friend of Kirsty's mother, Greta, when they'd lived as neighbours in an Old Town tenement, and had in fact nursed her in her last illness. When Callum came home from the war, there being no relatives to step in, she'd helped him to look after his two young bairns, Reid and Kirsty.

Not surprisingly, perhaps, he'd thought of marrying her, even though by then she'd been landed, as she put it, with her sister's baby to bring up.

'Aye, would you credit it?' all the neighbours had marvelled. That young madam, Beryl Ramsay, had dumped her love child on her sister and run away into the wild blue yonder! Well, London, as it turned out. No' many sisters would have taken on a babby like that, eh? And no' many men would have taken it on, either. But then Callum Muir was getting a mother in Lena for his own children, so maybe it wasn't too bad an idea to wed her, after all.

At first, things had gone well. Lena had been a fine wife to Callum and a kind stepmother to his children. Inclined to worry and rather fond of giving advice, maybe, but never strict or difficult. There'd been the excitement of the move to the new flat and the good news of Callum's promotion to supervisor at the sweet factory. Everyone had been happy – well, maybe not Angie – but then had come the great blow. One evening, Callum had had a heart attack and just died. 'Went out like a light,' as Lena mourned. A light had gone out of her life, anyway.

But she rallied. Took on a job at the sweet factory herself and kept the family going

18

somehow. Even managed to let Reid take up a place at college, and would have liked the girls to do the same, only Kirsty had chosen a different type of training, and Angie said never in this world would she go to college. Life went on. Had to, of course. As Lena said, they'd no choice.

The kitchen, where the women sat down to drink their tea at a Formica-topped table, was, like the rest of the flat, modern and easy to clean. Something to be grateful for, as Lena often said, usually adding that she'd never go back to the tenement. If only, though, somebody had remembered about the shops and the play areas and all the amenities they lacked! If only somebody would fix the lifts!

'Aye, it's grand here,' she murmured that evening. 'I mean, we've the space and the bedrooms, and the bathroom and everything, but it's no joke me having to walk up the stairs when I've been on my feet all day with my legs giving me stick. Maybe I'll write a letter to the council.'

'You're always going to write a letter,' Kirsty said with a laugh. 'But you never do.'

'Well, I might surprise you, then. Now who's going to give me a hand? Any minute now Reid'll be in, and he's to be out again quick because he's working at the pub.' Lena shook her head. 'Always keen to make a bit of money for me, but I say he's got his grant, we can manage.'

'Wish I could make a few bob at the pub,'

19

Kirsty said idly.

'Kirsty!' Lena's face was shocked. 'Whatever makes you say such a thing?'

'Might be exciting.'

'Exciting? I'll say! When the guys all start fighting and swearing and chucking broken glasses! I worry enough about Reid, never mind you.'

'Och, it was a joke.' Kirsty stood up. 'Come on, I'll do the veggies, eh? Angie, you can set the table.'

But Angie had mysteriously disappeared.

'Trust her!' Kirsty ran to the door and bawled, 'Angie, you're wanted!'

'Just putting on some dry socks,' Angie called back.

'Well, I'm no' doing everything!'

'I'm coming, I'm coming.'

'Oh, you lassies,' Lena sighed.

By the time Reid arrived, shaking off sleet, everything was ready. The previously made beef stew was bubbling nicely, the potatoes mashed, the carrots and cabbage steamed, and a pastry top hastily put together by Lena was browning in the oven.

'Hey, something smells good!' the young man cried, hanging his coat on the back of the door. 'And I'm starving!'

'Get ready, then, and we can dish up,' said Lena. 'Had a good day?'

'Fine, thanks.'

'Built any bridges?' Angie asked coolly.

'Sure – just finished that one over the Forth.'

20

He grinned. 'What do you think, cheeky? I'm still a student.'

Tall and thin, with unruly dark hair and a bumpy nose, Reid had his late father's looks. But his hazel eyes, Kirsty thought, were keener than her dad's had ever been. All her brother's intelligence shone from those eyes and it was not hard to tell that he was doing well on his civil engineering course at Heriot Watt College. Everyone in Pleasant Hill was sure that one day Reid was going to be a great man.

As they sat down to eat, he said cheerfully, 'See the lift's out of order again.'

'So, what's new?' Kirsty smiled across at her stepmother. 'Lena's going to write to the council about it.'

'Or I might just speak to that fellow who sometimes comes round to check things,' Lena said hastily. 'If I'm in.'

'That'd be best,' Reid told her comfortingly. 'No point worrying too much.'

'No, I hate worrying.'

Poor old Lena, Kirsty thought later, as she stood looking out at the lights of the flats opposite from the living room window. Hates worrying, but worries all the time. Would she herself be like that some day?

How cold it looked out there! The sleet had stopped falling; probably it was going to freeze. And the metal frames of the windows let in such a draught, it was like the wind blowing great guns down Princes Street. Something else to tell the council about, then.

21

She sighed and let the curtain fall, turning back to the room, where she was for the moment alone. Reid had left for the pub some miles away; he would not be back until late. Angie was on her bed, secretly smoking, and Lena was still pottering in the kitchen, tidying up.

What was there to do? Nothing. Maybe she should have agreed to go out with Dermot. No, she couldn't face it. Trekking all the way back into town; dancing just with him. If there'd been someone else, perhaps ... But there was no one else. Not yet, anyway.

She moved to the settee and flicked through the day's paper that Lena had brought back after work. Maybe she should read about the rest of the world and all its troubles, and then she would not feel so bad. Riots, military coups, strikes, violence – oh, Lordy. Now she felt guilty for complaining about her lot.

But her eyes went to the pictures of girls in short skirts rocking and rolling, and smart folk on their way to the French Alps or Switzerland for skiing. Just think of it! Being able to travel to the French Alps, or Switzerland. Or America, like The Beatles. Here were their photos again, the Fab Four, soon to be away on their fab tour. Why were some folk so lucky?

She folded up the paper and put it aside, as Lena came hurrying in.

'Have you no' switched on?' she cried. 'It's *Emergency – Ward Ten* tonight. Mustn't miss that.'

'Excitement at last,' sighed Kirsty, and turned on the television.

22

Four

Morning brought black skies and black ice, the sound of Cormack MacFall's bagpipes from the flat next door, and Dick Murdoch from upstairs thundering down to complain to Cormack's mother, Vinnie.

Where was Nesta Harvie, then? She was another who liked to pick a fight over Cormack's pipes, claiming they always woke her baby, but maybe she'd had enough of battling with fierce Vinnie, who could always give as good as she got. Seemingly only Dick was doing the fighting that morning, and he wasn't winning, as Vinnie had already sent him packing. The Muirs, having breakfast, could hear his feet running back up the stair and his voice shouting to his wife.

'Oh dear, will you listen to that?' Lena asked, setting out the cornflakes. 'Trouble again over Vinnie's Cormack. And him only practising, eh?'

'Bit early for practising,' Reid muttered. 'Any milk, then?'

'Come on, you know where the milk is,' Angie said irritably. 'Are we supposed to wait on you?'

'What's he practising for?' Kirsty asked, diplomatically passing the milk to her brother. 'I

23

mean, what's so urgent he has to wake everybody up?'

'A wedding on Saturday,' Lena told her. 'Seemingly, he earns a bit with his piping these days. No' bad, they say, though I canna tell. One piper sounds like another to me. Angie, what's wrong with your cornflakes?'

'I hate cornflakes, Auntie Lena.'

'Since when?' asked Reid. 'Thought it was porridge you wouldn't eat.'

'Och, I'm going to have toast!'

Up leaped Angie with set face and cold eyes, as the others exchanged glances and unspoken warning. *She's in a mood again. Say nothing.*

But as she sliced bread and fiddled with the cooker grill, a knock at the door and the hoarse call of Lena's name announced the arrival of Vinnie MacFall. Just 'popping in', as she so often did, when she'd run out of something she needed, though that morning all she wanted was to sound off about Dick Murdoch.

'Lena, would you credit it?' she demanded, her dark eyes burning, a work-worn hand fussing with her thick black hair. 'That guy coming down and threatening my Cormack – telling him what he could do with his pipes and all! No, thanks, I'll no' have any tea, I've to get to work. But what d'you think, then? The cheek of it, eh? And the poor laddie only practising!'

'And waking up the whole building,' Angie snapped, turning round from the grill. 'Mr Murdoch has a point, I'd say.'

Vinnie's face turned dusky red; for a moment she was speechless. 'Well!' she finally got out.

24

'Well, Lena, that's grand, that is! Your niece talking to me like that! And I thought I was among friends.'

'So you are, Vinnie, so you are,' Lena said hurriedly. 'Angie, there was no need for you to say anything to Mrs MacFall. Just get on with your breakfast, then.'

'I intend to.' Angie was coolly buttering her toast. 'Is there any marmalade?'

'Are we supposed to wait on you?' Reid asked with a grin and stood up. 'I'm away. Think I'd rather be at college.'

'And I'd rather be at work,' Kirsty said, putting her cereal bowl in the sink.

'Me too!' cried Vinnie. 'Lena, I'm away back to the boys.'

With a last furious glance at Angie, Vinnie took herself home, where her older son, Niall, a friend of Reid's, would probably be quietly getting ready for work, while Cormack fumed and sulked over Dick Murdoch's threats.

As everyone remarked, the two young men were very different, even if alike in their dark good looks. Since their father's death, it was always Niall who tried to keep the peace and act the man of the family; it was always Cormack who would only do as he pleased.

'Angie, come on,' Kirsty urged, glancing at the clock. 'We'll have to hurry if we're to catch that bus.'

'Just a minute – I want to say something to Angie first,' Lena cut in, with a rare show of authority. 'I'm no' pleased with you, Angie,

25

speaking to Vinnie like that. Kindly remember that she's a widow and has to do the best she can, like me.'

'Aye, well she's no' like you,' Angie muttered. 'She really irritates me, the way she spoils those two boys – especially Cormack. Everybody knows he's a tearaway, always hanging out with the lads from Briar and getting up to mischief, but the way Mrs MacFall talks about him, you'd think he'd angel's wings sprouting. It's ridiculous.'

'She is his mother...' Lena began, then stopped and flushed, as Angie's mouth tightened and she turned to leave the kitchen.

'I've to get the bus,' she said flatly. 'What did you do with my shoes?'

'Put your lace-ups on,' Lena ordered, recovering herself. 'It'll be terrible treacherous out there today, with the ice freezing the slush. Anyway, your other shoes are still wet.'

'Oh, just let's go!' cried Kirsty.

When the girls and Reid finally left the flat, it was to join the exodus of workers hurrying down the stairs on their way to work. They knew most people, of course, even if not to talk to, for folk didn't mix as much in Pleasant Hill as in the Old Town houses. And that morning, in fact, there were some people they thought it best to avoid anyway. Dick Murdoch, for one, whose cheekbones still glowed with spots of angry colour, and George Harvie, the husband of Nesta, and father of the woken-up baby, for another.

'Looks like they're both spoiling for a fight, eh?' Reid asked, keeping his voice down. 'And there's Cormack and Niall on the stair with no Vinnie in sight to do battle.'

'Thank the Lord for that!' Angie cried. 'Could not stand seeing her twice in one day.'

'I think Cormack can take care of himself,' Kirsty murmured, observing the young man's scowl. 'Probably he's spoiling for a fight as well.'

'It's OK, Niall's grabbed his arm, and Dick's hurried on with George. Folk have to get to work, after all.' Reid laughed. 'And the corporation buses wait for no man.'

'Better run,' Kirsty said.

As they hurried to the buses lined up at the terminus, the wind coming from some immensely cold place seemed to cut straight through everything they were wearing, sending Kirsty's spirits plummeting. She should have been relieved that there'd been no more trouble, but the intense cold and the lowering skies, which were not yet fully light, only filled her with gloom. And then the great grey blocks of flats around her seemed to be closing in somehow. Seemed suddenly desolate, as though not part of the landscape, or anything folk knew.

Yet they were homes, it was true, and better than most in the old days. Why be so despondent? She couldn't be sure. Oh, it was just the weather. January. Everybody felt depressed in January. Unless, of course, they could go to Switzerland or America. Or, somewhere. And not many people from the homes in the sky would be going anywhere. Except work.

'What's up?' asked Reid in her ear, just before she boarded her bus, with Angie following. He'd always been able to tell when she was down.

'Nothing. Well, I just feel a bit depressed. No' sure why.'

'That Monday morning feeling, eh?'

'But it isn't Monday morning.'

'That should cheer you up, then.' Reid waved goodbye, before turning to join the queue for his own bus. 'Bet this'll be your lucky day.'

Lucky day? As Kirsty and Angie found seats, Kirsty was faintly smiling. Trust Reid to look on the bright side. All she'd be doing, probably, was making that new customer's kilt for Burns Night. Still, it was what she liked doing.

'Nice, eh?' asked Angie as the bus began slowly to move away from Pleasant Hill. 'I mean, Reid can always make you feel better.'

Kirsty's eyes widened. 'He's like that with everyone.'

'Except me.'

'Ah, come on, that's unfair. He tries to make you feel better, too.'

Angie shook her head. 'You can tell you're his sister. I've always known the difference.'

Kirsty, looking out at the wintry street they were negotiating, sighed, then brightened.

'Shall we meet in our lunch hour, Angie? Come up to the shop and we'll go to a café. I'll treat you – what d'you say?'

'OK, I'd no' mind.' Angie's hard gaze suddenly softened. 'Thanks, Kirsty. You know, I do think of you as a sister.'

'And a friend?'

'And a friend.'

There's progress, Kirsty thought with satisfaction, and by the time she arrived at Macrae's was feeling quite her usual self.

Five

Mrs MacNee, still wearing her hat, was checking what her girls were working on that morning.

'Lil, if you're finishing off Mr MacEwan's kilt today, you'd better do a final press, as he's coming in to collect this afternoon. Not forgotten, have you?'

'No, I've no' forgotten, Mrs MacNee,' Lil answered shortly, not taking kindly to being reminded. 'I'm just about ready for pressing now, so everything's fine.'

'Good, good. Excellent. And Kirsty, you've worked out how many pleats you need for Mr Ferguson's kilt?'

'Twenty-six, Mrs MacNee.' Kirsty made a face, remembering the calculations, based on pattern repeats and spacings, that had been required. Still, it was part of the job and she didn't mind it too much; she'd always been good at arithmetic.

'I don't mind doing sums, but I hate working

out the pleats,' Lil said. 'Worst bit of the job, I always say.'

'Most important bit of the job,' Mrs MacNee retorted. 'That and measuring. Because a kilt has to fit and have the right number of pleats, or what'll it look like? I tell you, as I've told you before, a girl might be the best needlewoman in the world, but if she canna do her calculations, she's no good to me. Now, I'm away to take off my hat.' She beamed at her listeners. 'Lecture's over, eh?'

'Sometimes wonder how I ever made the grade,' Lil muttered, inspecting the kilt she was finishing as Mrs MacNee left them. 'I mean, there must be easier ways of earning a living.'

'Ah, you know you enjoy it,' Kirsty told her. 'And there's nothing better than starting out with a roll of tartan and finishing up with a grand kilt, is there? Wait till your Mr MacEwan sees his!'

'Hope he likes it, or I'll be in trouble. Is it no' coffee time yet?'

'Coffee time? Mrs MacNee's only just taken off her hat!' Kirsty grinned. 'Better wait for our break. We'll get shot if she catches us drinking coffee over the tartan!'

'Ever think what it would be like to have your coffee whenever you wanted?'

'All the time, Lil.'

Their coffee break came at last, and was taken in the tiny staffroom at the back of the shop, after which Kirsty, having worked out all her measurements and marked the material with tailor's chalk, said the time had come. She'd have to

30

start cutting.

'Another thing to worry about,' Lil remarked. 'I mean, you have to think what would happen if you made a mistake.'

Dermot laughed. 'It's you for the chop – excuse the pun.'

'No one here has ever made a mistake in cutting,' Mrs MacNee said coldly. 'Don't even think of it.'

'Always a first time,' he said cheerfully.

'Shouldn't you be back in the front shop?'

'I'll just finish this cigarette. I can hear the shop bell from here.'

'If you're smoking, you're supposed to be outside. We don't want our materials to smell of smoke.'

'Ah, Mrs MacNee, have a heart! It's freezing outside! And I'm nowhere near the tartans.'

'I should hope not!' She put her finger to her lips. 'Ssh, I think I hear Mr Macrae's office door. He must have just come in.'

'Better late than never,' Lil muttered to Kirsty. 'Think he was out on the tiles last night, after the cocktails, then?'

At the idea of the usually straight and correct Mr Macrae out on the tiles, she and Kirsty were almost giggling, only managing to control themselves when Mrs MacNee asked if one of them would kindly take in his coffee.

'Time we had another assistant, to do that sort of thing,' Lil declared boldly, making a great show of being busy as she damped a pressing cloth at the small sink. 'When's Mr Macrae going to appoint somebody?'

31

'Not at the moment,' Mrs MacNee replied, dropping her voice. 'Money's tight, with so much competition – kilt shops opening up all over the place these days. Mr Macrae thinks we should try to expand the hire business, and he'll do more to help Dermot.'

'Lucky me,' Dermot sighed, and stubbed out his cigarette. 'Ah, well, it's back to the coal face, eh?'

'Yes, we must get on – but who's going to take Mr Macrae his coffee?'

'I will.' Kirsty shook the coffee pot. 'Think I should make some fresh?'

'Oh, yes, for Mr Macrae, better make some fresh.'

Andrew Macrae was thirty-one years old. Tall and slender, he held himself well, having once served in a Highland regiment, and might have been handsome if he'd had a little more colour about him. But his eyes were grey, his hair dusty brown, and though he ran a shop full of bright tartans, he always wore a dark three-piece suit to work, with a white shirt and subdued tie.

'Oh, could you no' throw a pot of red paint over him?' Lil had been heard to ask. 'Just to brighten him up, eh?'

And if that was just one of her jokes, everyone appreciated what she meant.

When Kirsty carried in his freshly made coffee, he half rose from his chair behind his desk and thanked her with a pleasant smile. In fact, he was always pleasant to his staff, preferring to leave any sharp words required to Mrs MacNee.

Of course, if his mother had worked in the shop, she would have had no trouble in issuing sharp words, that being her forte, but Mrs Macrae had never worked anywhere and now, in late middle age, never would. For which blessing, her son's staff were duly grateful.

'Things going well?' Andrew asked, as Kirsty placed the sugar down on the desk.

'I'm just going to start cutting out a kilt for Mr Ferguson,' she replied. 'He's ordered a new one for this year's Burns Night.'

'Ah, yes, Tim Ferguson – I know him from Rotary. And you're about to start cutting? Not as bad as diamond cutting, anyway!'

'Diamond cutting?'

'Yes, that's the way the experts create good diamonds. With the cutting. If they make a mistake, they can ruin the stone.' At the expression on Kirsty's face, Andrew laughed a little. 'But don't worry, you're not going to ruin a piece of tartan, I'm sure. You're one of our most trusted makers.'

'Am I?'

'Certainly, you are. Mrs MacNee's star pupil.'

Her face bright pink, Kirsty excused herself, wishing Mr Macrae had not made his compliments, which were probably exaggerated anyway. But now, if her scissors slipped or something, she'd feel even worse.

In fact, all went well. By the time she was ready for her lunch with Angie, she had already laid out the prepared fabric on her table and had tacked, tapered and pinned, so that the kilt was

33

beginning to take shape.

'Just off?' Dermot asked, when she'd left everything tidy and was making her way through the front shop, well muffled up against the cold. 'Listen, if you wait five minutes, Mr Macrae's going to take over so I can get my lunch. Maybe we could go somewhere together?'

'Sorry, Dermot, I'm meeting my stepsister.'

His handsome face fell. 'Never have much luck with you, Kirsty, do I?'

'We can go some other time,' she said, softening a little. 'It's just, you know, it'll be all girl talk with Angie. You'd be bored.'

'Nae bother,' he replied stiffly. 'I understand. Here comes a customer, anyway – I'd better see to him.'

Oh, dear, why was life so complicated? Kirsty, plodding along gritted pavements, knew that Lil wouldn't mind going out with Dermot, yet he never asked her, because she wasn't the one he wanted. And the one he wanted – who was Kirsty – didn't want him. Thank goodness she was fancy free, though! How awful it must be to want somebody who didn't want you!

The lunch with Angie went well. She seemed to have come out of her bad mood and allowed herself to enjoy looking round the café and studying the menu just like anyone else. And when they'd chosen omelettes and apple pie, she even offered to pay half, though Kirsty said, no, no, it was her treat. And everything was so pleasant and easy-going, it was hard to picture

Angie as she could be – a stiff, cold-faced young woman sinking under the enormous chip on her shoulder.

'I feel the better for that,' Kirsty declared when she'd paid the bill and they were out again in the chill of the open air.

'Me, too.' Angie was even smiling. 'My turn to treat you next time. Thanks, Kirsty. See you tonight.'

'Aye, tonight.'

Back at Macrae's, unwinding her great tartan scarf, Kirsty marvelled at how much better people always felt after food. Maybe even Dermot would be more cheerful, once he'd had his lunch.

And he seemed to be, as he came hurrying towards her, his eyes alight.

'You'll never guess who's here!' he said in a stage whisper.

'Who?'

'Jake MacIver!'

'Jake MacIver? You mean, the fiddler?'

'Aye, the guy who has that programme on the telly, *Reel Time, Song Time*. He wants another kilt – from us!'

'Where is he then?' Kirsty asked, looking around with interest.

'Being measured in the fitting room by Mr Macrae himself.' Dermot shook his head. 'I thought I might do the measuring, but of course I never got a look in. Want to hang around, in case you're asked to make the kilt?'

'Me?' Kirsty's eyes widened. 'Oh, no. Mrs

35

MacNee will want to make it. I mean, Jake MacIver – he's well known.'

'She's out at lunch, and so's Lil. I have a feeling Mr Macrae's going to ask you.' Dermot knocked her arm. 'Anyway, here they come now.'

'Oh, Kirsty, just a moment, please!' Mr Macrae called, as he and a fair-haired young man in a dark jacket and cord trousers appeared from a fitting room. 'Mr MacIver, this is Miss Muir, one of our most experienced kilt makers. She'll be making your new kilt for you. Kirsty, would you show us Mr MacIver's tartan?'

'Of course, sir,' Kirsty answered, turning pale. 'This way, Mr MacIver.'

'Thanks so much, Miss Muir,' the young man replied.

Six

He was of medium height, the famous Jake MacIver, broad-shouldered and slim-waisted, with a wave to his fair hair and eyes of vivid blue. Of course, they were his trademark, those eyes. Everyone who watched his television programme of Scottish music and dancing knew his blue eyes and looked for their bright gaze, as he played his fiddle and smiled out at his audience. There were others in the band, of course, all very accomplished and cheerful, too, but Jake was the one folk remembered. His was the personality that drew them – that, and his blue eyes.

Now, as she unrolled the MacIver tartan for his inspection, Kirsty could feel his magnetism attracting her in the same way as it attracted his audiences. And making her feel ... could it be ... sort of special?

Don't be a fool, she told herself, as her hands smoothed over the tartan. This was just the way he made people feel who watched his show. She'd seen the effect on Lena. Experienced it herself. He couldn't resist turning on the charm for anyone who was around, could he? Kilt maker, or whoever. But why should she respond?

'This is our MacIver, sir,' she told him, trying to sound businesslike. 'It's the modern version – I don't know if you'd prefer the ancient?'

'Ancient? No, I like the modern colours. And best quality material.'

'All our tartans are one hundred per cent pure wool worsted.'

'Perfect. How about weight?'

'Thirteen or sixteen ounces per yard, and we'd need eight or nine yards.' Kirsty cleared her throat, which was hoarse, making her sound nervous. 'But we can easily get you a heavier weight if you prefer.'

'Up to twenty-one ounces,' Mr Macrae put in. 'Which is regimental weight, of course. I wore that myself when I was in the Seaforth High-landers.'

'No army weight for me these days, thanks all the same.' Jake laughed. 'Had enough of that when I did national service. Sixteen ounce will be OK, but I'd like to go for military pleating. Looks more attractive, don't you think?'

'The way the stripes are centred, yes, indeed. Many of our customers prefer the style. May I ask how soon you would be requiring your kilt?'

'No desperate rush. I have several kilts on the go. Some past their best. Think I'd better order two.'

'Two?' Mr Macrae's eyes brightened. 'No problem there, Mr MacIver. The only thing is, we do like to insist on a fitting before completion. Perhaps you could give us a ring in a week or so, to arrange that?'

'Certainly, I will. Many thanks, then. See you soon, I hope.'

'Dermot, the door, please!' Mr Macrae ordered, and Dermot sprang forward. But as Jake moved towards it, he looked straight back at Kirsty, whose gaze fell before his smile. Just one of the smiles he gave everyone, no doubt. Or, perhaps not. Perhaps it was a particular smile. When she finally looked up, he had gone.

'Two kilts – that's a satisfactory order,' Mr Macrae remarked. 'Could be a good advertisement for us. I wonder if Mr MacIver would let us use his name?'

'Probably cost a bit,' Dermot suggested.

'Yes, maybe we'd do best not to get involved. I wonder where he had his present kilts made, though? Glasgow, maybe, but he's an Edinburgh man. An old boy of the Academy, I believe.'

'I thought he didn't sound as Scottish as when

he's on his programme,' Dermot remarked. 'Probably lays the Scots on thick for that.'

He looked at Kirsty, who was keeping very quiet, and seemed about to speak when the shop door opened and Mrs MacNee and Lil came in together, bringing in a rush of cold air.

'Oh, it's freezing out there!' Lil cried, pulling off her scarf, gloves, and coat.

'Freezing!' echoed Mrs MacNee, who was taking off her coat but not her hat. 'Now, how come you're all standing here, then? Has something happened, Mr Macrae?'

'Not really. But we've had a rather well known customer in while you were at lunch.'

'Who?' cried Lil.

'Jake MacIver of television fame.' Mr Macrae's tone was cool. 'Very much admired, I'm told, though not my cup of tea.'

'Wants to buy two kilts, no' just one!' Dermot put in. 'How about that?'

'Jake MacIver?' Mrs MacNee cried. 'From the TV programme? Well!'

'Wish I'd been here,' Lil muttered. 'Why am I always out when anything interesting happens?'

'Did you tell him I could fit him in any time?' Mrs MacNee asked. 'I can always put that hire stuff to one side.'

'Actually, I asked Kirsty to make Mr Mac-Iver's kilts,' Mr Macrae said, flushing a little. 'As she was here at the time.'

'Kirsty?' Mrs MacNee stared. 'Oh, well, if it's arranged, there's no more to be said.'

'I don't have to make them,' Kirsty said quickly. 'It should be you, Mrs MacNee. It was just –

39

like Mr Macrae said – I happened to be here.'

'Nae bother. I'm sure you'll do a very good job. Now, I'd better take off my hat...'

As soon as Mrs MacNee had stalked away, reluctantly followed by Lil, Kirsty turned to Mr Macrae.

'I don't feel happy about making the kilts, sir. Maybe you could change the arrangement?'

'No, no, that might give the impression we don't know what we're doing.' He gave a harassed smile. 'I'm sorry, I should have thought of Mrs MacNee. I hope she'll understand.'

'Do you think she will?' Kirsty asked Dermot, when Mr Macrae had returned to his office.

Dermot shrugged. 'She's the senior kilt maker, eh? Should have been asked if a famous guy like Mr MacIver needs a kilt.'

'It was just that I was here. Mr Macrae's probably regretting choosing me now.'

'Aye, 'specially as they say Jake MacIver's got an eye for the lassies.' Dermot laughed heartily. 'Better watch your step.'

'He certainly needn't cast his eye over me!' Kirsty cried, suspecting as she hurried back to the workroom that he already had. But then she wasn't sure, was she? Maybe her imagination was working overtime. All she should really be thinking about now was whether or not Mrs MacNee was going to be cross.

Mrs MacNee, however, seemed just as usual as she stitched away at a kilt destined for the hire department, evidently having quickly recovered from her attack of wounded feelings. When she went out to speak to Mr Macrae about an order for sporrans, Lil gave a little laugh.

'Your luck's in,' she whispered to Kirsty. 'Madam's no' taken offence.'

'Oh, I hope not!'

'Och, I shouldn't worry. She's probably made kilts for all kinds of famous folk, anyway. And who's Jake MacIver, after all? He's no' exactly a film star!'

'Attractive, though,' Kirsty murmured.

'Think so?' Lil shrugged. 'I prefer taller men myself.'

Like Dermot? Kirsty wondered. Aloud, she said, 'You still seemed disappointed when you heard you'd missed him.'

'Anything to break the monotony, eh? Now all I've got to look forward to is my customer coming in for his final fitting. Won't compare with you fiddling round with all Jake's straps and buckles, will it?'

'I must get on,' Kirsty murmured, her cheeks flaming under Lil's amused gaze. 'And I wish you'd stop teasing.'

'Just something else to break the monotony,' Lil answered cheerfully.

The long afternoon passed slowly by, with Kirsty working hard on Mr Ferguson's kilt, thinking all the time that as soon as she'd finished it, she'd have to start on Jake MacIver's. Considering how many kilts she'd made over the years, it was ridiculous that she should feel so nervous at the idea of sewing for him, but already she could feel butterflies at the very thought.

41

It was a relief when Lil's customer arrived and she had to hurry off to check the fit of his new kilt, which meant she couldn't sit reading Kirsty's mind and smiling. At least Mrs MacNee wasn't one for teasing, and didn't in fact say much at all when she returned from Mr Macrae's office, only remarking that there would be another hard frost by evening.

'Best take care going down the Mound, Kirsty. Canna have you laid up with broken bones if you've to make Mr MacIver's kilts, can we?'

Seemingly, she hadn't quite got over her hurt feelings after all.

As usual, at the end of the day, the young people left the shop together, the girls clutching each other on the frozen pavements that rang like iron under their feet, while Dermot went sliding ahead, crying out, 'Hey, look at me! This is as good as an ice rink, eh?'

Lil obliged by laughing at him, but Kirsty was busy looking round at shadows in doorways, wondering if anyone might be waiting for her. Anyone? Who? Not Jake MacIver? Was she crazy? Why would Jake MacIver be standing in the cold, waiting for her?

He wasn't, of course. He might have been, though. If it had been a summer evening, he might have been watching out for her leaving the shop. It was the sort of thing he might do, if it was true he had 'an eye for the lassies'. As though she'd want anyone like that waiting for her! In fact, she wasn't even looking forward to seeing him again, when he came back to the

42

shop. Maybe she'd have a cold or something and be unable to go into work, then Mrs MacNee would have to see to his fitting. Yes, that would be ideal.

'Here's my stop!' she cried, as they reached the foot of the Mound. 'You folks take care, now, crossing that road!'

'See you tomorrow!' Lil and Dermot cried, but before they left her, Lil couldn't resist asking Kirsty if she was going to tell her stepmother about making Jake MacIver's kilts.

'She'll be thrilled, eh? Bet she watches *Reel Time, Song Time*!'

'I might tell her,' Kirsty answered coolly. 'And I might not.'

At which, Lil only laughed.

The awful thing was that Kirsty did tell Lena, and Angie and Reid, and Mrs MacFall and everyone, and basked in their interest in the most foolish way possible. Still, if it made her feel good to talk about the fiddler, and if folk were thrilled to listen, why shouldn't she?

'I was that sad when his programme finished the other week,' Lena had sighed. 'But just think, Kirsty, Jake MacIver might be wearing your kilt next time, because they say there's another series in the pipeline. It's no' often a celebrity comes into our lives, is it?'

'I wouldn't say he was exactly in our lives,' Angie commented. 'Only in Kirsty's.'

'I wouldn't say he was in mine at all,' Kirsty said swiftly.

Seven

Some days went by. Kirsty finished Mr Ferguson's kilt, and having pressed it, fitted it and received his thanks, as Macrae's received his cheque, began almost at once on the first kilt for Jake MacIver.

'Nervous?' asked Lil.

'Yes,' Kirsty answered shortly. 'Now, will you just let me get on?'

'Sorry.' Lil gave an apologetic smile. 'I'll keep out of your hair. Got plenty to do, anyway. Another Burns Night kilt, surprise, surprise.'

Kirsty made no reply. She was deep in the study of Mr Macrae's meticulous measurements for Jake's kilt – waist, hip, drop length – and preparing to do the usual calculations, taking into account the pattern of the MacIver tartan. The worst part of the job, Lil had called it, doing the calculations, but everything about the making of this particular kilt was going to be a strain, Kirsty could tell. If only the job had been given to Mrs MacNee as it should have been. If only she'd just had to make a kilt for some ordinary, easy-going customer like Mr Ferguson, or some tourist no one knew – anyone other than Jake MacIver.

Yet it wasn't his fame as an entertainer that was making things so difficult for her. She might

44

have been thrilled to be making a kilt for some other entertainer she'd seen on television, but she wouldn't have felt as strung up as she did now.

So, what was different about Jake MacIver? Might as well admit it – she was attracted to him. She thought he was attracted to her. There had been a clear line from his blue eyes to her that had held them both, and held her still, try as she would to pretend that she didn't want to see him again.

As she took down the roll of his tartan, Mrs MacNee's voice came piercing into her thoughts. 'Ready to start cutting, dear? Better keep your hand steady, then. Won't want to make a mistake with this kilt, eh?'

'No, Mrs MacNee.'

'You can lay the material out now – that table's clear. Got your tailor's chalk?'

'Yes, Mrs MacNee.' Kirsty could sense Lil listening as she sat stitching, and knew she was ready to have one of her laughing fits, but Kirsty herself had never felt less like laughing.

'I could give you a hand, if you'd feel happier?'

'I think I'll be all right.' Kirsty laid the MacIver tartan across the table and took up her shears. 'Thanks all the same, Mrs MacNee.'

'Well, you have done it often enough before.' Mrs MacNee gave a little laugh. 'So I'll leave you to it.'

But it was only after Kirsty had measured the length of the kilt and begun to cut that she moved away and left the workroom.

'Don't you dare say a word,' Kirsty whispered, turning round to look at Lil, but Lil now had herself well under control.

'Hey, I thought you were grand just then! So patient! I'd have socked her one!'

'Och, she's peeved and I don't blame her. Everything I know I've learned from her. Why wouldn't she be peeved?'

'Bet your hand was wobbling, though, while she was watching, eh?'

'No, steady as a rock,' Kirsty answered with a sudden grin, which faded as Dermot appeared and fixed her with a significant look.

'Telephone for you, Kirsty. It's Mr MacIver.'

She had to take the call in the front shop, where Dermot, within earshot, was making no effort to move away.

'Kirsty Muir speaking,' she said as firmly as possible.

'Ah, Miss Muir, this is Jake MacIver.' His telephone voice was soft and pleasant. 'I was wondering how things were going with my kilts? Any chance of a fitting yet?'

'I'm afraid I've only just started on cutting out the first one, Mr MacIver.'

'Not ready yet, then. So – when shall I look in?'

'Well – the end of the week should be OK.'

'Friday? Friday afternoon?'

'That'd be grand.'

'Till Friday, then. I'll look forward to seeing you.'

'Goodbye, Mr MacIver.'

'*Au revoir*, Miss Muir.'

46

When she had replaced the receiver, Kirsty looked at Dermot, who was of course watching her.

'Coming in Friday, eh?' he asked.

'Yes, Friday afternoon.'

'Must be keen.'

'Must need his new kilts.'

'I thought I heard him tell Mr Macrae there was no hurry.'

She shrugged. 'Customers can change their minds. Maybe something special's come up.'

'If you ask me, folk never look at his kilt anyway. He's the attraction, no' his kilt. Him and his blue eyes and that dimple in his chin.'

'I've got work to do,' Kirsty said, leaving him. 'And so have you – there's a lady over there looking at the scarves.'

'When's he coming in, then?' asked Lil. Mrs MacNee, who had returned to the workroom, looked up with interest.

'Friday afternoon.'

'As though you could be expected to have a kilt ready for fitting any sooner!' cried Mrs MacNee. 'Och, these men have no idea!'

'Wonder if he'll bring his girlfriend with him,' Lil murmured.

'What girlfriend?' Kirsty asked.

'No idea. But he must have one, eh? Fella like him?'

'They do say he's one for the lassies,' Mrs MacNee remarked.

Kirsty picked up her shears again. 'Was it Dermot told you that?'

'Maybe it was. Or did I read it in the paper?'

'Mightn't be true, then. Print all sorts of rubbish in the papers.'

'Always get things wrong,' Lil agreed. 'Still, he's no chicken, is he? Thirty at least. I'd say he'd been around.'

'Thirty?' Kirsty's shears halted. Jake MacIver as old as Mr Macrae? It didn't seem possible. 'I'd have said younger than that.'

Lil shrugged. 'Too old for you, anyway.'

'Who's talking about me?' cried Kirsty, glancing at Mrs MacNee, who was pursing her lips over the apron, the front part of the kilt she was tacking. 'I'm just the kilt maker.'

'And what's wrong with that?' Mrs MacNee demanded.

'Och, I was just teasing,' Lil said hastily. 'Never meant Kirsty was interested in Mr Mac-Iver.'

'I should think not. He's a customer.'

'And that's forbidden?' Kirsty asked sharply.

'There's no law against it, but it wouldn't be ideal. Women assistants getting off with men chatting 'em up.'

'Canna see many of the chaps who come in here chatting anybody up,' Lil said, laughing. 'Probably give 'em heart attacks if they tried anything on.'

Mrs MacNee bit off her thread and studied her work. 'I'm sure most of our customers are quite happily married men. Who's going to make us a cup of tea, then?'

'So, when's Mr MacIver coming in for his

fitting?' Lena asked eagerly when Kirsty arrived home. 'Have you heard?'

'Aye, it's Friday,' Kirsty answered with a sigh.

All this interest – other people's interest – in one man's kilt was beginning to form a burden weighing her down. If she'd had any sense, she'd have said nothing at all about Jake Mac-Iver's visit to Lena, or anyone else at Pleasant Hill, but then that wouldn't have prevented the fascination everyone was displaying at Mac-rae's, would it? Anybody would think they had royalty coming in for a fitting, or Elvis Presley at the very least. And the worst of it was, because she'd been chosen to be Jake's kilt maker, she had somehow become tangled up in the interest, as though something of him had rubbed off on her.

For two pins, she'd ask Mrs MacNee to fit his kilt for him, as she'd thought of doing before. Yes, that would do the trick. Shut everyone up about her, anyway. She'd say ... Well, what could she say? She had a cold? No one would believe her. She felt too nervous? That would make it seem like she too thought of Jake as Elvis or some royal personage or other. Couldn't let folk think that. Couldn't in fact get out of fitting the kilt she had made, and would just have to go through with it.

And as she lay awake that night, while Angie turned fitfully in her sleep, she knew she'd never been serious about not going through with it, anyway. Because she was longing to see Jake MacIver again, and was counting the days to Friday.

Eight

Friday came at last. Kirsty dressed carefully, putting on her best green jumper that matched the green in her kilt, and when she was alone in the cloakroom in her lunch hour, made up her face with an unskilled hand. She had a fine, fresh complexion, anyway, and normally considered a dab of lipstick quite enough, but now she gave herself the full works she'd just bought at a chemist's in the High Street – foundation, powder, eye make-up, lipstick, even a little rouge. Then she looked at her reflection in the mirror and wiped it all off before anyone saw it.

Heavens, what had she been thinking of? Talk about a giveaway! If the others saw her dolled up to the eyebrows, they'd see exactly what she'd been trying to hide, even at times from herself. At all costs, she mustn't let that happen. Must pretend that this afternoon was the same as any other, and this fitting just another fitting.

But as she studied the new kilt on its rack, while Mrs MacNee and Lil were out at lunch, she couldn't help thinking of Jake MacIver wearing it. And of how she would feel, standing close to him, as she'd stood close to so many men, of every possible height and weight, and tweaked the material over their waistlines, checking strap positionings, fastenings, length to

50

the knee and all that she had to do. But never before had she been interested in the men; only their kilts that she'd had to make sure were right. This time – well, this time it was going to be different.

All she could do was put on an act. Not look into the blue eyes until she'd finished her job. Not let him suspect that he was any different from her other customers. Keep very calm, very matter of fact. Already, she was wondering how she'd do it.

'Mr MacIver no' here yet?' Mrs MacNee asked, looking in at the door, still wearing her hat as usual.

'It's only two o'clock,' Kirsty answered.

'Thought he might have been early.' Lil, who had followed Mrs MacNee, was putting her hands to her cheeks, flushed with the cold.

'Plenty of time yet,' said the older woman and hurried away.

Lil, staring hard at Kirsty, asked, 'Hey, have you been wearing mascara?'

'Of course not!' Kirsty was blushing bright red. 'Keep your voice down, please.'

'It's all right. Madam's gone to take off her hat – her little ritual. Oh, you have, you know. You've still got a bit on your eyelashes. Damp your hankie and give it a rub. Want my compact mirror?'

'It's just from last night,' Kirsty told her, lying with difficulty. 'Went out with Angie. I'll go to the cloakroom and get it off.'

'Kirsty, have you got Mr MacIver's kilt?'

51

asked Mr Macrae from the doorway. 'He's here now.'

'Mr MacIver's here?' Kirsty cried, rubbing her eyelashes. 'He's early!'

'Never mind, let me have the kilt and I'll help him to try it on – I'll give you a call when we're ready.'

'Quick, use the sink at the back,' Lil said briskly, as soon as Mr Macrae had left with Jake's kilt. 'Here's a bit of cloth – don't worry, you'll soon have it off. There, you look fine. Should've been more careful last night, eh?' She gave a grin. 'Youno' supposed to leave that stuff on, you know.'

'Oh, shut up,' Kirsty muttered, aware that there had been no point in her little white lies. 'Thanks, anyway.'

'Better hurry along to see if they're ready. It's good he came early, after all. I thought he would.'

So much for being very calm, very matter of fact. As she made her way to the fitting room, Kirsty had never felt less prepared to meet anyone, star or no star, and had already decided not to look into Jake MacIver's eyes at all, even when she'd finished the fitting. Supposing there were still bits of mascara on her eyelashes and he could see them? When Mr Macrae called her in, she was still blushing like a schoolgirl, all hope of putting on any sort of act melting like Edinburgh's last snowfall.

Jake MacIver was wearing a white shirt and plain tie, woollen knee socks and black shoes –

and his new kilt, of course, which Kirsty could see at a glance was a perfect fit. Thank God and Mr Macrae's measurements for that!

The length looked right – a little above mid knee as he'd stipulated. The waistband clinched his slim waist just as it should. The pleats, as he turned slowly round for her inspection, swung beautifully.

Breaking the silence that had overcome them all, he said softly, 'Miss Muir, thank you. This is excellent.'

'Glad you're pleased.' Mr Macrae was polite, though not over-excited, Kirsty thought. It came to her suddenly that he didn't like Jake MacIver.

'It's good you think it's OK,' Kirsty murmured. 'But I still have work to do.'

'Mainly checking strap placings and buckle holders, things like that, the straps being the most important,' Mr Macrae told Jake. 'Now, you opted for three, Mr MacIver, for extra firmness, though the third sometimes pulls the top a little askew...'

'Really?' asked Jake, his eyes fixed on Kirsty. 'I'm sure Miss Muir will sort it out for me. Isn't that right, Miss Muir?'

Against all her intentions, she slowly raised her eyes to his, to find the blue gaze so gentle, so surprisingly kind, her heart lifted and she took courage to begin checking the kilt, only wishing that Mr Macrae would depart instead of watching.

But he showed no signs of moving, until suddenly a rap came on the fitting-room door and Dermot's voice could be heard calling that Mr

Macrae had a telephone call.

'A telephone call? Will you excuse me, then, Mr MacIver?'

'Certainly,' Jake answered politely, but grinned as Mr Macrae left them and breathed a long theatrical sigh.

'I thought he'd never go,' he whispered, and caught at Kirsty's hand.

Nine

For a moment, he said nothing, while to her, holding her breath, looking down at her hand in his, the two of them seemed frozen in time.

'Miss Muir, may I ask you something?' he asked at last.

'About the kilt?' Was that her voice? So squeaky? She felt ashamed.

'No, not about the kilt. I was wondering if you'd care to have a drink with me? After work. Just as a little thank you, you know. For doing such a terrific job.'

She cleared her throat. 'Oh, I couldn't, Mr MacIver. I'd like to, but I'll be expected home, you see.'

'You needn't stay long. Say, half an hour? That wouldn't hold you up too much.'

'I live out of town.' She hesitated. 'Pleasant Hill. If I miss my usual bus, I'd be pretty late and my stepmother would be worried.'

'She's got no phone?'

'In a council flat?' Kirsty shook her head. 'There's no phone.'

She had lowered her eyes, but he bent to look into her face.

'There's no need to worry. I can run you home in my car. Bet I can beat your bus, too.'

'You have a car?' Her eyes lit up.

'Sure. It's parked at my flat not far from here. Come on, what d'you say?' He pressed her hand again. 'Only half an hour, Miss Muir!'

'Half an hour,' she agreed.

'So, I'll meet you outside the shop – when? Five? Half past?'

'Some time after five.'

'Fine.' He released her hand and smiled. 'And when we meet, you won't still be Miss Muir, will you?'

'My name's Kirsty.'

'And mine is Jake.'

'Till this evening, then.'

When Mr Macrae returned, Kirsty, moving to the door, said she'd finished the fitting and everything was in order.

'That's good. Mr MacIver, we'll leave you to get changed, then. And if you'd like to give us a ring for your final appointment...'

'I'll be sure to do that, Mr Macrae. Many thanks to you both.'

She had to wait, of course, until he came out of the fitting room, wearing a tweed jacket and his old kilt, which was undeniably faded, even shabby.

'Told you it needed replacing,' he murmured, handing over his new kilt on its hanger and contriving to press her hand again, even under the watchful eye of Dermot. 'My fans won't know me in my super new one.'

'And you've got plenty of fans.'

'A few,' he agreed modestly. 'It's the telly that does it, of course. But it's mainly at concerts that folks see my kilt in full splendour – and my terrific knees, eh?'

She gave a genuinely happy laugh that made other customers stare and Dermot frown, but by then Jake was leaving, turning at the door to give her a look full of meaning. Oh, yes, the blue line was there again, holding her, sending her heart leaping. 'Until this evening,' he mouthed, and imperceptibly she nodded.

Or, perhaps not as imperceptibly as she thought, for as she began to walk slowly back to the workroom, Dermot appeared at her side.

'What's going on?' he asked bluntly. 'Between you and him?'

'What do you mean? Nothing's going on.'

'Come on, Kirsty. I've got eyes, you know.'

Her colour rose again, as her eyes sparkled. 'All right, he's asked me to have a drink after work. Just as a thank you.'

'A thank you? What the hell for? He's paying for the kilt, isn't he?'

'Look, I don't have to listen to you, Dermot. Will you excuse me? I have to get back to work.'

'What's up?' asked Lil, passing by with a swatch of tartans in her hand. 'Are you two having a row?'

'She's going out with MacIver,' Dermot muttered. 'Having a drink after work.'

'Never! Jake MacIver?' Lil put a hand to her lips as though to hide a smile. 'And I was only making a joke before!'

'What's so funny now?' Kirsty asked in a furious whisper. 'Is there any reason why I should not have a drink with Jake MacIver?'

'No, of course not – it's just ... a surprise, that's all.'

'Is it? Well, I think we should all get back to work. Folk are watching us.'

As Kirsty stormed away, Jake's kilt over her arm, Lil and Dermot exchanged glances.

'It's only a drink,' Lil said brightly. 'Nothing to get excited about.'

'What a lie,' Dermot answered.

At a little after half past five, they were both standing outside the shop, watching Kirsty stepping away with Jake MacIver.

'He came, then,' Lil murmured.

'Of course he came. Why shouldn't he?'

She shrugged. 'You never know with guys like him, what they'll do.'

'All I know is, she's asking for trouble, going out with him.'

'Like I said, it's only for a drink.'

'Tonight, maybe.'

'I bet that's all it'll be.'

'Hope you're right.' Dermot turned up his collar against the rain that had taken the place of earlier sleet.

'Mr Macrae didn't see them, did he?'

57

'No, and Mrs MacNee didn't, either.'

'Just as well.' He glanced at Lil, huddling in the doorway. 'Fancy a drink yourself?'

'Wouldn't say no.'

'Come on, then.'

And they began to run through the rain, straining their eyes to see the other couple ahead, but of Kirsty and Jake there was no sign.

Ten

Holding her arm firmly, Jake was steering Kirsty from the High Street into a side street where he told her he had a flat over a firm's offices.

'Not getting too wet, are you? We'll soon be in the car.'

'I'm fine, thanks. Got my umbrella and winter boots.'

'And I'm in my cords again.' He laughed down at her. 'Not being one who likes wearing a kilt in all weathers. What a great jessie, you're thinking, eh?'

'No, no, of course not.'

'Och, when you get to know me, you'll know I'm one for comfort. What's the point in suffering when you needn't?'

Kirsty, splashing through puddles step for step with him, felt a fluttering excitement as the casually said words echoed in her mind. 'When you get to know me...'

Was she going to get to know him? Was he talking about the future? Oh, get a grip, she told herself. Don't go down that road, reading too much into a half-hour drink, a few words lightly spoken. That was the way to trouble. Maybe she was already on the way to trouble, anyway, accepting this drink in the first place. Better be careful.

'Here we are,' he announced, pausing outside a stone-fronted building with a solid front door, its moisture glistening under a street lamp. 'Home, sweet home.'

'You go in this door?' she asked in surprise.

'No, no, there's one at the side, and then stairs. It's not bad up there. Quite spacious and warm – I get the benefit of the offices' central heating as well as my own.'

He was looking at her, studying her up-turned face, and for a moment she wondered if he might be going to invite her in, which had not been part of the original offer. But then he took out a bunch of keys and said, 'Here's my car. We can drive to the West End and I'll take you home from there.'

She didn't know much about cars, but could tell that this one was special. Long, low, with shining bodywork, it was a two-seater sports car with a proper roof, and purred so beautifully down the Mound and into Princes Street, she almost felt, in her passenger seat, like purring herself. Oh, see the poor folk at the bus stops, waiting in the rain! How she sympathized. Just for tonight, she wasn't one of them.

'What sort of car is this?' she asked Jake, as they came into the West End.

'A Lotus Elan. What do you think of it?'

'I've never been in anything so grand.'

'Och, it's not grand. Just a fine sports car. Can do top speeds if it ever gets the chance.'

She was silent for a moment, wondering what it would be like to own a car like this. To feel free as a bird. To have no need, ever, to stand in the rain in a bus queue. How different Jake's life was from hers, wasn't it? Or, indeed, from most people's.

'Where are we going now?' she asked quietly.

'Here,' he answered, drawing up outside a small hotel off Shandwick Place. 'This is a place you'll like. Nice quiet bar and soothing music. I chose it specially.'

'Did you?' She brightened. 'And you found a place to park.'

'I always find a place to park. The trick is never to think that you won't. Come on, then, hop out.'

As he'd promised, she did like the hotel bar. Though it was a new experience for her to be in such a place, just as it had been new to her to drive in the beautiful sports car, the bar was so quiet, so pleasant, that it wasn't daunting in the least. She found she could quite relax, as she settled into a comfortable chair, and even when Jake asked her what she'd like and she'd no idea, she didn't panic.

'I'm no' used to drinking much,' she admitted. 'The pubs here are still mostly for men.'

'Which is why I brought you to this hotel.'

'And it's lovely!'

'So, what will you have? Gin and tonic? Glass of wine?' His blue gaze was indulgent. 'Or, something soft?'

'I sometimes have sherry,' she said cautiously.

When a cream sherry was brought for her and a lager for him, they raised their glasses and smiled.

'To you, and my kilts,' Jake said softly. 'Thank you for coming.'

'Thank you for asking me, but I mustn't stay long.'

'Soon as we've had these drinks, we'll be on our way. That'll just give you time to tell me about yourself. And don't say there's nothing to tell!'

She laughed. 'Well, there's no' much. I'm just an ordinary person.'

'No one is ordinary, Kirsty. You look around at ordinary folk and you'll find they all think of themselves as unique. It's what happens to them that counts. Now, isn't that true?'

'I suppose it is. I'd never thought of it before.'

'Och, we're all VIPs in our hearts,' he said with a grin. 'And when I play my fiddle for people, I know that and make them know it too.'

'Which is why you're so popular.'

He shrugged. 'Hope so. But come on, tell me about this ordinary person who's not ordinary at all.'

Briefly, she told him of her life, finding as he listened closely that she didn't mind talking to him, even if he was only giving her the same VIP treatment he gave his audiences. He made her feel special, anyway, in a wonderfully warm way. Just like the sherry, really.

'Your turn,' she told him cheerfully. 'Tell me about the Academy boy who ended up on the telly.'

'Academy boy? Where'd you get that from?'

'You didn't go to the Academy?'

'Hell, no! My mother could never have afforded to pay Academy fees – my dad died years ago and she taught the piano to make a bit of a living. There were just the two of us.'

'I'm sure Mr Macrae thought ... Oh well, where did you go, then?'

'Heriot's. As one of Jingling Geordie's "poor fatherless boys".'

'Jingling Geordie – I've heard of him.'

'Aye, George Heriot, James the Sixth's goldsmith. He left money for widows' sons to be educated at the school, as some still are. I had a great education, but all I wanted to do was play the fiddle.' He set down his glass. 'And that's the story of my life.'

'Well, your mother must be very proud of what you've made of it.'

He hesitated. 'She died, three years ago.'

'I'm sorry.'

He covered her hand with his. 'You'll understand better than most what that meant to me. At least, she got to see I'd had some success, and that meant a lot. Look, we'd better go.'

How quickly the Lotus ate up the miles to Pleasant Hill, compared with the lumbering bus! And though Kirsty was worrying what folk would

62

think when they saw her arrive in such style, she still enjoyed the luxury and novelty of the drive.

If only there hadn't been the streetlights, though, outside the blocks of flats! Usually, she was glad of them, but as they drew up outside Clover, all she wished she could have done was to scuttle out and run in home, before watching eyes could see her, or Jake's car, or Jake himself.

'This is home?' he asked, craning his neck to look out at the buildings of Pleasant Hill, tall, grey and forbidding in the shadows cast by the lights. 'How d'you like it here, then?'

'It's all right. Better than the tenement, on the whole. I mean, more modern.'

'But a long way out.'

'That's the thing. Once I get home, it's a struggle to think of going out again.'

'You do go out, though?' Jake's eyes gleamed in the dim light of the car. He leaned forward and took her hand. 'If I were to ask you out again, you'd come?'

'Are you?' Her throat was dry. 'Asking me out?'

'Well, sort of.' He hesitated. 'I just wondered if you'd like to come and hear my lads and me play at a concert at the King's. There'll be us and another band, a couple of singers and some dancers. I could get you a ticket.'

Her eyes shone. 'Jake, I'd love to come. When is it?'

'Thursday. If I pick up my new kilt on Wednesday, I could give you the ticket then.'

'That'd be grand. Thank you. And thank you for the drink and bringing me back.' Her hand

63

was trembling on the door. 'Now, I'll have to go. It's been so nice...'

'I'll open the door for you.'

As he helped her out of the low-slung car, he stooped and kissed her swiftly on the cheek. Just a friendly peck, the sort Reid might have given her. Only Jake wasn't Reid.

'Till Wednesday, then.'

Once she'd run into the entrance of the flats, she paused to look through a side window. Saw him standing by the car, looking up at Clover, then get in and drive away. For some time after the car lights had vanished, she stood, watching. Then, as the lift was still not working, she ran up the stairs home.

They were all sitting, waiting for her – Lena, Angie and Reid – and as soon as she came in, fixed her with rounded, questioning eyes.

'Where've you been?' Lena cried in a high, strained voice. 'I've cottage pie drying up in the oven. We were all ready – where've you been, then?'

Eleven

'Anyone'd think I was a criminal,' Kirsty said to Angie when they were in their room, after a miserable meal of stiff cottage pie and solid rice pudding. 'Just for going out with Jake MacIver! I thought Lena liked him.'

'She does, on the telly.' Angie, lying on her bed, drew on a forbidden cigarette and flicked over the pages of a magazine. 'Not as somebody for you to have a drink with.'

'But where's the harm? It was just a thank you, for me making him his kilt.'

Angie smiled a knowing smile. 'And the ticket for the concert? What was that in aid of?'

'I wish I'd never told Lena about that concert.'

'Come on, you had to tell her. You'll no' be home for tea, if you go straight from work.'

'Better than ruining the tea, like tonight.' Kirsty groaned. 'I suppose she was right to get annoyed over that. But why go on about just going for a drink?'

Angie put her magazine aside and watched the smoke rising from her cigarette. 'It's obvious she's worried you might get hurt. I mean, somebody like him – he isn't the guy next door.'

'There's no future in it, you mean?' Kirsty's brown eyes had lost their softness. 'Honestly, Angie! I'm twenty years old. I'm no' thinking about the future, for heaven's sake! Just enjoying being with somebody—'

'Like him? Thing is, I bet Aunt Lena wouldn't have minded you having just the one drink with him. But the ticket for the concert – that shows he's really interested.'

'And that's a bad thing, is it?'

'Because he might get too interested. Or, give up being interested.'

Kirsty's lips tightened, her brow darkened. 'Angie, you ought to stop that smoking,' she said curtly. 'Or you'll be the one in disgrace.'

'I'm only telling you how Aunt Lena sees things. It's no business of mine what you do, Kirsty.'

'You're right about that. Och, I'll go and speak to her. Make her understand.'

Lena had washed her hair and was putting it into rollers, pulling down strands and snapping clips shut with such force that Kirsty was wincing. Oh, that poor hair! Bleached and rolled and forced into shape. Why couldn't her stepmother leave it alone?

'Look, I just want to say I'm sorry,' she said quietly. 'I mean about spoiling the tea. I thought I could get back in time.'

Lena shrugged as she fastened the last roller.

'Nae bother, Kirsy. But it's no' a bit of dried up pie that's worrying me.'

'Well, there's no need to be worried about Jake and me. I mean, what's one drink?'

'It won't be one drink, will it? If you're going to this concert at the King's. What happens after that, then?'

'Why, nothing. I just don't understand why you're so upset.'

'Well, I know why. I'm thinking of my sister.'

Kirsty's cheeks flamed. 'Beryl? How can you say such a thing? I've been out once with Jake and you think I'll end up like Angie's mother? You've no right—'

'Kirsty, it's just how it all began for her. I know, I remember. She went out with a fella she met when she was working at the stocking counter at Logie's in 1946. An air force pilot,

66

she said he was, looking for nylons for his sister. Nylons? For his sister? Would you credit it?'

'I suppose you couldn't get nylons?'

'No, and they'd wouldn't have been for his sister, anyway. But he fell for Beryl and started taking her out, spending money like water, wining and dining, and all of that. Then when she thought he was going to marry her, he just said it was out of the question, he wasn't the marrying kind. And the next thing she knew, he'd died in a flying accident, and she was in the family way. You ken what happened then.'

'I've never heard anything of Angie's father before.'

'No, well, all I could tell Angie was that he was dead – I mean, I never even knew his name ... But never mind all that now, Kirsty. Think of yourself. Jake MacIver's a grand fiddler, but he's out of your world, just like our Beryl's fella was out of hers. It all came to nothing with him, but by then she'd made her mistake.'

Lena leaned forward, the rollers in her hair grotesquely wobbling, and looked desperately into Kirsty's face. 'I don't want you to do the same,' she finished quietly.

'One drink is all there's been, Lena!' Kirsty cried. 'There's nothing between us!'

'Now's the time to nip it in the bud, then. Promise me you'll cancel that concert. When he offers you the ticket, you say you canna go. He'll understand why. Then you'll be safe.'

For a long time, Kirsty was silent, her shoulders drooping, her eyes downcast.

'I canna promise,' she said at last. 'It's no good

asking.'

Lena, her face working with emotion, stood up, throwing a towel around her shoulders.

'I might as well just dry my hair, then. But you tell Angie I can smell that cigarette of hers from here, and if I have to come in about it, she'll be in trouble.'

No one spoke over the cornflakes next morning, though Reid gave cheering smiles to the three women around him. Lena's mouth was set in a thin narrow line, while Angie, still brooding over her banned cigarette, was looking moody again and Kirsty defiant.

It was not that she didn't understand her stepmother's anxiety, now that she understood what had happened to Beryl. Rather that she just didn't see why Lena couldn't grasp the fact that things were different for her. A charming man had asked her for a drink and promised a ticket for a concert. Who was to say there'd be anything to follow? Who was to say he was truly interested, anyway?

But as she crunched her cereal without tasting it, she didn't let herself pry too deeply into her own emotions. Afraid, perhaps, of what she might find. Afraid of owning up to the fact that, more than anything in the world, she wanted true interest from Jake. And something to follow the concert. A genuine relationship. Even if she couldn't expect it.

No, she didn't put any of these desires into words she might have expressed. At the memory of his blue gaze always finding her, however, a small smile curved her lips, which, luckily, only Reid saw.

The young people were out on the stairs again, having said goodbye to Lena and receiving only a cool nod in return. Be glad to get to work, the girls said, and out of the 'atmosphere'.

'And where I can smoke, if I want to,' Angie muttered, at which Reid laughed.

'Over the clients? You'll be thrown out.'

'I mean, in my break!' she fired back.

'Morning!' Niall called, as he joined them, with Cormack trailing behind. 'Raining again.'

'Oh, thanks, that cheers us up!' Kirsty snapped, then seeing his face fall, relented. 'Sorry – I've just got the blues this morning.'

'That's all right, Kirsty, I know the feeling.'

Did he? She always pictured him as another Reid – not one to let things get to him. Ambitious, too, just like Reid, though better looking, as it happened – not that that had anything to do with anything. Both those MacFall boys were handsome, with their heavy-lidded dark eyes and straight noses, their rich black hair sweeping over fine brows; all inherited from Vinnie, of course, though in Niall's case, without the truculence. It was said that in character he was like his long-dead father, whereas Cormack followed his mother – which had always meant a difficult life for Niall, keeping an eye on him.

'I'm the one knows the feeling,' Cormack was muttering now, his eyes smouldering. 'I'm the one with the blues. And Ma's to blame.'

'What's she done?' Angie asked, with interest.

69

'Given in over me practising,' Cormack told her fiercely. 'Aye, to that lot up the stair! Just 'cause they complained to the Council, eh? If it was left to me, I'd go pipe right outside their door!'

'Don't you dare!' Niall cried, and giving an apologetic grin to the others, caught at his brother's arm. 'I'd better get this guy to the bus before he does something I'll regret!'

'Oh, lay off, I'm no' doing anything,' Cormack grumbled, shaking himself free and running down the stair with Niall after him.

'Poor old Niall,' Reid said with a laugh, as they followed. 'Who else'd want to nursemaid Cormack?'

'Suppose he thinks he should,' Angie said grudgingly.

'Niall's OK,' Kirsty stated. 'We talk some-times – he's got good ideas.'

Still wishing she hadn't snapped at him, she shrugged a little. Och, she'd enough on her plate to make her feel snappy, what with Lena going on.

'Still in the grumps over Lena?' Reid asked her, reading her mind, as he so often did. 'She's only thinking of you, you know. Keep quiet and see how things work out, is my advice.'

'You don't think I shouldn't go to Jake's concert?'

'You do what you think is right for you.'

'Well, I'm going.'

'And be prepared to take the risks,' Reid added. 'I forgot to mention that.'

'Oh, what risks?' Kirsty asked crossly. 'I can

take care of myself. Isn't that right, Angie?'

'Sure it is.' Angie laughed shortly. 'We don't need nursemaiding.'

Twelve

Dermot was waiting for Kirsty when she arrived at the shop. Even before she'd begun to unbutton her coat, he was at her side, fixing her with an unmoving stare.

'Well, how'd it go, then?' he asked coldly. 'Your drink with Mr Wonderful?'

'Very well.' Kirsty took off her scarf and shook back her damp hair. 'We went to a hotel in the West End. I had one sherry, he had one lager, then he took me home.'

'Took you home, how? Don't tell me, on the bus?'

'In his car.'

'Oh, he has a car.' Dermot's eyes flickered. 'Of course, he would have. And it's a good one, is it? No second-hand jalopy for him!'

'It's a nice car. Very comfortable.'

'Bet you spent a long time in it, eh? Because it was so comfortable?'

'We went straight to Pleasant Hill, we said goodnight, and I went in.' Kirsty's cheeks were reddening. 'Look, what is this, Dermot? Am I under interrogation, or what? You've no right to be asking me all these questions.'

'I know that,' he said hoarsely. 'But remember what it's like for me, thinking of you out with a guy like Jake MacIver? I bet he's had it easy all his life, never had to worry about money like the rest of us—'

'He has not had it easy all his life, Dermot. His dad died and his mother had to give piano lessons. He only went to Heriot's because he got one of those scholarships for poor fatherless boys—'

'Jake MacIver, a poor fatherless boy?' Dermot laughed heartily. 'Where's my violin? You'll have me sobbing into my hankie!'

'Here comes Lil,' Kirsty told him in an angry whisper. 'And I'm going to get on with my work!'

'No, Kirsty, wait!' He put his hand on her arm. 'Just tell me – are you going out with him again?'

'It's none of your business!'

'Temper, temper,' Lil said in the workroom. 'No' falling out with Dermot again, are you?'

'He's been questioning me as though I was in the witness box. Why is everybody going on about one drink, for heaven's sake?'

'He's just jealous, poor lad.' Lil hesitated. 'But you enjoyed yourself, eh?'

'I did, but I've had enough of talking about it, if you don't mind.'

'Fine. I understand. And Mrs MacNee's just at the door, complete with hat. We'd better get on.'

'Glad to,' Kirsty said, beginning to work a buttonhole on Jake MacIver's kilt.

She'd never thought it could happen, but when Jake came in on Wednesday for his final fitting, Kirsty experienced twinges of doubt when he greeted her in the fitting room. She'd so built him up in her mind that the reality, just for a fleeting moment or two, failed to measure up. But then there were those eyes of his meeting hers again, there was the softness of his voice, his way of making her seem so special to him, and all doubts vanished. He was exactly as she'd pictured him.

Of course, Mr Macrae had to be with them again, hovering round. If only he would go! Leave them alone, as he'd done before. Couldn't he get another phone call? Wasn't likely, was it? But then came an answer to a prayer. Dermot banged on the door to say that a man from Rotary was in the showroom, wanting a word with Mr Macrae.

A word with Mr Macrae? Oh, wonderful! Kirsty and Jake were alone, and Jake was smiling.

'Thank God for Mr Rotary,' he whispered. 'Let's hope he has a lot to say!'

She was so nervous, being so close to him again, her fingers were still fussing with one of the kilt straps, but he caught and stayed her hand.

'No more checking, Kirsty. Everything's fine.'

'As though you'd know,' she said shakily.

'I'm an expert on kilts – and other things.' He drew her against him, holding her lightly, running his hand through her pretty hair, almost, as

73

she knew, on the point of kissing her. When he didn't, she guessed he might be feeling the constraints of their situation, as she did, though when she turned her head towards the door, fearing to see Mr Macrae, he gently turned her back to look at him again.

'He's not there yet, Kirsty.'

'Will be, Jake.'

He sighed and after a moment let her go. 'OK, I don't want you to be embarrassed.'

'I just don't want to upset Mr Macrae. You can guess what he'd think.'

'My God, we were scarcely even holding hands! What year is this shop living in? I mean, is Queen Victoria dead, or not?'

'You're a customer; I'm supposed to be checking your kilt.' She blushed a little. 'I mean, you can understand he'd no' be too pleased.'

'Maybe you can understand it. Look, let me give you that ticket before anyone sees me and says it's not allowed.' He took the ticket from his jacket on a peg and pressed it into her hand. 'But, Kirsty, you'll be there? Promise? I want to see you again and I've booked a seat next to yours for the interval.'

'I promise,' she was beginning, when Mr Macrae came striding in, apologizing for leaving them, and she gave a guilty start.

'Kilt all right, then, Mr MacIver? It looks fine, I must say.'

'It's perfect. I think I'll keep it on. Could you have my old one wrapped for me?'

'Of course, provided the new kilt's ready to go. No problems, Miss Muir?'

74

'It's fine, I like it just the way it is,' Jake said before Kirsty could speak. 'Just wrap up the old one, please.'

'Very well, it will be a pleasure. Would you like to step this way?'

Jake looked back at Kirsty.

'Don't forget, there's my second kilt to think about, Miss Muir.'

'I'm going to be starting on it right away, Mr MacIver.'

'I'll be in touch, then.'

Their eyes met, then had to fall, as Jake went one way to have his kilt wrapped by a glowering Dermot, while Kirsty went another. But the thought of seeing him the following day went with her like a protective shield, making it easier not to mind that he had gone.

'Pleased with the kilt, was he?' Mrs MacNee asked, as Lil gave one of her indulgent smiles.

'Said it was perfect. In fact, he's gone off wearing it.'

'Never! It'd have needed another press, I'm sure.'

'He was insistent.'

'Oh, well...' Mrs MacNee shrugged. 'The customer is always right, I suppose.'

'Always,' Kirsty answered.

75

Thirteen

Some said the King's Theatre was old-fashioned, and perhaps it was showing its age a little,
dating as it did from 1906. But Kirsty, who knew
it from being taken to the pantomime when her
dad could afford it, loved its look of faded gilt
and crimson and wouldn't have had it any other
way. Especially not on Thursday evening when
she took her seat for the 'Scottish Winter Gala',
which was the title of Jake's show, for then she
could feel the magic of being in the theatre she
knew, while watching out for the man who had a
magic of his own.

As she waited for the familiar curtains to go up
and fanned herself with her programme, she
suddenly felt luck to be on her side. Not only
had she been given the chance to see Jake here,
and to know that he wanted to see her, but she
had made her peace with Lena. Or, at least, Lena
had made it with her, for that morning before she
left for work, her stepmother had suddenly
thrown her arms around her and said with a little
sob, 'Let's no' fight, Kirsty. I only want you to
be happy, and never to come to any harm.'

'Oh, Lena!' Kirsty, almost shedding a tear herself, hugged her stepmother in the hallway,
while Reid and Angie studiously looked the
other way. 'I never wanted to quarrel, and I will

take care, I promise. You'll see, I'll be OK.'

'Aye, well you keep to that, eh?' Lena stepped back, dabbing at her eyes. 'And have a good time at the concert. There'll be some grand tunes there, whatever else.'

'Only thing is, I don't know when I'll be back – I'll probably have to get the bus.'

'Nae bother, I'll expect you when I see you.'

As Lena heaved a deep sigh and turned away, the young people exchanged glances. They knew she had surrendered. She would say no more of her worries over Jake MacIver.

Oh, but who could have worries about Jake? Kirsty's heart was beginning to sing, as the auditorium grew dim and the brilliantly lit stage revealed Jake himself, and his MacIver Boys, opening the concert with the Bluebell Polka. How the audience loved it! How they loved Jake, too, and who could blame them? If he was charming, it was only natural for him to be like that. How could he be any different?

Now the dancers were coming in from the wings – men in kilts and Prince Charlie coatees, girls in white dresses with tartan sashes, as the MacIver Boys discreetly moved back and began to play 'Petronella', a reel Kirsty knew well. Soon, her feet were tapping, along with those of others around her, but from time to time, her gaze left the dancers and the band for the empty seat that was at her side. Here Jake would come, when he was free – he'd said so. No wonder her heart was singing!

* * *

77

He came at last, though not before a soprano and a baritone had followed the dancers, and then another band had had to play, with its leader trying to outdo Jake and failing. Finally a small choir had come on to round off the first half of the concert, to so much applause it was like having another item on the programme.

'Oh, Jake!' Kirsty murmured. 'It's been so lovely, but I thought you'd never come!'

'I thought it'd never end myself.' He quickly touched her hand and glanced round at people eyeing him, nudging their neighbours and smiling in recognition. 'But maybe we'd better go backstage to get some privacy.'

'Backstage?' She was thrilled. 'I've never been backstage in a theatre in my life! Can I see your dressing room?'

'Dressing room? Cupboard, I'd say. But come on then, before folk start getting their autograph books out.'

What a warren it was, then, behind the stage! Narrow passages, tiny rooms, performers darting in and out, calling, complaining, tripping over props and equipment.

'How ever do you find your way about?' Kirsty asked, bemused, but Jake only laughed and said you got used to it, as he threw open the door to a dressing room, which if it was not a cupboard, was certainly not much bigger.

'Come and meet the guys. Sandy Robson, accordionist – Rickie Innes – double bass – and Colin Smith, who plays anything that's going – flute, tin whistle, Scottish harp, whatever. Fellas, this is Kirsty Muir, the world's best kilt maker.'

78

'Hi, Kirsty! Made a good job of his lordship's kilt, then!'

'Better make ours next, eh?'

'Aye, mine's falling apart. Held up with kilt pins!'

They greeted her with grins and friendly badinage. Tall, melancholy Sandy. Black-haired, Celtic-looking Rickie. Freckle-faced, blond Colin. All in white shirts and kilts of their own tartans, which, according to Kirsty's expert eye, were not too badly made and not in quite such bad repair as they'd joked.

They seemed pleased to see her, yet not, perhaps, surprised. Had Jake already mentioned her? Or had other girls been here before her, at other shows? Instantly, she put that thought from her mind, as the band members pulled up a battered chair for her and asked if she'd like coffee. Rickie had just volunteered to get it.

'Volunteered, I don't think!' he exclaimed. 'So, I'll make that five, eh?'

'Unless Kirsty'd like an ice?' asked Sandy.

'Oh, coffee will be fine, thanks.'

'Enjoying the show?'

'It's wonderful! Really wonderful!'

'Amazing, how folk still like the trad music, eh? I thought it'd die a natural death when the pop stuff took over, but no, we're still going strong.'

'Our music will never die,' Jake said seriously. 'There's room for all sorts in this world, surely?'

'Aye, that's right,' Colin agreed. 'I'm a Beatles fan myself, though I still want to play our music, no' theirs.'

Jake nodded. 'Just what I mean. But here comes the coffee. Drink up, lads, time's getting on.' His eyes went to Kirsty and, as she finished her coffee, he came over to whisper in her ear. 'Did I mention privacy? Have to find that later. Wait for me at the front of the theatre and I'll give you a lift home.'

A lift home? She was filled with joyous relief. They would see each other when the concert was over. Find their privacy, as he'd promised, be really alone. As her great eyes glistened and her face was lit by smiles, the men in Jake's band studied her without speaking, until a bell rang in the distance and they leaped up.

'Can you find your seat, Kirsty?' Jake asked hastily. 'We're on in a couple of minutes.'

'I can find it,' she cried, feeling she was on wings.

The second half of the concert was even better than the first, for she was relaxed; content to enjoy the music because she knew she could be sure of seeing Jake later. And when she came out of the theatre into the chill of the night air, she didn't mind that she would have to wait for him. It was only to be expected that he'd have things to do. He couldn't just walk out after a performance.

In fact, his beautiful car came gliding up rather earlier than she'd thought, and as she slid into her seat beside him, she felt so happy she could scarcely speak.

'Had a good evening?' he asked, negotiating the theatre traffic with casual skill.

She gave a long contented sigh. 'You know I have.'

'That's good. I just wanted you to hear my music, meet my lads.'

'It was all perfect, Jake. Out of this world.'

'And interesting, wasn't it, that talk of pop music with the guys? I must admit, I see no reason why people can't enjoy different sorts of music. Bet you like discos, don't you, Kirsty?'

'I go to them sometimes.'

He glanced at her, smiling. 'Shall we go to one?'

'You and me? Hard to imagine you at a disco, somehow.'

'I've another plan, anyway.'

They were leaving the West End, where they'd had that first drink – strange how far they seemed to have come, even since then. Already, she could not picture a life without seeing Jake.

'Another plan?'

'Yes. Do you have any dancing shoes? Scottish dancing shoes?'

'Yes, I've got dancing shoes.' She hesitated. 'Why d'you ask?'

'I was just wondering if you'd done any Scottish dancing?'

She smiled. 'I do work in a kilt shop – I'd be expected to know a bit about the dancing. As a matter of fact, I learned it at school, and then my stepsister and me once went to classes at the kirk hall – near where we used to live.'

'That's excellent.'

'You're asking me to go to a ceilidh, or something?'

'No.' He paused for effect. 'A ball.'

'A ball?' She stared. 'Where? Which ball?'

'The Valentine Ball, at the Assembly Rooms. It's a sort of Highland ball, really.'

'Oh, Jake, I ... I'm no' sure...' She swallowed hard. 'Will you be playing for it?'

'As a matter of fact, I'm not. I'd be going just as your dancing partner.'

Her dancing partner ... Such beautiful words!

'Aye, in my doublet and my new kilt. And you'll be in your white dress with your tartan sash. Don't worry, I'll get them for you. They'll be my present.'

'No,' she said with sudden firmness. 'I can get the white dress and sash myself. Cost price from the shop.'

'You're coming then?'

'Oh, Jake, I don't know what to say – I've never been to a ball like that.'

'It's just another dance, dear Kirsty, and you've been to plenty of those.'

'But the people – I won't know anyone.'

'You'll know me. Won't I be enough?'

'My dancing partner,' she said fondly. 'Jake, I don't know if I'm on my head or my heels – it's all happening so fast...'

'No point hanging about. I'll get the tickets, then.'

For the rest of the drive home, she was silent, her thoughts whirling. How was she going to buy one of the shop's white dresses without telling everyone where she was going? They weren't expensive, there was no problem there, and she'd long wanted one of the silk sashes for her own, but she could just imagine Dermot's face, or Mrs MacNee's, if she said why she wanted a proper Scottish dancing dress and the sash to go with it.

'You're going to the Valentine Ball?' She could hear Mrs MacNee's scandalized voice as though she was actually in the car. 'With Mr MacIver?'

'Going to the ball, with *him*?' That was Dermot. 'Talk about Cinderella, then. Who's he think he is, the handsome prince?'

'What's this I hear about you and Mr MacIver attending the Valentine Ball?' Mr Macrae would be asking. 'A customer?' And Lil would be smiling her little smiles.

'Penny for them?' asked Jake as they neared Pleasant Hill. 'I seem to have given you food for thought.'

'No, it's OK. It'll be all right. I'm just a bit – stunned, I suppose.'

'Mind if we stop here? Not quite at your door?'

She looked around, saw that they were in a side road, with the blocks of flats some distance away, and that there was no street lighting overhead. She turned to look at Jake.

'Yes, you've guessed it,' he said quietly. 'I want to kiss you away from the audience. If that's all right with you?'

'All right?' she asked huskily. 'Oh, Jake, what are you talking about?' And went into his arms.

How long they spent, clasped together, kissing as though the end of the world was upon them and they had to make their mouths meet as fast

83

as possible, she couldn't guess, but it was only when they were too breathless to go on that they drew apart.

'I've been thinking of this all evening,' Jake whispered against her face. 'Being with you, kissing you. Oh God, Kirsty, you're so lovely ... But I know I mustn't keep you.' He smoothed his hand down her cheek. 'Try not to look too guilty, my darling, when you see your step-mother, or she'll never let me take you out again.'

'I'll be as calm as a cucumber,' she said, laughing nervously, as he began to drive slowly towards Clover. 'But I don't think she'll say anything, anyway.'

When he came round to open the door for her, she climbed out reluctantly and gazed into his face.

'Shall I see you again before the ball, Jake?'

'Have you forgotten? You're making my second kilt. I'll be coming in for a fitting.'

'If I make it exactly like your first one, you won't need a fitting.'

'I'm having a fitting,' he said solemnly. 'But could you fix it so that Mr Macrae is called away on business first?'

She was smiling when she let herself into the flat, forcing herself to appear very calm, very relaxed, even when three pairs of eyes were fixed on her again.

'Enjoy the concert?' Reid asked – the first to speak.

'Look cold,' Angie commented. 'Red in the

face, anyway.'

'Look happy,' Lena said quietly. 'Did you get a lift back?'

Reid sighed, as Kirsty nodded. 'Wish I'd seen the car – next time, eh?'

'If there's a next time,' Angie murmured.

'Oh, there's sure to be a next time.' Lena got up. 'I'll put the kettle on, eh?'

I needn't tell her about the ball just now, Kirsty thought. *I can leave it till tomorrow.*

Fourteen

In a way, it was disconcerting, telling Lena about the Valentine Ball, for, as they'd all thought, she seemed to have resigned herself to putting up no opposition.

'It's your life, Kirsty, your decision what you do,' she said tiredly. 'If I think you're going to burn your fingers, well, you don't think so, so we'll no' argue.'

'Lena, I just don't want to worry you, that's all.'

'Och, let it go. What's one more worry?'

With that, Kirsty had to go to work with worries of her own – principally buying the white dress and the silk sash and not letting anyone know.

'How can I do it?' she asked Angie and Reid at the bus stop. As though they would know.

85

Certainly, Angie only shrugged, but Reid after a moment or two gave his opinion that Kirsty had better buy the dress and sash somewhere else.

'What, and lose the discount?' she cried.

'There speaks a good thrifty lassie! Come on, it'd be worth it. Tell you what – I'll give you something towards it – out of my pub money.'

'No, thanks all the same, Reid. I've got a few pounds in the Post Office I can spend if I want.'

'Why do you no' just tell 'em at Macrae's that you're going to the ball with Jake MacIver and let 'em lump it?' asked Angie. 'I would.'

'Because I know Mr Macrae wouldn't approve of me going out with a customer, and neither would Mrs MacNee. And I'd never hear the last of it from Dermot.'

'Better do what Reid says, then.'

'Aye, you're right,' sighed Kirsty. 'Think I will tell Lil, though. It's such a strain, keeping secrets from everybody.'

Naturally, Lil was excited to hear about the invitation to the Valentine Ball, saying that this was serious stuff, and that Jake must be really keen.

'I think he's really fallen for you, Kirsty. I mean, he'd never take somebody who didn't matter to a do like that.'

'Promise you won't tell the others?'

'Cross my heart and hope to die. Why would I tell 'em, anyway?'

'You might tell Dermot. I've seen you talking to him quite a bit lately.'

86

'Aye, well we've been out for a drink a couple of times. But if you don't want me to tell him, I swear I won't say a word. Can I come with you to buy the dress, though?'

'Sure, we can go in our lunch hour. Just hope no one recognizes me. I mean, if it got back to Mr Macrae that I'd been shopping at another kilt shop, he'd wonder what was going on.'

'Mightn't matter what he thinks,' Lil said cheerfully. 'Since you might be moving on, eh?'

Kirsty put her finger to her lips and shook her head. 'No talking like that, Lil. It's just pointless.'

They chose a kilt shop at the other end of the city, as far away as possible from Macrae's, where Kirsty found a simple white dress that made her look as slender as a wand, and a beautiful sash in her own tartan to wear at her right shoulder.

'Oh, look at you,' Lil moaned in the fitting room, where it was now Kirsty's turn, after checking on so many customers, to study herself in a mirror. 'Makes me feel like a house end. I'll just have to go on a diet.'

'Think it's OK?' Kirsty asked, turning round to try to see the dress at the back.

'Perfect!'

'Lovely,' said the young assistant. 'You look like you should be on that *Reel Time* programme, eh?'

'I'm going to a ball,' Kirsty murmured, flushing. 'The Valentine Ball.'

'The Valentine Ball? Aren't you the lucky one, then?'

'I am.' Kirsty's eyes met Lil's. 'Very lucky indeed.'

'I still don't believe it,' she murmured, when they had left the shop and were on their way to a café for a quick lunch. 'I sometimes think I'm dreaming and will have to wake up.'

'These things happen when you least expect 'em,' Lil said sagely. 'But don't go around being grateful all the time. Jake can think himself lucky, too.'

'Oh, come on, what am I giving him?'

'No' too much, I hope,' Lil said cheekily, and at the look on Kirsty's face, laughed and knocked her arm. 'Only joking.'

But Kirsty, though she nodded easily, wasn't sure Lil's words were funny, for she often thought of how her relationship with Jake might progress. How much might he expect? How much would she be prepared to give? Or to risk?

At the back of her mind now was always Beryl. 'I don't want you to do the same,' Lena had said darkly, meaning make the same mistake. Yet, more and more, Kirsty was coming to understand how Beryl had allowed herself to make it, and wondered how much she could trust not Jake, but herself. Should she try to find out about precautions? Trouble was she didn't know where to start.

When Jake came in some days later, though it was only to collect his second kilt, he still tried it on, under Dermot's supervision, and afterwards Kirsty slipped into the fitting room, supposedly to check buckles and straps.

'Thanks, Dermot,' she said pointedly. 'You'd better no' leave the front shop too long.'

His face very red, Dermot walked out, and Jake shook his head.

'Oh dear, oh dear, we've upset him, haven't we? But I had to have my chance to be alone with you – especially as your Mr Macrae doesn't seem to be around.'

'He's away today, but the others know I'm here with you. We mustn't stay too long.'

'Secrets, secrets.' He kissed her lips. 'Why must everything be kept under wraps?'

'It's easier, that's all. And there's another thing – nobody here knows about the ball, except my friend, Lil. So you'll no mention it, eh?'

'Another secret?' He groaned. 'We'd better make our arrangements now, then. But first, did you get the dress?'

'Oh, yes!' Her face brightened. 'And the sash. They're lovely.'

'I wanted to buy them for you. At least, let me pay now. I haven't given you anything.'

'Look, it's all right, I wanted to get them. Let's talk about the arrangements.'

It was decided that he would pick her up from home at a little before eight and they would drive to the Assembly Rooms in George Street. If he couldn't park, they'd try one of the New Town squares and take a taxi from there.

'You always say you can park anywhere,' she said with a smile.

'Yes, well, I expect I'll find a place. Just keep your fingers crossed that it's not raining or snowing or whatever, in case we have to walk a bit. Of course, I could always drop you off first.'

'No, no, I'm no' going in without you!'

Very firmly, she said she must go, and took his new kilt from him to have it wrapped.

'And then I write my cheque?'

'If you like.' She stood looking at him for a moment. 'I was wondering...'

'Yes?'

'When you collect me for the ball, would you like to come in for a minute? Meet my family?'

Was there just the slightest hesitation from him before he spoke? She couldn't be sure. Anyway, he seemed to like the idea.

'Why, of course, Kirsty. I'd like very much to meet your folks. Wish I'd someone to introduce to you, but there it is – I'm all alone.'

'Not now,' she wanted to say, but only smiled sadly for him as they turned for the door.

'Till the ball, then,' he said softly. 'I have to go to Glasgow for a few days, but I'll be back in good time. Don't forget to look out for the postman on the fourteenth.'

'The postman?'

'You haven't forgotten what day it is?'

Valentine's Day? Of course not. But she hadn't thought of receiving a valentine. As she and Jake left the fitting room together, her heart was singing again, even though Dermot was looking grim, and when she arrived home that evening with Angie, there was more good news.

'Guess what?' cried Angie, trying the lift. 'It's working!'

'Never!' Kirsty leaped in. 'Just in time, then.'

90

'Time for what?'

'Jake will be coming in to meet you all before we go to the ball.'

'Oh! Better practise my curtsey.'

'No need to be like that. He's nice. You'll see.'

'OK, sorry. Wonder what Auntie Lena will say?'

'I think that's very polite, wanting to come in to meet us,' Lena said, when told. 'It's only right, after all. How about you meeting his folks, Kirsty?'

'He has no one. His parents are dead and he was an only child.'

'Poor fellow.' Lena shrugged. 'Still, he seems to have managed all right on his own, eh? Some men have no interest in families.'

Fifteen

From time to time as she was dressing for the ball, Kirsty's eyes would go to the card by her bed. Her valentine. It bore no signature, of course, but she knew it was from Jake, partly because of what he'd said, partly because its picture showed a man serenading a girl on a balcony, who was throwing him a rose. And the man was playing a violin.

'Clever Jake, to find that,' Angie had said. 'Now mine's just got sweet peas in a vase. Do I look like a sweet pea?'

'Maybe it's meaning that you're sweet?'

'Well, I'm no' sweet, am I?'

All the same, Angie had been smiling. Seemed she was pleased somebody had sent her a valentine. Who could it have been? Kirsty wondered. Niall MacFall, maybe? Was he interested in Angie? It had come through the post, but that might have been a way of putting Angie off the scent. At least Kirsty knew who'd sent hers and had a beautifully warm feeling inside, thinking of it.

'Time's getting on,' Lena called through the door. 'Your young man'll be here soon.'

'Coming,' Kirsty answered, applying lipstick with a trembling hand. Oh, how she suddenly wished she didn't have to go! Meet all those strangers. Have to remember the dances. Have to be a credit to Jake, who'd paid for her ticket. Have to enjoy herself.

'How do I look?' she asked Angie, who'd put her head round the door.

'Amazing. Canna recognize you.'

'Is that a compliment, then?'

'It's just I've never seen you in a dress like that – and with the sash and all...' Angie's voice trailed away, until she cried strongly, 'Come on out and show Auntie Lena!'

'Oh my, is that you, Kirsty?' Lena whispered. 'I don't know what to say! Reid, come and look at your sister!'

'Wow!' He grinned. 'A dead cert for *Reel Time, Song Time*, eh?'

'The girl in the shop said that,' Kirsty murmured. 'It's the sash, that's all.'

'And you've got your ma's Cairngorm brooch to fasten it, eh?' Lena's voice trembled. 'I remember her with that brooch. Your dad gave it to her, she once told me—'

'Someone at the door!' cried Angie. 'I'll go.'

It was Jake.

When Angie brought him in, he seemed keen to smile, to be introduced, but then his eyes went to Kirsty, who was standing still as a statue, and he too stood still.

'Kirsty?' he whispered, as though not sure.

But it was only that the pretty girl he knew had become, in her white dress and sash, with her copper hair shining and her brown eyes enormous, quite suddenly beautiful. That was what had surprised them all, as people are surprised sometimes by a bride's beauty on her wedding day. Another dimension seemed to have been granted, perhaps only for a little while – but something of it would linger always.

Kirsty herself was the first to recover and make the introductions.

'Lena, this is Jake MacIver. Jake, this is my stepmother. My brother, Reid, my stepsister, Angie – this is Jake MacIver.'

There were murmured greetings as Jake shook hands with Kirsty's family. Then her family looked at him.

'Wow,' Reid might have repeated, for Jake was in full evening dress, with high-necked velvet doublet and silver buttons, jabot, sporran, sgian dubh (or small dagger), tartan hose and laced black shoes. Never had they seen anything like it, except in pictures, and that was how he seemed for a moment – a picture come to life.

But Jake's social gifts did not desert him and he was soon filling the stunned silence. Talking easily to Lena about how she liked the flat; to Reid about his engineering course; to Angie about how it was to be a young person in Edinburgh. Was she one for the pop concerts, or maybe the traditional stuff played by an old chap like him? Both, he hoped.

'I'll bet you know we all watch your programme,' she answered smartly, and he smiled and bowed, then glanced at his watch.

'Kirsty? It's been so pleasant, but I'm afraid we'll have to go.'

'Yes, I'm ready. I'll just get my cloak.'

Wrapped in the tartan cloak she'd bought in a Macrae's sale some years before, she hesitated in the doorway.

'Goodnight, then. I ... might be late back.'

'Have a good time!' cried Lena.

'We will,' Jake said. 'So happy to meet you, Mrs Muir – Reid – Angie.'

'And you,' Reid said. 'Can I come down and see the car?'

'Liked your family,' Jake told Kirsty as they sped towards the centre of the city. 'Reid, now, he's clever, as you said. Could tell that from his eyes.'

'I've always thought that.'

'And your stepmother – you've been lucky, there. She's one who cares. Isn't that true?'

'It's true. She's been wonderful to Reid and me.'

'And to her niece, I should think. Angie. So lovely, Kirsty, but so sad. What's the story? Can you tell me?'

'Angie's never known her mother. She wasn't married and left Angie to Lena to bring up. That's all we know.'

'I'm sorry.' Jake gave a sideways glance at Kirsty. 'But I shouldn't pry. Let's think about the ball and the good time we're going to have. All eyes will be on me, thinking I'm a lucky devil, dancing with such a beautiful girl.'

'You're looking pretty good yourself, Jake.'

'In my doublet? Think I'm going to be too hot. Wish I'd worn my Prince Charlie coatee. Story of my life, eh? Always making wrong choices.' He smiled as they drove into George Street. 'Maybe not always. Hi, look, do you think I can squeeze in there?'

Sixteen

As so often happens, Kirsty's nervousness evaporated as soon as the evening actually began. Could it have been true that she'd not wanted to come to the ball? Looking round the long elegant ballroom, with its chandeliers and exquisite flower arrangements, its little gilt chairs and tables at the side, she couldn't believe she'd ever thought such a thing.

She knew she looked right, and she felt right too, even amongst these smart people – the men in their doublets or Prince Charlie coatees, the women in white dresses or more elaborate gowns, with tartan sashes over the shoulder just like hers. And all so full of confidence. Knowing everyone, and being known. Radiant with the expectation of the ball to come.

Of course, it was true that Kirsty didn't know anyone except Jake, but it didn't matter, for he seemed to know everyone. Members of the band, the dancers in their sets, people passing with drinks – there was always someone to say, 'Hello, Jake!' and send eyes over her as his partner.

And then she'd be introduced and the next thing she knew she'd be flying through the reels, holding strangers' hands and exchanging smiles, or stepping gravely through a strathspey, still smiling, still feeling she was on Cloud Nine.

How lovely it was to do the old dances she'd once known so well! The Eightsome, the Foursome, the Duke of Perth, Monymusk, Hamilton House ... How all the steps came back to her, though it was some time since she'd gone with Angie to the dancing in the kirk hall. But she and Jake were careful not to go first couple, so that they could check what the expert dancers did, and there were always folk ready to call out, 'Set to me!' or 'Set to partner!' or 'Cast off, cast off!'

'Didn't tell me you were so good,' Jake murmured, as they retired to the gilt chairs after a particularly lively jig. 'Someone taught you well at that kirk hall.'

'You're right. An old dragon – used to scare the wits out of us, but we learned the steps.'

'Kirsty, I'm proud of you.' He glanced at his watch. 'Not long to supper and I could do with it. Would you like a drink now?'

'Oh, please! Something long and cold.'

After she'd watched him move away, admiring her own handiwork in the swing of his kilt, she sat back in her little chair, ready to take a breather and cast a critical eye over the kilts of those still dancing. So absorbing was this for her that she didn't at first hear someone calling her name.

'Kirsty?' the voice repeated. 'Whatever are you doing here?'

And then the voice penetrated and she scrambled to her feet, her colour fading.

'Mr Macrae?' she stammered. 'Good ... evening.'

He was wearing the Prince Charlie evening dress – the formal coatee with a black tie and waistcoat, plus silver-topped sporran, plain stockings and black laced shoes – all of which made him look quite distinguished, almost handsome. Not that Kirsty was able at that moment to appreciate his looks. All she wanted was to be spirited out of his sight before Jake came back with her drink, when all her efforts at secrecy would be proved to be a waste of time.

Oh, please, let him be delayed, she prayed, *please!* But that was a waste of time too. For she could hardly be at a ball such as this without a partner, and she would have to tell Mr Macrae who it was.

'I'd no idea you were coming to the Valentine Ball,' Mr Macrae was saying, wonderingly. 'Are you ... you're not alone, are you?'

'No,' she was beginning, when a waiter arrived with drinks on a tray, followed by Jake, who was pointing out his table.

'Sorry I took so long,' he said cheerfully. 'It's like a rugby match at the bar, but this chap's saved the day.'

'Here's Mr Macrae,' Kirsty said quietly, and sank into her chair.

'Why, Mr Macrae, how nice.' Jake was giving his famous smile, showing no sign of anything except pleasant surprise. 'Won't you join us? May I order you something to drink?'

'Thank you, no, I must rejoin my partner.' Mr Macrae's tone was cold, his eyes frosty. 'Good to meet you both. Kirsty, I'll see you tomorrow.'

'Yes, Mr Macrae.'

As he left them, they saw a fair-haired young woman come hurrying up to take his arm, and then they were both lost in a crowd of dancers leaving the floor as a reel came to an end.

'Everything all right, sir?' asked the waiter.

'Fine, thanks.' Jake put a note on his tray and as the waiter withdrew, turned to Kirsty.

'You're looking worried. Not about meeting Macrae, I hope?'

'I'm sure he's going to tick me off tomorrow.'

'Because I asked you to this ball? I'm not even a customer now. What the hell has it got to do with him, if you go out with me?'

'He'll know it all started in the shop. It's the sort of thing he doesn't like.'

'And I have the feeling he doesn't like me. That's what's wrong.'

'Why wouldn't he like you, Jake?'

He shrugged. 'Plenty of men don't. But he's the same as his shop – fifty years behind the times. Why don't you leave? Go somewhere more up to date.'

'I don't want to go anywhere more up to date. I like Macrae's. They've been good to me there.'

'OK, they won't want to lose you. My guess is he'll not say much. These things happen. I can't be the first man to buy a kilt who's fallen for the kilt maker.'

Fallen for the kilt maker ... Had he really said that? Her spirits lifted.

'No, but you're famous, you see.'

'Can't see why that should matter.'

'I think it will.'

'Och, don't worry about it. Drink up and let's go and find some supper. I'm starving – don't know about you.'

As she obediently took up her glass, he leaned forward, holding her with his direct gaze.

'Promise me you won't let this spoil our evening, Kirsty? When we're having such a good time?'

'Of course I won't.'

All the same, it was hard not to think of tomorrow, when she'd have to face her boss. Only by remembering those special words of Jake's could she put it out of her mind.

* * *

They were fortunate not to bump into Mr Mac-rae and his partner again, which meant they were able to enjoy the rest of the ball well enough. And then of course there was the end of the evening to bring another kind of enjoyment, when they parked back at Pleasant Hill in their secluded spot. This time it was Kirsty who kissed first, and passionately, too, then sat back to look at Jake with melting tenderness.

'Thank you – for being so kind.'

'Kind?' He shook his head. 'Not many have called me that.'

'Well, you've been very kind to me. Very understanding.'

'Have I?' He held her hands against his face. 'If I have, it's because you're such a sweet, loving girl.'

For some time, she rested against him, and he stroked her hair and gently kissed her.

'I'm glad you've stopped worrying about your Mr Macrae,' he said quietly.

'Have I?'

'Yes, you're thinking of me for a change.'

'For a change? You've no idea how much I think about you.'

'Well, if it's the same as I think about you, it's a lot.' Suddenly he held her closer. 'Ah, Kirsty, we've so much to look forward to, you know, you and I. Why waste time worrying about a chap at work?'

'A chap? You mean my boss.' She gave a delighted little smile. 'Tell me what we have to look forward to, then.'

'Well, being together. Going to concerts –

dances – the theatre. There's so much I want to take you to, or show you. My recording sessions, for instance. In Glasgow.'

'Recording sessions?'

'Of my programmes. We'll be starting on them soon, getting the new ones ready for the autumn. You could come through to Glasgow to watch, be a part of the studio audience. Would you like that?'

'Would I? Oh, Jake!'

They began to kiss and caress in earnest, forgetting time and weariness, thinking only of each other, until Jake reluctantly drew away and said he'd better get her home before her stepmother came looking.

'Have to keep on the right side of your Lena, you know.'

'It's all right; she knows I'll be late.' Outside the flats, she pressed his hand. 'Thank you again, Jake, for everything.'

'I'm the one who should be thanking you. I've had a wonderful evening, dancing with the best-looking girl at the ball.'

They kissed briefly and arranged to meet two days later, when Jake returned from engagements in Perth. He would be waiting for her as before, outside the shop at half past five.

'And no worrying about what Grey Man says, eh?'

'Grey Man?'

'You know who I mean.'

Laughing, she stood at the door to Clover and watched him drive away, then took the stairs, rather than the rattling lift, for it was very late.

No one was about when she let herself into the flat, but when she tiptoed round the bedroom, Angie asked sleepily, 'Had a good time?'

'The best.'

'We all admired your Jake – quite the charmer, eh?'

Her Jake? Kirsty smiled in the darkness.

'What did Lena say, then?'

'Said she could see why you'd been bowled over.'

'But...?'

Angie yawned. 'How d'you mean, "but"?'

'I bet there was one.'

'You shouldn't worry. Night, Kirsty. I need my sleep.'

'Me too.'

But Kirsty knew she'd get very little.

Seventeen

As Kirsty had expected, Mr Macrae asked to 'have a word' with her as soon as he arrived at the shop rather late the following morning.

'Ten o'clock, you'll notice?' Lil had murmured, when they'd heard his office door bang. 'Wish I was the boss.'

Almost immediately, he'd appeared at the workroom door, looking for Kirsty and requesting coffee.

'Certainly, Mr Macrae, Kirsty will bring it to

you,' Mrs MacNee told him. 'If you want to see her anyway.'

And no one missed her unsaid question. Why should he want to see Kirsty at ten o'clock on a Saturday morning?

Especially, Lil added to herself, when he looked as though he could have done with the morning in bed.

'Think he's got a hangover?' she asked, as Kirsty carried away the coffee tray as if she was going to execution. 'Must have been somewhere exciting last night.'

'The Valentine Ball,' Mrs MacNee told her confidentially. 'He always takes Miss Grier to that. Maybe you remember her? I think you made her a kilt once.'

'Oh, yes, I do. Tall and fair. Well-to-do.'

'Aye, her mother's a friend of Mrs Macrae's. Between you and me, I think Mildred wouldn't mind being young Mrs Macrae.'

'Oh, yes? So, what are her chances?'

'Who knows? But if his mother thinks any girl would be good enough for him, she'd be the one.'

His eyes were not as cold as at the ball, Kirsty noticed, as she set Mr Macrae's coffee on his desk. In fact, his smile was just as friendly as usual, but it didn't make her feel any better. She hadn't been called in to his office for nothing, that was for sure.

'Thank you, Kirsty.' He took a sip of the coffee. 'Could do with that. Late night last night, as you'll know. Why didn't they have the ball

103

tonight, I wonder? Then we could have had a rest tomorrow.'

'I suppose they wanted it on Valentine's Day.'

'Yes. Well, take a seat, please. I'd just like to have a quick word.'

She sat down facing him and stared at her hands folded on her lap while he drank more coffee.

'The thing is,' he began, after a pause, 'when I saw you at the ball with Mr MacIver, you can understand I was a little surprised. I wasn't aware that you knew him.'

Kirsty stayed silent.

'I presume you first met him here? In the shop?'

'That's right.'

'And he asked you out – at one of his fittings?'

'Yes, for a drink.'

Now he's going to tell me he doesn't approve, she thought. *He's going to say that it isn't the sort of thing for Macrae's, and what would his father have said in the old days? Or his mother today, come to that?*

But when he spoke again, it seemed Mr Macrae had something different on his mind. 'You'll forgive me for seeming to interfere, Kirsty, but it was in my shop that this began and I feel somewhat responsible.'

'Responsible? Why?'

'I gave Jake MacIver the opportunity, if you remember. I asked you to make his kilt.'

Not Mrs MacNee. Of course she remembered. As though she could have forgotten how close she'd been to missing the love she shared with

104

Jake ... She felt cold at the thought.

'What of it?' she managed to ask.

'Well, because you were his kilt maker, he was able to take advantage of seeing you. Able to ask you out, as some men do when they meet a pretty girl in a shop. I was worried about it from the start...'

And all the time hovering around, Kirsty thought. As though she couldn't take care of herself!

'You'd no need to worry,' she told him. 'Jake isn't like the men you mentioned. He isn't just amusing himself. He's serious. We both are.'

'Kirsty, you scarcely know the man.' Mr Macrae leaned forward. 'I'm telling you, now's the time to end this relationship before it's too late, before you get hurt!'

Her face was scarlet, her eyes enormous, filled with the pain of his words.

'There'll be no getting hurt for me,' she said in a low voice. 'Can I go now?'

'No, hear me out. Look, Mr MacIver is very well known. He moves in a different world from yours. And I've heard it said that he's – to put it kindly – a bit of a ladies' man. Everywhere he goes, women are attracted to him, as you are.'

'And he's attracted to me,' she said quickly. 'As soon as we met, I knew, because girls always know. I knew what he felt, because I felt the same. He loves me, and I love him.'

Mr Macrae looked down at his desk. 'Has he said that? Has he told you he loves you?'

She hesitated. 'He doesn't have to tell me. Like I said, I know.'

'Oh, Kirsty, Kirsty!' Mr Macrae leaned his head on his hand, then sat up, straightening his shoulders. 'Will you at least think about things very carefully? Try to see this relationship as something temporary? Then, when the break-up comes, you'll be ready, you see. To say good-bye.'

Break-up. Goodbye. The words struck straight to her heart, and for a moment she couldn't speak. But then it came to her in a flood of sweet relief, that there had been no break-up and would be none. There would be no goodbye.

What had Jake said to her only last night? 'We've so much to look forward to, you and I...' And when she'd asked him what, he'd said, so simply, 'Being together.' That was what they wanted, that was what they had. There was no need to be afraid of Mr Macrae's warnings. No need to take any notice of him at all.

She stood up, putting his empty coffee cup on her tray. 'I think I'd better get back to work, sir. I've a lot to do.'

'You haven't listened to a word I've said, have you?'

'I have, sir, and I know you mean well. But honestly there's no need to worry. So, can I go now?'

'Yes, you go,' he said tiredly. 'I've done all I can. There's no more to be said.'

Moving back to the workroom, his words echoing in her ears, she was reminded of her stepmother, suddenly letting go of all opposition in the face of Kirsty's own defence of Jake Mac-Iver. Didn't that prove she was right?

But when Mrs MacNee fixed her with a piercing look and asked if there was a problem, she suddenly felt so exhausted, so drained of all energy, she simply decided to tell the truth.

'Mr Macrae's worried because I went to the Valentine Ball with Mr MacIver,' she said, sitting down at the table where she'd left a kilt she was stitching. 'But it's no' really anything to do with him, is it?'

And, as Lil said afterwards, it was worth a week's wages, to see the look on Madam's face, to discover she could be completely lost for words and quite unable for a moment or two to express her disapproval. Of course, she made up for it pretty quickly, but as the tide of words flowed over Kirsty, it was plain to see that, as she took up her work, her mind was somewhere far away.

Eighteen

When Kirsty and Jake met on Tuesday evening, it was in driving icy rain. They had made no plans, but as they stood outside Macrae's, their umbrellas locking together, their faces cold and damp, Jake said, 'To hell with this! Let's have something to eat and go to my flat – OK?'

'Oh, yes,' Kirsty said, great dark eyes shining in the street lights. She had wondered for some time when this would come – when he would ask her to his home. And what it would mean. If anything. 'I'd like to see your flat, Jake.'

'Sorry I can't cook you a meal, the kitchen's empty. Maybe next time, eh?'

'I didn't even know you could cook.'

'A dab hand, I promise you. But let's find a taxi, we're getting soaked.'

He looked up the High Street and waved, and Jake being Jake, a taxi immediately materialized out of the darkness and they were driven away, leaving Lil and Dermot, who'd just left the shop, staring after them.

In a little restaurant close to the Castle, they had steaks and French fries, and Jake ordered himself a half bottle of wine, as Kirsty said she didn't care for it.

'You just need to get used to it,' he told her. 'Wine makes a meal.'

'It makes me feel woozy. I like to know what I'm doing.'

He laughed. 'Sensible girl. But listen, what did the Grey Man have to say to you the other day? No, don't tell me, let me guess. He was warning you off me. Am I right?'

At the pink flush that rose to Kirsty's cheeks, he nodded.

'I see I am. I knew he was never going to be mad at you. It's Big Bad Wolf MacIver he's blaming, isn't it? For leading you astray?'

She drank some water. 'Let's no' bother about him, Jake.'

'No, tell me what he said. I'd like to know.'

'Just that we ... moved in different worlds. And

I shouldn't go out with you.'

'He said that? The hell he did!' Jake's blue eyes were snapping angrily. 'What gives him the right to tell you what to do?'

'He feels responsible for me.'

'Because he pays your wages? He definitely belongs to another age.' Jake leaned forward. 'I bet he said other things about me, didn't he? Not just that rubbish about different worlds?'

'Look, he's no' important. Why bother about what he says?'

'Because if he's been taking my reputation away, I want to know. Has he been doing that? That's important to me, if anything is.'

After a long moment, she said reluctantly, 'He said women were attracted to you.'

'That's a crime, is it?'

'And that you were ... a bit of a ladies' man.'

Jake sat back, bright colour burning on his cheekbones. 'And what exactly did he mean by that?'

'I'm no' sure.' Kirsty remembered Dermot's phrase, 'one for the lassies', echoed by Mrs MacNee, but thought better of mentioning it, as Jake was looking so angry. It was a side of him she'd never seen before, but she didn't blame him for it. Mr Macrae had been taking his character away, and should be held to account.

'Look, I'm nearly thirty years old. Does he imagine I wouldn't have met a few women, had a relationship or two? You wouldn't have expected that, would you, Kirsty?'

'No, of course not,' she replied, though she wished it hadn't been true.

109

'I'm sure you've had your share yourself, haven't you? That guy who follows you round in the shop is clearly smitten. I bet you've had a load of admirers.' Suddenly Jake smiled, and covered her hand with his. 'But you haven't had as much time as I have, have you?'

She shook her head. 'Lets no' talk about the past, eh?'

'You mean mine, don't you?' He released her hand. 'Shall we skip coffee and go? I'll get the bill.'

When they came out of the restaurant, they saw that the rain had stopped and decided to walk to Jake's flat. The air was chill but refreshing and though she had no idea what lay ahead, Kirsty felt better. Less weighed down by the memory of Mr Macrae's warnings, and Jake's anger over them. Hopeful that this step forward would not somehow end in disaster.

But why should it? As Jake tucked her arm into his, she felt a warm radiant confidence fill her being. For it couldn't be denied – they were in love. That was all that mattered.

'What do you think, then?' he asked, escorting her into his living room. 'Pretty modern, eh? As you can see, I'm not a mahogany, loose-covers sort of guy.'

'It is very modern,' she said cautiously, looking round at the black leather furniture of the living room, the porridge-coloured carpet and stark white walls. 'And is that the kitchen over there?'

'Yes, designed it myself. All stainless steel.

110

Then I found out that stainless steel's not stainless at all.'

'Don't tell me you do the cleaning?'

'No, I have a very conscientious lady who comes in three mornings a week. Gets annoyed if I mess the place up. But, of course, I do what I like in my music room – she's not allowed in there. Come on, I'll show you round.'

His music room, officially the dining room, was wonderfully untidy, with music and fiddles stacked on tables and chairs, a desk piled with papers and folders, two telephones, and a clarinet, bookshelves overflowing with scores and paperbacks, musical dictionaries and encyclopaedias, a record player with a heap of records, and, in pride of place at the window, an upright rosewood piano.

'My mother's,' Jake said quietly. 'Still in good nick. I play it, as a matter of fact.'

'You play the piano as well as the violin?'

'Sure. But I'm no pianist. Just strum away, you know.'

'Strum away now, then. Please!'

'What do you want? Reels? Chopin? Ragtime? You name it, I'll vamp it.' He grinned. 'My mother's despair.'

For some time, he sat at the piano, entertaining her with a repertoire that stretched from classical to pop music, from jazz and ragtime to sweet old Scottish melodies, until he swung round and cried, 'That's enough. I'll put the coffee on.'

But when he'd filled the percolator and placed it on a gas flame, he slowly turned to look at her.

111

'Kirsty,' he said hoarsely. 'Oh, Kirsty.'

And she went to him and he held her. At first, they just stood together, listening to the coffee bubbling in the background, but as the kisses came and their passion rose, Jake stretched out his hand and turned off the percolator.

'To hell with the coffee,' he murmured. 'I didn't finish showing you my flat. Didn't show you the bedroom.'

This is it, she thought. *This is what we've both been waiting for.* Everything Lena had said to her, everything Mr Macrae had warned her against was forgotten. All thoughts of future hurt, of ending up like Beryl, were already winging their way out of this modern kitchen and over the roofs of the city, as though they'd never been, for all she wanted was to be with Jake. And in his bed.

His face, as she looked at it through a haze of her own delight, was lit by such feeling, she wondered that they were still where they were. Still in the kitchen, where the coffee, if no longer bubbling, was filling the place with its own special smell.

'Jake,' she whispered. 'Jake?'

Eternity seemed to pass before she saw that he was looking at her with eyes that had somehow lost their famous brightness.

'It's no good, Kirsty,' he said, as though from a long way off. 'He's spoiled it.'

'Who? Who's spoiled it? What are you talking about?'

'That old stick Macrae.' Jake pushed back his damp fair hair. 'I'm what he says I am, aren't I,

112

wanting to have sex with you? When you're so young, so sweet. You trust me, and you're doing what I want to please me—'

'No, that's no' true! I want to make love with you, I do. I may be young, but I'm no' a child, and girls these days, they don't have to wait, like in the old days.' She tried to smile. 'Come on, you say Mr Macrae's fifty years behind the times, but you're the same, eh? Trying to protect me?'

'If you were like all those other girls you talk about, maybe I'd feel different,' he said quietly. 'But you see, Kirsty, you're not, and I suppose Mr Macrae's made me see that. Let's leave it for now, see how things go.'

'Why should we? Look, I've thought about it, and it's my decision as well as yours. Does that no' count for anything?'

She put her arms around him, desperately trying to regain what they'd shared only minutes before, but it was too late. He gently released himself.

'Think we'll have to have that coffee after all.'

'Jake, I love you. I want you. Why won't you listen to me?'

'I will, I will, but not now. Don't ask me. I'm trying to do the right thing.' Putting her aside, he was about to turn on the flame under the coffee again, but she touched his hand.

'No coffee, Jake. Just take me home.'

They were silent on the drive to Pleasant Hill. Only when Jake had taken them straight to Clover, rather than stopping at their special

113

place, did Kirsty clear her throat to speak.

'I suppose we won't be meeting again?'

'We shouldn't,' he answered gloomily. 'You're too much of a temptation.'

His way of sweetening his pill? She stared up at the windows of the flats of Clover, feeling almost battered with the let down from the promise of love to the reality of farewell.

'I'll say goodbye, then,' she said quietly.

'Goodbye? Kirsty, you're not serious?'

'Seemingly, it's what you want.'

'No, no. That's not true. I don't want to say goodbye to you.' He took her hand and kissed it. 'I just need a bit of time, to forget what that fellow said of me. I mean, he warned you against me, didn't he? And maybe he was right.'

'Jake, how can you say that? He was wrong about you, just plain wrong! We love each other. That's what makes the difference.'

She was happy again, bruised feelings forgotten, her heart rising, even singing. There would be no farewell, no goodbye. If they were not to make love at present, it didn't matter. They could wait for marriage. Just as long as they were to keep on seeing each other.

She kissed him on the lips, then sighed with a contentment she'd thought she would never feel again.

'Jake, I'll say goodnight.'

'Kirsty, darling, goodnight. Have you forgiven me?'

'What's to forgive? Will you be in touch?'

'Sure, I will. Right this minute. Would you be able to come to the Glasgow studio next week?

For one of our recordings? I'll send you the details.'

It was true, then. As she ran up the stairs home, she could hardly believe her luck. There was to be no goodbye.

Nineteen

The weeks that followed were wonderfully free from strain, because, of course, the burden of secrecy had been lifted. Everyone now knew that Jake MacIver had become Kirsty's 'young man', to use Mrs MacNee's phrase – or, as younger folk said, her 'boyfriend'. Neighbours at Pleasant Hill learned to recognize his splendid car, and to try to catch a glimpse of the tv star himself, while at Macrae's, even Dermot and Mr Macrae had to accept that he was part of her life. No more could be said against him, though Mr Macrae's grey eyes on Kirsty were thoughtful, and at times rather sad.

Meanwhile, Jake was as good as his word in taking her to things she would enjoy. Whenever he could arrange to be with her and she was free from duty at the shop, they went out together. Sometimes to the theatre or art galleries, more often to ceilidhs and concerts where Jake and his boys would be playing, or dances where he could partner her and she, in her dancing shoes, would find a skill and energy she'd never dreamed she could possess.

It was a magical time for her, only marred by the continuing regret that she and Jake had not become lovers. Maybe it was foolish to want it so much when she'd done nothing yet about taking precautions – although, with Beryl's experience finally returning to her mind, she'd got as far as looking up the address of the Family Planning Clinic in the telephone directory. Still, the more she was with him, the more she wanted him, and wondered often how it might be for Jake himself. All this hovering on the brink of passion, never giving in – didn't he care?

'Are you still remembering what Mr Macrae said about you?' she ventured to ask once, but he only laughed and put his fingers over her mouth.

'Ssh, don't tempt me to forget. I'm being a good boy.'

What could she do? She was sure in her mind that he felt they should wait for their marriage, and she supposed it made sense that she should wait too. One day, he would propose, and she wished it could be soon, but in the meantime there was life to enjoy. And she did.

Best of all the outings for her were the broadcasts in Glasgow. She had never been so thrilled than when she got to go behind the scenes and see how the *Reel Time* programmes were put together. To watch the dancers, to listen to the music of Jake's Boys, to meet the 'boys' again, and feel a part of the show with them. She could scarcely wait to tell her family all that she'd seen, and soak up their interest. Even Lena

116

seemed impressed, even Angie stirred herself to show enthusiasm, while Reid confessed to a certain surprise.

'I'll have to hand it to him, Kirsty, Jake Mac-Iver's certainly pushing the boat out for you,' he remarked one teatime.

'You're surprised?' she asked spiritedly.

'Well, he's no' your usual laddie next door, is he?'

'And I'm the usual lassie? That's been said before.'

'Needn't stop him wanting to take Kirsty out,' Angie murmured. 'He seems really keen.'

'Time will tell,' Lena snapped, beginning to clear the table. 'But there's more to being keen than taking folks out. Anybody want to help with the washing-up? I'm going out to bingo with Vinnie.'

When her stepmother went into her bedroom to get ready, Kirsty followed her in and stood leaning against the door, watching her powder her nose and dab on lipstick.

'You still don't like him, then?' she asked casually.

'Jake MacIver? I've always said he was a charmer.'

'I mean, for me. You'll have to admit, he's doing his best to make me happy.'

'Taking you out? Wining and dining? Spending money like water?' Lena laughed shortly. 'Sounds familiar.'

'I know what you're talking about, Lena, and it's no' the same for me, no' the same at all.'

'Aye, well, I'm just waiting for the wheels to come off your cart and that's all I'm going to say.'

'Right, then, we know where we are!' Kirsty cried. 'Maybe you'll understand about me and Jake one day.'

'Aye, the day you come walking in with his ring on your finger, Kirsty. That's when I'll understand.'

'Well, that'll happen, you'll see – that'll come.'

'And nobody'll be more pleased than me if it does.'

Lena tied a little scarf at her neck and shrugged herself into her coat.

'Now, I'm away. I'll see you later – unless you're out on the town by then.'

'If only she could be glad for me,' Kirsty said to Angie later. 'It'd make such a difference to me, if she'd accept Jake.'

'She's worried, that's all.' Angie, on orders from Lena, was slowly sorting out laundry for ironing. 'I mean, you're no further forward, are you? You go out a lot, but there's nothing permanent.'

'We have an understanding.'

'Oh, right.'

'Don't you believe me?'

Angie shrugged and plugged in the iron. With lowered eyes, she asked, 'Have you been to bed with Jake?'

'No!' Kirsty flushed. 'We're waiting.'

'Because you have this understanding?'

118

'Look, do you mind? I don't want to talk about it. What about us talking about you and your life? Why'd you never go out to things? Join something, have some fun? All you do is go to work, come home and read magazines, or do a job or two for Lena if she makes you. Life's passing you by, Angie!'

'No need to worry about me. I've got my own interests and they're enough.'

'What interests?'

'Do you mind?' Angie mimicked. 'I don't want to talk about 'em.'

'Och – I'm away to watch the telly!' Kirsty cried. If only there'd been one of Jake's programmes to watch...

In the end, she shared the ironing with Angie, and then they made a cup of tea and settled down to watching *The Saint* on the box until Lena and Reid returned home.

Twenty

One pleasantly light evening in April, Kirsty and Jake went for one of their drives out, this time to Cramond, a village by the River Almond where it flowed into the Forth near Edinburgh. There had been a Roman fort there once, and in later times, iron mills. Now, it was just a pleasant place to walk by the water, watch the yachts from the sailing club, or have a meal.

Kirsty had managed to get away on time from the shop, which was not so easy now that they were staying open later for the evening visitors, and Jake had booked dinner at the inn, which turned out to be splendid.

'I'm so hungry, I could eat anything,' Kirsty remarked. 'But this is special, isn't it?'

'Certainly is. Sure you don't want any wine, though?'

'No, thanks. But I'm going to have a pudding, even if I do put on pounds.'

'You'll never put on pounds,' he said with a smile, but as he called for the dessert menu, she felt – she didn't know why – a little apprehensive. There was something different about him tonight, though she couldn't say what. Maybe he was just tired – as she was herself, but she always brightened when she was with Jake.

'I'll have the raspberry gateau,' she announced. 'We could share, if you like?'

'No, no, you have it. I'll wait for coffee. Then maybe we could get some air before we go back to the flat.'

For a little while, after dinner, they moved to the little harbour, where they watched the owners of the moored yachts 'messing about in boats', and Jake said idly he wouldn't mind trying sailing one day. Of course, he had very little time.

'Want to go back, then?' he finally asked.

'Yes, I'd like to,' she answered casually, wondering as she always did if this visit might bring what she was waiting for. The words that would change her present understanding with Jake into the engagement she wanted – not just to have a ring on her finger, but to be wholly one with the man who had become her world.

In the small hallway of the flat, she hung up her jacket and moved into his living room, still filled with evening light, and sank on to his sofa with a sigh of contentment.

'I do love being here,' she murmured. 'Come and join me.'

'Want a soft drink, or anything?'

'Oh, no, thanks – after that raspberry gateau, I feel I'll never want anything ever again.'

He laughed a little and came to sit next to her, kissing her briefly, but then, drawing away, he lit a cigarette.

'You're smoking?' she cried in surprise. 'That's something new!'

'Something old, as a matter of fact. I gave up years ago, but now and again, I still feel like one. You don't mind?'

'No, no.' But she was puzzled. 'Why d'you feel like one tonight, then?'

'Och, no reason. Have something to discuss with you, that's all.'

As her eyes widened, he waved smoke away from her and suddenly stubbed out his cigarette in a large glass ashtray she'd never noticed before.

'Hell, I don't need it.' He smiled. 'The thing is ... something's come up – for the boys and me.'

'Something good?'

'For us, yes. Very good. It's ... a tour of America.'

America ... Somewhere she had always wanted to go. Hadn't she said so to Angie, that time
they'd spoken of The Beatles? Her lips parted,
her eyes shone.

'Jake, that's wonderful! I never dreamed you'd
be going to America!'

'Nor did I. Seems our sort of music has a big
following there. Not just with the Scots who've
emigrated.'

'How long will the tour be?'

'Plans haven't been finalized, but we'll be
away quite some time. That's the down side, of
course.'

'Down side?'

'Well, it means we won't be seeing each
other.'

She waited a moment for this to sink in, then
gave an uncertain smile.

'But I can come, Jake. I can leave Macrae's.
Go anywhere with you.' Her eyes were so dark,
so anxious, that he looked away. 'You know
that's true.'

'Darling, I'm so sorry. I can't take you.' He
leaned forward and put his arms around her. 'It
just wouldn't be possible.'

'Why?' She twisted free. 'Why wouldn't it be
possible?'

'Well, we'll be going to all sorts of places, you
see. And there'll be travel and accommodation
arrangements to be made, which might not be so
easy for you as a girlfriend. I know it's the
sixties, but some folk over there, in some of the
states, might – you know, get the wrong idea –
might not approve.' As she kept her eyes on him,

saying nothing, he shook his head. 'I just don't want to make things difficult.'

'I don't see what's so difficult. I bet Sandy's taking Gina, isn't he?'

'Sandy and Gina are married. The other guys won't be taking anybody.'

'I'm no' just "anybody",' she said slowly. 'We love each other. We have an understanding. I can be the same as Gina.'

He looked up. 'Understanding?'

'To be married.' Her voice trembled. 'That's true, isn't it? We are going to be married?'

'We never actually said that, Kirsty.'

'We didn't have to say it, we knew it! We had an understanding...'

'Kirsty, there was never anything like that between us.' At the look in her eyes, he cried to her in desperation, 'For God's sake, be fair! I never said anything about commitment. In my job – my life – I decided long ago marriage wasn't for me. Some men can cope – Sandy, for one – but I have to feel free, to put the music first. A wife – children – they'd be wonderful. I know I'm missing out ... but, it's the way things are.' He kissed her swiftly. 'You can understand, can't you? You can see how it is?'

But she couldn't answer him. His news had been too much. Too sudden. The change, from all that she'd had and hoped for and what she had now – how could such a thing be accepted? It was as though he had hit her. Dealt her a physical blow. She even put up her hands to her face as though to shield herself. But there was to be no shield for what she would have to endure.

She dropped her hands and sat very still.

'Kirsty,' Jake said, watching her, 'I feel so bad about this. I never thought...'

He put his arms around her, but she unloosened them without a word.

'I can see it's been a shock for you.' He shook his head. 'Thing is, I never thought you'd take it so hard. But I'm to blame. As soon as I saw the danger signals, I should've prepared you. When you kept telling me you loved me—'

'That was a danger signal?' Kirsty's eyes flashed. 'My love?'

'I'm sorry, that was the wrong thing to say. What I meant was – all I meant was – I should have realized we were getting in too deep. Look, I think you could do with some tea, or something, Kirsty. You're so pale...'

'I don't need any tea. I'm all right, I'm going home.'

'No, no, stay. Stay till you feel better. I can't let you go like this...'

Stay till you feel better. She could have laughed. But a numbness was gradually moving through her, as great cold deadens in water or snow, and she knew that for a time at least the pain would be held at bay. Best to get home then, quickly, before the tears came and Jake saw her cry. 'I'll get my jacket,' she told him, moving slowly to the hallway.

'Kirsty, wait! I have to talk to you – make you understand – I never meant any of this to happen. I've been stupid – a complete fool...'

'No.' She looked at him briefly with her wounded eyes. 'I was the fool.'

* * *

When she had found her jacket, he helped her to put it on, and said if she really insisted on leaving, he'd take her back.

'No need. I'll get the bus.'

'You don't realize how late it is. Your last bus will have gone.'

He waved a hand to his uncurtained windows, from where they could see that the sky, growing dark at last, held only a few remaining streaks of light touching the clouds.

'I can get a taxi,' she told him, wondering if she had enough money in her purse. She had never needed money on her outings with Jake.

'Oh, come on, what's the point in that? Let me drive you home, at least.'

And with such weariness overtaking her that she felt almost ill, she went with him down the stairs to the car.

At Pleasant Hill, after their silent journey, he parked where they used to park when they'd been happy, some way from Clover. Kirsty kept on staring straight ahead, but Jake turned to look at her.

'I just wanted to tell you, Kirsty, whatever you think, I do care for you. I always wanted to be with you. Maybe that's what was wrong – I didn't want to let you go.'

'You have let me go.'

'It should have been earlier. Before ... before anyone could get hurt.'

'It'd have always been too late.'

'It's true, there was always an attraction

125

between us, wasn't there? Right from the start.'

She moved her head impatiently. 'Can we go now, please? I want to get home.'

Outside Clover, he seemed loth to say goodbye, as though the longer he kept her, the better he'd feel, but Kirsty only wanted to leave him now. She stepped out of the car.

'Will you be all right?' he asked, hurrying round to help her.

She made no answer to that, and when he tried to take her hand, held it away.

'Goodbye, Jake. I hope you enjoy America.'

'I'll be back, you know.'

'I won't know.'

He winced and sighed.

'OK, you don't want to see me again, but will you try not to think too badly of me? We had some good times, didn't we?'

For the first time since he'd given her the news that had changed her life, she looked at him. At the beloved face; the eyes that even in this dusky light were such an amazing blue; the fine mouth and dimpled chin. What was she to tell him? Yes, she would try not to think badly of him? No, she would only be trying not to think of him at all? It didn't matter what she said. His heart was his own, probably always would be. She would have to work hard in the future to be like that. Once her wound had healed.

'Goodbye, Jake,' she said again and, opening the main door to the flats, quietly closed it behind her. Only once she was on the stairs did the tears begin to flow.

Twenty-One

Kirsty had been lucky. Everyone had been asleep when she let herself into the flat, even Angie. There had been no one to see the tears. It was different, of course, in the morning.

'Oh, Kirsty, what's wrong?' Angie asked, as soon as she saw Kirsty's red eyelids, but Kirsty only shook her head, snatched up her clothes and ran to the bathroom.

How terrible she looked in the mirror! Her eyes so red, her face paper-white. She didn't even recognize herself.

Couldn't go to work, she thought. Couldn't face everybody at Macrae's, or even her own family. And all the folk in the flats, who'd watched her going out, who'd waited to see Jake MacIver, and Jake MacIver's car – how was she going to tell them?

Och, what did it matter? Nothing mattered, except the hard lump in her chest, the pain she'd known would come and now had come, the heartache she could not avoid.

Slowly, she washed in cold water. Saw a little colour come back into her cheeks, before she dressed and put on some make-up. There, she looked better, eh? Good enough to go and face the family.

'Morning,' she said shakily, sitting down and

pouring herself tea.

'Oh, lassie!' cried Lena. 'What's happened to you?'

They were all so sympathetic, so supportive. Reid said Kirsty had only to say the word and he'd go round to MacIver's flat and kick his teeth in, while Angie said, as she'd always thought, nobody could be trusted. Even Lena refrained from saying 'I told you so', but as she shook out the cornflakes, declared that one thing was for sure: she'd never again watch *Reel Time, Song Time*.

'Never watched it, anyway,' Reid remarked.

'Boring, really,' Angie added. 'Just one Scottish dance after another, eh?'

'To be fair to Jake, he never did ask me to marry him,' Kirsty said, not listening. 'I just all along thought ... we had an understanding.'

'Have to be very careful about understandings,' Lena said after a pause. 'Have to make sure two people are involved, no' just one.'

Angie, staring at her cereal, suddenly pushed it away and stood up. 'I'm away,' she announced, and left them to sit staring after her.

'Why, what's up with her?' Reid asked, and Lena sighed heavily.

'She'll be thinking of her mother,' she whispered. 'This has brought it all back, eh?'

'You mean what's happened to me?' cried Kirsty. 'It's no' the same at all, I've always said so!'

'Aye, well, you've been lucky,' Lena told her, beginning to clear the table. 'Maybe.'

As Kirsty showed her outrage at the idea she'd been 'lucky', Reid shook his head at her, as though to say 'leave it', and she subsided into silence.

Perhaps she had been lucky, after all. Luckier than Beryl, anyway. She might be feeling devastated, as well as angry and foolish, but at least she'd no need to regret any love-making with Jake MacIver. What a risk she'd been prepared to take! Thanks to him, it had never happened.

But need she be grateful to him? 'I'm being a good boy,' he had once said, but the idea came to her now that perhaps, however much he'd have liked to have sex with her, he'd been playing safe for *himself* in holding back. She'd wanted marriage, but if they'd never made love, she couldn't make things difficult for him, could she? He'd always be able to say that he hadn't let her down.

Or was she being too cynical? Perhaps she should be grateful to him, after all, that there had been no sex and no baby, and she hadn't ended up like Beryl. Yes, she'd better admit it, she should think herself lucky. Once she'd got over her broken heart.

'Hey, are you going to work this morning?' asked Reid, looking into her thoughtful face. 'You're miles away, but time's getting on.'

'You could take the day off,' Lena suggested. 'Say you're no' well. Which is true.'

'I'm going in to work,' Kirsty said firmly. 'I'll bite the bullet.'

'You needn't tell folks what's happened, though. Just say that Jake MacIver's gone to

America. By the time he comes back, they'll have forgotten about him.'

'No, I want them to know. I've had enough of secrets. I'll tell them and put an end to the whole thing.'

'Aye, draw a line under it,' Reid agreed. 'Then you can begin to forget about it yourself.'

Forget? Kirsty lowered her eyes. Maybe.

Strangely enough, it wasn't too bad, telling people at Macrae's. They were all so surprised, then so nice about it, taking her part, finding fault with Jake, that she came through feeling rather soothed.

Mrs MacNee had known all along, of course, that he was not to be trusted. Hadn't they all heard about him and the lassies? And you could never trust a man with a smile like his, aye, and a cleft chin and all; Kirsty was well shot of him. Lil, hugging Kirsty, had agreed, and Dermot, with the same idea as Reid, had declared that for two pins he'd go round to MacIver's place and sort him out. What a rotter, eh?

As for Mr Macrae, he had been so kind when he'd spoken to her in his office that Kirsty had nearly burst into tears in front of him. Like Lena, he never said 'I told you so', only that he hoped she wouldn't let this experience spoil things for her in the future. There would be other admirers, others wanting to take her to dances and balls.

'Hope not,' Kirsty said grimly. 'I've thrown away my dancing shoes.'

'Oh, why, in heaven's name?'

She shrugged. 'Didn't fancy wearing 'em

again. On the way to the bus this morning, I put 'em in the outside bin.'

And so she had, while Angie, looking pale and gloomy, had watched and approved, though Reid had said it was a pointless exercise, before hurrying ahead for his bus. But Niall MacFall, who had been standing by, gave Kirsty a sympathetic look and touched her arm in support as she turned away.

'I do hope you will soon get round to replacing those shoes,' Mr Macrae was murmuring now, as she came back to the present.

'Doubt it,' she said shortly.

'Well, just see how things go, Kirsty, see how things go.' After studying her face for a moment, he put an encouraging hand on her shoulder. 'Look, why not take the rest of the day off? I'm sure Mrs MacNee won't mind, and you probably need a little time to yourself today.'

'It's very kind of you, Mr Macrae, but I think I'd be happier getting on with my work. I've a kilt to make for Dr Lindsay.'

'If you're sure, then.'

'Thank you, Mr Macrae, I'm sure.'

Back in the workroom, cutting out the Lindsay tartan under the sad eyes of Mrs MacNee and Lil, Kirsty felt, if not at peace, that she was at least weathering the storm. How long it would last, how much buffeting she would have to face, she'd no way of knowing. Time would tell. Yes, of course, that was what everyone said – time, the great healer, would do the trick. Just let time go by and she'd be footloose and fancy free ... If only she could hibernate till it happened!

Just keep going, she told herself. Hang on to all those encouraging things folk liked to say. Like Niall MacFall telling her on the way to the bus that broken hearts could be mended.

'Aye, sometimes by the folk who break 'em,' he'd finished firmly.

'Had experience?' Angie asked, raising her eyebrows.

'No, but I've heard it happens.'

'Won't happen this time,' Kirsty declared.

'How about someone new?' His tone was light. 'That happens, too.'

She shook her head. 'I don't want anyone new. Don't want anyone at all.'

Niall smiled a little. 'Looks like you'll have to mend your heart yourself, then.'

'Oh, I will. That's a promise.'

She didn't believe it, but she felt good, for a moment, saying it.

And still felt good, thinking it, in the work-room, cutting out Dr Lindsay's kilt. With any luck, one day it would be true.

PART TWO

PART TWO

Twenty-Two

At half past five precisely on Christmas Eve, Mr
Macrae clapped his hands and cried, 'Dermot,
lock the door! Let the revels begin!'

His little joke, of course. Everyone was waiting for it, he said it every year. And every year
they laughed dutifully, for with only five on the
staff, not counting Mrs Mill, the cleaning lady,
who lived in Portobello and never wanted to
come back in the evening, there were hardly
enough to have what you could call a revel.
Why, Mrs MacNee wouldn't even let Dermot
bring in mistletoe, for which in fact Kirsty was
grateful, not wanting to be kissed either by Mr
Macrae or Dermot himself.

Still, it was pleasant to have a get-together in
the shop, which they had decorated with holly
and balloons, where lights twinkled on the arti-
ficial Christmas tree they brought out every
season, and the door was firmly shut against
customers. No more folk could come rushing in,
hoping to find a last-minute present of a scarf or
a brooch, or hire a kilt for a party they should
have thought about before. Peace, eh? Until they
came back after Boxing Day for the start of
the New Year sales. No need to think about
that now, though. They turned their attention to

the buffet.

The food was always good. Mrs MacNee's finger sandwiches and mince pies; Lil's sausage rolls (made by her mother); Kirsty's bits on sticks (all her own work); and Dermot's savouries from a local baker. And then of course there was Mr Macrae's wine. After a glass or two of that, it didn't take long – happened every year – for the little get-together to turn quite merry, but what matter? Nobody was driving, and it was Christmas.

'Oh, will you look at Mrs MacNee?' Lil whispered to Kirsty. 'She's as red as a beetroot! What'll Mr MacNee say when he comes to collect her?'

'Same as he says every year,' Kirsty answered. 'No' much.'

'Aye, talk about dour, eh? But he's nice enough. Listen, you'd better have something else to eat, Kirsty – you're looking a bit floaty.'

'Wine always goes to my head, but what can I do? Can hardly drink lemonade at our revels, eh?'

They both laughed, until Lil pressed Kirsty's arm and said quite seriously, 'Ah, it's so grand to see you happy again, Kirsty! You're just your old self again now, aren't you? And once you never thought you would be.'

'I'm OK.' Kirsty lowered her eyes for a moment and pretended to be debating what to have to eat. 'It took time, but I came back in the end.'

'They say everybody does.'

136

'Maybe. Think I'll have a mince pie.'

As she sampled Mrs MacNee's delicious pastry and brushed sugar from her lips, Kirsty knew that she would have to change the subject. Better she might be, but talking about the long sad months she had just endured only brought back something she'd rather forget.

Jake MacIver had been on television, but she'd never watched him. He'd had the cheek to send her postcards from America, which she'd thrown away. She'd read in the paper that he was at present touring in the north of Scotland, and had crumpled up the page. So far, so good. She'd managed to excise him from her mind as far as possible. But talking about the experience of losing him brought back the memory of pain, if not pain itself, and she quickly thought up something else to say.

'Lil, I think it's so grand what you're doing, you know, you and Dermot. I mean, the evening classes.'

Lil's face lit up. 'Our bookkeeping? Och, Mam thinks I'm crazy, taking on something new, when I've got a good job already. But I only started to keep Dermot company and then I found I enjoyed it. I'm no' saying I'm any good—'

'Bet you are, then!'

'Aye, well it seems to come easy to me, and I think Dermot finds it a help that I'm with him, you see. Only he's more serious than me – about moving on, I mean, to a new job.'

'Can imagine he'd find it a bit boring here, just selling all the time.'

'And doing so much. He definitely needs another pair of hands, but there's no hope of that.'

'No hope of what?' Dermot asked, coming up with a face almost as scarlet as Mrs MacNee's. 'And what are you two lassies doing huddled in this corner, anyway? Leaving me stuck with the boss.'

'Well, he's gone off for our little presents,' Lil remarked, watching keenly as Mr Macrae made his way with some concentration to his office. 'Stand by for your handkerchiefs, Dermot.'

It had been a practice of old Mr Macrae's that all his staff received, not only a small bonus at Hogmanay, but also a gift at Christmas – perhaps handkerchiefs for men, scent of some sort for women – and his son had continued the tradition. Now that they'd finished most of the food and daren't drink any more wine, he was ready to distribute his offerings, just as his staff readied themselves to be grateful.

'Rather have my New Year bonus, all the same,' Dermot muttered, but after Lil knocked his arm in rebuke, pressed again to ask them what they'd meant in saying there was no hope.

'No hope of another assistant, that's all.'

'Well, you're right there, but what I want to know is why. I mean, the hire business is booming and there's talk of expanding the ladies' stuff – how am I supposed to do all that extra work?' Dermot frowned and shook his head. 'I've a good mind to say something to His Nibs – mebbe this very night – tell him I need some help.'

'That's just the wine talking,' Lil told him and

138

put a finger to her lips. 'Here he comes, so pipe down.'

'Yes, be quiet, Dermot,' Mrs MacNee put in, pronouncing her words very carefully. 'Mr Macrae ... wants ... to speak to us.'

Twenty-Three

Standing before them with his small bag of presents, Mr Macrae looked for once quite colourful, his cheeks highly flushed, his grey eyes sparkling. Quite handsome, Kirsty thought vaguely, as he held up his hand for attention. But what did he want to say, apart from 'Merry Christmas'?

Seemed he first wanted to thank them, for all their hard work for Macrae's Kilts in 1964.

'It's paid off, I can tell you, as we've had one of the best years I can remember, with really excellent sales figures. So good, in fact, I'm happy to tell you that I'm now able to fund the appointment of a new assistant. Just what we've all been waiting for, I think?'

There was a short silence, then an astonished whistle from Dermot and an exchange of looks between Kirsty and Lil. From the superior smile on her face, it was plain that Mrs MacNee already knew about the new appointment and hadn't breathed a word.

'Is this assistant going to be a kilt maker?' Lil

asked swiftly. 'Or for the front shop?'

'Oh, for the front shop, of course,' Mr Macrae replied. 'That's where the help is needed – right, Dermot? The hire business and ready to wear are doing exceptionally well, but we also want to stock more for the ladies. More and more visitors, particularly Americans, are interested in ladies' kilts, and I think we have to meet that interest. Which is why I'm planning to appoint a young lady to the new post.'

'Couldn't we have had another man?' Dermot asked. 'I'm outnumbered here.'

'Now, now, Dermot, Mr Macrae knows what he's doing,' Mrs MacNee said sternly. 'Just be grateful that you're going to have some help.'

'I'll bet she'll no' be interested in football,' he said sulkily, in spite of Lil's efforts to shut him up, and in the end she gave an exasperated smile and said maybe it was time he went home.

'That's all right, we'll all be going home, just as soon as I've given everyone my little tokens of appreciation.' Mr Macrae smiled round from face to face. 'As usual, my mother has chosen the gifts and is so sorry she wasn't able to join us tonight – friends visiting, you understand.'

'Oh, what a shame,' Lil murmured, as Mrs MacNee hurriedly told Mr Macrae to be sure to give his mother their best wishes for Christmas.

'Of course, of course. Now what have I got? Mrs MacNee, this one's for you ... and Lil, this is yours. Dermot, I hope you like handkerchiefs?'

'Oh, lovely, lavender water!' cried Lil, tearing off the paper from her present. 'Thanks so much,

Mr Macrae.'

'Aye, and for the hankies.' Dermot dabbed at his moist brow. 'Just what I wanted, eh?'

'And I've got eau de cologne! Oh, I can smell it already.' Mrs MacNee gave a beaming smile. 'Too kind, Mr Macrae, too kind.' She dropped her voice to a sibilant whisper. 'But Lil, where's our ... you know what? Quick, run and get it from the workroom, then.'

'Hang on. Kirsty hasn't got her present yet.' Lil was staring at a wrapped box in Mr Macrae's hands. 'That looks like an awful big bottle of scent, eh?'

'Perhaps because it isn't scent,' Mr Macrae replied, quietly. 'Like to open it, Kirsty?'

'Looks like a shoe box,' Dermot observed. 'Bet it's one of ours.'

'Oh, no, it couldn't be a shoe box!' Kirsty said hastily. 'I mean – I wouldn't be getting shoes.'

But the box she unwrapped was indeed a shoe box, and the present inside was a pair of shoes. Dancing shoes. Macrae's Scottish dancing shoes in, as Dermot had predicted, a box from Macrae's own stock. Kirsty flushed poppy-red, and kept her face lowered as those around her stared at the shoes still in the box, but she made no effort to speak.

'You never did buy another pair, did you?' Mr Macrae asked her softly. 'That's why I thought these would make a perfect present. Something you really needed, you see.'

'Your mother didn't choose 'em, then?' Mrs MacNee asked him bluntly.

'Well, no, not these.' Mr Macrae laughed

141

rather uneasily. 'Hope I haven't made a mistake, have I, Kirsty? They're the right size, aren't they?'

'Oh, yes. Yes, they're right. They're ... lovely.'

Finally, she raised her eyes to his and found the grey gaze so warm, so sympathetic, it was hard to remember how she'd once thought it frosty cold. *Come on, smile*, she told herself. He was only trying to be kind. Didn't realize how the sight of dancing shoes like these brought back memories that she'd buried at the very back of her mind.

'Lovely,' she said again, and gave a smile that was immediately answered by his look of relief. 'Thank you very much, Mr Macrae. It's a very thoughtful present.'

'And you're a very lucky girl,' Mrs MacNee remarked, as Lil gave a wondering smile, and Dermot's face remained impassive.

'Better go and get you-know-what,' he said out of the side of his mouth, and Lil, giving a squeal of remembrance, ran off to the workroom.

'Shall we clear away?' Mr Macrae asked smoothly, pretending he had no idea of what was afoot, though he went through the ritual every year.

'Och, yes, we'll tidy up,' said Mrs MacNee, looking back for Lil. 'At least everything's paper, nothing to wash.'

'Got it!' whispered Lil, hurrying back, and Mrs MacNee put out her hand.

'Give it here, then. Mr Macrae, sir, it's our turn now, to wish you a happy Christmas and present you with this small gift from us all.'

'Mrs MacNee – all of you – how kind, how very kind!' He was undoing ribbon, tearing off the paper. 'Now, I wonder, what can it be?'

'My idea,' Dermot said modestly. 'If you'd got one, thought you could always do with another.'

'Why, it's a photo album! Perfect!' Mr Macrae gave a charming smile. 'Now I can put all those snaps floating around at home into proper order. I can't thank you enough. It's a grand present, it really is.'

Searching for something else to say, he was saved by a great knock on the shop door and a hoarse voice crying through the letterbox, 'Are you there, Vera?'

'Och, it's Donald!' Mrs MacNee cried. 'Girls, I'll have to leave you to tidy up. Where's my coat, then?'

'And your hat,' Lil said.

'Aye, and my hat. Dermot, will you open the door, then? He'll not want to be waiting in the cold.'

In came Donald MacNee, short and stocky, with greying hair and eyes in retreat below shaggy eyebrows, who only nodded as he was wished a merry Christmas and asked his wife if she was ready.

'I've just to put on my hat, Donald.'

'You're looking awful red.'

'He speaks,' whispered Lil. 'Amazing.'

'It's just the wine,' said Mrs MacNee.

'Does that, eh?'

'Won't you have a drink yourself, Mr Mac-Nee?' Mr Macree asked politely, but Donald shook his head. He wasn't one for wine, thanks

143

all the same, and he and Vera had to be away.

'Such a grand evening,' Mrs MacNee sighed, departing with her arm in Donald's, and her present in her bag. 'Don't forget to leave everything ship-shape, girls. Have a lovely Christmas!'

'And you, and you!' they cried, and then there was the whizz round to tidy up, put the paper cups and plates in the bin, brush up the crumbs, stack the bottles at the back, and get themselves ready to face the cold.

'Dermot and I are going for another drink,' Lil told Kirsty. 'Aren't we awful? D'you want to come?'

But Kirsty, conscious of Mr Macrae beside her, said she'd better get home, and there were more exchanges of Christmas wishes and promises to have a good time, until Lil and Dermot finally departed and Kirsty and Mr Macrae were alone.

'Ready to leave?' he asked, taking out his keys.

'Yes, I'm away for the bus.'

'I'll see you to the stop, then.'

'There's no need to do that,' she exclaimed, as they left the shop and Mr Macrae locked the door behind them.

'It's no trouble. Always plenty of drunks around on Christmas Eve, you know.'

'I can look after myself, thanks all the same.'

'Come on.' He hooked her arm into his and as they walked up the High Street together, she said no more.

Twenty-Four

The truth of the matter was that Kirsty was bemused. Why this sudden wish of Mr Macrae's to walk her to the bus? Why the present of the Scottish dancing shoes? It was almost as though – and the idea was crazy – almost as though he was attracted to her. Mr Macrae? Attracted to her? No, no, he'd never allow it. He was the boss, she his employee. And he had his own girlfriend, anyway. Kirsty had seen her. So, what this was all about, she couldn't be sure.

Still, there he was beside her, as they walked with care down the frosted pavements, her arm in his, his face constantly turning towards hers as she looked away. Ahead were the Christmas lights of Princes Street, where late shoppers were hurrying in and out of shops ready to close, while at their left, beyond the Mound's shimmering tree, the silhouette of the Assembly Hall seemed to pierce the sky. In the distance, in spite of its lighting, the castle brooded darkly, but then the castle could appear to brood even in the daytime. It was what folk expected.

Christmas Eve. A time of magic, Kirsty had always thought as a child. What was she doing now, walking along with her boss?

'You didn't think I might like to see you to

your bus?' he asked, as they approached the stop.

She turned her large eyes on his. 'Just wondering why you should. I mean, you don't usually.'

'You're usually with Lil and Dermot.' He hesitated. 'And maybe the time wasn't right.'

'The time wasn't right to see me to the bus?'

'For us to be alone. Away from the shop.'

'The time's right now?'

'Oh, I think so.' His eyes were on the buses moving slowly through the congested traffic, and she guessed he must be wondering which one was hers and how long he'd got. Suddenly, he turned back to her. 'I wish I could've driven you home, Kirsty, but I knew I'd be drinking and didn't bring my car.'

'The bus'll be OK.' She smiled. 'I catch it every day.'

'Yes, but what's it like on Christmas Eve? Full of drunks, as I say?'

'Still too early for drunks.'

'Well, if I can't see you home, I'll have to ask you here.' He took her hand in its woollen glove, moving her out of earshot of the queue. 'Not the best place, you'll be thinking, to ask a girl out? But it'll have to do. Will you come with me to the Hogmanay dance at the Crown Park Hotel, Kirsty? There'll be Scottish dancing as well as ballroom – that's why I wanted you to have the shoes.'

Surrounded by noise from traffic and crowds, it was as though they were suddenly wrapped in silence, only aware of each other, he waiting on

146

her reply, she trying to accept that what she'd suspected was in fact true. Mr Macrae was attracted to her. That was his reason for walking her to the bus stop, and for giving her the shoes. Whatever she'd tried to tell herself, she'd already known it.

'What do you say?' he asked, as she stood with lips parted, staring into his face.

'Mr Macrae—'

'Andrew, please.'

Andrew? He was asking her to call him Andrew?

'I ... don't know what to say...'

He gave one of his nervous laughs. 'Shows you haven't a previous engagement for Hogmanay, then. At least, I hope you haven't.'

'I've nothing planned.' She waited a moment, trying to think of a way to put her question. 'But, isn't there someone else ... someone you usually take to dances?'

'You mean Miss Grier?' His tone was easy, his face open. 'The girl I took to the Valentine Ball? We've known each other since we were children. Only go out occasionally. She has her own friends.'

'I see. Well, the thing is ... I'm no' so sure about going dancing again, really. I've sort of given it up.'

'I know, and that's got to be changed, Kirsty. You're so nearly better—'

'I *am* better!'

'So nearly ready to move back into the world, but just hesitating over something that reminds you of ... other times.' He put his hands on her

147

arms, his eyes on her in the lurid glare of the street lighting, very direct, very intense. 'Kirsty, you have to make the break. It's time. Time to put on your dancing shoes and become a part of things again. You've mourned for that fellow long enough.'

Her eyes moved from his. She saw her bus approaching and stepped towards the queue.

'I'll go with you to the dance,' she said quickly. 'I'll put on my dancing shoes. But here's the bus, I have to go.'

'Kirsty, that's splendid!' He seemed genuinely delighted. 'You've made the right decision, to enjoy yourself again. You'll see; it'll make all the difference.'

She made no reply to that, but said she'd see him after the holiday.

'Yes, when I can give you all details of the dance. And then the day after Boxing Day, we'll be having the interviews for the new assistant. Something of interest, I should think?'

'Oh, yes. Well, for Dermot. Goodnight ... Andrew.'

'Goodnight, Kirsty, take care. And enjoy your Christmas!'

She waved her hand, waited her turn and at last climbed on to the loaded bus. The windows were so steamed up, she could scarcely see him, but her last glimpse showed him standing with his hand raised in farewell and a smile lighting his pleasant face.

Back at the flat, where a tiny tree winked coloured lights and paper chains hung from picture

148

rails, she found only Lena at home. She had just finished covering the Christmas cake with almond paste and was dubiously studying her handiwork.

'Doesn't look much, eh? But it's too late to put the royal icing on – should've done it before.'

'Looks fine,' Kirsty told her, nibbling some of the spare marzipan from the snowstorm of sugar and ground almonds that seemed to have spread everywhere, from kitchen table to worktop, to floor. 'Put that little Santa on and it'll be grand. Where is everybody?'

'Reid's working at the pub – gets extra money for tonight – and Angie's gone for drinks with the Logie's crowd.' Lena's brows bent into a frown. 'Och, I sometimes think she does things just to spite me, Kirsty. Imagine! Taking a job at Logie's where her mother used to work! She knew it'd upset me.'

'I'm sure she never meant to do any such thing.' Kirsty was putting on the kettle. 'Angie's no' like that.'

'Aye, but she knows what happened to Beryl, and she still chucks up the hairdresser's job and takes counter work, where she'll probably meet some man just like her ma did.'

'She's on perfumery, though, isn't she? No' the stockings and tights.'

'Och, what does it matter which counter? She's put herself where men go to buy presents for women. Next thing, she'll be involved. Mark my words.' Lena sat down in her chair and sighed. 'Anyway, how'd you get on? Enjoy your Christmas party?'

149

'Yes, it went well.' Kirsty busied herself making tea and pouring a cup for her stepmother. 'Something odd happened, though.'

'Oh, what? Is there a digestive biscuit in that tin? I've eaten so much marzipan, I feel like something plain.'

'Mr Macrae asked me to go to a Hogmanay dance at the Crown Park Hotel.'

'Mr Macrae!' Lena almost choked over her tea. 'Kirsty, what on earth's going on?'

'Nothing. He just said I should go dancing again. I said I'd given it up but he sort of insisted.' Kirsty passed the digestive biscuits. 'Anyway, I ended up saying I'd go.'

'Oh, this is bad news, Kirsty, going out with the boss!' Lena's face was crumpling into lines of worry. 'Out of the frying pan, into the fire! Whatever are you thinking of?'

'I knew you'd get yourself into a state if I told you about it, but this dance doesn't mean a thing. Honestly. Mr Macrae's just a very nice chap, that's all. Likes to help folk on the staff.'

'Takes 'em all to Hogmanay dances, eh? Oh, Kirsty, I'd have thought you'd have learned your lesson!' Lena mournfully dipped a biscuit into her tea. 'Instead, we're starting all over again with worry, just like with Jake MacIver.'

'We are *not* starting all over again!' Kirsty cried. 'There's no risk, no worry, this time, because I don't care about Mr Macrae the way I cared about Jake.' As her stepmother gave her a long hard stare, Kirsty lowered her eyes. 'And that's the truth,' she finished.

'You're all right, then,' Lena said softly. 'Let's

hope he'll be all right, too.'

Kirsty gave a sudden laugh. 'Oh, come on, Lena! He's the boss; I'm one of his kilt makers. He's isn't going to be broken hearted whatever I do. And what's one dance, anyway?'

'It's a start, Kirsty. And everything has to start somewhere.' Lena stood up. 'But listen – that sounds like Angie. Let's hope she's got no news to worry me.'

'Smell my clothes!' Angie cried, throwing off her coat and scarf. 'Smell the smoke! Och, I feel like getting into the bath, clothes and all!'

'You're a fine one to talk,' Lena told her. 'You and your own secret smokes, eh?'

'Aye, well it's different when it's just me. And folk were breathing alcohol fumes all over the place as well.'

'Apart from that, did you have a good time?' asked Kirsty.

Angie shrugged. 'It was OK. Just the usual thing.'

'Never met anyone?' Lena asked casually.

'No, I never met anyone. Give over worrying.' Angie and Kirsty exchanged glances. 'Hey, that cake looks good, though. Can I have a bit of the almond stuff? And is there any tea in the pot?'

'I'll make some fresh.' Lena passed Angie a few marzipan pieces. 'Guess where Kirsty's going at Hogmanay, then? Oh, you never will. The Crown Park's Hogmanay dance with her boss from work. What do you think of that?'

'Mr Macrae?' Angie smiled. 'Get you, Kirsty!'

'Oh, come on,' Kirsty muttered.

151

'But what'll you do for dancing shoes? You threw your others away, eh?'

'You never!' Lena cried.

'She did,' said Angie.

'It's all right,' Kirsty answered reluctantly. 'Mr Macrae's given me a new pair.'

There was a silence, while Lena refilled the kettle and Angie scraped up more marzipan.

'Fancy,' she said at last.

'That's lucky,' Lena murmured.

'Let's put our presents under the tree!' Kirsty cried, leaping up. 'Then it's me for bed.'

'Aye, we'll none of us be long.' Lena made Angie's tea. 'Needn't wait up for Reid. He'll be late.'

'Merry Christmas, then,' Kirsty said, when she'd put her wrapped presents under the tree. 'We'll have a nice easy day tomorrow, shall we?'

'Christmas Day, are you joking?' Lena cried. 'Apart from anything else, we've Vinnie and her boys coming in for their dinner. They had us last year, if you remember.'

'Oh, help!' Kirsty and Angie cried together. 'Goodnight!'

Twenty-Five

The candidates for the assistant's post were due to arrive at two o'clock on the afternoon of 28th December. There were four of them, all women, and though the middle of the sales seemed a difficult time to hold an interview, everyone at Macrae's was on the lookout for the hopefuls.

'Och, the suspense is killing me!' Lil cried, striking a pose in the front shop as the time drew near for the candidates to arrive. 'I mean, supposing we don't like the new girl? She's got to fit in.'

'She'll fit in,' Mrs MacNee said shortly. 'I'll see to that. I'm interviewing, if you remember, with Mr Macrae.'

'But has he got the same ideas as you?'

'Of course.' Mrs MacNee patted her hair and straightened the tartan scarf at her neck. 'We both know what to look for in a girl who wants to work here. And having the interviews at sale time will show the candidates just how busy things can be.'

'Mr Macrae thought of that?' asked Kirsty. 'Did seem a funny time.'

'Mr Macrae always knows what he's doing, Kirsty. Now, you two had better go and help Dermot – I see several customers turning over those reduced jackets. Aye, and there's a lady hovering round with a skirt. Be quick, now, it's nearly two o'clock.'

On the dot of two, the four candidates arrived together to be received by Mr Macrae and Mrs MacNee, who gave them a brief tour of the front shop, while the fascinated Dermot and Lil kept swivelling their heads round from customers to survey the 'possibles'. Afterwards, it was Kirsty's duty to show the girls into the workroom to await being called, one by one, to Mr Macrae's office, and to tell them something of kilt making, though, of course, they wouldn't be involved in that.

Already, she'd made up her mind which one she'd like to see get the job, and that was a rather sad-looking girl wearing a suit that seemed too big for her, and who was struggling with a cold. But she was sweet and could be a friend, Kirsty thought, while the cool blonde who was sitting tapping her foot looked as though she considered the whole place beneath her, and the redhead was too truculent. As for the fourth girl, she was so mousy, it was hard to notice her at all.

'So, what you do all day is just stitch kilts?' Anita Keith, the blonde, asked Kirsty, indicating by her tone what she thought of that.

'Wee bit boring, eh?' asked Julia Cooper, the redhead, whose dark eyes were like stones.

'Quite difficult, I'd say,' Prue White, the girl with a cold, managed to get out before she sneezed, while Meriel Lammond, the mousy one, kept her eyes down and made no comment at all.

'It is extremely interesting,' Kirsty said sharply, 'and requires a long training. Your job will be just to sell.'

'With that dark-haired fellow?' Anita Keith asked. 'Seems a bit young to me.'

She exchanged looks with Julia Cooper, and Kirsty was guessing that they were probably both thinking they could eat poor Dermot for breakfast, when Mrs MacNee sailed in and called in clarion tones, 'Miss White, please!'

'Oh, dear,' Prue gasped, putting her handkerchief to her nose. 'I'm afraid I'm going to sneeze again.'

And as she followed Mrs MacNee from the workroom, silence fell.

'Oh, quick, tell me, who d'you think will get it?' Lil asked, hurriedly catching Kirsty as she made tea for the candidates after their interviews. 'I'm so terrified it'll be that blonde, eh?'

'Miss Keith?' Kirsty grinned. 'I'll resign if she does.'

'Did you see the way Dermot was looking at her?' Lil was carefully renewing her lipstick. 'His eyes were out on stalks, I'm telling you. Oh, I'll die if she gets to work with him!'

'I don't know what you're worrying about, Lil. You're a blonde, aren't you?'

'Bottle blonde. She's natural, you can tell, and as cool as a cucumber. In no time, she'll have him wrapped round her little finger, I know, I've seen girls like her before.'

'Lil, she hasn't even been appointed yet.' Kirsty put some biscuits on her tray and prepared to carry it away. 'Look, stop worrying. I'll tell you what's going to happen. They won't choose the blonde, because Mrs MacNee won't like her. They won't choose the redhead, because Mr Macrae will think she's too bossy, and they won't choose the poor girl with the cold because she'll put them off, sneezing all over 'em. So, it'll be Miss Lammond, the mousy one.'

'Never! Oh, fingers crossed, you're right!'

'You'll see, I am. Now, I'd better take the girls this tea. They've all had their turns and they're sitting biting their nails, poor things.'

'Well, I'm no' going to feel sorry for that blonde character, whatever you say,' Lil declared.

The candidates had all finished their tea and were looking at their watches.

'D'you think they'll tell us today?' Prue White asked nervously. 'Or write us a letter?'

'Who knows?' Anita was searching in her bag. 'Anybody mind if I smoke?'

'No smoking,' Kirsty told her. 'Look at all this tartan around you.'

'Oh, honestly – what a set-up! As though I want to work in this place, anyway!'

'I'd like to work here,' Prue whispered.

'I wouldn't mind,' said Julia.

Meriel Lammond said nothing.

The door to the workroom suddenly opened and Mrs MacNee again appeared. As all eyes went to her, she looked directly towards Meriel.

'Miss Lammond, will you step this way

please?'

Aha! thought Kirsty. *Lil, you can uncross your fingers now.*

'I knew I wouldn't get it,' Prue said, blowing her nose. 'They just wanted me to go.'

'I'm not bothered,' Julia muttered.

'I've applied to be a doctor's receptionist,' Anita announced, rising and sweeping towards the door. 'That'll be much more my cup of tea. Do we get any expenses, by the way? I had to come in from Musselburgh.'

'Better speak to Mrs MacNee,' said Kirsty, who was shaking Prue's hand.

'I'm really sorry you didn't get it,' she said in a low voice. 'Have you tried Logie's? My sister works there.' And as Prue's reddened eyes filled up and it seemed another sneeze was on its way, added hastily, 'When your cold gets better, eh?'

Later, when the defeated ones had departed and things were quiet in the front shop, Mr Macrae brought the newly appointed assistant round for introductions. Smiling, he called his staff forward to greet her.

'Listen, everyone, I'd like you to meet Miss Lammond, our new assistant, who'll be coming to us shortly after New Year. She's recently moved here with her parents from Perth, where she worked in a dress shop, but tells me she's looking forward to working with kilts and tartan now. We hope she'll be very happy at Macrae's doing just that! Miss Lammond, meet my staff!'

Under the benevolent smile of Mrs MacNee, Lil, looking immensely relieved, was the first to

157

shake Meriel Lammond's hand, followed by Dermot, seeming dismayed, and finally Kirsty, still feeling rather pleased with herself for singling out this colourless girl for success.

But was she so colourless? As she put out her hand to be shaken and flung back her pale brown hair, Kirsty properly saw her face for the first time and realized she'd been mistaken. This was no mouse, but a good-looking young woman, with a straight nose, a delicate mouth, and eyes as blue as Jake MacIver's.

Oh, what a fool I've been, thought Kirsty, *to be taken in by lowered eyes and pale brown hair!* But then there was no question of Miss Lammond trying to take anyone in, was there? Why ever had that phrase come into Kirsty's mind? As she smiled and said her welcoming words, she dismissed it, for the new assistant seemed really very pleasant – softly spoken and polite.

'Everyone has been so nice,' she murmured, as Mr Macrae came up to take her back to the office for various formalities. 'I'm sure I'll be very happy here.'

'I'm sure you will,' Kirsty told her.

'I think she'll fit in all right, don't you?' Lil asked, after Miss Lammond had gone home and closing time was drawing near. 'What a bit of luck, eh, that they didn't land us with that blonde?'

'What was wrong with the blonde, anyway?' Dermot asked. 'I think she'd have drawn in the customers.'

'Drawn in the men, you mean.'

158

'Well, it's mainly men who buy what we sell.'

'Thought we were hoping to do more for ladies now.'

'Little Miss Lammond can look after them,' Dermot muttered. 'Probably be scared of the fellas.'

It was plain to Kirsty, gazing from one face to the other, that neither Dermot nor Lil had really looked at little Miss Lammond. Would be interesting to see what happened when they did.

'Nearly time to lock the door!' she called. 'I'm looking forward to getting home tonight; it's been a long day.'

'Going anywhere nice for Hogmanay?' Dermot asked, tying on his scarf. 'Lil and me are going to be out on the town. Want to come?'

'Thanks, but I've got something fixed up.'

'Oh, that's good,' Lil said warmly. 'So glad you're going out these days, Kirsty.'

For a moment, Kirsty hesitated, remembering Mr Macrae's special smiles and snatched moments for special words. Seemingly, Dermot and Lil hadn't noticed those either, which was just as well.

'Yes, it's good,' she agreed at last, hoping she was right.

Twenty-Six

Out came the white dress again, and the tartan sash, as Kirsty prepared to get ready for the Hogmanay dance.

She didn't feel the same, though, as when she'd dressed for the ball with Jake MacIver. How could she? Everything then had been magical, bathed in golden light. The present, the future, she'd thought all the delight would just go on and on, because she'd been so dazzled by what was happening, she couldn't see anything as it really was. Only when Jake had taken the light from her had she been able to use her eyes again, and that had been so painful, she didn't like to think of it.

Which was why she'd thrown her dancing shoes away, and had wanted to do the same with her white dress, until she'd decided to show some spirit and keep it. Why should Jake Mac-Iver's behaviour make her waste anything more? Maybe, one day, she'd get it dyed and wear it for discos – which would make sense. But in the end she'd left it to hang forlornly at the back of the wardrobe, the tartan sash tangled round its waist, from where she'd had to rescue it for the Hogmanay dance.

'I'll wash it for you,' Lena had offered, but

160

Kirsty had said no, thanks all the same, she was tired of running away from things and would wash and iron the dress herself.

'That's right; you have to move on, eh? Maybe going out with Mr Macrae'll no' be a bad idea, after all. I mean, why shouldn't you enjoy yourself again, if you can?'

'As long as I don't enjoy myself too much?' Kirsty asked dryly.

'Ah, well, you did say you weren't keen on him.' Lena's gaze was wary. 'Should be no danger there.'

'Och, there'll be no danger with Mr Macrae! Andrew, as he's asked me to call him.'

'Andrew? Fancy. But no' at work!'

'Oh, no.' Kirsty laughed at the very idea. 'Even Mrs MacNee never calls him Andrew at work.'

It being New Year's Eve, everyone was out when Andrew came to collect her for the dance. Lena had gone with Vinnie to a special bingo session, while Reid was as usual working at the pub, and Angie – surprise, surprise – had graciously agreed to be Niall's guest at his firm's Hogmanay party. And that, Lena had said, before rushing out, fully made-up and smelling of Christmas scent, was the best news she'd heard in a long time.

'No lying on her bed, smoking and reading, for this holiday!' she'd cried. 'Could be the turning point, eh?'

'Could be,' Kirsty had agreed, interested in the news, though she had her doubts that Vinnie MacFall would be happy about it. 'Don't wait up for me, eh? I'm not sure when I'll be back.'

'We're all seeing the New Year in after bingo,' Lena had told her with pride. 'I don't know what time I'll be back, either!'

It was left to Kirsty alone, wrapped in her tartan cloak, to wait near the main door and keep a lookout for Andrew's car, a large family saloon – not, of course, a sports car. Not that she cared what sort of car he had, except to think that he was lucky to have one.

Punctual as ever, he arrived at half past seven, as he'd said he would, and as soon as he saw her hovering in the entrance to the flats, leaped out to show her into his passenger seat.

'There you are, Kirsty! All set, then?'

'Yes, Mr— I mean, Andrew.'

'So – first stop, the Crown Park. I think you'll like it. Bit out of town, but none the worse for that. Does very nice food, I can promise you, and has a pleasant atmosphere. Ambience, I believe they call it these days, don't they?'

She could tell he was nervous, as he drove away from Pleasant Hill. Smiling too much, talking too much – always signs. But why should he be nervous, taking her out? Surely she was the one who should be feeling anxious about an evening with her boss, someone she'd never regarded as a person she would meet socially? In fact, she did feel ill at ease, but that was very different from the nervousness she'd suffered before the Valentine Ball with Jake. Then, she'd wanted so much to fit in, be a credit to him. Tonight, she just felt she shouldn't be

162

where she was. In this car, going to a Hogmanay dance, with a man who might ask her to call him Andrew, but would always be Mr Macrae to her.

'Family all out?' he asked as they drove on through built-up areas, making for the outskirts of the city, watching occasional fireworks shooting upwards, listening to the bangs.

'Oh, yes, all got plans for tonight.'

'I don't really know about your people, you know. Why don't you tell me about them?'

She told him, finding it a relief to have something to talk about, and then was able to sit back while he told her he only had his mother now. His father, as Kirsty knew, had been dead for years, but there had been a brother who'd died as a baby, something Kirsty had never heard. Poor Mrs Macrae. Maybe the loss of that baby explained her close hold on the one who'd survived. So, poor Mr Macrae too.

'Soon be there,' he told her. 'The Crown Park's within reach of Turnhouse, but really in the country. Probably be packed tonight, though it's not that well known as yet.'

Was that why he chose it? Kirsty wondered cynically. So they'd be unlikely to meet people he knew? Then she felt a little ashamed of the thought, when he was so obviously hoping to please her. *Relax*, she told herself. *It's New Year's Eve. Your chance for a new start. Be happy.*

Twenty-Seven

And the Crown Park, on New Year's Eve, was certainly the place to feel happy – or at least pampered. A large white building, ablaze with lights, filled with flowers; spacious, beautifully furnished, clearly no expense spared anywhere. And the clientele, dancing in the two ballrooms – one for Scottish dancing, one for modern – were the same. No expense had been spared on them, either, whether on clothes, hair-dos, jewellery, cigars, or whatever luxury they fancied.

How this place smells of money, Kirsty thought, looking at herself in the cloakroom mirror when she'd deposited her wrap. Other gorgeous scents, of course, but mostly money. So, did her dress look too plain? Her tartan sash quite ordinary? At least she had some colour herself, for her copper hair shone, burnished, in the light, and her cheeks were already flushed.

'How lovely you look,' Andrew murmured when she joined him. 'Your dress is perfect. Is it one of ours?'

'I've had it some time,' she replied obliquely, and told him he looked very well himself, in his Prince Charlie evening dress, which was true. No one could have called him the 'Grey Man' then.

'Oh, I'm no oil painting! Bit of a stick, I some-times think. But let's have a drink and then go for the reels, shall we? I'll have to admit to you that I'm not one for the modern stuff.'

'I shouldn't think they do rock and roll here,' she told him with a smile. 'More like the foxtrot or the quick step.'

'But those are what I call modern, anyway.'

She hadn't expected to enjoy it, and it was true that on first hearing the Scottish band, she did feel a twinge or two, but dancing the reels again gave her back a pleasure she'd thought she'd lost for ever.

Just as at the Valentine Ball, all her old favour-ites were there to set her foot tapping again, and then she was away, setting to the men, pousset-ting round to change position, taking Andrew's hand and dancing down between the couples, smiling, even laughing, until she returned with him to their seats and tried to get her breath back.

'Kirsty, that was wonderful!' Andrew cried. 'I'd no idea you were such an accomplished dancer.'

Accomplished. Such an Andrew Macrae sort of word. Still, she was pleased with the compli-ment, accepting it gracefully. And if Jake Mac-Iver had said much the same in different words, she'd forgotten it. Or at least had chosen to forget, and studying Andrew's face bent towards hers, she felt a great lightening of her heart. She really was better, wasn't she?

And lucky too, to be here with someone who

could so absolutely be trusted. True, he was her boss – she still thought of him as Mr Macrae – but it came to her now that she needn't think of him that way. She'd accepted his invitation to come to this dance; maybe she owed it to him to forget who he was, and think of him as just a man who wanted to be with her. And to call him by his first name, if that was what he wanted.

'Andrew,' she said earnestly, leaning a little forward, 'I want to tell you that you were right to give me those shoes. I'm really enjoying dancing again and being here. Thank you.'

His face lit up and he took her hand. 'Kirsty, it's so sweet of you to tell me that. I can't tell you how happy it makes me. I've waited such a long time for this, you see.'

'A long time?'

'To be with you. To ask you to go out with me.'

Her expression changed. She sat back in her chair, letting his hand go. 'I'm sure it's understandable you would want to be careful. You being the owner of the shop, me being an employee.'

'No, no! It's not that at all!' Scarlet spots burned on his cheek bones. 'It was because you were too young.'

She laughed. 'I'm twenty-one. Still young, some folk would say.'

'Twenty-one, but not seventeen,' he said doggedly. 'The gap's still there between us, but not quite as much as before, because twenty-one is closer somehow to thirty-two, than seventeen is to twenty-eight. If you understand me.'

166

'Oh, yes, I think I do.'

'I'd always been attracted to you, you know. Did you never sense that?'

'No. No, I never knew.'

'You told me once that girls always knew.'

She looked down. 'Maybe I got that wrong. It was only when you gave me the shoes that I thought ... you might be interested in me.'

He nodded. 'That was the first time I could let you see that I was. I wanted to tell you how I felt when you were twenty, but before I got my courage up, it was too late.'

'I'd met Jake,' she said after a pause.

'You'd met Jake. You'll never know what I felt then. And what I'd have liked to do to him – when things went wrong.'

'He knew what you thought of him, anyway.'

'I'm glad to hear it. I'd have wanted him to know. Where is he now, anyway? Back from America, I suppose?'

'Oh, yes. Touring in the north, I think. Does it matter?'

'Not at all.' He caught at her hand again. 'Listen, shall we go for supper? It'll not be long now, to the bells, and that'll be the end of 1964.'

And I shan't be sorry, thought Kirsty.

At just before midnight, all the hotel guests gathered in the main ballroom, where the Scottish band had played for dancing and was ready now to play the company into the New Year. A great television screen had been wheeled into the corner, showing revellers at Edinburgh Castle waiting for the firing of the gun that would

167

signal the end of 1964, and as the moment grew closer, the counting began.

'Ten – Nine – Eight – Seven – '

Couples, Kirsty and Andrew among them, were clasping each other's hands, their eyes on the screen, ready to savour the last moment of the old year, the first of the new...

'Six – Five – Four – Three – Two – One!'

And then to the thud of the gunfire and the cheers of the crowd, the sound of church bells and a sudden television shot of Big Ben in London, everyone began crossing arms and singing 'Auld Lang Syne', kissing and hugging and making toasts. The year 1965 had arrived.

At their little Christmas party in the shop, Kirsty had not wanted to be kissed under mistletoe by her boss. But now, in the ballroom of the Crown Park Hotel, surrounded by others all embracing, it seemed the natural thing to exchange kisses with Mr Macrae who had become Andrew. And to hold him as tightly as he held her, until they both drew apart, breathing hard, and Andrew cried, 'Where's your glass, Kirsty? We have to make a toast. To 1965!'

'To 1965!' she repeated, feeling a sudden, happy optimism.

Going home in the car it was to be expected, perhaps, that each would feel a little self-consciousness. Seeing in the New Year, they'd forgotten who they were; had been swept up in the excitement around them, which of course had had to fade. In fact, they hadn't stayed long after

168

the toast, as Andrew had expressed himself worried about getting Kirsty home. Didn't want to be in trouble, keeping her out too late. Her stepmother wouldn't even be back, she'd told him, but still, they hadn't stayed.

Glancing at her as he drove through empty roads, Andrew said awkwardly, 'Sorry, I got a bit carried away back there, maybe.'

'It is Hogmanay,' she said with a smile.

'That's right. Glad you didn't mind, anyway.'

Exchanging kisses? No, she hadn't minded. What else would they have done at Hogmanay? Yet the kisses had been more than they might have been, as they both knew.

After driving for some time without speaking, Andrew asked suddenly, 'Enjoy it tonight?'

'Oh, I did!' she cried truthfully. 'It was a lovely Hogmanay – one of the best!'

'I thought so too.' He gave her a quick glance. 'Like to come out with me again?'

Kirsty, gazing at the quiet road ahead, had been wondering if this question would be coming. Still hadn't decided how to answer.

'Please don't tell me you can't because I own the shop,' Andrew said into her silence.

'Well, what will folk say?' she asked at last.

'We needn't tell them, need we?'

More secrets. She moved uneasily, fiddling with her bag. Did she want to be involved? It would be easier not to be. And yet, it was true, she'd enjoyed herself that Hogmanay, and it had been thanks to Andrew. For the first time in months, she'd felt herself part of the world again, her confidence in herself restored, and

169

though at the beginning of the evening, she'd felt it was all wrong to be with him, somehow all that had changed. Someone wanted her again. And the thought was balm to her hurt.

'I'd like to go out with you,' she said quietly. 'If you're sure about it.'

'Kirsty, I've never been so sure of anything in my life. As I've said, this is no snap decision for me. I've been waiting a long time to make it happen.'

'There might be difficulties, though.'

'They won't matter. We'll see that they don't.' Andrew smiled into the darkness. 'I didn't drink all that much tonight, you know – thinking of the driving again – but I feel as though I'd had a magnum of champagne. Kirsty, listen, when can we meet?'

They arranged to have dinner some days later, and for the time being at least to keep their meetings secret.

'It would be easier,' Andrew said carefully. 'If you're happy about it?'

'Think I'll have to be.'

'No, no, it must be what you want.'

'Well, what I don't want is to tell Mrs Mac-Nee.' She laughed, and so did he. 'Imagine it!'

And where would be the point? She had no way of knowing how long she and Andrew would want to go out together. Why make it public now? Better to keep quiet, and not let folk think there was more to it than there ever could be. As for Andrew's mother – it was up to him what he told her. Kirsty needn't worry about that at all.

'You agree, then, we'll keep this to ourselves?' Andrew asked.

'I agree.'

'Sure?'

'I'm sure.'

They exchanged smiles and drove on.

When they arrived back at Pleasant Hill, it was to find it still hopping with New Year celebrations. Fireworks fizzing into the air, a bonfire crackling on waste ground, dark figures running around, banging on doors and calling to one another in hoarse voices.

'Heavens, this is worse than usual,' Kirsty protested, as Andrew parked his car, and more dark figures arrived to inspect it. One she recognized as a young fellow from Briar, who was smoking and grinning as Andrew handed her out, and called, 'Got any spare cash, mister?'

'You'd better get home before your mother sees you!' Kirsty cried, at which there were roars of laughter and, scarlet-faced, she told Andrew she'd better hurry in.

'I'll come with you,' he declared, and taking out a handful of money from his overcoat pocket, gave it to the boys.

'Here, have a good New Year, but just keep out of our way, eh?'

'Sure, mister, sure!'

'Where do we go in?' Andrew asked, but Kirsty put her hand on his arm and shook her head.

'Don't leave your car,' she whispered. 'I'll get home and see you after the holiday. Thanks

171

again, Andrew, I had a wonderful time.'

'Not quite my idea of saying goodnight,' he said ruefully. 'But I'll see you soon, dear Kirsty. And all my thanks for a marvellous evening.'

Relieved to see his car leaving the area, she turned to go into Clover, her head spinning. Like Andrew, she had not drunk much during the evening, but unlike him, she couldn't say she felt she'd had a magnum of champagne. Was just pleasantly tiddly, perhaps, at the thought of a new life in 1965.

Twenty-Eight

So much had been occupying her mind, Kirsty had forgotten that the new assistant, Miss Lammond, was due to start work after the New Year. But Dermot hadn't, and when Kirsty arrived early at the shop, she found him looking glum.

'Hasn't arrived,' he told her. 'That new lassie. I felt sure she'd want to make a good start.'

'Oh, Miss Lammond, you mean? We're early, Dermot. There's plenty of time for her to come yet.'

'Aye, maybe. So what's brought you in before time, then? Weren't too tired after Hogmanay?'

'No, no, it was very nice.'

Kirsty, unbuttoning her coat, couldn't help smiling as she pictured Dermot's reaction if she'd told him how she had in fact spent

Hogmanay. Back in the shop, it was almost too hard for her to believe it herself. Had she really been dancing with Mr Macrae? Had they kissed and embraced as the New Year came in? Yes, it was true, she'd kissed the owner of Macrae's Kilts, but he'd been Andrew by then, hadn't he? Made it seem possible, to remember that.

'Still can't understand why they didn't appoint that smart blonde,' Dermot was muttering. 'She was a looker, eh?'

'Listen, how d'you think Lil would feel, to hear you going on about that blonde?' Kirsty asked him, fixing him with a hard stare. 'She'd be upset, eh?'

'Lil? Upset?' Dermot seemed surprised at the idea. 'She'd have no reason to be, Kirsty. I mean, she's special, eh?'

'Is she?' Kirsty's eyes softened. 'Ah, that's nice. But does she know? I mean, d'you ever tell her?'

'I'm no' one for talking.'

'What?' She gave a peal of laughter. 'What was it Burns said? "O wad some power the giftie gie us, to see oursels as ithers see us." Dermot, don't you realize you talk all the time?'

'Ssh,' he said hastily, 'someone's coming.'

It was Miss Lammond.

'Hi,' Dermot said. 'Come on in.'

'Thought I'd be early on my first day,' she told him, half smiling. 'Didn't even know if the door would be open.'

'Our cleaning lady opens it. She waits to leave till one of us is here.'

He was staring at the new assistant as though

173

trying to tell, Kirsty guessed, why she should seem different. The hair was different for a start. Still mouse-brown, but shorter and away from her face, so that the good features Kirsty had observed were now more apparent. And the intensity of the blue gaze she was now training on Dermot was also something he probably hadn't expected, as he'd scarcely looked at little Miss Lammond before.

Oh dear, thought Kirsty, *I hope he takes that interested look off his face before Lil arrives.* She moved forward herself to shake the new assistant's hand, reminding her that she was one of the kilt makers.

'Oh, yes, and it's Kirsty, isn't it? I'm Meriel.'

'Meriel,' Dermot repeated, also putting forward his hand. 'I'm Dermot, remember? Dermot Sinclair. In charge of sales – apart from Mr Macrae, of course – so you'll be working with me.'

'I'm looking forward to it,' she said quietly. 'Kirsty, is there somewhere I can put my coat?'

By the time Kirsty had shown her the cloakroom and where they made the coffee, Lil and Mrs MacNee had arrived, to give Meriel another friendly welcome. As Lil took in the face and new hairstyle, however, her eyes sharpened, and her smile, it seemed to Kirsty, was a little forced. It didn't surprise her, when they were alone in the workroom, that Lil should immediately begin to talk of Dermot's assistant.

'Well, what's happened to little Miss Mousy, then?' she demanded. 'I mean, she's a cool one, eh? Turns out to be real stunner, and never gave a hint.'

'No, she seemed to want to play herself down when she was here.'

'Just for the interview, d'you reckon? Maybe she thought this was an old-fashioned shop and she'd do better not to look too smart?'

'Maybe. Anyway, they did prefer her to the blonde.'

'Aye.' Lil's expression grew dark. 'And I was glad they did. Now, I'm no' so sure.'

'Oh, come on – Dermot's never going to be interested in Meriel!' Kirsty cried, trying to forget the look she'd seen on his face. 'He's keen on you.'

'But he'll be with her all the time.'

'And you're a thousand miles away? Lil, you're here, too, remember?'

'Yes, I suppose I am.' Lil's brow cleared. 'Och, I'd better get to work, before Madam comes back from taking off her hat. Listen, did you have a good Hogmanay, then?'

'Oh, yes, grand, thanks.'

As Lil continued to look at her questioningly, Kirsty hurriedly began threading a needle.

'So, how was yours?'

'Oh, lovely. We went to the Tron Kirk, of course, for midnight, and then back to Dermot's and on to Mam's – I've no idea what time I got to bed!'

'You've really no need to worry about Dermot,' Kirsty was beginning to reassure her, when Mrs MacNee came bustling in with a self-satisfied smile.

'Miss Lammond – Meriel – seems to be settling in nicely, eh? I think we made a good appointment there.'

'Oh, yes,' Kirsty agreed, as Lil said nothing.

'I'm sure she'll be quite an asset. Dermot must be so relieved to have someone like her to help in the front shop.'

'Did you tell her she'd have to take a turn at doing the coffee?' Lil asked, unrolling a bale of tartan with a thump. 'She could start by taking a cup to Mr Macrae – I think I heard his office door bang. Late again, eh? Wonder where he spent Hogmanay?'

'Now, is that any of our business?' Mrs Mac-Nee asked. 'And it's not coffee time yet.'

'I'll take his in,' Kirsty said, keeping her eyes on her sewing. 'I don't mind.'

'I should hope not. What's to mind about it? And I think we should let Meriel off on her first day. She has a lot to learn all at once. I'm going to instruct her in measuring myself.'

'Your coffee, Mr Macrae,' Kirsty was able to say some time later, when she took the tray into his office.

'Kirsty!' He leaped up from his desk. 'Ah, it's good to see you!'

'I do work here, you know.'

'Yes, but it's hard to see you alone. I've been thinking about you so much since Hogmanay. Have you been thinking about me?'

'Oh, yes.' She stirred his coffee. 'Better drink this before it gets cold.'

'Who cares?' He came to stand close to her

176

and took her hand. 'Still all right for our dinner date? Shall I collect you from home?'

'Might be best. Except that we have to come back into town.'

'No problem there, with the car.'

'That's true. I still think of the bus journey, I suppose. Mr Macrae, I have to go now, otherwise folk'll be wondering what we're talking about.'

'Mr Macrae, Kirsty? What happened to Andrew?'

'Not possible to call you that here.'

'When we're alone, you could.'

'But then I might forget when we weren't.' She laughed, knowing she was needling him a little. 'What would Mrs MacNee say, if I did that? Called you Andrew in the shop?'

His face sagged, but he said at once, 'To hell with it – why shouldn't you?'

'You know what we agreed.'

'Yes, I know.' He pressed her hand, as she took up her tray. 'At least, try to be the one to bring the coffee, anyway. That'd be something to look forward to.'

'No promises. We have Miss Lammond now, and Lil thinks she should take her turn.'

'Miss Lammond? Oh, God, I'd better go and have a word.' He flung himself into his chair and swallowed some coffee. 'Why is life so difficult, Kirsty?'

You don't know the half of it, she thought, but only smiled and withdrew.

By the end of the day, it seemed clear to all that

Meriel Lammond was going to prove herself an asset to Macrae's Kilts.

'She's a natural!' Mrs MacNee declared to Andrew when he looked in at the workroom. 'Took to kilt measuring as though she'd been doing it all her life. I had to be impressed.'

'She did work in a dress shop,' Lil put in shortly. 'I expect she had to do plenty of measuring there.'

'Why, you know that's not the same as measuring for kilts!' Mrs MacNee cried, scandalized. 'It's a very specialized job, it takes time to learn, but she seemed to get the hang of it straight away. And then Dermot tells me that she's been learning fast where everything is, and doing very well with her first customers. Such a nice manner, he says. I think we're going to be very pleased with her, Mr Macrae.'

'Sounds like it,' he agreed. 'There seems to be a lot more to her than we thought.'

'Och, I can always tell what lassies are going to be like.' Mrs MacNee pursed her lips a little. 'There's no way they can pull the wool over *my* eyes, I'm telling you.'

'That's why I wanted you in on the interview,' Andrew murmured, his eyes wandering towards Kirsty. 'Well, it's nearly time to shut up shop, isn't it? Been a good day back at work, I think, even if the sale is pretty well over. Goodnight, everyone.'

'Goodnight, Mr Macrae!' they chorused, as he left them, only glancing back once to where Kirsty was tidying her table. But she was careful not to raise her head.

'How was your first day, then?' Dermot asked Meriel, as they fastened up their coats and prepared to leave. 'Not too tiring, was it?'

'Not at all. I really enjoyed it. Thanks for being so patient.'

'Nae bother.' He hesitated. 'It's really grand, having help, you know.'

'It must have been far too much for you on your own.'

'That's right. You've hit the nail on the head. Well, tomorrow I'll be able to go through the hire business with you, eh? That side's really taking off.'

She kept her bright gaze on him. 'Do I get to serve the men as well as the women?'

'Oh, yes. Well, if there are too many for me.' He grinned. 'Find 'em more interesting?'

'Everyone's interesting, aren't they?' She smiled. 'If they're customers?'

'You bet.'

'Ready to go, Dermot?' called Lil, as she and Kirsty came to the shop door.

'Aye, all set. Which way for you, Meriel?'

'I get the Twenty-Three or the Twenty-Seven. I live in Trinity.'

'So do I! Lil lives in Canonmills, so we can all get the same bus.'

'How nice,' Lil said coolly. 'Hope you don't feel left out, Kirsty, having to go to Pleasant Hill.'

'Come along now. Are you going out, or staying here?' Mrs MacNee interrupted. 'I want to lock the door.'

There were four of them, then, to walk down the Mound, instead of three. Luckily it wasn't icy – no need, therefore, for anyone to take Dermot's arm, and, after a backward glance, he walked ahead with Meriel, while behind came Kirsty and Lil.

'So, this is the new regime, is it?' Lil asked, as the wind sent them bowling towards Princes Street. 'To think I was worried about that blonde!'

'Lil.' Kirsty took her arm. 'Settle down, eh?'

'What d'you mean? I hope I'm allowed to speak these days?'

'If you go on like this, you'll just make yourself look foolish. It's the girl's first day. Nothing's happened to upset you. Give it a rest.'

'I can see the way things are going, Kirsty. Soon as I saw her this morning, I knew how it would be.'

'You're imagining the whole thing. But if you go on about it, you might make it happen.'

Lil put a hand to her hair that was whirling across her unhappy face. 'You think so?'

'Aye. Just be yourself and really nice to Meriel, and remember that Dermot cares for you. It was only this very morning, that he told me you were special.'

'He said that?' Lil's voice was almost lost in the wind. 'I was special?'

'His very word, and he meant it.' Kirsty let Lil's arm go. 'No need for you to be miserable, then.'

'Maybe not.' Lil sighed and slowed her steps

180

as Kirsty's bus stop loomed. 'I've just got into a state, I guess. But why does life have to be so difficult?'

'Mr Macrae said that same thing to me this morning.'

'Mr Macrae?'

'When I took in his coffee.' Kirsty, reddening, could have kicked herself for mentioning his name. 'Must've been upset over something,' she added quickly.

'Nothing difficult in his life, that's for sure,' Lil said firmly. 'Here's your stop, then. I'll have to catch up with the others.' She paused, then suddenly gave Kirsty a quick hug. 'Thanks, Kirsty. You're a good friend.'

'You coming, Lil?' called Dermot, standing with Meriel at the edge of the pavement.

'Coming!' she called back, and ran to join them.

Just hope I'm right about Dermot, Kirsty thought, standing shivering in her queue. He was a nice enough fellow, surely he could be trusted? But how about Meriel?

Twenty-Nine

Before Andrew came to collect her for their dinner date, Kirsty sat in the kitchen of the flat with Lena and Angie. Reid, of course, was out – not working at the pub for a change, but studying at the college library. He had Finals that summer.

'Very nice,' Lena observed, of Kirsty's new dark blue dress she'd bought at a New Year sale. 'What there is of it.'

'Skirts are short these days, Lena,' Kirsty told her.

'All right if you've got the legs, eh?' Lena unfolded the evening newspaper. 'Still wish you were going out with somebody more your age, though.'

'Somebody like Niall?' Angie asked dryly.

'Aye, why not? He works hard and he's ambitious, like our Reid. You could do a lot worse yourself, Angie.'

'No matchmaking, Auntie Lena. I'm no' interested in marriage at the moment.'

'You will go out with Niall again, though?'

'Maybe. Maybe not.'

'Oh, Angie!' Lena heaved a great sigh. 'Why are you two lassies so difficult, eh? There's Kirsty here, going out with her boss and she knows there's no future in that, and there's you, Angie, turning down a nice steady fellow like

182

Niall. Good-looking, too.'

'I haven't exactly turned him down, when he's never asked me anything.' Angie laughed carelessly. 'As a matter of fact, I think he's got someone else to think about.'

'Who?' Kirsty cried, interested and a little surprised. But then, why shouldn't Niall have his secrets the same as anyone else? No reason. Still, she was surprised.

'Canna say, but I saw him once, talking to a girl in George Street. Probably somebody from where he works.'

'What did she look like?'

'Quite smart. Red hair, I think. Didn't take much notice.'

'So, why did he take you to the Hogmanay dance?' Lena asked sharply. 'If he's keen on somebody else?'

Angie shrugged. 'Maybe she couldn't come. Or was another fellow's partner.'

'We don't know if he's keen, anyway,' Kirsty pointed out, but Lena shook her head.

'Well, I'll bet plenty of fellows were looking at Angie, anyway – and thinking Niall was a lucky man!'

'Here we go again.' Angie sighed, rolling her eyes. 'You'll never rest till you've got us walking down the aisle, Auntie Lena!'

'That'll be the day.' Kirsty laughed. 'But women are supposed to have careers today, you know, instead of expecting meal tickets from husbands.'

'What a piece of nonsense! Women will always want husbands. Who says they're just meal tickets?'

Kirsty, glancing at the clock, buttoned on her best coat. 'Lena, I'd better go down and see if I can see the car. Andrew said he'd be here by seven.'

'No' asking him up first?'

Kirsty hesitated. The thought of bringing Andrew to meet her family reminded her too much of Jake MacIver's coming up before the Valentine Ball and exercising all his charm, as though it mattered. In any case, she and Andrew were not at the stage of seriously wanting to meet families. Never would be, come to that.

'Maybe another time,' she said at last, and Lena nodded.

'Just as well, as I never tidied up after tea.'

'As though he'd care about that! Anyway, it looks fine.'

'Next time, then. If you're keeping on with him.'

'I'm no' sure what I'm doing. Except that the future doesn't come into it.'

'That's right,' Angie told her. 'Have a good time, and live for the day, eh?'

'What a way to think,' Lena muttered.

As usual, Andrew was exactly on time, and, as he had said, returning to town, even on a winter's night, presented no problems in his comfortable Rover.

'Seems no distance at all,' Kirsty murmured as they drove into a parking place near the cathedral in the West End. 'You've no idea what a trek it is from our place in the bus.'

'I can imagine,' he said sympathetically, locking the car and putting her arm in his. 'Did you find it hard to make the transition from the Old Town to Pleasant Hill? Or were you too young to notice?'

'Oh, no, I wasn't too young. I can remember a lot about the old days, and there were things we missed at first. But life's a lot easier in the flats, you know, even if we are a long way out and the lifts don't always work.'

She glanced at his face, so serene below his trilby hat. 'Andrew, mind if I ask whereabouts you stay, then? I know it's south side, never heard where.'

'It's the Grange. Holm Road. Pretty quiet.'

'Big old houses there, aren't they?'

'Yes, pretty big, Victorian, on the whole. I could easily make a separate flat for myself out of the top floor of ours, but haven't got round to it yet.' He hesitated. 'To be honest, I'd rather move out altogether – have my own place. But I couldn't leave my mother on her own.'

'I can understand you wouldn't want to do that.'

He looked down at her and smiled faintly. 'Can you? Some people think I'm crazy. Listen, let's see if we can find this restaurant. It was recommended to me, but I've never been to it. I'm told it's very good.'

Out of the way for him, Kirsty thought. Like the Crown Park, not a place he was likely to see people he knew. But why was she being so cynical again?

'I'm sure it'll be lovely,' she said quickly. 'But

185

I'd better tell you that I don't know much about restaurant food. Plain, is what we're used to at home.'

'You'll be all right here, I promise you. They specialize in good Scottish food. Joints, game, steaks, and hearty puddings. Sound OK?'

'Sounds fattening!'

'You've no need to worry on that score, Kirsty. You're beautifully slim.'

They easily found the restaurant, which was in the converted ground floor of a large old Victorian house. Not at all smart, just comfortable and welcoming, with a crackling open fire and a handful of tables, all occupied, except for one in the corner, which was theirs.

'It's just as I said – it's lovely!' Kirsty cried, as a waiter hung up her coat and she took her seat opposite Andrew, her eyes shining as she looked around.

'Think I made a good choice?' he asked lightly.

'Oh, I do!'

As she turned her eyes on him, it seemed to her that he seemed younger than in the shop, perhaps because he was happy. Happy to be with her? She didn't know whether to be flattered, or worried. Or was it just her imagination at work again?

It was a relief, in a way, when the waiter brought the menus, and they had something to study apart from each other. And, certainly, studying the dishes on offer was a wonderful way to be sidetracked from perplexing thoughts.

'Oh, my, what shall I have?' Kirsty sighed. 'They all seem gorgeous.'

After Andrew had ordered wine for himself, they chose a starter of smoked salmon pate, followed by pheasant with game chips and bread sauce. Defeated by the pudding menu, Andrew settled for cheese, but Kirsty was reckless and went for a Scottish trifle, named Typsy Laird.

'How d'you feel?' he asked later, when she had laid down her spoon.

'Wonderful. Except that I may never move again.'

'We'll have coffee, though?'

'Oh, please. Then I might sober up.'

He grinned. 'You haven't drunk anything.'

'I had that Typsy Laird.'

'They only frighten the sponge with a spoonful of whisky. But I know what you mean. Remember the magnum of champagne I didn't have at the ball?'

They both laughed, and Kirsty, looking at Andrew, thought, if he's happy, so am I. Yet, wasn't it all a bit like Cinderella? Tonight it was as though they were at the ball again. Tomorrow, they'd be back at the shop, Andrew would be Mr Macrae, she a kilt maker. Seemed hard to think of it.

When the coffee came, she drank it eagerly, finding it strong and fragrant, then touched Andrew's hand where it lay on the table.

'Thank you for this evening, Andrew.'

His look now was serious. 'There'll be more, won't there? We'll go out again?'

'If you want to.'

'I think you know I want to.'

187

'But if we do – are we still keeping things a secret?'

'That's what we said.'

'Somebody will be sure to see us,' she whispered. 'They always do.'

'Why should they? If we're careful?'

'You can go anywhere in the world, I've heard folks say, and somebody from home will turn up beside you. I bet that'd be Mrs MacNee.'

He didn't smile. 'Let's worry about that if it happens. All I want now is a promise from you to come out with me again.'

'Where?'

'Anywhere! Restaurant, cinema, theatre – you name it, we'll be there.'

For a brief chill of a moment, she was reminded of Jake and all his promises of what they might see and do, but she hurriedly pushed the memory from her, saying maybe it was time to leave. Apart from themselves, there was only one other couple left, and the waiters were looking hopeful.

'I'll get the bill,' Andrew said, rising. 'Though I'm like you, I don't want to move.'

All the way home, through sleet that threatened soon to be snow, Kirsty kept wondering how and where they would say goodnight. Would Andrew find somewhere quiet for their kisses – naturally, there would be kisses – or would he drive her straight to her door and hope no one was about? At this time of night and in this kind of weather, there probably wouldn't be a soul to see them, but she couldn't imagine Andrew

188

risking onlookers. He was not the sort to rush things, anyway, and even though they'd exchanged kisses and hugs at Hogmanay – well, that was Hogmanay. Whatever he did, it would soon happen. Even in driving sleet, this car did good time. They'd soon be reaching Pleasant Hill.

Still, as his windscreen wipers worked overtime and visibility grew worse, she told him she was worried about his own drive home. 'Supposing it's snowing by then?'

'No need to worry. I have winter tyres fitted and the Rover's fine in snow, anyway. All I want is to get you home safely.'

Then she knew that they would not be dallying in any side road; would be driving straight to Clover's entrance, and if anyone should be hanging about, there might well be no kisses after all. Maybe that would be for the best. As she'd remembered during their dinner, tomorrow he'd be Mr Macrae again; she his employee. Kissing him tonight might not be easy.

Easy, though, was just what it was. As soon as they arrived at Clover, Andrew's sharp grey eyes had pierced the darkness and checked that no one was in sight.

'No young figures setting off fireworks tonight,' he said with a grin. 'Only lighted windows.'

'Curtained windows,' Kirsty told him. 'And we're not that late. They'll still be watching TV.'

'And not us, you mean? Oh, Kirsty!' He took her in his arms. 'If they all had binoculars train-

189

ed on us, it wouldn't stop me kissing you.'

'You haven't yet.'

For answer, he drew her close, pressing his mouth to hers with a confidence and passion she hadn't expected from so quiet a man, even after their embracing at Hogmanay. But how foolish she'd been, not to think he'd be experienced in love! He was over thirty, after all, and had always had a social life of his own, as they'd known at the shop, even if he'd seemed so colourless.

The truth of the matter was, as Kirsty was beginning to realize, he'd never been as colourless as they'd thought him. No Jake MacIver in show or charm, he was attractive in a different way, which was why, now, in his arms, she'd forgotten about work tomorrow.

'The ritual goodnight kiss,' he said, as he released her. 'Didn't mind, Kirsty?'

'No, I didn't mind. You asked me that before, at Hogmanay.'

'Because I want you to feel as I do,' he responded quietly. 'It's not always easy to tell what girls want.'

'They don't always know,' she said with truth.

'But you did want me to kiss you, Kirsty? That wasn't just a ritual for me, I can promise you.'

'I wasn't sure what I wanted,' she said after a pause. 'Because sometimes I remember who you are. But when we kissed just then, I forgot.'

'Thank God for that!'

'You're really very good,' she said with a laugh. 'At kissing.'

'And so are you.'

190

But when he made to hold her again, she shook her head.

'I'll really have to go, Andrew. There's work in the morning.'

'Don't remind me.' He groaned. 'The only ray of sunshine is that we'll meet again, won't we? When you bring in my coffee, we'll fix it up?'

'As long as Miss Lammond doesn't have to take her turn.'

'I'm relying on you,' he said firmly, and slowly and finally they made their farewells, she facing the weather long enough to run into the flats, he to begin his drive back to the Grange. And they'd been right about the snow; it was just beginning to replace the sleet, falling in thick white cottonwool flakes that whirled with Andrew's thoughts as he drove himself home.

Thirty

It was strange, but no one at the shop seemed to notice that there was anything between Mr Macrae and Kirsty, though Kirsty had felt sure that as the weeks went by, somebody would see something.

'Love and a cold cannot be hid' went the saying, but she wasn't expecting anyone to notice love as such, for she wasn't in love with Andrew and didn't believe that he was in love with her.

191

Only very much attracted, which wasn't the same. Probably, he'd have liked to go to bed with her, but with no thought of marriage he wasn't the sort even to suggest it, and certainly she didn't want it.

But they did like being together when they could; they did like their outings, their kisses and light love-making, and if their relationship was not one between true lovers, it was a relationship all the same. Which was just why Kirsty had thought folk would spot it. But so far, no, they'd been safe.

Even from the far-sighted blue eyes of Meriel Lammond? Had she never wondered why Kirsty was always on hand to take in the boss's coffee? It seemed not, but then she had concerns of her own, such as the job she was still learning and the presence of Dermot, who, if there were no customers about, always seemed to be hovering around her. Kirsty wondered what Lil thought of that and guessed it would be enough to prevent her noticing anything else.

As for Mrs MacNee, the idea that Mr Macrae might be interested in Kirsty would be so incredible, she'd not be likely to see his fond looks in her direction, or her unexplained willingness to serve his coffee. Maybe one day, though? They couldn't expect to get away with it for ever.

Sometimes Lil and Kirsty spent their lunch break together, so that Kirsty could listen afresh to Lil's fears over Dermot and make soothing remarks. She was happy to do what she could,

192

viewing it as a sort of therapy, but the melancholy fact was that she knew Lil was right about Dermot's feelings. Anyone with eyes could see that he had fallen from a great height for Meriel; had been dazzled by her beauty and novelty and could no longer save himself. What was there to say?

'You still see Dermot, don't you?' she asked Lil one windy day in March, when they were having a comforting lunch of pies and chips and tomato sauce. 'I mean, that must prove something.'

'Prove what?' asked Lil. 'He daren't say anything to me, and hasn't fixed up anything with her.'

'But I think it shows he still wants to be with you.' Kirsty rather desperately ate a chip or two. 'That's the way I'd see it.'

'Aye, well I might, if he didn't talk about her all the time. Och, it's Meriel this, it's Meriel that. How she wants to change the shop round – put the hire kilts here, the ladies' clothes there – or whatever. I just switch off when he starts up, but what does that tell you, Kirsty? When a fella never stops talking about a lassie?' Lil's eyes filled with tears and she pushed away her half-eaten lunch. 'Oh, I know what I'm facing. What you faced, eh? No point putting it into words.'

Kirsty, flushing, pushed her own plate away and said she'd get some coffee. 'And how about a cake, Lil? An almond slice, or a doughnut?'

'The last thing I want is a cake,' Lil said savagely and took out a packet of cigarettes. 'But I'd no' mind a coffee.'

193

Over the coffee, as Lil drew on a cigarette and seemed calmer, Kirsty reminded her that whatever she had faced, it was over now. She was quite her old self.

'Aye, prettier than ever,' Lil said slowly. 'I was thinking the other day, how well you were looking.'

'There you are, then.' Kirsty, still rose-red in the face, drank her coffee. 'If things do come to an end between you and Dermot, remember, it isn't the end of the world. Plenty good fish in the sea.'

'You've found someone else, eh? Aye, that's it. I see it now.' Lil was managing a smile. 'Kirsty, you sly boots, why'd you no' say?'

'There's no one else, Lil,' Kirsty told her quickly, crossing her fingers till they ached. 'I'm just happy to be free, that's all. So might you be.'

Lil's smile faded. 'Takes time, to be free. And anyway I'm no' sure – I mean, supposing ... supposing things aren't the way I think?'

Oh, Lil ... Kirsty could have groaned, but on that pseudo-optimistic note, they went back to work.

'Lost in thought?' Andrew asked that evening. They were sitting in an Edinburgh cinema, waiting for the start of the 'big picture', which was *A Fistful of Dollars* starring Clint Eastwood. Andrew's choice, only accepted by Kirsty because she thought Clint 'very dishy'. Andrew had said, if he'd known that, he'd have taken her to see *Cleopatra* with Elizabeth Taylor, which was

194

being shown again elsewhere.

'Ah, well, Richard Burton's in that,' Kirsty had countered. 'He's dishy too.'

Now, as Kirsty finished an ice-cream, Andrew asked again if she had something on her mind.

'Maybe I shouldn't talk about it.'

'Everything is safe with me.'

'Still, it's other people's business.'

Andrew gave her a long look from his shrewd grey eyes. 'Think I can guess what's troubling you. It's Lil, isn't it?'

She put her little wooden spoon into the empty ice-cream tub. 'How did you know?'

'Part of my job, to know about my staff.'

'So, you'll know why I'm upset?'

He nodded. 'Dermot has fallen for his new assistant. I suppose it was always on the cards. Meriel's a very lovely girl.'

Kirsty's eyes narrowed. 'You think so?'

'Well, she's one of those girls who can look plain or beautiful, whichever she chooses. Mostly, she looks beautiful, I'd say.'

'I'm glad she has another admirer.'

Catching up Kirsty's hand, Andrew laughed. 'Come on, Kirsty! This is just the same sort of thing as your admiring Clint Eastwood. Meriel Lammond means nothing to me.'

'She's done a lot of damage to Lil, is all I can say. And Dermot will probably end up being hurt as well.'

'You think she's encouraging him?'

Releasing her hand from Andrew's, Kirsty had suddenly become very still, staring towards a

195

couple just taking their seats in front of them.

'Seemingly,' she whispered. 'She's with him now.'

'Oh, hell!' Andrew said softly.

Thirty-One

As the cinema lights went down, and the film's opening titles began to roll, both Andrew and Kirsty sat stiffly in their seats, not saying another word, as though not to speak made them invisible. A waste of time, of course. Before the first scene had begun, Meriel had turned round, her eyes shining, even in the half-light from the screen, and said, 'Why, hello, Mr Macrae and Kirsty! Dermot, here's Mr Macrae with Kirsty, sitting right behind us.'

The film seemed to last for ever and what it was about, Kirsty had no idea. After giving her a rueful look, Andrew appeared to be watching it, but Kirsty could think of nothing but Meriel's smile. Of course, she and Andrew had always known that sooner or later someone would see them together – or at least, Kirsty had known it. Sometimes she'd thought Andrew just kept his head in the sand, hoping he could go out with her as long as he liked without any problems.

There were, in fact, no real problems. No reason why they shouldn't have a relationship. Except they'd both known that what they had would change, once folk knew about it. Some wouldn't approve. Andrew's mother wouldn't approve. Decisions might have to be made. They'd both just wanted to put discovery off as long as possible – keep their pleasant status quo – but now they knew that that was probably over. Meriel Lammond had ended it for them, and it remained to be seen what she would do now. If anything.

For there was always Dermot to consider. He had neither looked back at Andrew and Kirsty, nor spoken. And the way he sat slumped with his head down, Kirsty knew that, like her, he was not watching the film.

In other circumstances, he would certainly have been fascinated by seeing her with Mr Macrae, but now he was just terrified that she would tell Lil about seeing him with Meriel. And it came to her mind that perhaps if they all agreed to say nothing, all would not be lost. Even so, things would never be the same for her and Andrew. Because Meriel Lammond and Dermot knew.

When the film ended and the lights went up, the four from Macrae's blinked a little but stayed in their seats, as people around them rose to leave. Finally, Meriel turned round again to look at Kirsty and Andrew. She smiled, but did not speak, while Dermot kept his face averted.

'Enjoy the film?' Andrew asked politely, putting on a good imitation of himself as the usual Mr Macrae.

'Oh, very much, thanks,' Meriel answered.

'How about you?'

'Always like Clint Eastwood.'

'Dermot's the same. He chose the film, didn't you, Dermot?'

Dermot slowly turned round, his eyes meeting Kirsty's and falling away. He cleared his throat. 'Yes, I thought it'd be good.'

'We have to make tracks,' Kirsty said brightly. 'See you tomorrow, eh?'

'Oh, yes,' Meriel agreed. 'Goodnight, then.'

'Goodnight,' the others echoed.

'Had to happen,' Kirsty told Andrew, as they walked to the car. 'Couldn't be helped.'

'Not the end of the world, anyway,' he said cheerfully. 'If people know about us.'

She looked at him strangely. 'You've always gone on as though it was.'

'I just thought it might cause difficulties, if someone like Mrs MacNee knew we were seeing each other.'

Only Mrs MacNee? What about his mother? His friends at the New Club, the Rotary, etc? The owner of Macrae's Kilts dating one of his workers? Sure, that sort of thing happened. Happened all the time. But could lead to trouble, eh? Kirsty could almost hear the voices. Knew Andrew could hear them too.

'I don't think we need worry,' she said shortly. 'Meriel probably won't tell Mrs MacNee. Why should she? We could do a deal, anyway. She says nothing and I say nothing, about Dermot taking her to the pictures and in the most expensive seats.'

'Why, Kirsty, darling, what is it?' Andrew, opening the car door for her, was looking down at her in surprise. 'You sound so – I don't know – bitter. Not like you at all.'

'Maybe I'm tired of the way folk go on, Andrew. Dermot cheating on Lil. You and me and our secrets.'

'You wanted secrets as much as I did,' he told her, taking his seat at the wheel. 'If you remember, when I asked you if you were happy about keeping things to ourselves, you said you were. You didn't want to tell people, either.'

'OK, I didn't. But now I've changed my mind.'

'Because Meriel Lammond has seen us?'

'Yes!' Kirsty's eyes flashed. 'Why should I have to worry over someone like her seeing me in the cinema? Why should I have to tell lies to Lil when she asks me if there's anybody in my life? I've had enough, Andrew. I've had enough of secrets.'

'And so have I,' he said quietly. 'Listen, when we agreed not to tell people at work about us, you did tell your stepmother, didn't you? But I've never told my mother.'

'I never thought you would.'

'You didn't? Well, I feel I should have done. The only reason I held back was because ... well, she's inclined to go on a bit.'

'And wouldn't think me suitable as a friend for you.'

'Ah, now, I didn't say that.'

'Come on, we needn't spell it out.'

'Kirsty, it's true you work for me, but my

mother wouldn't have anything against that. We're not grand people, just have a good business that gives us a comfortable living. My grandfather worked in a flourmill at one time, my dad made kilts in the early days, just like you. Why shouldn't you and I go out together?'

'She'd be worried, all the same, if she knew about you and me. I live in Pleasant Hill, I went to the local school. Don't tell me she wouldn't rather see you going round with somebody like Mildred Whatshername.'

For a moment Andrew was silent, then he gave a brief sigh. 'How did you know? How do women always know?'

'I'm right, eh?'

'You're right. Mildred's the one for me, according to my mother. That's because she knows her parents and all her relations, they go to the same kirk, they meet at the same houses. What's forgotten is what I want. And I want to be with you.'

'You'd be a brave chap, then, to tell your mother that.'

'So, I'm brave.' Andrew took Kirsty into his arms and held her close. 'How about coming to tea with my mother next Sunday, then? I think it's about time.'

'He's serious,' Lena declared later, when Kirsty had returned from the cinema, Reid had returned from the pub, and Angie had stirred herself over this latest development to leave her bed. 'Asking you to have tea with his mother, he must be.'

'Think you're right,' Reid said thoughtfully.

'A chap like him wouldn't get involved other-wise.'

'Aye, he's a gentleman,' Lena said, pouring herself another cup of tea. 'I took to him straight away, that time you brought him up, Kirsty. So different from Jake MacIver, eh?'

'Seem to remember you thought Jake was a charmer,' Angie murmured, yawning.

'My very point! He's no' sincere. Tries to butter folk up, when he couldn't give a toss for 'em. But Mr Macrae, he's really nice. He's genuine.'

Yes, Andrew's one visit to her home had been a success, Kirsty recalled. They'd been going out to some dance and she'd suddenly decided he should come up and meet Lena, because she knew Lena wanted it. From the start, they'd hit it off, with Andrew just being pleasant and courteous, and Lena responding with smiles and blushes.

When Reid and Angie appeared, there had been the same easy chat, and though, to be honest, Kirsty thought Jake had acquitted him-self just as well, perhaps that had been only his professional manner working, while Andrew had remained himself. Anyway, she'd been glad she'd changed her mind about inviting him up, though had never in all the world expected to be asked back to Holm Road, in the Grange.

'I don't know what you mean by serious,' she said now, fiddling with the teaspoon in her saucer. 'He's just sick of secrets, like me.'

'Don't you want him to be serious?' Angie asked.

Kirsty, aware of Lena's eyes on her, moved uneasily in her chair. 'Doesn't matter what I want. He won't be planning to ask me to wed.'

'So, why take you to see his ma?' asked Reid.

'I've told you. He doesn't want to keep things from her any more.'

'Keep you from her, you mean. So, what did you say when he asked you to go for your tea with her?'

'I couldn't think what to say. I was amazed.'

'You did say yes, though.'

'Aye, I did. Of course, I've already met Mrs Macrae at the shop, so it'll no' be that different, seeing her at home.'

'Who are you kidding?' Reid asked with a laugh. 'It'll be different, all right.'

'I'm just trying to convince myself, OK?' Kirsty sighed. 'First problem is – what to wear.'

'I'm sure you'll have worked it out by Sunday.' Reid stood up. 'Now, why don't you lassies get off to bed and I'll clear the cups for once?'

'Heavens, is the sky falling?' Angie asked.

'Want to talk?' she asked Kirsty later, in their room.

'No,' Kirsty answered after a pause. 'Thanks all the same. To tell you the truth, I don't know what to say.'

Thirty-Two

Dermot was at work before Kirsty the following morning, as she'd known he would be; fortunately, Meriel had not yet arrived.

'Kirsty!' As soon as she came through the door, he was at her side, a cigarette in his hand, his face showing his strain. 'Hope we can have a word? About last night?'

'You'd better put that cigarette out first. Mrs MacNee will smell it the minute she gets here.'

'Aye.' Dermot opened the door and stubbed out his cigarette on the pavement. 'Needed a smoke, though.'

'I'll bet you did.' Kirsty took off her coat and looked at him coldly. 'But you needn't worry, I won't say anything to Lil.'

He breathed a sigh of relief. 'Kirsty, you're a pal. Thanks. I appreciate it.'

'I'm no' going to tell her, Dermot. You are.'

His eyes flickered and he stared away. 'Ah, no. No, Kirsty, I can't do that.'

'You'll have to. You owe it to her. How can you leave her to think you still care, when you're seeing Meriel Lammond? That wasn't the first time, was it, last night?'

He shook his head. 'No. I asked her out pretty early on. Couldn't help myself. I knew it was the

203

wrong thing to do, me still being Lil's fella, but when Meriel said she'd go, nothing on earth would've stopped me seeing her.' He put his hand to his dry lips. 'Nothing'll stop me now, Kirsty. That's the way it is.'

'You think you're in love with her, eh?'

'I am in love with her.' He hesitated. 'You know how I used to feel about you? And then me and Lil began to hit it off and went out together? This is different. This is like I've no say in what I do any more, or think, or anything. I'm just ... sort of ... driven.'

As Kirsty said nothing, looking uneasily around for someone else to arrive, Dermot touched her hand.

'Weren't you the same, Kirsty? With Jake MacIver?'

'And look what happened to me,' she said in a low voice.

'And now ... now you're seeing Mr Macrae?' He gave a faint smile. 'Gave me a shock when I saw you with him at the flicks, I can tell you. Meriel said she'd no idea.'

'No one has any idea. At the moment.'

'I won't say anything, Kirsty.'

'Don't worry about it. And you can tell Meriel that, too.'

'Oh, she's already said she'll keep quiet about it. It's your business and no one else's.'

'True.' Kirsty gave Dermot another long cold look. 'But things are different for you, Dermot. What you do matters to Lil. You're going to have to tell her how you feel, because she has to know. It's her right.'

204

'I know that; nobody better,' he said quietly. 'But I feel so bad, Kirsty. What can I say? For God's sake, tell me what to say!'

'How can I do that, Dermot?'

'She's still my Lil. I can't hurt her.'

As his eyes pleadingly met hers, the shop door banged, and Meriel came in.

'Morning,' she called. 'It's nice, too. Quite spring-like, for once. Goodbye, winter!'

As she went off with her coat to the cloak-room, Kirsty and Dermot continued to stand facing each other, not speaking, just waiting. For Lil.

As soon as she saw his face, of course, Lil knew what Dermot was going to say to her. Not that he could say it then, but when they moved to a corner of the front shop, it seemed obvious that he was about to arrange a meeting where the axe would fall. Even Meriel looked apprehensive.

'This wasn't my doing,' she whispered to Kirsty, following her into the workroom.

'No? You agreed to go out with him.'

'He wouldn't leave me alone. Anyway, I didn't know then how keen Lil was.'

'It's Lil he really cares for, Meriel. He's never going to have a proper relationship with you, is he? You've just somehow got in the way.'

'I am quite fond of him, as a matter of fact.'

'Quite fond?' Kirsty's eyes were snapping when Mrs MacNee came in, still wearing her hat, and asked what Lil was doing in the front shop.

'And you, Meriel, shouldn't you be back there,

or have you and Lil swapped places?'

'Sorry,' Meriel said, gracefully removing herself, while Kirsty began to set out her work, and Mrs MacNee frowned over the order book.

'If that Campbell of Cawdor tartan doesn't come today, we're really going to be in trouble, Kirsty. Colonel Campbell wants his kilt for a trip to a clan gathering in Canada, and Lil should have started on it by now, but where's the tartan? I'm going to have to make a phone call. Kirsty, are you listening?'

'Yes, Mrs MacNee.'

'I'll just go and take off my hat, and hurry up Lil. I want her to get on with the Anderson boy's kilt, so's to be ready for Colonel Campbell's. Maybe I can get the material sent special delivery.'

'Yes, Mrs MacNee.'

Kirsty, watching her go, sighed with relief, for Lil, pale as wax, had just slid into her seat. Already, in some strange way, she seemed a shadow of herself, her face all eyes, making Kirsty's heart go out to her in fellow feeling. She had never been interested in Dermot herself, good-looking though he was, but to Lil he was everything, and not so long ago it had seemed she could be everything to him. Now, as she'd said to Kirsty, she was facing what Kirsty had had to face, and though she'd refused to spell it out, they both knew what it was. The end of dreams.

'Asked me to meet him in the lunch hour,' she told Kirsty tonelessly. 'Says he wants to talk. I say he needn't bother. I know what he

206

wants to say.'

'You're meeting him, though?'

Lil shrugged. 'Might as well.'

Kirsty's face, too, seemed all eyes. Great eyes fixed on Lil with such sympathy that Lil had to look away. A thought seemed to strike her.

'You're no' saying much, Kirsty. Usually, you try to take his part, eh?'

'Lil, I do not!'

'Well, you make out he still cares.'

'I think he does – deep down.'

'Deep down? Thanks for that. And up top, it's all Miss Mousy, is it?'

'She's dazzled him, that's all. If you wait, he'll come to his senses.'

Lil picked up the Anderson boy's kilt she was working on and studied it with unseeing eyes.

'I don't think he wants me to wait, Kirsty.'

Thirty-Three

To take her mind off her problems and Lil's, Kirsty, in her own lunch hour, decided to walk down to Logie's, maybe buy some new tights, have a coffee with Angie. Andrew had had to visit some new suppliers in Perth that day, which meant she couldn't talk things over with him, but it didn't really matter. They'd already made arrangements for the tea with his mother. No need to worry, then ... As though she could stop worrying! She had to admit, though, she was better off than poor Lil.

Logie's, where Angie was now working, was a smart store close to Jenners in Princes Street. Perhaps not quite as smart as it had been in earlier years, but still pricey and a good place to work. Angie had been lucky to get in – just as her mother had been, maybe. But then, with her looks, she always seemed to find it easy to get jobs. One thing she hadn't told Lena, though, was that she'd switched from Perfumery to Stockings.

'Och, working with scents gave me a headache,' she explained to Kirsty, who'd said the change would only upset her aunt.

'You know how she'll see it, Angie – you back where your ma was.'

Angie had been unmoved. 'If she finds out, I'll just tell her what I told you – I had headaches. Stockings and Tights – suits me fine.'

'Nice if you've found something you like at last,' Kirsty had sighed.

On that April day of unusual warmth, the great department store seemed airless, but Kirsty still enjoyed its atmosphere of luxury. Once through Logie's doors, you could forget your troubles for a while, and just pretend you were one of the 'haves', for a change. Buy anything you fancied, put it on your account, and there you were – it was yours! See all those well-dressed women looking at things they didn't need? That was how life was for them, eh?

Och, I'd soon get tired of it, Kirsty thought,

and sent her eyes roving round for the stocking counter. Showed how often she shopped in Logie's, when she didn't know where it was.

'Just there by Scarves and Gloves, Madam,' a young assistant told her, and Kirsty wanted to giggle. Madam? But she could see Angie at her counter, all right, busy with a customer, and sank for a moment on to a nearby chair, not wanting to interrupt.

Never having seen her stepsister at work before, she found it interesting to watch her for a little while, then gradually began to wonder. Was Angie actually serving this customer? Was the woman even a customer at all? There were no stockings being shown, and something about Angie's attitude, and the way the woman was leaning forward, a large envelope in her hand, seemed strange.

As Kirsty sat back in her chair, now not wanting to be seen, the woman laid the envelope on the counter and Angie, unsmiling, picked it up and bent down, presumably to put it away. When she straightened up, she and the woman shook hands.

'You'll be in touch?' Kirsty heard the woman say.

'Aye,' Angie answered. 'Thanks.'

Then her customer, if such she was, came towards Kirsty and walked past her, giving her the chance to see that she was in her thirties, with a pleasant, rather square face, and thick ginger hair. Probably not one of the wealthier of Logie's clients, but then not badly off either, for her tweed suit was good and her handbag was leather. But who was she?

'Who was that?' Kirsty cried, hurrying up to Angie's counter.

'Who was who?' Angie asked, taking down some packets of stockings from cabinets behind her.

'That lady you were talking to just then.'

'Oh – a customer.'

Kirsty shook her head. 'No, I'm sure she knew you. She gave you an envelope.'

'I tell you, she was just a customer.' Angie hesitated. 'Returning some stockings, that's all.'

Why was she lying? Kirsty, not feeling she could press further, hesitated as a slight flush rose to Angie's cheeks and her hands kept straying over the stockings on her counter.

'Were you wanting tights, or something?' she asked after an awkward silence. 'I could buy them for you at staff discount, if you like, and you could pay me back.'

'Fine, that'd be nice. Could we have a coffee afterwards?'

'Sorry, I went on early lunch today. Why didn't you tell me you were coming in? We could've fixed something up.'

'Yes, I should have done. Well, I'll just take the tights then. Let's see what shades you've got.' Kirsty smiled. 'Don't often shop at Logie's, do I?'

All the way back to the High Street, Kirsty puzzled over the identity of the woman at Angie's counter, and by the time she'd stopped at a café to buy herself a sandwich, was rather more worried than intrigued. She didn't like mysteries where her own family was concerned, and yet somehow felt she couldn't question Angie further. There had been a look in her stepsister's eyes, as they'd said goodbye, that had said as clearly as any words, 'Kirsty, leave it.' Seemed that Kirsty was just going to have to.

Thirty-Four

Back at the shop, Kirsty's thoughts were with Lil.

'Is she back yet?' she asked Meriel.

'Lil? Not yet.'

'And Dermot?'

Meriel shook her head. 'Maybe they're not coming back this afternoon.'

'Can't just take time off like that! They'll come back.' Kirsty hesitated. 'Dermot, anyway.'

But it was Lil who came through the shop door first, her face pale and set, her blue-grey eyes flinty. When she saw Meriel, she immediately looked away. To Kirsty, she gave a short nod.

'Where's Dermot?' Meriel asked.

'Coming.'

'I'm supposed to manage on my own?'

'It'll no' kill you, will it?'

Head held high, Lil strode off to the cloak-room, followed by Kirsty, who, as soon as they'd closed the door, grasped Lil's arm.

'Lil, tell me what happened – I've been worrying about you.'

'There's no need to worry.' Lil, freeing herself, splashed her face with cold water. 'It isn't the end of the world, getting dumped, is it?'

'Can feel like it, sometimes.'

'Aye, well, I'm just so angry, Kirsty. I said I knew what I'd be facing, knew what was going to happen, but now it's come, I don't believe it. I mean, I don't believe that he could throw me aside for that girl out there, when we'd so much going for us! That's true, eh? We were right for each other!'

'You were, absolutely right,' Kirsty hurried to agree, for she had seen the tears glistening in Lil's eyes and knew that her anger was not going to last long. At any moment, she was going to break down, and must be comforted, helped to get through the afternoon, at least. The last thing she'd want would be for Meriel to see her tears. And then of course there was Mrs MacNee...

'We went to the gardens at lunch time,' Lil was saying dully. 'Bought some rolls and sat on the grass. Then Dermot started going on. Och, you should've heard him! It was like a speech. I swear he'd been rehearsing it.'

Kirsty was sure he had.

'How he'd been hit by a bolt from the blue – couldn't do a thing about it – never meant it to happen – never meant to hurt me. Och, I could've thrown my sandwich in his face! But I just sat there and let him go on, and then I left him and ran back here. Where he is now, I've no idea. The pub, I expect.'

212

'Oh, Lil! I just wish I could do something.'

'It's OK, it's OK.' Lil's voice had begun to waver. 'I'll get through this. Somehow, I will. I'll no' let the two of them see how I feel.'

'I know you won't believe me, but Dermot does care for you,' Kirsty said quickly. 'He told me and I think it's true. He was dreading having to hurt you.'

'Did though, eh?' Lil's eyes, swimming in tears, were glittering. 'But when did he talk to you about me?'

'This morning. Because I saw him at the cinema with Meriel last night.'

'They were at the cinema?'

'Yes. So, this morning we talked. He told me how he felt – kind of crazy, I suppose. That's the thing, you see – he can't think straight. But he knew he had to tell you about Meriel.'

'And he has.' Lil turned aside. 'That's all I need to know, Kirsty.'

Longing and failing to find some crumb of comfort, Kirsty could only stretch out her arms to her friend, then let them fall, as a loud rapping on the cloakroom door made them both jump.

'Girls, are you in there?' came Mrs MacNee's voice. 'Kirsty? Lil? What's going on? Where's Dermot? No one's come back from lunch!'

'Sorry, Mrs MacNee,' Kirsty mumbled, hastily opening the door. 'Lil's got a headache, we were looking for the aspirin...'

'Now you know the aspirin's not kept here! I have it in my cupboard.' Mrs MacNee's sharp eyes rested on Lil's ravaged face, and she loudly clicked her tongue. 'Goodness, lassie, whatever have you been doing, then? Better come with me. Kirsty, make some tea.'

'Yes, Mrs MacNee.'

'And take a look outside to see if you can see Dermot coming – I've never known him so late back.'

'Dermot's here!' Meriel cried from the front shop. 'Just this minute walked through the door.'

'And about time, too!' Mrs MacNee, halting on her way to the first-aid cupboard, stared at the wilting Dermot, who was propping himself up at the counter by the door. Then she sniffed the air.

'Dermot – have you been drinking?'

'Been to the pub,' he said carefully. 'What's new? I often go to the pub.'

'What's new is that this time you've had too much! Oh, whatever would Mr Macrae have said to you if he'd been in today? Thank heavens, we've no customers at the moment. I can smell your breath from here!'

'Sorry, Mrs MacNee.' Dermot put his hand to his brow. 'Think I did have ... one too many.'

'Well, go and wash your face in cold water and make yourself a coffee. Kirsty's got the kettle on.' Mrs MacNee, shaking her head in disbelief, hurried Lil away for her aspirin, while Dermot wavered off to wash his face and Meriel wrinkled her fine nose.

'If there's anything I can't stand, it's folk who can't hold their drink,' she murmured to Kirsty. 'I thought Dermot could do better than that.'

'Maybe you of all people might show a bit of sympathy,' Kirsty said coldly.

214

'I told you, all this has nothing to do with me. I'm not responsible for Dermot's feelings.'

'Here comes a customer, better do your stuff.'

As Meriel, putting on a smile, went forward to greet a young man who was looking vaguely round the hired kilts, Kirsty stamped away to make the tea. What a day this had been! And it wasn't over yet.

It came to an end at last, with Dermot recovering himself pretty well after a strong coffee, and Lil saying little but doggedly stitching away at the Anderson boy's kilt, while Kirsty and Mrs MacNee kept watch.

'Don't have to be Sherlock Holmes to see what's happened,' Mrs MacNee whispered to Kirsty, when they were getting ready to leave. 'Dermot and Lil – they've split up, eh?'

Kirsty nodded. There was no point in denying it.

'Over Meriel, I expect. I always did think we'd have trouble there.'

Her eyes widening, Kirsty stared. 'You did?'

'Oh, yes, I've been around long enough to recognize trouble. Ssh, Meriel's coming. I'll say no more.'

Marvelling at the senior assistant's idea of her own perceptive abilities, Kirsty was glad to be out of the shop, walking with Lil to her bus stop. Where Dermot and Meriel had gone, neither of them knew, but were glad to be on their own, free to talk again at last.

'Thing is, Lil, there's something I should've told you,' Kirsty said, making a decision. 'I feel bad I've never told you before, as a matter of fact.'

'Seems everyone's feeling bad,' Lil observed grimly.

'You might laugh.'

'Oh, try me!'

'But you didn't ask who I was with at the pictures, did you?'

'Never thought of it.'

Kirsty cleared her throat. 'It was Mr Macrae.'

For a moment, Lil stood still on the pavement. 'What did you say, Kirsty?'

'I said it was Mr Macrae. I've been going out with him since Hogmanay.'

Though not laughing, Lil was smiling – a strange, incredulous smile. 'You are joking. Aren't you?'

'No. I've been going out with him and I've enjoyed it. He isn't like he is at work, Lil. He's no' dull and grey, he's sweet and kind, and got a lot more personality than you'd think.' Kirsty fixed her eyes on the crowds making their way home down the Mound. 'And he's made me forget Jake MacIver.'

'Well...' Lil seemed unable to take her eyes off Kirsty's face. 'Well, I don't know what to say. I'd never in the world have guessed. But isn't it ... sort of awkward? Him being Mr Macrae?'

'To me, he's Andrew.'

'Oh. Yes, well, I suppose he would be. I suppose you wouldn't call him Mr Macrae if you were going out with him.' Lil finally looked away from Kirsty to the buses lumbering down Princes Street. 'Lot older than you, though.'

'Not that much. Ten – eleven years.
'It's no' serious, is it?'
'Serious? Och, no.' Kirsty was very casual. 'But I'm going to tea with his mother on Sunday.'
'To tea with Mrs Macrae? Oh, Kirsty! And you say it's no' serious?'
'Here's the bus,' Kirsty said quickly. 'Lil, I'm thinking of you. If there's anything I can do—'
Lil's smile was now a little crooked. 'Just for the minute, you've taken my mind off Dermot,' she said softly 'Best of luck, then. For the tea party that's no' serious.'

Thirty-Five

On Sunday afternoon, the day of Kirsty's visit to Mrs Macrae, Lena and Vinnie were on a coach trip to Portobello, while Reid was watching a football match somewhere with Niall.

'So, there's only me to see you go,' Angie said, with a wry smile. 'Bet that suits you, eh? Not having Lena to fuss over you? She's got you engaged already, because of this tea invitation.'

'I told her that wasn't going to happen,' Kirsty answered absently, as she studied herself in the hall mirror. She was wearing a new suit of tobacco brown and already worrying over the length of the skirt. 'Think this looks like a mini, Angie? I'm sure Mrs Macrae won't approve.'

'It isn't a mini-mini.' Angie lit a cigarette. 'I shouldn't worry about it. Anyway, she must know what the fashions are like.'

'Think I look OK, then?'

'Perfect. Your Andrew will think so, too.'

Kirsty, with a last look in the mirror, said she'd better go down. He might be early.

'Aye, and the lift's no' working again, so you've to do the stairs.'

'I'm wondering why I'm so nervous.' Kirsty took the spring flowers she'd bought for Mrs Macrae from their bucket of water, and shook their stems. 'I mean, it's no' as though I'm on approval, or something.'

'Maybe you are, though.'

'No. Why does everybody keep thinking I'm going to get wed?'

'Because a man would never take a girl home unless he'd got marriage in mind. I mean, if he hasn't, what's the point? It'd only give her the wrong ideas.'

Kirsty frowned as she wrapped the flowers in plastic. 'Andrew knows I've no ideas like that.'

'But does his mother know that?'

'Oh, please don't make me feel worse! At least it's only tea, eh? I'll be back soon and then it'll all be over. Bye, Angie.'

'Bye, Kirsty.'

But as Kirsty tapped her way down the stairs, she was surprised to find Angie following her.

'Hey, what's up? Have I forgotten something?'

'No, I just wanted to ... wish you luck.'

Flinging her arms round Kirsty, Angie gave her a long hard hug. 'Take care, eh?'

'Take care?' Kirsty, freeing herself from Angie's thin arms, examined her flowers to see if they'd been squashed. 'Why should I? Mrs Macrae won't eat me!'

'Well, I'll be thinking of you anyway.' Angie, retreating up the stair, smiled and waved. 'Bye again, then.'

Kirsty, running out of the main door, was in time to see Andrew's car just arriving. She did not look back.

'Looking very smart,' Andrew told her as they drove away from the flats. 'Is that a new outfit?'

'Saw it in a wee shop in the High Street. Do you like it?'

'Very much. The colour suits you really well.'

Should she mention the skirt? Kirsty decided not to; after all, there was nothing she could do to change it then, and she had good legs, anyway. Not that Mrs Macrae would be impressed by that. Probably would prefer a young woman visitor to arrive in floor-length tweed. Probably would prefer a young woman visitor not to arrive at all.

Glancing at Andrew, it didn't improve her spirits to see his look of strain. Seemed that her visit was going to be as much of an ordeal to him as to her. Why ever were they going through with it? Angie's remarks echoed in her mind, but she couldn't believe that Andrew was considering marriage with her. They liked being together, but that was all. They'd never behaved like people in a special relationship, never spoken of love. But then Jake MacIver had never spoken of

219

love and she'd thought...

Never mind what she'd thought. What she had with Andrew was different. He'd know that as well as she.

What had he meant, though, when he'd said 'I want you'? Just that he wanted to be with her, rather than Mildred. She gave a little sigh. No need to worry.

'Here we are,' Andrew murmured, and turned into a quiet street where the houses were large and stone-built, and the front gardens wide. There were flowers, trees with blossom, an atmosphere of comfort, privilege and good Edinburgh values. And Andrew, Kirsty thought as she stepped out of the car, would be the perfect resident.

'Welcome to Holm Road,' he said lightly, and put his hand on her arm. 'Let's go in.'

Thirty-Six

Inside, the house was like the outside. Solid, comfortable, a haven for the respectable. Large rooms, long windows. Dark panelling in the hall, and wood block flooring; the dining room, briefly glimpsed, was the same. Patterned loose covers in the drawing room, where they were to have tea, and dark old pictures, china ornaments and flowers. A fire burned in the grate of the handsome fireplace, where fire irons shone, and even the coal in its scuttle looked as though it might have been dusted.

Not a room for 1965, or folk like Jake Mac-Iver, who wasn't, as he'd said, a 'mahogany, loose-covers sort of guy'. But none the worse for that, was Kirsty's opinion, for the serenity of this place appealed to her. If a room like this had been part of your home, you'd be protected all your life, even if you had to leave it. You'd be cushioned. And if you'd experienced life in a tenement, you might quite fancy being cushioned.

However, as the woman who'd been sitting by the fire now rose to greet her, a cold wind seemed suddenly to blow round Kirsty, reminding her that she was only a guest here. And not a very welcome one, if Mrs Macrae's grey eyes resting on her were anything to go by.

'Mother, here's Kirsty,' Andrew said bravely. 'You'll remember her, of course. Kirsty, please meet my mother again.'

'Of course I remember Miss Muir.'

Mrs Macrae, a well-preserved woman of sixty, with greying fair hair and a hawk nose, put out a dry hand for Kirsty to shake. 'One of our best kilt makers – isn't that right? Oh, are these lovely flowers for me? How kind! Do sit down near the fire. It's turned cold again, hasn't it?'

Exactly so. Though the words were friendly enough, the grey eyes in the austere face remained as chill as the weather Mrs Macrae had mentioned, yet really it was no more than Kirsty had expected. Andrew's mother must still be struggling to come to terms with what she'd

221

only recently been told. It would be unlikely that her welcome would be warm.

'Kirsty, not Miss Muir,' Andrew corrected his mother now. 'She's rarely called that, even at work.'

'Yes, well, you must forgive me, Andrew, but I'm old-fashioned, you see. It takes time for me to get used to people's first names.'

'Nevertheless, Mother, Kirsty is the name to use here.'

'As you please.' She smiled briefly. 'Perhaps you'd like to put these flowers in water for me, and switch on the kettle?'

'You'd like me to make the tea?'

'Yes, dear, why not? The caddy's by the teapot.'

'Very well.'

'And bring in the trolley, would you? It's all ready.'

As Andrew reluctantly left them, his mother turned to Kirsty.

'I have a wonderful housekeeper, you know, but she doesn't come in at weekends, so I'm afraid it's had to be all my baking today.'

'I'm sure it'll be lovely,' Kirsty murmured.

'Hope so. But now I thought if I sent Andrew to make the tea, you and I could have a little chat.'

A little chat. Kirsty, folding her hands, said nothing.

'Now, I understand that you and my son have been going out together for some time? Since Hogmanay, I believe?'

'That's right. We went to the dance at the

Crown Park Hotel.'

'I didn't know, you know. He never told me.'
Mrs Macrae's fingers were turning the beads at
her neck. 'There was a time when he'd look in to
tell me about his evenings, but he hasn't done
that for some time.'

Kirsty, looking down at her hands, remained
silent. She was beginning to hope she would not
have to feel sorry for Mrs Macrae.

'I must say, Miss Muir – I mean, Kirsty – I'm
rather surprised that I've been kept so much in
the dark about my son and you. You've been out
together quite a lot since Hogmanay, haven't
you? And never said a word to anyone?'

'Some folk think it isn't a good idea for someone like Andrew to go out with staff. We didn't
want to get involved ... explaining...' Kirsty,
floundering, ground to a halt.

'Yes, I understand why he wouldn't want to
tell Mrs MacNee and people,' Mrs Macrae said
impatiently. 'But his own mother!' Her look
sharpened. 'Or, was he thinking of Mildred, I
wonder? Have you met Miss Grier, Kirsty?
She's the daughter of very old friends of ours. A
lovely girl, in every way.'

'I've seen her.'

'Yes, well, her mother asked me only the other
day how Andrew was, and it never even occurred to me that she was trying to tell me Mildred
hadn't seen him. Now I'm beginning to understand. He didn't want to tell me about you
because he knew I'd be thinking of Mildred.'

Kirsty gave a nervous little cough. 'He has told
you now, though, hasn't he? We're both of us

223

tired of secrets, that's the thing.'

'Tired of secrets?' Mrs Macrae grew pale. 'Does that mean ... does that mean ... you have something ... to announce?'

'Announce?' The colour rose to Kirsty's brow. 'No, no, there's nothing to announce.'

'He hasn't ... proposed?'

'No, he hasn't proposed.'

A great light seemed to come over Mrs Macrae's face and her grey eyes glowed.

'I'm sure it's for the best, my dear. I don't know if you're disappointed, but you're much too young for Andrew, you know. Probably you'd want a very different sort of life from his. Dining and dancing is all very nice, but when it comes to settling down that's different, isn't it? Not something girls want these days. And you've years ahead of you before you need even think about it!'

As Mrs Macrae sat back in her chair with a triumphant smile, Kirsty, stunned by the flow of words, turned her great eyes to the door where Andrew had appeared.

'Tea's up!' he cried cheerfully, and rolled in the trolley.

Thirty-Seven

During tea, which was delicious, with feather-light scones and walnut cake, Mrs Macrae moved into her hostess mode, talking brightly to Kirsty about her family and her life, making her feel welcome at last.

How sad that she'd lost her parents so young! Mrs Macrae and Andrew knew what it was like to be bereaved. But at least Kirsty had been lucky to have a caring stepmother, and then she had a stepsister, too, and a clever brother. Made so much difference to have a happy family background, didn't it? And an interesting job – or, at least, Mrs Macrae hoped Kirsty found her kilt making interesting.

'I love it,' Kirsty said honestly. 'I'd never change.'

'Andrew, isn't that nice to hear?' his mother asked him, as she gave him more tea, and rather dazedly he agreed. It was easy to see that he was mystified by her friendly manner, perhaps believing that Kirsty had worked some sort of charm, though she knew herself that his mother was only relieved because she now saw Kirsty as no threat.

Poor Andrew! Still, it was good to see him sitting back in his chair, the lines of strain fading from his face, making him seem young and happy again. Perhaps now was the time to go, while the atmosphere was pleasant. It would be so easy to make a mistake here; you could never be sure when everything would change.

There were polite farewells. Offers to help with the washing-up, which were at once refused. Thanks for the lovely tea, the flowers, everything. And then they were in the car and Andrew was backing out into the quiet road, his mother waving in the cold wind, and they could heave long sighs of relief. The visit was over.

'Sorry you didn't see the rest of the house,' Andrew said, as they drove through empty streets slumbering under the great Sunday shutdown. 'I wanted to show you round, but I knew Mother would come with us, and I thought you'd probably had enough, anyway. Maybe next time, eh?'

'There'll be one?' Kirsty asked.

'Sure there will! Your visit was a great success.'

'Think so?'

'Of course. You did the trick, Kirsty. My mother liked you. I knew she would.'

'I don't know whether she liked me or not, to be honest.'

'Of course you do! Heavens above, if she hadn't liked you, you'd have known it fast enough!'

'I think I'd better tell you what she asked me, Andrew. When you were out making the tea.'

'What? What did she ask you?'

'If you'd proposed.'

There was a long, long silence. So long, that Kirsty eventually turned her head to look at Andrew. Driving carefully as he always did, he seemed calm enough, but his hands gripping the wheel were white, the knuckles shining.

'Andrew?'

'So, you told her I hadn't?'

'Of course!'

He gave a short laugh. 'That explains a lot. She thinks everything's OK. Mildred's safe. Well, she's got another think coming.'

The words hit Kirsty like a blow to the heart. So real, she caught her breath in a gasp and for some moments could not speak. 'She's got another think coming.' What could he mean? Except what Kirsty knew he meant. So, had she been walking blindfold for all these weeks? Had everyone else been right and she wrong?

Gradually, she realized that Andrew had driven into a quiet lane on the way to Pleasant Hill, and that the car was stopping. Had in fact stopped.

'Andrew, what ... what are you talking about?' she stammered, as they turned to face each other.

'Are you saying you don't know?' He put his hand to his brow. 'Kirsty, you must know I love you and want to marry you. Why do you think I've been taking you out all this time? Asking you to meet my mother at my home?'

'Andrew, I'd no idea,' she said shakily. 'No idea at all. I never thought ... never...'

'Never? Never thought about marrying me?'

His eyes were so hurt, so baffled, she wanted to throw her arms around him, comfort him. Cry, 'Yes, yes, of course I've thought about marrying

227

you!' But she was still so shocked at her own blindness, she could do nothing except raise her eyes, now so clear, to his face, and read there all that she'd been missing for so long.

'Folk have been saying you were serious,' she murmured, touching his cheek. 'But, honestly, I never thought so.'

'Why? Why, for God's sake, didn't you think I was serious?'

'Because once before I thought someone was. And he wasn't.'

'Jake MacIver,' he said with a groan. 'You compare me with him?'

'No, no. Don't say such a thing! It's just that I probably remembered him without meaning to, that's all. And then I didn't think we wanted ... you know ... anything permanent, anyway.' When he did not speak, she added, hesitantly, 'There was a lot against it, wasn't there? I mean, you thought so. That's why you wanted it kept secret.'

'That's not why I wanted it kept secret!' he cried. 'The truth is I was afraid you'd be frightened off, if people knew and criticized. I was all the time afraid that you'd give me up, for one reason or another.'

'I never knew that.'

'Didn't want you to know.' He shrugged and half smiled. 'Had to remember how people regard me. Steady Mr Macrae. Not the sort of chap who'd be ... so dependent.'

'You could have talked to me, Andrew. Why would I want to give you up, anyway?'

'There was your age – you might have found

some younger guy. There was Jake MacIver. I used to dread he'd turn up again and you'd not be able to turn him down.'

'That would never have happened!'

'You underestimate him. And what you felt for him. I always had to think of that.'

'Why didn't you just ask me to marry you? I'd have known then what was going on.'

Andrew held his brow again, as though it pained him. 'Didn't dare. Because you might have said no. I couldn't risk the chance that I might lose you. Then, when you agreed to visit my mother, I began to think you must realize ... what was in my mind.'

He felt for her hand and held it.

'But now you say you've never even thought of such a thing as marrying me, and I feel ... Hell, I don't know what I feel. Like somebody in a bubble that's burst, maybe. Because you're not going to accept me, are you?'

'I don't know,' she said slowly. 'It's all been such ... a surprise. And I've been so stupid. I mean, never seeing what was there. Maybe, deep down, I still didn't think it could happen – marriage between Mr Macrae and me.'

'For God's sake, let's forget Mr Macrae! I can make you happy, that's the thing. You've always said we were happy together. And I could be a good provider—'

'Oh, Andrew, you don't have to tell me all that!' She put her arms around him. 'I know it already.'

'Will you consider me, then?' He kissed her gently. 'You don't have to love me, the way I love you. That can come later. It often does, you know, when there's a happy marriage. And that's what we'd have, I promise you.'

'Yes, I know. And I think I do love you, Andrew, in my own way, but I just need some time...'

'Take all the time you want, sweetheart. I can wait.'

They exchanged a last long embrace, then Kirsty put her hand to Andrew's brow. 'Have you got a headache? I thought you looked to be in pain.'

'Splitting,' he admitted. 'I wanted us to have a meal, but...'

'After all that walnut cake? And I've got a headache, too. What a couple of crocks, eh? Shall we go back now?'

'I'll take you home,' he said quietly.

At the door of Clover, she kissed him again, briefly.

'There's something I haven't said, isn't there?'

'What's that?'

'Thank you.'

'What for? Offering you something you're not even sure you want?'

'It's wonderful, what you've offered me, Andrew. Don't think I don't appreciate it.'

For some time, they looked steadily into each other's faces.

'I'll see you tomorrow.' Andrew took his seat at the wheel again. 'Don't worry – I won't ask you for your answer so soon.'

After she'd watched his car until it was out of

sight, Kirsty turned and began to climb the stairs. She felt exhausted, as though her legs would hardly support her, and the headache she'd mentioned was beating like a cruel drum at every step she took.

Oh, God, what was she to say to him? He was so kind, so loyal. Married to him, she need never have fears for his love or commitment. And then there would be the comfortable lifestyle – most girls she knew would think her lucky to be given the chance of it. Why not accept, then? Maybe she would. She just needed time to think...

But she was not to have time to think, for as soon as she'd opened the flat door, Lena came running and flung her arns around her.

'Oh, Kirsty, thank God you're back! Angie's gone. She's run away to London and Reid's going after her. But how will he ever find her when he doesn't know where to look?'

Thirty-Eight

There was a note.

'Vinnie and me found it when we came in,' Lena said, staring at the kitchen table where the folded note still lay. She was in the blue dress and jacket she'd worn for her trip, while Vinnie, noisily making tea, was startling in vivid red, with a matching band over her black hair. 'And we'd had such a lovely day, eh?'

'Aye, it was grand,' Vinnie agreed. 'The lads had had a good match, and just come home and all. And then to find that note! Whatever can the lassie have been thinking of, then? But Angie's's always been difficult, eh?'

'I wouldn't say that,' Lena retorted. 'Sometimes difficult, mebbe. But she's no' had a good start in life, remember.'

'I don't believe this,' Kirsty was whispering, as she collapsed into a chair. 'She was fine when I left, hadn't packed or anything, and never said a word...'

But she had, she had. She'd thrown her arms round Kirsty and said she wanted to wish her luck. She'd said 'take care' for no reason at all, except that she was really saying goodbye, and Kirsty had been too preoccupied with her own affairs to notice. Oh, why had she not tried to find out what was going on? Made Angie talk to her? But, then, all the time she'd been planning this, Angie had not talked to any of them. The fact had to be faced: she didn't want her family to know what was in her mind.

'Kirsty, you're awful pale,' Lena suddenly observed. 'Poor girl, I'd clean forgotten you'd been to Mrs Macrae's. Didn't upset you, did she?'

'No, it went well, but never mind that now. Can I see the note?'

'Have some tea first – that'll make you feel better,' Vinnie said comfortingly. 'It's true, you're as white as a sheet.'

'But where's Reid?' Kirsty asked, as she drank the tea. 'Hasn't gone off already?'

'No, no, he's just away with Niall to the phone box. Wants to ring up some lecturer at the college who comes from London. Thinks he might tell him where to find somewhere to stay.'

'Somewhere cheap, I expect,' Vinnie murmured, looking in Lena's biscuit tin and selecting a custard cream.

'Somewhere near King's Cross, maybe. That's where the Edinburgh train comes in.' Lena sighed and began to slice bread for sandwiches. 'But where'll poor Angie be staying, I'm wondering? A young girl like her knows nothing. She's nowhere to go, no idea where to find Beryl, though she thinks she has. Kirsty, see what you make of her note – it's there, on the table.'

'Dear Auntie Lena,' Angie had written in her large pointed hand, 'this is just to say I'm away to London to find my mother. I've some new information and I think I might be lucky. Sorry I never told you, or Kirsty or Reid, but I knew you'd all try to stop me. Don't worry about me. I've money saved and I'll be OK. I'll keep in touch. Love, Angie.'

'Doesn't tell us much, eh?' Lena asked, as Kirsty laid the note down.

'She does say she'll keep in touch.'

'I'll believe that when it happens. Oh, to think of her down there, roaming the streets, or whatever she's doing. Every day, there's girls like her go missing. Sometimes, never found.'

'Don't think about it,' Vinnie told her quickly. 'And Angie must've had some plan, eh, or she wouldn't have gone?'

'She says she's got new information,' Kirsty said after a pause.

'Aye, but never says what!' Lena cried. 'Wants to keep us in the dark!'

Something was stirring in Kirsty's mind and she wanted to speak of it, yet couldn't be sure. And would it help, anyway? If only Reid would come home!

And soon enough Reid did come home, striding into the flat with Niall, both unwinding their football scarves, their faces lighting up at the sight of Kirsty.

'Hi, glad you're back!' Reid cried, giving her a hug, as Niall stood aside then took his turn to hold her close for a moment or two.

'Everything OK at Mrs Macrae's?' Reid asked.

'Yes, yes, but what's it matter now? Did you have any luck?'

'Yes, I did.' He flung himself into a chair, stretching out his long legs. 'I got through to Dr Howard – he's one of our lecturers, lives near the British Museum but hasn't gone home yet. He told me I could ask at the King's Cross information bureau for lists of accommodation, but it'd be better to try to book something before I went. So he's given me a couple of addresses and I'll try them tomorrow morning.'

'You'll ring London?' Vinnie asked in hushed tones. 'That'll set you back a bonny penny!'

'All in a good cause and I've got my pub money. Hey, do I see sandwiches, Lena? I'm starving.'

'Just a few cheese and tomato to keep you

234

going till I cook something.'

As Vinnie poured fresh tea, Lena passed the plate of sandwiches to the two young men, her face puckered with worry.

'Thing is, Reid, what about your studies? I know it's the Easter holidays, but you've got your finals coming up, eh? I should be the one going to seek Angie.'

'Ah, come on, Lena! I'm the one with the time off, and I'd be better at finding my way round London.' Reid took a sandwich. 'And you need not worry about my revision. I'm up to date, and I'll soon get back to it, anyway. I've no plans to stay long in London.'

'I'd just like to know how you're ever going to find Angie, though. I mean, you've nothing at all to go on!'

'I'm going to look for Beryl, Lena. I'll have a much better chance with her, and when I find her, then I'll find Angie.'

'Reid,' Kirsty declared, 'I'm coming with you.'

Thirty-Nine

Of course, Kirsty had known that Lena wouldn't approve, but she would not be dissuaded; she'd already made up her mind.

'No arguments.' As her stepmother opened her mouth, Kirsty put up her hand. 'Look, I'll be all right, Lena, there's no need to worry. After all, I'll be with Reid.'

'Hey, hey, who said I was going to take you along?' he cried, then grinned. 'Only joking. Of course, I want you to come.'

'Wish I could come too, but I'm at work,' Niall said glumly, at which his mother's fine eyes flashed.

'Now, why would you want to go rushing off to London, Niall? That'd be a piece of nonsense, that would.'

'Look, I've said, I'm at work, anyway.'

'And neither can you rush off, Kirsty!' Lena cried. 'You've to go to work, too! What would Mr Macrae say, if you never turned up?'

'He'll let me go, I've got some holiday owing,' Kirsty answered smoothly. 'I'll phone him this evening. But there's something I want to say first – this new information – I think I might know who might have given it to Angie.'

The eyes on her were widening, the voices

crying as one, 'Who?'

'Well, I saw a woman talking to her in Logie's once. Didn't seem to be about stockings. She gave Angie an envelope, and I'm wondering now if she's someone who knew Beryl.'

'Knew Beryl?' Lena repeated, catching her breath. 'Aye, could be. But did Angie no' say who she was?'

'No, she wouldn't tell me. Said she was a customer, but she never bought anything.'

'What did she look like? If she knew Beryl, I'd know her.'

'Describe her exactly,' Reid ordered. 'This is our one lead, Kirsty.'

'I only saw her as she walked past me.' Kirsty was frowning, trying desperately to call up the image of the woman in Logie's. 'I'd say she was about thirty-five. She had a big face, sort of square, and big eyes – I think dark. She looked kind to me, sort of good-natured.'

'What colour hair?' asked Lena, twisting her hands hard together.'

'Ginger. I can be sure of that.'

'Ginger.' Lena sighed. 'Aye, Kirsty, she did know Beryl and I know her. She's Junie Binnie. Was Binnie, that is. Oh, Lord, what's she called now? She did well, married a chap with his own photography business in Stockbridge. Moffat, that's it! Art Moffat was the one she married.'

'Was she a good friend of Beryl's?'

'Sure she was, in the old days, when we were all in the tenements. I was her sister's friend, Peggy, but we've lost touch.' Lena had leaped to her feet and was pacing up and down the room.

'Kirsty, we'll go to see Junie tomorrow. I'll ask for an hour or two off. Meantime, shouldn't you be going down to speak to Mr Macrae, then?'

'I'll go down and ring him now.' Kirsty stood up. 'Got any change?'

'I have.' Niall took coppers from his trouser pocket. 'Want me to go with you to the phone, Kirsty? Frighten off the kids?'

'That's OK, Niall, thanks.'

But he went with her anyway and they ran down the stairs together.

'No kids,' she said forcing a smile as they reached the phone box, but all that was running through her mind was a heartfelt prayer that she might get straight through to Andrew and not have to speak to his mother. But, oh her head! Felt like a whole orchestra was pounding her now, not just a drum.

'Are you all right?' Niall asked, heaving open the door of the phone box. 'You've lost all your colour.'

'Just a headache.'

Looking at her with concern, he said he'd wait outside and, moving into the smoky, stuffy interior, Kirsty braced herself to make her call.

Oh, thank God, Andrew himself answered and though she could tell he'd been hoping she had different news, he said at once that she must take the time off for London. Find her sister as a priority, but be sure to ring him every evening so that he knew what was happening. And money? How was she off for money? When she said she was OK – which in fact, she wasn't, at least until

238

she'd been to the post office to take out some savings – he made her promise to tell him if she needed more.

'Safe journey, dear Kirsty,' he murmured at last. 'And good luck.'

Good luck. Everything came down to that. There was Angie, hoping for it in her London search for Beryl, and Kirsty and Reid, hoping for it in theirs. At least there had been this piece of luck in finding Junie Moffat, Beryl's friend. Tomorrow, they'd find out how good that was.

Putting down the slippery handset, Kirsty left the box and stood for several moments, gratefully breathing in the fresh air as Niall moved forward to take her arm.

'Everything OK?'

'Fine, thanks. I can have the time off.'

'I expect he was quite sympathetic, eh? Your Mr Macrae?'

'Oh, he was. He'll help all he can.'

'That's good.'

They turned to go back, walking slowly, Kirsty feeling a little better, now that she'd spoken to Andrew, and taking comfort, too, from Niall's presence. Somehow, that arm of his holding hers gave strength. Made her feel that things after all might work out. They'd find Angie. Wouldn't they?

'I know it's pretty pointless, telling you no' to worry,' Niall said as they returned to Clover and climbed to their flats. 'But maybe I'll say it anyway. Remember, you've got this lead now – the woman who met Angie – and you've got Reid. He'll find Angie, all right. Just wish I could've come with you.'

'I do, too.' Kirsty pressed his hand. 'Thanks anyway, Niall.'

He shook his head. 'What for? Haven't done anything. But, Kirsty, good luck, eh?'

There it was again, the hope for good luck. *Just pray it'll come tomorrow*, thought Kirsty.

Forty

In fact, when they first arrived at Art Moffat's studio and made themselves known to Junie, the Muirs thought they might well have no luck with her at all.

Though she made them very welcome, inviting them up to her pleasant flat, while her mystified husband attended to his clients, she explained, as she served coffee, that there wasn't a lot she could tell them. It was lovely seeing Lena again, and meeting her stepchildren, too, but telling them where Beryl was and where Angie might have gone in London, she simply didn't know.

'That poor girl from Logie's,' she murmured, as she handed chocolate biscuits, 'she's just clutching at straws, eh?'

'Please, Junie, tell us everything you can,' Lena said hoarsely. 'Because we know she's in London somewhere and we have to find her.'

'Oh, I know, I know. Maybe I shouldn't have

spoken to her like I did, but I couldn't resist it.'
Suddenly, Junie's large brown eyes were shining. 'She looked so like Beryl, you see. That was it. I thought I was seeing things, going back in time, for there she was, on the stocking counter, eh? Just like Beryl at seventeen!'

Very much as Kirsty had described her, Junie was in her mid-thirties, trim and fit looking, with a square-jawed, kindly face and thick ginger hair. She had two children, she told them, one five, one six, both at the local school, and she mustn't be late in collecting them, as they came home for their dinner. Reid said that was all right, they wouldn't keep her; they had to catch a train for King's Cross in the early afternoon.

'You're going to King's Cross? To find Angie? Oh, well, I'll get on then.'

What had happened was that after seeing the new assistant on the stocking counter on several occasions, Junie had plucked up courage to ask her if she was related to Beryl Ramsay, an old friend of hers. Well, they should have seen the girl's face! You'd have thought it was Christmas! She'd said she was Beryl's daughter, Angie Ramsay, and they'd ended up going for a coffee, with Angie pleading for any bits of information Junie could give her. Seemingly Lena had had very little in the way of news from Beryl, so when Junie was able to tell her that she'd had letters right up to 1959, Angie was over the moon.

'But I couldn't really help her,' Junie said sadly. 'I told her that Beryl had been working in

241

a London hotel, and I gave her the letters I'd had, so that she could see if they were any use, but come 1959, Beryl's letters just stopped and I never heard from her again.'

'Was there an address on these letters?' Reid asked.

'Just the hotel.'

'Have you got that?'

'Oh, yes, it's in my old address book. I'll get it for you.'

The Danby Court. She wrote it on a piece of paper for him and Reid put it in his wallet, glancing quickly at Lena and Kirsty. Here it was, then. A piece of luck at last.

'This is great,' he told Junie. 'A real lead to Beryl.'

'Do you think so?' Her look was troubled. 'Well, Angie was pleased about it, but I never thought it'd be enough for her – and I never thought she'd go to London.'

'I think now she's always been keen to find her mother,' Lena said in a low voice. 'It's been a ... what d'you call it ... an obsession.'

Junie's expression changed to one of sympathy.

'I feel that sorry, you know, and I must admit I never understood how Beryl could have done what she did. I mean, it's never easy, bringing up a bairn and no' married, but plenty manage with no harm done. But Beryl said she was too young, didn't she? Said she couldn't face it, and you'd be a better mother, Lena, than she could ever be.'

'Suited her to think so,' Lena muttered.

'Well, you've been wonderful,' Junie said warmly. 'Everyone agrees on that. And Angie really appreciates what you did for her.'

'She does?'

'Och, yes!' Junie smiled. 'You can be sure of it. If she's gone seeking her own mother, it's no' because she doesn't think of you as her mother, anyway.'

'Maybe we should be going,' Lena said, blinking tears away. 'And give you all our thanks, Junie, for your help. It's been grand, eh, meeting up again? What happened to Peggy, then?'

'She's married and over in Glasgow, but I'll tell her I've seen you.'

After shaking hands with Kirsty and Reid, Junie kissed Lena on the cheek and told her to let her know about Angie and how she got on.

'If she does find Beryl, I'd really be glad to know,' she finished. 'I've often wondered why she stopped writing.'

'Think something happened to Beryl?' Kirsty asked when they were in the street outside the studio.

Reid shrugged. 'Who can say? It's possible.'

'We'd have heard,' Lena said. 'No, I bet she just got married.'

'Why stop writing to Junie because she got married?' Kirsty asked, but Reid said conjecture was pointless. What they needed were facts and they wouldn't get those until they were in London.

'So, Kirsty, we'd better make that train. Lena, are you coming to Waverley? We're going to

243

pick up our cases from the Left Luggage and snatch a bite at the café.'

'Got to get back to work.' Lena's face was bleak. 'Look, you'll keep in touch? Just wish I had a phone.'

'Of course we'll keep in touch. We'll report progress every day. Maybe ring you at work.'

'And you're sure you'll be OK for money?'

'Positive. You've helped us, I've got my pub money, and Kirsty's taken something out of the post office.' Reid kissed his stepmother's cheek. 'As I say, we won't be in the big smoke too long. We're going to find Angie and bring her back. Mission accomplished.'

'Oh, Reid, if only you're right,' Lena sighed.

'Feeling better?' Reid asked Kirsty, as the King's Cross train began to glide slowly out of Waverley Station.

They'd collected their cases, had their sandwich, and now were in their seats, saying farewell to one city, thinking about another.

'Why d'you say that?' Kirsty whispered, glancing at their fellow passengers in the corridor compartment, glad to see that they were reading newspapers. 'I'm OK.'

'Thought you were looking a bit worried, when you said goodbye to Lena.'

'Well, it's the first time I've left her, I suppose. First time I've ever been to London, come to that.'

'Remember, I went on a school trip once? Thought it was too big.'

'They say it's really exciting these days.'

244

'Couldn't care less about that. All I care about is that we've got somewhere to stay. Paid off, ringing Dr Howard, eh?'

'And the bed and breakfast place this morning. Better no' tell Vinnie how much that cost!'

'Well, we got a couple of rooms out of it. Worth it, eh?'

For some time, they looked out of their windows, watching the outskirts of Edinburgh passing by – small houses, industrial units, places they'd never seen – until they reached open country. When the other people in the compartment folded their papers and disappeared to the buffet, Kirsty leaned forward.

'Reid, I'm really glad I'm with you.'

He grinned. 'Make you feel safer?'

'Hey, I can take care of myself. No, it's just that it's right what Niall says: if anybody can find Angie, it'll be you. Though I'm a bit surprised, to be honest, that you're so worried about her.'

His grin faded. 'You think I wouldn't be worried about a kid like her roaming round London on her own?'

'Sorry, I should've said worried enough to go seeking her.'

'Look, if I'm worried about anything, I sort it out. That's me. That's how I am.'

'Yes, that's true.' Kirsty smiled apologetically. 'Sorry, again. I suppose I'm no' thinking straight.'

'You've got a lot on your plate,' he told her kindly, missing her wry smile as he stood up and stretched. 'Listen, I'm still hungry. How about us going to the buffet, too, and seeing what they've got?'

'Told you it was good to be with you, Reid!' she told him, leaping up and following him down the swaying corridor. But he didn't know the half of it, did he? And wouldn't for some time. How long before she could think of answering Andrew, then? How long before she and Reid could say those lovely words: 'Mission Accomplished'?

'You're still looking worried,' Reid whispered as they reached the buffet car. 'We'll find Angie all right – and look, they've got sausages!'

Forty-One

In spite of her worries, a part of Kirsty was genuinely thrilled at coming to London. Too big, Reid had said of it, and so she felt it to be, even just seeing it from King's Cross, even driving in the taxi they'd extravagantly taken to their B & B off the Euston Road. So many people. So much traffic. So many houses, streets, buildings of every sort. Still, it was exciting; different. Made her feel she really was in a famous capital city.

Edinburgh, of course, was also a capital city, but then Edinburgh was home and familiar, and London was not. She might not be seeing the famous attractions yet – Buckingham Palace, the

246

Mall, the Houses of Parliament, the River Thames, all the sights she'd love to see – but there was still a new experience here for her. And though Angie's image was always with her, she felt she couldn't turn away.

'Don't be too disappointed by the Towers,' Reid was whispering in her ear. 'Dr Howard knows we can't afford high prices, so this place he's suggested isn't going to be the Ritz.'

'I know that!' she retorted. 'No need to tell me what we can afford.'

'Yes, well, I'm just saying, it's in the Euston Road area, and you know where that comes on the Monopoly Board!' He grinned. 'Nowhere near Mayfair.'

'As long as there's a decent bed for me at this house, I won't be worried.'

'This is it, folks,' called the taxi driver. 'This is the Towers – and don't ask me why the name. Never had any towers that I know of, but Mrs Vince is all right – you'll be OK here.'

So they were, considering that they'd told themselves not to expect too much. If there were no towers in sight on the gaunt Edwardian terraced house Dr Howard had recommended, there were at least a few daffodils in the strip of front garden, and pot plants in the narrow hall. And though their rooms were tiny, the beds were clean, the towels not too threadbare, and Mrs Vince, the proprietor, was welcoming.

Could have been worse, was their verdict, even though the 'English Breakfast' didn't qualify to be called 'Full', the bacon being skimpy and the eggs very small, and there was no chance of porridge or a kipper. Still, the toast was hot, and the waitress was very sweet and kept telling them to 'talk some more' – oh, she did love their accents!

'Should come up to Edinburgh,' Reid told her gallantly. 'Listen to us all the time, then.'

'So far away, though. I mean, it's another country, ain't it?'

So it is, Kirsty thought, and visions of Angie trying to find her way around this foreign country of London made her heart sink.

'Reid, let's get directions to Beryl's hotel,' she said urgently. 'Let's be on our way.'

'You want to move to the Danby Court?' Mrs Vince asked coldly. 'You're booked in here for two nights, remember.'

Standing behind her reception desk in the narrow hallway, she reminded Kirsty of Lena, particularly when she was upset by someone in the family. There was the same narrowing of the eyes, the same nervous edginess and tightening of the lips, which made Kirsty hurry to explain the truth of the matter.

'Oh, we're no' wanting to move out, Mrs Vince! We just want to look up somebody we know who might have once worked at the Danby Court.'

'Aye, that's all,' Reid agreed. 'Thing is, we've got the address, we know it's in Bloomsbury, but we need directions to get there.'

'Oh, well, I can help you then.' Mrs Vince's

248

brow cleared and she gave a gracious smile. 'I know the Danby Court – it's off Great Russell Street. Pretty big and impersonal, you know, but smart. You'd be best to take the underground – I'll give you details. Want a guidebook as well? With map?'

Well equipped with information, they left the Towers to make their way to the tube, Reid quietly smiling over Mrs Vince's final call: 'Now, remember, if there's anything else you want, you've only to ask!'

'How about a nice fat juicy kipper for breakfast?' he murmured to Kirsty. 'Always knew we should've booked in at the Ritz, after all!'

But Kirsty, when they reached the draughty platform, was already burying herself in the guidebook, to read about Bloomsbury. Seemed an interesting sort of place, filled with pleasant squares, colleges and theatres and the homes of literary people. She should really find out more. But as their train arrived, she slipped the book into her bag, knowing she couldn't take a real interest in anything then. Except the Danby Court and what they might find there.

Forty-Two

The Danby Court was huge. Six or seven storeys of red-brick elegance: elaborate plaster decoration around the rows of windows, a massive entrance opening straight on to the street, where taxis seemed to be constantly arriving. A truly daunting place.

'Oh, dear, it's smart, all right,' Kirsty whispered. 'Think they'll want to talk to us?'

'Why not?' asked Reid, but she noticed he was fingering his tie and looking rather uncertain.

'You're never nervous?' she asked with an uncertain laugh of her own.

For a moment, as they stood on the pavement, watching the flow of arrivals moving through the swing doors at the entrance, he did not reply. Then he shook his head.

'I'm thinking about Angie, Kirsty. I have the feeling she might be here, ahead of us. I mean, this is where she'd be bound to come.'

'She is ahead of us, so it would have been yesterday she'd have come.'

'And what might she have found?'

'We won't know unless we go in.' Kirsty, feeling it was time to take the initiative, grasped her brother's arm. 'Come on, then.'

As they'd expected, the hotel vestibule, filled

with people, was vast, with acres of soft carpeting stretching away towards a curving staircase and, beyond, a row of lifts. There were chairs and sofas, some occupied; small tables, shaded lamps, and, to the right of the entrance, a long mahogany reception desk where two young women were dealing with newcomers.

Had Beryl ever worked here? Kirsty was wondering. Had Angie really come asking for her? Suddenly, the whole object of their visit seemed to become unreal to her. She couldn't even imagine going up to those smart young women and asking for their help. Couldn't imagine Angie doing that, either. Looking with longing eyes at the swing doors to the street, she felt ashamed to think that if she'd been on her own, she might have hurried through them. No, no, she'd have to pull herself together. They'd come all this way to find Angie, and find her they would.

'Will you ask at Reception, or shall I?' she said huskily to Reid, and felt a great rush of relief when she saw that his own certainty of purpose had returned.

'I'll ask,' he declared. 'That crowd of folk's gone now. Leave this to me.'

'Booking in, sir?' asked the tall blonde receptionist he approached during the fortunate lull, her green eyes going over his casual appearance and lack of luggage, before moving to Kirsty's anxious face and hands clutching a guide book.

'Er, no.' Reid produced a confident smile. 'We're down from Scotland, seeking some

251

information about a family member who once worked here.'

'I see.' The receptionist's eyes appeared to glaze over. 'Well, I'm not sure I can help you, sir. I've not been here very long. Maybe you'd like to speak to the Assistant Manager?'

'No, no, Julia.' Her colleague, dark-haired and a little older, was moving swiftly nearer, her face bright with interest. 'I think I can help on this. We had a young woman in yesterday, asking that very same thing.'

A young woman? Reid and Kirsty exchanged glances. A young woman asking questions? It had to be Angie.

'Did she give her name?' Reid asked urgently.

'I don't know, I wasn't on duty yesterday,' the blonde girl put in hastily. 'Gwen, can I leave this with you?'

'Like to come this way, sir?' the older woman asked smoothly, and over the thick, muffling carpet, Reid and Kirsty followed her to a table and chairs near the lifts. They were not holding each other's hands, but felt they should have been, for the trek to the table seemed endless and they could hardly bear the suspense.

'The young lady did give a name,' the receptionist named Gwen told them, her eyes moving from Reid to Kirsty and back again to Reid. 'But may I ask yours?'

'Reid and Kirsty Muir, from Edinburgh. We're brother and sister and think the young lady who spoke to you must have been our stepsister, Angela Ramsay. We've somehow got separated – weren't sure if she'd arrived here or not.'

'Ramsay. That's right. That's the name she gave.' Gwen seemed relieved that they should know it. 'She told us that she was trying to trace a relative named Beryl Ramsay who'd worked here up to 1959. I was able to check our staff records and I found she'd been an assistant housekeeper with us – before all our reorganisation – from 1955.'

'Was there any forwarding address given for her?' Reid asked quickly.

'I'm afraid not. Your relative asked me that, but I couldn't help.'

'Well, is there anybody still here who might have known her?' Kirsty asked quickly.'

'Yes, there is.' Gwen rose. 'The head housekeeper. Like to meet her? I took the other young lady up to meet her, too.'

Forty-Three

In her little office, next to a store with the largest collection of linen imaginable, Mrs Frome, the housekeeper, seemed thrilled to meet them. She was a plump woman of forty or so, with a plump woman's pretty, unlined face, and dark hair stiffly permed. As soon as Gwen had introduced them and hurried back to Reception, Mrs Frome gave them chairs and offered them morning coffee.

'Got my own Cona coffee maker here, you

253

see,' she said, smiling happily, 'and a few biscuits. Chocolate Bourbon? My favourite. There
we are, all set.'

'This is very kind,' Reid murmured. 'It's good
of you to see us.'

'Oh, but I'm so excited! All this interest in
Beryl after so long!' Mrs Frome snapped a Bourbon biscuit in half and took a bite. 'And you
could've knocked me down with a feather when
that lovely young girl came up yesterday. Oh,
my, she was Beryl to the life. I knew at once she
must be her daughter, though she didn't say.' She
hesitated a moment. 'So what's it all about,
then? I mean, why come looking now?'

'That girl you saw – Angela Ramsay – is our
stepmother's niece,' Kirsty said quietly. 'And
our stepmother is Beryl's older sister.'

'The one who brought the girl up?

'That's right. Angela had always wanted to
find her mother and when she found out lately
that she'd worked here, she came down to London herself. My brother and me – we thought we
should come too, but she didn't wait for us.'

'So, you see, we need to find them both,' Reid
went on. 'If there's anything you could tell us,
we'd be grateful.'

'Oh, my! Well, I'll do what I can, but it'll not
be much help, I'm afraid. I've quite lost touch
with Beryl.'

Mrs Frome leaned forward to refill their coffee
cups.

'Now, I did know that she'd had a baby when
she was young, and that her sister had taken it.
She used to talk to me a lot, because we were

quite close at one time. So many of the girls here come and go, you know, and a lot of 'em are from abroad, just passing through, you might say, and you never get to know 'em, but Beryl, she stayed.'

'She ever tell you why she didn't come home?' Reid asked bluntly.

'No, dear, she never did. But I know she'd had a tough time to begin with – moved from job to job, and had a couple o' men interested, but when they heard her story, that was it.' Mrs Frome shook her head. 'I remember she said, if she ever met Mr Right, she'd tell him nothing at all.'

For a little while, there was a silence. Reid and Kirsty finished their coffee and put the cups on Mrs Frome's tray. Offered more biscuits, they politely declined, after which Mrs Frome began to talk again.

'The girl who came yesterday, she looked like Beryl, all right, but I'd say she was different, really.'

'How exactly?' asked Kirsty.

'Well, she struck me as being ... what's the word ... oh, I can't think – means easily hurt...'

'Vulnerable?' Reid suggested.

'That's it. Yes, vulnerable. Now, Beryl never was. Maybe I'm speaking out of turn, and I was fond of her, you know, but I think Beryl was a bit on the hard side.' Mrs Frome nodded her head. 'Hard-boiled, as the Yanks say. A lovely girl, but I have to admit it, out for Number One. I mean, look what happened when she left!'

'What?'

'Well, I knew she'd met someone. A professional man, she said, and he was very keen. Only called him Carl, never mentioned his surname, but he phoned up once when she was out and gave his name as Carl Eade, so I got to know. Teased her about him, asked if there were going to be wedding bells, but she was miffed with me and wouldn't say a word.' Mrs Frome sniffed a little. 'I felt sure, all the same, she'd invite me to the wedding, if there was one, but all she did was come up one day and say she was off. Wouldn't say where, wouldn't give any address, just said she'd keep in touch. And that was that.' Quite breathless with remembered indignation, Mrs Frome sat back in her chair. 'Never heard from her again.'

'Never heard from her again?' Kirsty cried. 'You mean you don't know if she ever got married? Or where she went?'

'Not a clue, dear. She didn't even leave an address with the office, and of course she lived in at the hotel, so there was nowhere else to check. Not that I'd have bothered.'

'Thanks very much, anyway,' Reid told her, rising. 'You've been very helpful, Mrs Frome, and given us a lot of your time.'

'No trouble at all. I've been so interested, you know, talking to you young people, you and that sweet girl.' Mrs Frome pressed her soft hands to theirs. 'It's been a trip down Memory Lane for me.'

Someone knocked at the door and a young woman put her head round. 'Mrs Frome, can I just see you about the new pillowslips – oh, sorry, didn't know you had visitors!'

'Just coming, Noreen.'

As the girl withdrew, the housekeeper showed Reid and Kirsty into the corridor and walked with them to the lift.

'I do hope you find your sister and Beryl, my dears. And if you do find Beryl, you could say Cora would like to be remembered. Mustn't hold grudges.'

'I suppose our sister didn't mention where she was staying?' Kirsty asked, without hope.

Mrs Frome shook her her head. 'Afraid not. Well, she'd no reason to. She knew I wouldn't get in touch – I couldn't tell her any more.' As she pressed the down button on the lift for them, Mrs Frome gave a smile. 'Except, I remember now, I did tell her to try Somerset House. I mean, if Beryl ever got married to that Carl Eade, there would be a record there.'

'Exctly right,' Reid murmured as the lift appeared and they stepped in, giving a last wave to Mrs Frome's plump, smiling face. 'Somerset House, here we come.'

And when they arrived at the grand eighteenth-century building in the Strand that housed the public records they needed, the first person they saw was Angie.

Forty-Four

She was sitting on a bench in the entrance hall, a forlorn young figure in jeans and blue jacket, a canvas bag at her feet, a notebook on her knee. All around her, people were passing by, hurrying about their interests, but she seemed oblivious, her eyes fixed only on space.

For a long moment, Kirsty and Reid stood motionless, watching her as though she were unreal, a shadow. Then Kirsty shrieked, 'Angie!' and saw the fair head jerk up, the eyes widen in recognition and an unbelieving smile light her stepsister's face.

'Kirsty!'

Leaping forward, Angie flung herself into Kirsty's arms. 'Oh, Kirsty, is it really you? Did you come to find me? And Reid, too? I canna believe it!'

'You can believe it.' Reid was grinning broadly, holding her close. 'You don't mind? You're no' angry at us?'

'Angry at you? I'm over the moon. I was beginning to think I'd never see anyone I knew ever again!'

'That's London for you. Millions of people, yet you're all alone.' Reid's grin had faded. 'Why didn't you just tell us what you were going to do? We could've all come together.'

'I never thought you would. I thought you'd stop me.'

'Never mind now,' Kirsty said quickly. 'Listen, Angie, have you had anything to eat today? You look so pale, so weary—'

'I'm staying at a hostel – they don't do breakfast.' Angie shrugged and put back her long hair. 'Had some coffee somewhere.'

'Right, let's find a café and stoke up,' Reid said promptly. 'Then we'll come back and see if we can check the marriage certificates.'

'I've done that already.' Angie stooped to pick up her canvas bag, perhaps to avoid their looks of surprise. 'Well, I got somebody to help me. And I copied everything down in my notebook.'

'But what did you find?' Reid cried. 'Anything to help, or not?'

Angie straightened up, swinging her bag. 'Oh, yes, my mother is married. She married a dentist called Eade in Dulwich, in 1959. But of course, I don't know where they live now. I was just sitting here, wondering what to do, when I saw you.' She gave a long sigh. 'An answer to a prayer, I can tell you – if I'd thought of praying.'

'A dentist?' Reid was smiling. 'He'll be in the telephone directory. Sure to be. Girls, I reckon we're home and dry.'

'If they're still in London,' Kirsty pointed out. 'They could be anywhere.'

'OK, we'll check. Soon as we've had something to eat. A big steak, with chips, I say, and to hell with the expense. My treat, anyway.'

'I won't say no,' Angie said, letting Reid take her bag as they walked out into the Strand.

259

'There was a charge to look at the records – I wasn't expecting it – money seems to go nowhere in London.'

Thank God we found her, Kirsty thought, glancing quickly at Reid, who was rolling his eyes and sighing. *I bet she hasn't a bean.*

After a good meal at a local café, they all felt better, which perhaps went to prove Kirsty's theory that life always seemed easier after lunch. Until, however, Reid suggested making a move, when Angie's new confidence seemed to wither and she shrank into her chair.

'Where d'you want us to go?' she asked fearfully.

'Well, to check the directories, of course.'

'And ... and if we find an address, we go there?'

Reid studied her with some puzzlement. 'Isn't that what you've come here to do?'

'Oh, yes.' Angie's eyes were wandering round the café. 'Only maybe I should ring up first?'

'That might be best,' Kirsty said.

'But then she might say she doesn't want to see me.'

'You're not scared, are you?' Reid asked gently. 'Not hoping you needn't face her? No need to worry. It'd be only natural to feel a bit like that.'

'I am scared,' Angie answered slowly. 'Now that it might be going to happen. I've wanted it for so long, as long as I can remember. I can't bear to think how it'd be ... if she ... turned me down.'

'Whatever happens, you'll have to try to see her. You've come so far, there's no going back now.'

'Think how you'd feel, going home, if you'd never given her the chance to meet you,' Kirsty said persuasively. 'You'd never forgive yourself, and this whole trip would have been for nothing.'

'Aye, that's true.' Angie straightened her shoulders and tried to smile. 'Let's find the London phone books, then.'

'Why, I bet they've got them here!' cried Reid. 'You girls stay here and I'll ask.'

While he went across to the assistant at the cash desk, Angie and Kirsty looked at one another.

'Might not even be listed in London,' Kirsty murmured.

'I hope they are. You're right, I have to face her.' Angie's lip suddenly trembled. 'And I want to.'

'They're giving Reid the books now,' Kirsty told her. 'He's looking up the name.'

Both girls were silent, watching Reid turning pages. Then he handed back the directories and returned to their table.

'Got him,' he said quietly. 'There's a chap of that name with LDS after his name and two numbers, one for surgery, one for home. In Dulwich. Looks like journey's end.'

'Oh God,' Angie whispered.

'Want to ring up first? Or just go?'

'Just go,' Angie replied. 'Then she'll have to see me.'

Forty-Five

Beryl's home in Dulwich proved to be a large Edwardian house in a pleasant, tree-lined road. There were two gates, one leading up a short drive to the main front door, the other to an extension, in keeping with the original, which had been built at the side. A sign over its door read 'Surgery', and a brass plate on its door bore the name 'Carl Eade, LDS, Dental Surgeon'. Two cars were parked outside.

'Oh, nice,' Reid commented, looking up and down the road. 'What you'd call "leafy", eh? And this whole district's nice, according to your guidebook, Kirsty.'

'Very nice,' she agreed, glancing at Angie, who was smoking yet another cigarette as they all stood still, looking at the house. 'Got a picture gallery and a famous school, good shops, big houses – Angie, maybe you should put that cigarette out now.'

'Why? I bet my mother smokes.'

'You've no idea what she does. Living here, she might be quite diffferent from what you think.'

'Come up in the world, you mean?'

'Don't you think so?' asked Reid.

Angie gave one of her shrugs. 'If she has, she'll be less likely to want to know me.'

'More likely, I'd say.'

'What happens now, then?' Angie asked, finally throwing away her cigarette.

'You go up to the front door and ring the bell,' Kirsty told her.

At once, Angie's truculence vanished and her face took on a hunted expression.

'I'm no' going in without you folks,' she whispered. 'Don't even think it.'

'You have to speak to your mother on your own,' Reid declared. 'After all, you came on your own, eh?'

'I know, I know, but I feel different now.' Angie shook her head. 'I tell you, I couldn't walk up to that door on my own if you paid me. Reid, Kirsty, come with me, eh? Please?'

For a long moment, they held out, refusing to give in to the pleading blue gaze fixed on them, but in the end Kirsty yielded. If it was the only way to get Angie to her mother's door, so be it, and Reid, throwing up his hands, said the same.

'Against my better judgement,' he added. 'What's your mother going to think, when three of us turn up?'

'No idea what she's going to think, anyway,' Angie muttered.

'If she's in,' Kirsty added.

But even Angie by that stage didn't want her mother to be out.

Mrs Eade was not out, but was 'having her rest', said the young woman who opened the door to them.

'Could you tell her there's someone to see

263

her?' Reid asked, as Angie said nothing.

'What name?'

'Ramsay.'

'I'm just here to look after George,' the girl said doubtfully. 'But I'll see what she says. You'd better wait here.'

They didn't have long to wait. Within a few minutes, a fair-haired woman in her thirties appeared at the door and stared out at them, stricken. With her fine nose and brow, her blue eyes and pretty mouth, there could be no doubt who she was, for she was as like Angie as her own reflection. Nor was there any doubt, as she pulled a loose blue jacket around her, that she was pregnant.

'My God,' she whispered, her eyes on Angie. 'Oh, dear God, your name's Ramsay? You're not ... you're not Angela, are you?'

'I am,' Angie said in a low voice. 'I'm Angie. I'm your daughter.'

'My daughter?' Beryl's hand flew to her lips. 'Look, you'd best come in – come inside, please!'

She'd lost her Scottish accent. Put it behind her, perhaps, as she'd put so many things. But as she hurried them into a large, comfortable sitting room at the back of the house, she was beginning to take control of herself again. They could almost see her mind working, as she thought about what to do with them, these young folk who'd come to her, this daughter from the blue.

'Greta's children,' she murmured, her eyes passing over Kirsty and Reid to Angie. 'Lena's stepkids. I remember you when you were little. I remember your mother, too. But sit down, sit down.'

Easing into a chair herself, she held her hand to her back and asked, breathing hard, 'How did you find me?'

'Junie Moffat told me you'd worked at the Danby Court.' Angie, waxen pale, could not seem to take her eyes from her mother's face. 'I work in Logie's, just like you, and she sort of recognized me.'

'Junie?' Beryl sighed. 'I never thought of her. So, you all came down and – let me guess – Cora Frome told you about Carl?' She leaned forward a little, her gaze on Angie. 'But why? Why did you want to find me, for God's sake? After all these years?'

'I've always wanted to find you,' Angie answered steadily. 'All my life. But I didn't know how to start looking.'

'Always wanted to find me...' Beryl sat back. 'I still don't know why.'

'Because you gave me away.'

There was a silence. Beryl's face had grown red, she was breathing fast. 'What else could I've done?' she cried at last. 'My folks were dead, I was only seventeen. I could never have coped. Give me credit, I never went round the back streets, trying to get rid of you, but when you were born, I knew I couldn't look after you. So, I asked Lena to take you.'

'Asked?' Kirsty repeated. 'We were told you just left Angie and went.'

'All right, I went. I ran away. I knew Lena would make a far better mother than me, and

265

she'd already been told that she could never have kids.' Beryl's eyes were snapping fire. 'But don't think I had it easy down here! The first years were terrible. You young folks, you've no idea – no idea at all! But I swore that if I ever got the chance to lead a decent life, I'd take it and just forget the past. Cut it right out. All of it! And that's what I've done.' After another long trembling silence, she stood up. 'And that's what I'm going to keep on doing. I'm sorry, I'm truly sorry, Angie, but that's the way it's got to be.'

'Mummy!' shouted a high voice, and as Angie slowly rose to her feet, followed by Reid and Kirsty, a small blond boy ran into the room and flung himself into Beryl's arms.

'Mummy, I want you!' he cried. 'I don't want Pammie. I want you to play with me. Now!'

'This is George,' Beryl whispered over his fair head. 'He's upset, because I've to rest so much. The baby's due in July and I've not been well.'

'I'm sorry, Mrs Eade.' The young woman, who was evidently Pammie, came hurrying forward to snatch up the little boy. 'He's very fretful. Shall I give him his tea?'

'Yes, take him to the kitchen, and I'll be along in a minute.'

When George had been carried out, howling, Beryl turned to the young people.

'I'd offer you a cup of tea,' she said quickly, 'but my husband will be finishing his afternoon surgery soon. You'll understand, it would be easier, if he didn't see you.'

'You mean if he didn't see Angie,' Reid retorted. 'She's come all the way from Scotland to

266

find you, and you want her to go? Just like that?'

'What can I do for her?' Beryl cried. 'Angie, you understand, don't you? I can't take you into my life, there's just no place. No point, really, in you ever coming to find me. I mean, what could you expect?'

'Nothing.' Angie was already turning away. 'I never expected anything.'

'A bit of interest, maybe?' asked Reid. 'A question or two about her life? The life you gave her, Mrs Eade, if you remember.'

'Why, she didn't even know she had a wee brother,' Kirsty cried. 'And he'll never know he has a big sister!'

'It's how it is. I'm sorry.' Beryl was becoming agitated, her eyes watching the door, her hands fluttering towards her visitors, as if she would physically move them on their way. 'I'm sorry. I mean it. I wish things could be different. Look, I'll try to keep in touch, eh? I'll write. I always sent money, you know. I never left everything to Lena.'

They moved to the front door, which Beryl flung open for them, looking out towards the extension, to see if she could see her husband coming.

'Goodbye,' she cried, her voice cracking a little. 'Goodbye, Angie. I hope all goes well for you. Remember me to Lena. And I will write, I promise.'

But Angie, turning her head, gave her a long last look. 'No,' she said quietly, 'don't write. It'd be a waste of time. You wouldn't want me to reply.'

267

Forty-Six

At eleven o'clock the following morning, Kirsty and Reid were back at King's Cross, Angie with them this time.

Since the meeting with her mother, she'd scarcely spoken, though the Muirs had talked and talked, trying to find some crumb of comfort to give her. But what comfort could they find? Her mother had rejected her, not once, but twice. How could they reconcile her to that?

After an evening meal in a Dulwich café, Reid had decreed that Angie was not to return to her hostel where she couldn't even get breakfast, but should go back to the Towers with Kirsty and himself, where he was sure Mrs Vince would find her a bed. Then they'd all be together and leave next day for the station.

'I came down by overnight coach,' Angie said tonelessly. 'It was cheaper than the train.'

'Overnight coach?' Kirsty cried. 'No wonder you've been looking so tired. Look, you're coming back with us.'

'If you say so.' Angie put her hand on Kirsty's arm. 'Thanks, then. Thanks for everything. I don't know what I'd have done without you and Reid.'

'There's no need to thank us,' Kirsty answered, hugging her. 'We're family!'

Later, at the Towers, where Mrs Vince did indeed find a room for the poor young girl who looked so weary, Kirsty used the pay phone to ring Andrew.

'Good news!' she told him. 'We've found Angie. We'll be coming back tomorrow.'

'Kirsty, thank God! I've been half out of my mind, worrying. What can I do to help?'

'Could you ring my stepmother at the sweet factory and tell her what's happening? I'd be really grateful.'

'Of course, I will. And I'll meet your train, if you tell me when you're due to arrive.'

'Andrew, that would be grand. Thank you! We get in at eight. See you then.'

'All my love, darling.'

'And mine to you.'

Dear Andrew ... Why did the thought of giving an answer to his proposal weigh like a stone over her heart?

Putting her head round Reid's door, she told him of her call to Andrew and that Mrs Vince was serving tea and biscuits in the lounge if anyone wanted them, but Angie had already gone to bed.

'Poor kid,' he muttered, as he emptied his wallet and counted his remaining money.

'Well, she has got us, Reid, even if her mother doesn't want her, and it's true what I said, we're family.'

'More or less,' he answered.

'More or less? What does that mean?'

'Ssh. I'm just trying to work out if we've enough to get home, after I've paid the bill here.'

'I've enough for Angie's ticket.'

'You have? Thank God for that.' Reid grinned. 'I'm going to have to be pulling pints again, soon as we're back.'

'And you've your studying to do!'

'Don't worry, that's all in hand.'

'Well, you've been very good, taking time for Angie.'

'Just wish she'd had more luck here.' Reid's face darkened. 'If you ask me, she's well shot of a mother like Beryl. We've all done a damn sight better with Lena.'

'She'll be thrilled when Andrew tells her we're coming home.'

'Aye. I'm pretty keen to get back myself. Tea and biscuits in the lounge, did you say? Let's go down.'

Economising on a taxi next morning, they took the tube to the station, and even with luggage, managed well enough, arriving at King's Cross with time to spare.

'Busiest station in the country,' Reid commented, after they'd bought ham rolls for the journey and were battling through the crowds of travellers. 'Apart from Waverley in Edinburgh. Let's find the platform, eh?'

'You go on, I'll just get some magazines,' Kirsty said, stopping at a bookstall.

'Don't lose us.'

'Don't worry!'

She had bought a couple of magazines – one for Angie, who might be stirred from her apathy to read it – and was on her way towards her platform when she came to a halt. And froze. Jake MacIver, carrying a violin case, was coming towards her.

At first, she could tell, he was as stunned as she. But then he rallied, gave his smile, and took her hand.

'Kirsty? This is amazing. You're here – in London?'

'Leaving London,' she answered, immediately pulling her hand away, determined to let him see that this meeting meant nothing to her. 'I'm going for the Edinburgh train now.'

'And I've just arrived. I'm meeting the fellows – we're en route for Europe.' His blue gaze was as bright as ever. 'But this is wonderful, to see you again. Couldn't we have a drink, or coffee, or something? How long have you got?'

'No time at all.' She began to walk away, not looking back. 'Goodbye, Jake,' she called over her shoulder.

'Taxi rank, is it, sir?' Jake's porter asked, arriving with his luggage on a trolley.

'The taxi rank, yes,' Jake answered, watching Kirsty's slim figure disappearing down the platform, before slowly turning away.

Forty-Seven

'What's up?' asked Reid, when Kirsty joined him and Angie.

'Nothing,' she answered, though she knew she couldn't deceive him. Reid could always tell when something was wrong. Besides, her hands clutching the magazines were trembling. 'I was just worried in case I missed the train.'

'It's coming in now,' he told her, not pressing, just observing.

'Yes. I'm OK, then. Hope we can find seats.'

'We'll squash in somewhere.'

In fact, she was happy enough to sit separately from Reid and Angie, who had seats together in a corridor compartment. Seeing Jake again had shaken her more than she cared to admit, and it would be easier not to have to talk to those who knew her so well. Surrounded by strangers reading newspapers or opening packets of sandwiches, she could just let her churned spirits settle, and go over and over the little encounter, try to work out if it meant anything, or not.

No, she'd been right, it meant nothing. She no longer loved Jake MacIver. Yet the sight of him had stirred up so much that had made her unhappy, she knew she couldn't just dismiss it. She had put on a good act. Probably convinced him that his power over her no longer worked; not that he'd wanted it, anyway. But with memories so potent, there were still traces of that power for her. Maybe always would be, which meant she hoped she would never see him again, and turned her thoughts to Andrew, waiting in Edinburgh for her answer.

After a while, she was surprised to feel hungry and made her way back down the corridor to the compartment where she'd left Angie and Reid. Time for her share of the ham rolls Angie had put in her canvas bag, and afterwards they could go to the buffet car for a cup of tea.

Where were the two of them, though? Why was it always so difficult to find people on a train? After peering in at several compartments, and even opening the door to one that wasn't theirs, she found them. And stared.

They were alone. Reid had his arm around Angie's shoulders, while Angie was leaning against him, breathing quietly, her long fair hair trailing across his chest, her eyes closed. She was asleep.

As Reid's eyes met Kirsty's, he smiled and put a finger to his lips.

'She's flat out,' he whispered. 'Exhausted.'

'Where is everyone?' Kirsty whispered back.

'Gone to the buffet.'

Kirsty, still staring at her brother, sat down in someone's seat.

'You seem to be looking after her, Reid.'

'She needs looking after.'

'I never thought you'd want to, though.'

'You never knew what I wanted.'

'You put up a good smokescreen.'

He smiled again. 'Maybe it's clearing.'

As the train gave a sudden jolt and began to put on speed, Angie began to stir. Slowly, she sat up, pushing back her hair, stretching and yawning.

'Have I been asleep?'

She turned to look into Reid's watching eyes, and for the first time since he and Kirsty had met her in Somerset House, her sweet mouth melted into an uncertain smile.

'Hope I didn't snore?'

'It's all right,' Kirsty told her. 'You don't snore, Angie.'

'Kirsty, where did you come from? And where is everybody?'

'Gone to the buffet. Have you got those rolls we bought?'

But as they sat together, eating their picnic and discussing what they might afford at the buffet, Kirsty had the strangest feeling that she was set apart from Angie and Reid. Was she playing gooseberry? It didn't seem possible.

Certainly, though, there seemed to be something between these two. An attraction they were at last admitting to themselves. And why shouldn't they admit it? However Kirsty had thought of her, Angie was no relation of hers or Reid's, and Reid had never wanted to think of her as part of the family. How long had he been scrapping with her and loving her at the same time? How long had she been feeling the same? Without, perhaps, even realizing it?

The more Kirsty watched them, the more she

thought it possible that love could be coming to these two. A real love; a shared love. And one she found herself envying from the bottom of her heart.

Hours later, when Andrew had brought them all to Pleasant Hill and Reid and Angie had hurried into Clover, she still sat in her seat next to his and looked into his face.

'It's no' dark yet,' she whispered.

'So? I don't care if it's dark or not.'

'People can see us, that's all.'

'Let them.'

He took her in his arms and for some time they exchanged long and satisfying kisses, until Kirsty pulled away.

'Andrew...'

'Yes?'

'I've made up my mind.'

'Oh, God. If it's bad news, don't tell me.'

'It's good news.' She ran her hand down his face. 'Well, sort of.'

'Sort of? Please don't play games, Kirsty. You know what this means to me.'

'It means a lot to me, too.'

And that was true, she thought, as her eyes searched his face. Love, security, freedom from worry – they'd be hers. And the image of Jake MacIver need never trouble her again.

'All I'm saying is that we should have an understanding, Andrew. You know, before we make it official.'

'Let me get this straight. Are you accepting me?'

'Yes. Yes, I am!'

'But not without strings.' His eyes were suddenly a little cold.

'An understanding isn't strings!'

'It's another secret, though, isn't it? We said we'd had enough of secrets.'

'Well, I told your mother we weren't going to announce anything, and this way we could prepare her, couldn't we?'

'I don't see why my mother should come into this.'

'Mothers always come into things.' Kirsty lowered her eyes. 'I thought you'd be pleased – that I was saying yes.'

'Oh, Kirsty!' Andrew's grey eyes were beginning to shine, his expression to soften, as he took her again into his arms. 'Don't you know I'm willing to accept whatever you offer me? If it means you'll come to love me – some time.'

And she would. She'd see to it. Keep her side of the bargain, and make him happy. A wonderful sense of well-being glowed within her, staying with her even when Andrew had finally driven away, and she was home again and embracing Lena.

'Thank God, you're all back,' Lena was murmuring, dashing a tear away from her eyes. 'I was so worried, you know, till that sweet man said you were coming home.'

'No need to worry,' Reid told her. 'All safe and well. Mission accomplished.'

Kirsty gave a little sigh. Mission accomplished ... For now.

PART THREE

Forty-Eight

Back home. Back to work for Kirsty and Angie. Back to college for Reid. Everything the same as before, on the surface, at least. But below? Below, Kirsty could sense something bubbling away, just like lava that bubbled away under a volcano – and sometimes erupted.

At first, it seemed remarkable to her that Lena had never sensed it too, but Kirsty was sure she hadn't, for she'd have said, her stepmother not being one to keep her feelings to herself. Perhaps, in the first days after her family's return from London, she'd been too busy brooding over her sister's behaviour to allow room for anything else in her mind.

'I canna get over it,' she said privately to Kirsty. 'The way Beryl treated Angie! Just didn't want to know, eh?'

'I suppose she never did want to know,' Kirsty replied. 'Left that to you.'

'But when Angie had worked so hard to find her, and she could see what a grand lassie she'd turned out to be, you'd think that would have made a difference.'

Kirsty shrugged. 'Beryl's made this new life for herself, that's the trouble. Doesn't want Angie coming in, rocking the boat.'

'Aye, and she's had to cut herself off from everybody she used to know. Of course, she'd already cut herself off from me, but you'd think she'd still have sent word when she got wed. And told me about the wee nephew!' A tear had trickled down Lena's cheek. 'That cuts deep, that does! Never to tell her own sister!'

Kirsty hesitated. 'The woman she worked with at the hotel said she was quite fond of Beryl, but thought she was – you know – rather hard.'

'Hard? Aye, it's true.' Lena dabbed at her eyes. 'Takes after ma dad. Nice enough man, but never thought about anybody but himself. First, second, all the time – that was him. My mother always used to say, "never expect anything from your father and you'll no' be disappointed". And good advice it was, too.'

'Think Angie must have heard it,' Kirsty said sadly. 'I don't believe she ever really expected anything from her mother. Just had to find her, that was all.'

'Aye, well, she can settle down now, and live her own life. I've noticed she's been looking a lot happier.'

And Reid? Kirsty was careful not to say anything.

So was Reid, so was Angie. Never said a word about their feelings to anyone. Probably because the time wasn't right. The great hurdle of Reid's finals still lay ahead, and until they were over, it was Kirsty's guess that silence would be kept. Yet their eyes, their faces, said so much. How was it that Lena didn't see?

Were the cornflake packets at breakfast getting in the way perhaps? Reid was now only seen first thing in the morning and last thing at night, for he was working flat out for his exams, and by the time he came home, Lena would be in front of her telly, not looking at either him or Angie. In the mornings, though, when they were at the kitchen table, how could she miss the glances and smiles, the accidentally touching hands, the whispered conversations? Where were the old snappy remarks, backchat, the flashing eyes?

Sometimes, Kirsty felt the differences so keenly, she talked too much in an effort to cover up, but Lena didn't notice that either. Just carried on, with various bits of Clover gossip. How Nesta Harvie was having another baby – more worry to come over noise, eh? And Dick Murdoch had moved jobs again, this time to the Highways department – and let's hope he stuck to that, eh? And Vinnie was worried about Cormack – no, not over his piping, he'd given that up – but in case he turned into one of those dropouts you heard about. Just hoped he wasn't into anything serious, eh? With the lads he knew from Briar.

'Hope not,' Kirsty had murmured, glancing at Reid, who seemed not to be listening. 'What does Niall think?'

'He says there's probably nothing to worry about. But if anybody can deal with Cormack, it'll be Niall.'

'Such a good, steady lad,' Lena had added, glancing at Angie, who, like Reid, wasn't listening.

Looking back, Kirsty wondered if it was at this time that Lena had suddenly become aware of all the hidden bubbling of change she herself had been sensing for so long. Whatever it was, something alerted her, for when she next found Kirsty alone, it was to say, 'Is there something those two aren't telling me, Kirsty?'

Forty-Nine

'Those two?'

'Kirsty!'

'Oh, you mean Reid and Angie? Well, they haven't told me anything.'

'Aye, but I can tell by the look on your face that you know what I'm talking about. They're acting like ... like they're sweet on each other.' Lena's mouth tightened. 'Now, that canna be, Kirsty. They're brother and sister, eh?'

'No, they're not. They're no relation to each other at all. And Angie's only your niece, so it's right what Reid says – she isn't even our step-sister.'

'Is that right?' Lena's look was perplexed. 'Well, even if it is, they've been brought up together, so how can they fall in love? Why, they've never even got on! Always scrapping and needling – are you telling me that's all changed?'

'They've never said so, but I think it has. Down in London, they must have begun to realize how they felt.' Under her stepmother's scrutiny, Kirsty was twisting uncomfortably. 'You won't say anything, eh?'

'I will!' Lena cried. 'They're under my roof; I have to know what's going on!'

'There's nothing *going on*, Lena! They're no' even going out together, because Reid has to study. Oh, look, I bet they'll be telling you anyway, soon as they can.'

'And when'll that be?'

'When Reid's finished his exams. I think there'll be changes then.'

For some moments, Lena sat, pondering, then she shrugged. 'OK, I'll leave it for now, but I'm shell-shocked, and that's the truth. I am. Never in this world did I think those two'd turn into love birds.' She fixed Kirsty with a long, considering look. what about you, then? Have you any secrets you're no' telling me? I feel I'm on shifting sands with all you young folk. What's going to come out next?'

Kirsty who had lowered her eyes, slowly raised them to Lena's face. 'Andrew and me – we have an understanding.'

'I knew it! I knew there was something you were keeping quiet about! So, it's an understanding? Since when?'

'Since I got back from London. I'm sorry, Lena, I never told you before – it only happened the day Angie ran away, so I never had the chance – but Andrew asked me to marry him after that tea with his mother. I said I'd like time

283

to think about it.'

'Time to think! Oh, Kirsty, why d'you need to think? A dear man like that, wanting to marry you and give you a lovely life, and you've to think about it!'

'I had to be sure,' Kirsty murmured. 'How I felt.'

'Oh, my Lord! He'd make you happy. Isn't that enough?'

'I did say yes in the end. That's why we have an understanding.'

'But no' a proper engagement?'

'That'll come later.'

Lena, still studying Kirsty's face with incredulous eyes, shook her head. 'You settle for a ring and never mind about an understanding. Make it official, get wed, and be happy, that's my advice.' She lowered her voice. 'And don't go round comparing Andrew Macrae with that MacIver fellow, either. What you had with him would never've lasted, anyway. Never does.'

'I would never compare Andrew with Jake!' Kirsty cried. 'Except to say Andrew's a million times better!'

That same evening, when she and Angie were in their beds, ready to put out the light, Kirsty, though she'd told Lena to say nothing, suddenly decided she would speak to Angie herself. Ask her outright if there was anything between her and Reid. Just see what she would say.

'Angie?' she ventured. 'Can I have a word?'

'Why not?' Angie asked, clicking off the bed-side lamp.

'I was just wondering...' Kirsty fell silent, her will to interrogate Angie evaporating, now that she had the chance to do it.

'What?'

'Oh, nothing. It's OK.'

'Goodnight, then.'

But Kirsty had thought of something else. A way, perhaps, to work her way round to finding out what she wanted to know.

'Angie, mind if I ask you...?'

'Oh, for goodness' sake, Kirsty, get on with it!'

'Well, I was just thinking about that valentine you got this year, when Andrew never thought to send me one. Said he was too old, would you believe?'

'Yes?' Angie groaned. 'What of it?'

'You got one the year before too, didn't you? Do you still think Niall sent them?'

'How should I know? Valentines aren't signed. What's it matter, anyway?'

'Maybe it wasn't Niall, after all.' Kirsty waited a moment. 'Maybe it was Reid.'

From the other bed, there was no sound. Then Angie snapped the light back on and stared across at Kirsty.

'Oh, Kirsty,' she said softly. 'What a round-about way to ask me what's going on, eh? I never thought you were so devious.'

'Just asking, that's all,' Kirsty muttered, blush-ing. 'The thing is, Lena's been asking, too. Asking me. I told her to say nothing to you about it.'

'Thank God for that.' Angie paused. 'Has it been that obvious, then?'

'Since we got back from London. Though I
285

had my suspicions on the train.'

Angie sighed, then gave a radiant smile, stretching out in her bed like a cat in the sunshine.

'Och, so what? We don't really want to hide it, Kirsty. It's just that it's easier. You know what I mean?'

'Aye, I do,' Kirsty said with feeling.

She sat up against her pillow, looking curiously at the new Angie, now so calm, so serene, so lacking in all those sharp edges that had once surrounded her like a protective fence. Was this what love could do? Love, happiness, the feeling of being wanted? But hadn't her family always wanted her? Maybe it had been too hard for her to believe it – especially where Reid was concerned.

'When did you realize ... that you cared for each other?' she asked a little hesitantly, fearing that Angie would think her prying. But Angie seemed willing enough to talk.

'Well, it was all sort of gradual. Never hit me out of the blue, or anything!' She laughed and played with a strand of her long hair. 'In fact, when we were kids, I never took much notice of Reid at all. Then, when I grew up a bit, I kept looking at him and thinking, if I'd met him somewhere else, instead of here, would he have liked me? Because I knew I wanted him to, but it seemed to me that he didn't. He never treated me the same as you, Kirsty.'

'Because he didn't want to think of you as his sister, Angie. Or, part of the family.' Kirsty smiled. 'But not because he didn't like you.

Quite the opposite, as it's turned out.'

'Aye, we both of us got things all wrong. Until we went to London.'

'And everything was different?'

'Everything was different. Being together, away from home, we just seemed ... to see the truth of things.' Angie sighed with satisfaction. 'And that was it.'

'So, what's next?' Kirsty asked, feeling that she knew anyway.

'Why, we'll get wed, of course. As soon as Reid's finished his exams.'

'No engagement first?'

'Don't want to wait. It's bad enough waiting now.' Angie gave Kirsty a look full of meaning. 'Imagine what it's like, eh? Being so close every night? And so far apart?'

Kirsty slid down in her bed and pulled her sheet around her. 'I can imagine,' she said quietly. 'Better put the light out now, Angie. We should get some sleep.'

'OK. 'Night, Kirsty.' But after she'd put out the light, Angie leaned across and touched Kirsty's shoulder under the sheet. 'It's been good to talk, eh? For me, anyway. But you've no' said much. How are things with you and Andrew?'

'Fine. We've an understanding.'

'Kirsty, that's grand! We could have a double wedding! Except Reid and me'll only be running off to a register office.'

'That'd do me,' Kirsty said. 'Some time.'

Fifty

Time was, when Kirsty went into work, she could always feel relaxed. Able to put away any worries she might have while handling her beloved tartan. Able to shut out the world, as she immersed herself completely in creating her next kilt.

But since the split between Lil and Dermot, all that had changed. There was strain in the atmosphere now, which affected the whole shop, and though Andrew always managed to put on a cheerful look, even Mrs MacNee and Meriel seemed watchful, as though waiting for more trouble. As for Lil, she'd quite lost her natural ebullience and had become pale and morose, while Dermot carried out a kind of balancing act; on the one hand, trying to please Meriel, on the other, trying to comfort Lil. Which, of course, he could not do.

As the early summer days passed by, Kirsty found herself wondering if matters would ever come to a head. Sometimes she discussed it with Andrew, but he had no solutions. He could scarcely sack Lil for being miserable, or Dermot for letting her down, especially when their work had not suffered. If anything, they were working harder than ever, as though trying to prove that their misfortunes were not harming Macrae's, and Andrew said he didn't want to lose either of them. But Kirsty was convinced that eventually one would go – just hoped it would not be Lil.

On a dismal day in June, Lil asked Kirsty at lunchtime if she'd like to take sandwiches and walk down to the Queen's Park. If she was not seeing Mr Macrae, of course.

'Why, you know I never have lunch with Andrew!' Kirsty replied. 'He's always got people to meet, or some business thing on. It'd be grand to get out for some fresh air.'

'Fresh is the word,' Lil said wryly. 'Or you might just say cold. What's happened to summer this year? Might be too nippy for the park.'

'Oh, come on. It'll do us good.'

They were fond of the walk to the park, which took them down the Royal Mile from the High Street to the Canongate, at the foot of which was the Palace of Holyroodhouse and the Queen's Drive. In fact, they thought themselves lucky to be so close to this most historic part of the city.

Practically a neighbour of the Queen, eh? Not that she was often there, but she'd probably be up soon for the annual garden parties, when you could see all the guests arriving – the great and the good and the ordinary folk who'd done something special. Sometimes, the sun shone on the best hats and morning suits, but this year the weather was probably going to be of the Arctic kind.

Just like today, they thought, as they looked through the ornamental gates of the palace, then made their way into the vast stretch of land that was the park. In spite of the chill, there were plenty of people about, some even struggling up Arthur's Seat, the extinct volcano that was Edinburgh's great landmark, or making for one of the three lochs where the birds swooped and fluttered. But the girls only wanted to find somewhere out of the wind.

'I'm no' so sure now that this was a good idea,' Lil told Kirsty, as they sat shivering on a bench, eating egg sandwiches. 'How about trying to get coffee at that little café in the Canongate? I know one of the girls there, she might squeeze us in.'

'My treat,' Kirsty said promptly. 'As you made the sandwiches. Quick, let's go!'

Oh, what bliss, to be at a little table found for them by Lil's friend, Margie, at the back of the Canongate café, with steaming hot coffee and thickly buttered scones in front of them!

'Now this *was* a good idea,' Kirsty said with a laugh, and even Lil managed a smile.

'Did you say that Reid was beginning his finals today, Kirsty?'

'That's right. Very important time for him.'

Kirsty did not add that it was an important time for Angie, too, for that was still, for the time being, a secret. If all went well, of course, there would be no more secrets and a wedding instead, but maybe Lil didn't want to hear about weddings, anyway.

'Thing is, I've got an exam coming up as well,' Lil went on, as she cut her scone. 'At the bookkeeping class – tomorrow, in fact.'

'Lil, I'd no idea!' Kirsty's face was full of
290

pleased surprise. 'Oh, I feel bad – I'd clean forgotten you were doing that course, and here you are sitting the exam! That's grand, to keep going, in spite of...'

'In spite of being dumped?' Lil shrugged. 'I told you I wasn't going to let those two get me down. Dermot gave up, of course, couldn't face going to classes with me, but I kept on and I'm hoping to do well.'

'You will, I know you will.'

'Aye, well there's a purpose behind it all. That's why I wanted to talk to you, Kirsty.' Lil drank some coffee, took a deep breath. 'The truth is, I'm thinking of leaving Macrae's.'

'Leaving Macrae's?' Kirsty's eyes widened. Here was confirmation of what she had feared, but she already knew she wasn't going to accept it. Most definitely, she shook her coppery head. 'Oh, no, Lil, you can't do that. You can't leave. You're a kilt maker; it'd be a terrible waste. All those years! And what would I do without you?'

'You'll be leaving soon yourself. I'd be the one who'd have to do without you.'

'Why should I be leaving?'

'Well, you'll be getting married, eh? Don't tell me Mr Macrae will want his wife to keep on making kilts for all his Rotary friends?'

Kirsty was silent. Maybe it was hard to believe, but she had never once thought of what would happen to her job if she married Andrew.

'There's nothing planned,' she said after a pause, during which Lil watched her with a sympathetic look in her blue-grey eyes.

'Bet you've got an understanding, haven't you?'

'Look, let's talk about you, Lil. You can't leave, and that's all there is to it. Why, what would you do? A clerical job? Is that what you want? Or are you just wanting to get away from Dermot?'

'I'm no' denying that I want to get away,' Lil answered, the pink colour rising to her cheekbones. 'But I don't admit to being chased out. I could do with a change; I'm tired of kilt making. If I pass my exam, I'll try for an office job and see how I get on.'

'All right, I'll have to wish you luck, then.' Kirsty took out her purse. 'Now, it's time to go back. I'll get the bill.'

'Well, I hope you will wish me luck,' Lil gasped, hurrying after her up the Canongate. 'You wouldn't have me stay on if I'm no' happy, eh?'

Kirsty stopped, smiled, and suddenly flung her arms round Lil. 'Of course not! If it's what you want, you go for it. I'm just feeling blue because I'll miss you!'

Lil hugged her back. 'Like I said, you'll probably be gone yourself. Moving on to a new life.'

'I suppose I might.'

The two girls walked on, dodging the tourists, and at Macrae's, they halted.

'Haven't you made up your mind yet?' Lil asked softly. 'You don't sound too sure.'

'Oh, I am! Andrew's a wonderful person. I'd be happy with him.'

'So, why don't you get engaged?'

'Oh, that'll come. Plenty of time.' Kirsty

pushed open the door of the shop and stopped.

Looking at the racks of ladies' clothes was a fair-haired young woman in a fashionable boxy jacket and short skirt. Kirsty had only seen her once before, but remembered her very well. She was the Macrae family friend, Mildred Grier.

Fifty-One

As the girls stood for a moment in the shop doorway, Dermot appeared, looking worried as usual, and put his hand on Kirsty's arm. Not looking at Lil, he said in a whisper, 'Thank goodness you're back – can you do me a favour?'

'Depends. What is it?'

'Could you look after this lady for me? Meriel's no' come back from lunch and I'd like to get away.'

Kirsty, unwilling to get involved with Mildred Grier, said she'd things to do. 'Maybe Lil...'

But Lil was already marching off, and Dermot's expression was so woebegone that Kirsty groaned and gave in.

'OK, I'll cover for you. But Meriel's lucky Mrs MacNee's away to the optician's this afternoon, or she'd be in trouble, coming back late.'

'Och, you know what she's like.'

'Supposed to be very efficient.'

'Aye, but plays by her own rules.' Dermot had

managed a smile. 'Thanks, Kirsty. I'm starving.'

'Well, don't go for a liquid lunch, eh?'

'Oh, Lord, will you never forget that one time! Look, I'll see you later.'

And I, thought Kirsty, putting aside her coat, *will have to speak to Miss Mildred Grier.*

'May I help you?' she asked politely, and the young woman swung round. She was tall – several inches taller than Kirsty – and quite thin. Able to look good in her expensive clothes, but somehow not seeming sure of herself – perhaps, Kirsty guessed, because she was one who tried too hard. See how she was smiling so eagerly now, as if trying to please a shop assistant she didn't even know.

'Oh, thank you, that's very kind. I was just looking at the skirts.' Her Scottish voice was soft and pleasantly modulated. 'They're lovely, aren't they? My tartan's MacGregor.'

'We have several skirts in the MacGregor,' Kirsty told her smoothly. 'Are you interested in a kilt, at all?'

'Oh, I already have a kilt – it was made here, as a matter of fact – but I thought maybe a skirt would be nice to have, too.' Miss Grier was looking round a little vaguely, and Kirsty took down one of the skirts and held it for her to see.

'Perhaps you'd like to try one on, Madam? There's a fitting room just here.'

'Yes, well, maybe later.' With a sudden air of decision, Miss Grier fixed her large blue eyes on Kirsty. 'I wonder – would it be possible to have a word with Mr Macrae? I'm just ... you know ...

calling on the off chance.'

'He may still be at lunch,' Kirsty began, keeping her face expressionless, when Miss Grier, her eyes shining, interrupted her.

'It's all right, thanks – look, he's here!'

As Andrew came striding into the shop, she called his name and took a step towards him.

'Mildred!' He had stopped in his tracks, staring, but was quickly recovering himself. 'How nice! I didn't know you were coming in today.'

'It was just a spur of the moment thing – I was passing.' She was flushed, her eyes still very bright. 'I thought I'd see how you were.'

'Fine, fine.' He kissed her cheek. 'Come into my office and we'll have a chat.' Suddenly becoming aware of Kirsty, he gave a rueful smile, to which she returned a half smile of her own.

'So, you got to serve Miss Grier?' Lil asked, when Kirsty finally returned to the workshop. 'What was she after? Nothing wrong with that kilt I made, I hope?'

'No, no, said she wanted a skirt. Really just wanted to see Andrew.'

'And did she?'

'Aye, he came back from lunch and took her into his office. Looked a bit shattered, to be honest.'

Lil gave her a considering stare. 'You didn't mind?'

Kirsty was bent over her sewing. 'Mind what?'

'Well, Mr Macrae entertaining Miss Grier.'

'No, why should I? I feel sorry for her, to be honest.'

Lil shook her head. 'Shows you're no' jealous, then. Plenty of women would be hopping mad if their man had gone off chatting to an old flame.'

'I wouldn't call her an old flame. She's just someone he took to dances. He's never been interested in her.'

'Pull the other one! Why'd he take her to dances, if he wasn't interested?'

'He told me he wasn't and I believe him.'

'There you are then, you're no' jealous. Anybody with the green eye would never have believed him.' Lil clipped off some threads. 'I mean, look at me with Dermot. I was jealous, all right.'

'That was different.'

'Aye. And talking of Dermot, you should never have let him go off and leave you to do his work. Why should we help him out, because his darling Meriel can't come back on time? I wish Mrs MacNee had been in today; she'd have sorted 'em both out.'

'Had to go for reading glasses. Says she's tired of holding everything two feet away from her eyes.'

It was some time later that Meriel came sauntering into the workroom, curious to know about Mr Macrae's visitor. He'd been saying goodbye to her at the door, and taking his time about it as well. Rather plain, Meriel thought her, but well dressed. Nice suit with the new boxy jacket – would have cost her a bit.

'You should know, seeing as you once worked in a dress shop,' Lil said snappily. 'That was

Miss Mildred Grier, used to be Mr Macrae's girlfriend.'

'Sort of,' Kirsty amended. 'He took her to dances now and again.'

'Really?' Meriel's clear eyes rested on Kirsty's face with interest. 'So, why'd she come in to-day?'

'Supposed to be thinking about a skirt. If you'd been back on time, you might have sold her one.'

'The way she was looking at Mr Macrae, I don't think it was skirts she came to see,' Meriel remarked coolly.

At the end of the day, when everyone had gone except Kirsty, Andrew came up to her at the door, where they'd drawn the blinds, and kissed her long and deeply.

'Sorry about Mildred,' he murmured. 'I don't know why she suddenly decided to come in to see me.'

Doesn't he? Kirsty thought.

'Anyway, you didn't mind, did you? We only talked for a while and then I said we'd be in touch and she said she ought to go. I thought of taking her out for a cup of tea, but you might not have been happy about that, I suppose.'

'Why, you could have taken her for tea, Andrew. I wouldn't have minded.'

'Oh, I thought you might.' In the dusky light, it was impossible to read his expression, but he sounded surprised and a little hurt. 'You once thought she was someone I cared about.'

'But then you told me you didn't.' Kirsty

shook his arms. 'Were you thinking I'd be jealous?'

'Well, I would have been myself. If anybody from your past had called here to see you.'

She stiffened and let her hands fall. 'There's no one from my past likely to call here, Andrew. Look, I'd better go for the bus. You know what Lena's like when I'm late.'

He sighed and took out his keys. 'Wish we'd been going out tonight, Kirsty. We don't go out enough, you know. Let's have dinner tomorrow and book for that play at the Lyceum. That should cheer me up.'

As they locked up and left the shop, she didn't ask him why he needed cheering up. It might have been because of her. Or it might have been because of guilt over Mildred Grier. Better not to find out, either way.

Fifty-Two

Unflappable Reid didn't seem too worried over sitting his finals. He left that to Angie, who hovered round like a wraith as he left every day for another exam. Or, to Lena, who said she was biting her nails for him, so she was, and she wished she'd never promised Kirsty not to ask him what his plans were.

'I mean, what's going to happen when he gets this degree?' she muttered to Kirsty one evening, when Reid was revising in his room, and Angie reading in hers. 'Wedding bells, or what?'

'I wouldn't be surprised, Lena.' Kirsty was making an effort to do some mending – not her favourite job. 'Will you look at these tights? They're no' worth saving, are they?'

'One time, you'd have tried, though.' Lena shook her head dolefully. 'But we live in a throwaway society, so they say. Chuck 'em out, then.'

'No need to look so glum.'

'I'm thinking of this wedding. Are they serious? In my opinion, Angie's too young. She should give herself time. To look around, enjoy life.'

'All she wants is to be loved.'

'Well, we love her, eh?'

'She's grateful, Lena, for all you've done, she really is. But...'

'I'm no' her mother. Aye, I know. Nothing can make up for what Beryl did, eh?'

Kirsty rolled up the throwaway tights. 'Except that Reid can offer something different,' she said softly.

'I'd better start saving up,' Lena said after a pause. 'Though there mightn't be much time. How much do weddings cost these days?'

'How long's a piece of string? They won't want a splash. It'll be a register office ceremony and a drink afterwards, that's all.'

'Never!' cried Lena. 'We'll have to do better than that!'

First came the day when Reid came back from

college looking pale and drawn. The women of the family were at the table, pretending to eat ham salad; actually, they were just waiting for him. They knew the results were being posted up before lunch, and that he'd gone out early to wait for them. Afterwards, come what may, good or bad news, he'd be having a drink with his friends. 'Don't wait tea, eh?' he'd said as he went out.

No, no, they wouldn't wait tea. Just couldn't eat anything, that was all.

'Oh, why doesn't he come home?' wailed Angie, throwing down her knife and fork. 'He knows what it's like for us.'

'He'll be with his pals,' Lena told her. 'Said he would. Said we shouldn't wait. Have some more tea.'

'I don't want any more tea!'

'Listen, I think he's here,' cried Kirsty. 'Oh, God, he's opening the door.'

They sat in silence, three women frozen to their chairs, as he came slowly through the doorway, shoulders drooping, eyes cast down.

'Reid?' cried Lena. 'Did you get 'em?'

'Reid!' Angie shrieked. 'Why don't you give us the news?'

He's done badly, Kirsty thought. *He wouldn't look like that, if he'd done well. Oh, Lord, what do we say? It means so much – it's his whole career – all his plans with Angie...*

Then she caught a sudden glint in her brother's eyes and leaped to her feet.

'Reid, stop teasing! Tell us what you got!'

'Ta-ra!' he cried, and threw his arms wide, a

300

broad grin splitting his face. 'A First, is all. Sorry, folks, I couldn't resist it!'

'Reid!' cried Lena, shaking her head, but laughing, as he kissed her and twirled her round, then hugged Kirsty, who was laughing too while, in the background, Angie quietly burst into tears.

'You rotter, eh?' Kirsty was whispering. 'Nearly took me in, too. And oh my word, smell your breath! How much did you have?'

'Ah, come on, hardly anything. Half a pint. Had to celebrate.'

But he was already moving towards Angie, who was standing very still, letting the tears drift down her cheeks, and as he said her name, she came to him. Went into his outstretched arms and leaned her head on his shoulder, then raised it so that they might kiss. And watching the kiss, Lena gave a long, trembling sigh.

'What were we saying about weddings?' she asked Kirsty.

Afterwards, they all felt hungry and sat down to eat again, with Lena adding more buttered rolls, more ham, more tomatoes, and a pile of new potatoes – because of course Reid was a man and needed to stoke up. Which would have made Angie furious at one time, but only caused her to exchange a smile with Kirsty now.

Fresh tea was made and the special treat of a strawberry cake sliced – for a celebration as it turned out, not the consolation it might have been. And then Reid sat back and said, covering Angie's hand as it lay on the table, 'Lena, we have something to tell you.'

'As though I don't know what it is!' she cried.

All he and Angie wanted, Reid said, was to get wed as quietly as possible, with no fuss and the smallest outlay they could get away with. Which would surely suit Lena?

'No, it wouldn't, Reid. I'm no' one for wasting money putting on a show, but you have to have a wee bit of a celebration to mark the day. I mean, it's important, eh?'

'Most important thing in our lives.' Reid and Angie exchanged smiles. 'But the truth is, Lena, we haven't got much choice. None of us has any cash to spare.'

'I've a bit put by.'

'Best hang on to that. You've done enough already, helping with the trip to London.'

'Couldn't you get some pub work?' Kirsty asked.

'No time. We want to be wed as soon as we can. Thing is, I'm applying for jobs now. I've got an interview with a Glasgow firm next week.'

'Glasgow?' Lena frowned. 'I suppose it's no' so far away. Edinburgh would have been better, though.'

'The Glasgow firm's more what I want.'

'Well, you could still stay on here. If you got it?'

Reid glanced at Angie. 'It wouldn't be so easy, Lena, commuting to Glasgow for the sort of work I'd be doing. I'd probably be on a training scheme to begin with, then away on projects, you see. I wouldn't be working nine to five.'

'We thought we'd do best to get a flat in Glasgow,' Angie put in. 'I could get a job there easily enough.' She put her hand on Lena's arm. 'Like you say, it's no' far away. I'd always be over to see you.'

'Sounds good,' Kirsty commented cheerfully.

'Just got to get the job.' Reid laughed.

'Oh, you'll get the job,' Lena told him.

'No question,' Kirsty chimed.

After agreeing to leave wedding plans until after the Glasgow interview, Reid and Angie went out together to celebrate, and Kirsty and Lena sat down to watch television.

'Aren't you meeting Andrew?' Lena asked, fiddling with the channels.

'Thought I'd stay in – see how things went for Reid.'

'Well, now we know.'

As Lena sighed heavily, Kirsty put her arm round her shoulders. 'Why so gloomy? Looks like they'll only be going to Glasgow.

'It's the break, though. Has to come, eh? To every family?' Lena sniffed. 'You'll be next.'

'Nothing's planned.'

'I'll see you have a nice wedding, anyway.'

'Let's get Angie's over first.' Kirsty opened the evening paper. 'Now, let's see what's on.'

It was late when the young lovers returned to the flat. So late that Lena and Kirsty had both retired to bed, though Kirsty was not asleep, and she was willing to bet that neither was Lena. There were murmurs and subdued laughter from the living room, then silence, and Angie appeared at the side of Kirsty's bed.

'Goodnight,' she whispered.

Kirsty's head shot up. 'Angie, where are you going?'

In the half light of the summer night, she could just make out Angie putting a finger to her lips. 'Where d'you think?'

'To Reid? But what'll Lena say?'

'We're engaged, aren't we? And don't worry, we're organized.' She laughed softly. 'See you in the morning.'

As she glided away, Kirsty lay back, her thoughts in turmoil. Young Angie in Reid's bed? And 'organized', as she put it? But then, it was true, they were engaged, and as Kirsty herself had once said to Jake MacIver, girls didn't need to wait for marriage these days.

Why should she feel so taken aback, then? It wasn't as though she wanted to sleep with Andrew. Oh, but to think of Angie, who'd always been the little sister, moving ahead of her, being the experienced one, leaving Kirsty at the starting line, so to speak.

Better try to get some sleep, she told herself. And better not think what Lena was going to say in the morning.

In the event, Lena made no comment in the morning, as Angie slipped back into her own room to collect her clothes. But when Reid was heard singing his head off in the bathroom, she turned to Kirsty at the table where she was setting out the breakfast things.

'Hear that? Hear what Reid's singing? "Get

304

me to the church on time". Hasn't waited for the church himself, eh?'

'It's the modern way,' Kirsty ventured.

'Oh, yes, so folks tell me.' Lena gave her a sharp look. 'Think I should have a word with Angie? I'm responsible for her, you know.'

'I think she's responsible for herself now, Lena.'

'And if I do say anything, what good would it do?' Lena slapped down cereal bowls. 'Way they're going they'll be married before you can say knife, anyway. I might as well keep quiet.'

'That'd be best,' Kirsty said with relief.

Fifty-Three

'Well done, Reid!' Lil commented, when Kirsty gave her the news of his success next day as they hung up their jackets. 'And well done me.'

'You've passed your bookkeeping exam?' cried Kirsty.

'Aye, I have. And though I say it as shouldn't, I think I deserve a pat on the back. In view of the circumstances.'

'I think you do, too. You've shown a lot of—'

'Guts?' Lil laughed shortly. 'It was more a question of not losing face. Just didn't want to give certain people the satisfaction of seeing me fail.'

'Ah, come on, Dermot would never have

wanted that!'

'OK, a certain person, then. Better say no more.'

'What comes next then?' Kirsty asked hesitantly. 'You're never still thinking of changing jobs?'

'I'm thinking just that. Thing is, I know I've a lot more to learn about bookkeeping and general accounts, but I'm sure I've done enough to look for an office job.' Lil showed a marked copy of the adverts page in the local paper. 'I've already started looking, as a matter of fact.'

'Oh, Lil!'

'Oh, Kirsty!' Lil mimicked. As they moved out to the workroom, she took Kirsty's arm. 'Isn't You-Know-Who tempting you with a diamond ring, or something? He'd have you engaged tomorrow, if he could, and next thing you'd be married and away!'

'We've already got one wedding coming up,' Kirsty told her. 'Reid and Angie are going to get wed as soon as Reid gets a job, which might be in Glasgow.'

'Reid and Angie!' Lil's face was a study. 'Why, I never thought of such a thing! Isn't she sort of his sister?'

'No relation at all. And they're really in love, Lil. You should see them together.'

'Should I?' Lil sat down and threaded a needle, squinting at the thread, not looking at Kirsty. 'Well, there you are, then. You can have a double wedding.'

'That's not on the agenda,' Kirsty only had time to say before Mrs MacNee came bustling in, still, of course, wearing her hat, which was a summer straw with artifical daisy trimming.

'Morning, girls!' she cried. 'And a sunny one, for a change. Maybe it's turning out nice again, as that comedian used to say.'

'Maybe,' they agreed.

When Kirsty took Andrew's coffee in to him, he leaped up, closed his door and kissed her passionately – a pleasant little custom he'd lately taken up, though she had her misgivings.

'Supposing someone follows me in, Andrew? What would they think?'

'Might be the best thing that could happen.' He took a sip of coffee. 'I don't give a damn who sees us now.'

'Oh, well, never mind – I've got some news. Two pieces, as a matter of fact.'

'News? Sounds interesting. Come and sit on my knee and tell me.'

'Just for a second, then.'

Perched on his knee, she told him of Reid's success, which made him gave a long low whistle.

'A First? That's terrific. I always knew he was a clever chap. The world'll be his oyster now. What's the second piece of news?'

'Reid and Angie are engaged. They're going to be wed, as soon as Reid gets a job.'

Seeing his grey eyes widen, she gave an amused smile.

'I'm sort of getting used to everyone's amazement. Maybe I'd better say straight away that they aren't related in any way.'

'I understood that.' He looked at her thought-
ully. 'Still, it's a surprise. Angie's been like a
sister to you both, hasn't she?'

'Never to Reid. He never thought of her as
family.'

'Well, well.' As Kirsty slid from his knee and
straightened her kilt, Andrew still seemed lost in
thought. 'They'll be getting married, then?' he
asked at last. 'Reid won't have any trouble in
finding a job, I imagine.'

'He's got an interview in Glasgow next week.'

'And they'll want to be married as soon as
possible?'

'Oh, yes. Thing is, they haven't a bean. It'll
just be a register office wedding and then a few
friends meeting afterwards.'

'Why, Kirsty, I could help there. I'd be glad
to!'

'Oh, no, Andrew, thanks all the same. We
couldn't let you do that.'

'I tell you, I'd be glad to help give them a good
send off. Why not?'

'No, no, Reid could never accept. They don't
care about making a splash, anyhow. Just want
to be wed.'

'Just want to be wed.' Andrew suddenly seized
Kirsty's hand and clasped it strongly. 'They're
not the only ones. When are we going to make it
official, Kirsty?'

'Andrew, this isn't the time to go into that.
Better give me your coffee cup—'

'To hell with my coffee cup.' He drew her into
his arms, gazing intently into her eyes. 'Hasn't
it made you want to think about your own

wedding, Kirsty? Seeing Reid and Angie so happy? We could be the same. We're going to be the same. One day. It's always one day, isn't it? Never today?'

'I've said I'll marry you, Andrew,' she said, releasing herself from his arms. 'And I mean it. Just ... don't rush me, eh? Just let me come to it in my own time?'

'What else can I do but that?' he asked sombrely, his eyes as wintry as his mother's could be. 'You're in the driving seat.'

'Something wrong?' asked Mrs MacNee as she passed Kirsty leaving Andrew's office, her look serious, her colour high.

'No, no, why should there be?'

'Well, you were so long in there, we were beginning to think you'd got lost.'

'Mr Macrae was just ... asking me how things were going.'

'As though he doesn't know!'

'In trouble?' Dermot asked, appearing from the front shop as Mrs MacNee returned to the workroom. He grinned in his old way. 'What've you been up to, then?'

'Nothing that would interest you!' Kirsty snapped, then halted. 'But here's something that might. Did you know that Lil's thinking of leaving?'

His grin faded. 'Lil is? No, I didn't know. Why ... why would she do that?'

'She's just passed her bookkeeping exam – the one you didn't get to take. Now she's looking for an office job. She'll soon be gone, is my guess.'

He was silent for a minute or two. 'I never thought she'd want to leave,' he said finally. 'But, thanks for telling me.'

'Just don't tell Lil I did, OK?'

'No need to worry about that. Lil never lets me talk to her about anything these days.' Slowly, he walked away, his shoulders drooping, while Kirsty, her mind back with her own concerns, went to wash the coffee cups.

Fifty-Four

How well things worked out for someone like Reid, Kirsty came to think in the weeks that followed. Had he been born lucky, as well as clever? Hard to say, but certainly arranging his life seemed to give him no trouble, and she couldn't help envying him.

Of course, he got the job in Glasgow, and even though he said he would only be part of the training scheme to begin with, he'd be earning enough to marry on. Just as they'd planned, he and Angie could then give notice of marriage to the registrar, providing the required four weeks' notice.

They could even have a little reception at an Edinburgh café, now that Reid, with the prospect of earning, was willing to spend what savings he had left and Lena was keen to make a contribution. Afterwards, there would be a honeymoon – not in some exotic place, but in the tiny flat they'd rented in Glasgow. What could be sweeter? Oh, my, what a lucky pair!

'Aye, you might say that,' Lena commented. 'But they've not always had it so easy. At least, Angie hasn't.'

'No, but whatever Reid touches seems to turn to gold,' Kirsty answered. 'If you see what I mean.'

'He's clever, he works hard, there's no luck about it. All I say is that they're far too young to be taking all this on. They should've waited till Reid was more settled in his job.'

'Are you joking? He'd never make Angie wait a minute longer than she has to!'

'Who's waiting?' Lena asked coolly. 'Och, things are very different for young folk now from when I was young.'

At which, Kirsty hurried away before Lena thought to ask why she was one who was waiting so long.

Stitching all day at work, Kirsty had never been one for home dressmaking, yet when she set her mind to it, she was good at it and knew that now was the time to get the sewing machine out, when money was so tight. The wedding day had been fixed for the end of August and early in the month, she, Lena and Angie took a day off from work to shop for material and patterns for their oufits.

'I can do a bit, you know,' Lena promised. 'I used to make you lassies plenty of clothes in the old days, eh?'

'Sure you did, and very pretty they were,' Kirsty told her. 'So, all offers of help will be gratefully received.'

'As long as you don't look at me!' Angie cried. 'I've enough trouble sewing a button on. Don't tell Reid, will you? I don't want him to know until after we're married that I'm no good at darning socks.'

'Darning socks?' Lena cried, laughing. 'Why, as I told Kirsty, we live in a throwaway society now. Who darns socks these days?'

'Come on, let's get going to the shops over the Bridges,' Kirsty said, marshalling her troops. 'Logie's is too expensive, even with your discount, Angie. Now, what colours d'you have in mind, then?'

'Anything but white,' Angie declared, and grinned at Lena's expression. 'And I'm no' thinking what you're thinking, Auntie Lena. It's just that nobody wears white for a register office wedding, do they?'

'And I'd always pictured you girls getting married in white,' Lena said mournfully. 'Kirsty, it'll have to be you.'

'I'm only thinking pink,' Kirsty said hurriedly.

'For now,' Lena murmured.

As the great day in August approached, wedding fever began to take hold for the women of the family, with Kirsty rattling away on the sewing machine, Lena writing out lists of things to do and spring cleaning the flat, in case 'folks came back', and even Angie stirring herself to help, when not going through to Glasgow to work on the flat, while Reid began his training.

Earlier, it had been her task to write out informal invitations to everyone in Clover and quite a number besides, which had made her smile a little.

'Talk about a quiet wedding!' she'd remarked. 'This has snowballed. Are you sure you want all these folk from the sweetie factory to come, Auntie Lena?'

'There's just a token few, Angie, and you're inviting lassies from Logie's, eh?'

'Well, how about you, Kirsty? You want Lil and Dermot?'

'Oh, no, they don't really know you,' Kirsty had said quickly. 'And they won't want to go anywhere together now.'

'So, it's just Mr Macrae?'

'Yes, I'd like Andrew to come.'

'I should think so too, after his kind offer!' Lena exclaimed. 'Imagine wanting to help pay towards Angie's reception!'

'Suppose he is family,' Angie said idly. 'Sort of.' She'd looked thoughtfully at an inky finger. 'Kind of wish we could've taken him up on it.'

'Of course you couldn't take him up on it!' Lena cried. 'The point is he might be "sort of" family, but he isn't family. Not yet.'

'All in good time.' Kirsty had risen from the machine. 'Want to try your dress on, Angie? I just need to check the hem.'

'Oh, yes, please!' Angie cried.

'Canna keep Andrew waiting for ever,' Lena had whispered, while Angie disappeared into her room. 'It's no way to treat a man, Kirsty, keeping him dangling.'

'Plenty of folk have long engagements, Lena.'

'Aye, but you've no' even announced it, eh?'

'I told you, we have an understanding.' Kirsty hesitated. 'I do care for him, you know.'

'But does he?'

They said no more as Angie, in her unfinished blue wedding dress, came swaying in, turning like a model on the catwalk, to show off her slender loveliness.

'What d'you think?' she asked, and gave a delighted smile as Lena said she'd never seen a prettier bride, and Kirsty, running to pin up the hem, asked who would care about white, if they could look like Angie in blue?

'It's all thanks to you, Kirsty,' Angie said seriously. 'Making me this lovely dress. I really am grateful.'

'Me, too,' Lena said. 'Have you seen my two-piece?' She turned to Kirsty with sudden concern. 'But what about you, Kirsty? Mustn't forget yourself now!'

'Soon as I've finished this hem, I'll start on my suit,' Kirsty promised. 'And then I've to find a hat.'

'Aye, it'll soon be the great day.' Lena gave a little sniff and hastily turned away her head. 'Before you know it, Angie, you'll be away.'

'I know,' Angie answered, and gave a radiant smile.

Fifty-Five

On the morning of the wedding, Andrew drove up to Clover in his newly polished car to collect Angie and her two witnesses, Lena and Kirsty. Looking immensely elegant in a suit of dark grey with a white carnation in his buttonhole, he caused quite a stir amongst the watchers from the rest of Pleasant Hill as he ran up to the main door.

'Hey, are you the bridegroom?' somebody called, at which he smiled, and shook his head, glad to be drawn inside by Kirsty who had been waiting for him.

'As usual, punctual to the minute,' she said, closing the door and kissing him swiftly. 'It's so good of you, Andrew, to take us to the register office.'

'You know I'm glad to be of help.' His eyes went over her, in her new pink suit and matching hat. 'How lovely you look, Kirsty! As beautiful as the bride.'

'Och, no, wait till you see Angie! But guess what?'

'What?'

'The lift's no' working!'

As they ran up the stairs together, they were both laughing, which made Lena, looking out from beneath a large cream cartwheel hat, open her eyes in surprise. She'd never seen Andrew Macrae laughing before and thought how young it made him seem. Maybe Kirsty was thinking the same?

'Come in, come in, Mr Macrae – I mean, Andrew,' she said now. 'We're all ready, and it's that kind of you to give us a lift, we really appreciate it.'

'Don't mention it. I'm only too pleased to be able to drive you smart ladies into Edinburgh.'

'Smart? Wait till you see Angie. Angie, where are you, pet? Andrew's here. It's time.'

Out came the vision in blue who was Angie, and Andrew had to admit that he'd never seen anyone look better. What was it about weddings, then, that transformed women? Somehow, the magic never seemed to touch men, however elegant, in quite the same way. Perhaps they just didn't feel like women about weddings? Yet he did, thought Andrew. Oh, God, he did. He wanted a wedding, all right, to this little pink-suited witness, who was still smiling at him and breathing hard, after their run up the stair.

'Pity I couldn't have taken Reid and his friend as well,' he said hoarsely, but Lena shook her head.

'No, no, we couldn't have Reid seeing Angie before the wedding. He's stayed the night at Vinnie's; he'll make his own way in.'

'As long as he's there!' Angie cried. 'Oh, I'm that nervous, I'll never survive!'

'What a piece of nonsense!' Lena was adjusting her hat and locking the door. 'Come on, now, down the stair and away. Soon as you see Reid, you'll feel better.'

Which of course was true. Having run the gauntlet of the watching neighbours and driven smoothly through the Saturday traffic to the register office, as soon as Angie saw Reid waiting for her, she felt so relieved, she could have burst into tears. But then there was her make-up that Kirsty had spent so long applying – she shouldn't cry, she told herself, and hugged Reid instead, exchanging with him a long ecstatic kiss that was only ended by somebody calling them in to some room they didn't even see. To be married.

Soon, it was all over. The rings were on their fingers, all names had been signed, there had been more kisses and embraces, and then Angie and Reid, Mr and Mrs Muir, were outside being pelted with confetti by Vinnie and Niall, folk from Clover, Reid's friends from college, and Angie's friends from Logie's.

'Hang on, hang on!' Reid cried, laughing and running his hands through his hair. 'We want to reach our taxi!'

'See you at the reception,' called Andrew, guiding Lena and Kirsty to his car.

'Aye, see you at the café!' shouted Vinnie, her new hat a brighter red even than her old one, sliding over one eye. 'Come on, Niall, it's no' far.'

'Leave something for us!' called Dick Murdoch, grinning, as Reid and Angie climbed into their waiting taxi. 'Och, only joking!'

* * *

'Phew!' gasped Reid. 'I'm glad that's over!'

'Oh, no,' Angie replied, looking blissfully back at the confetti throwers. 'Now I've done it, I'd like to get married all over again.'

'To me, I hope?'

She felt for his hand and turned the ring she'd bought him.

'What do you think?' she whispered.

Fifty-Six

In the café, the guests sat at tables for four.

'No top table, all democratic here,' Reid announced to laughter. 'And no speeches,' he added, to applause. 'Help yourselves from the buffet, sit where you like and feel free to move around.' Cheers all round.

'This isn't too informal for you?' Kirsty asked Andrew, sitting next to her, keeping her voice down so that the young men opposite – college friends of Reid's – shouldn't hear.

He looked a little put out. 'I see you still think of me as an old stick in the mud. Of course it's not too informal for me. I find it a pleasant change from the usual thing.'

'Andrew, I never think of you as an old stick in the mud! How can you say that?'

'Sorry. If it's not true.'

'It's not true!'

'Let's have a little toast, then.' He touched her glass with his. 'To our wedding, whatever it's like.'

'To our wedding,' she echoed, and drank.

Reid's friends began to make conversation, until as the meal continued it became clear that people were on the move.

'Do we have to circulate?' Andrew whispered. 'Seems a new idea – I've only moved round at drinks parties before.'

'Typical Reid,' Kirsty answered, at which his friends laughed before moving on themselves, as Lena arrived to capture Andrew to sit with her and Vinnie, and Niall slipped quietly into Andrew's place.

'Hi, Kirsty! Mind if I sit here?'

'Of course not, Niall. How smart you're looking, then!'

It was true. Seeing him clearly for the first time in a formal dark suit, she was struck by his elegance. And some subtle difference about him. Was it his clothes that made him seem no longer just the boy next door? She didn't think so.

'In my interview suit?' He laughed. 'Nothing like as smart as you. You look terrific.' He glanced over at Angie, still sitting with Reid. 'Angie, too. She's beautiful.'

Kirsty, studying him as he turned back to her, wondered again about his possible feelings for the girl he'd called beautiful who'd married his best friend. Was he secretly suffering? Or, was it true what Angie had suspected, that there was someone else in his life? A mysterious girl at the electronics firm? How little one ever knew about what was in other people's hearts, she mused, then flushed a little as she met his gaze and hoped he couldn't read her thoughts.

'Can I get you a dessert?' she asked quickly, but he leaped to his feet and said he'd bring one to her.

'What'll you have? Black Forest gateau, trifle, or fruit salad?'

'I see you've checked them out already!'

'Too right, I always check out the puds.'

'Black Forest gateau, then, please.'

'And one for me. I'll be back in a jiffy.'

'No one's joined us,' she remarked, as he came back with their gateaux, at which he smiled.

'That's fine, we can have a good old talk again. I'm going in to work earlier these days, so I don't see you on the bus any more.'

'We always liked to talk,' Kirsty murmured.

'We did.'

For some moments he sat, twirling his spoon, not eating the mass of chocolate sponge and cherries on his plate, his eyes resting on Kirsty. How dark they were! Like his mother's and Cormack's, except that theirs so often seemed to be flashing or smouldering, showing their feelings for all to see, while Niall's ... Kirsty wasn't sure at that moment what Niall's showed. They were fine eyes, anyway.

'How's work going?' she asked, beginning to eat, as he did the same.

'Very well. My evening classes are a great help. I'm really beginning to think I'll make an electronics engineer one of these days. Of course, I'll never be in quite the same class as

Reid – he's special, as you know. Probably be going abroad pretty soon.'

'Abroad?' Kirsty stared. 'We never heard that.'

'Well, that firm he's with has a lot of overseas contracts on the go.'

'Where, exactly?'

He shrugged. 'All sorts of places. Mauritius, Fiji, Singapore – could be anywhere.'

'I wonder what Angie thinks about that?' Kirsty said thoughtfully. 'She's never been abroad.'

'She'll go where Reid goes. They're so much in love, eh? Like one person.' Again, there was the intense gaze levelled on Kirsty's face. 'And how are things with you, then? Will you and Mr Macrae be tying the knot soon?'

She hesitated. 'I don't know about soon. We have ... an understanding.'

'I see. I told you, didn't I, that your heart wouldn't stay broken?'

'You said I'd mend it myself, which I did.'

'But I think I said someone new might mend it, too.'

'Did you?' She seemed to be hesitating again, unwilling, it seemed, to speak of Andrew and herself. 'Mr Macrae – Andrew – isn't really someone new. I've known him for years.'

'In a different way.'

Why are we talking about my heart? she wanted to ask. Why not yours, Niall? Does that need mending, too? But she only looked around and said she couldn't see Cormack. Had he not come? She knew he'd been invited.

'You know Cormack – a bit of a law unto

321

himself these days. Never know what he's up to.'

'He'll settle down.'

'Sure he will.'

Before Kirsty could say more, clapping sounded again as Angie and Reid cut their wedding cake, and she looked up to see Andrew returning to their table.

'Coffee's on its way, with the wedding cake,' he told her, glancing at Niall, who leaped to his feet.

'Have you met Niall, Andrew?' Kirsty asked. 'Our neighbour, and Reid's friend.'

'Oh, yes, we met outside the register office. Hello, Niall. But don't get up. I'll sit opposite, shall I?'

'Sorry, Mr Macrae, I took your place.'

'No need to apologize, we were meant to move round. And do call me Andrew, please.'

He pulled out a chair and sat down facing them, seeming for the moment rather like a teacher waiting for his pupils' answers. But when the coffee and wedding cake arrived, he relaxed and became his pleasant, easy self again, until one of Reid's friends called for silence.

'No speech,' he promised, 'but I'm taking Reid and Angie to the station now. So, could you all rise to drink a toast to the bride and groom before we go? If you haven't got any wine left, there's more coming round now.'

'The bride and groom!' everyone cried, watching Reid and Angie lovingly kiss, and then the reception was over.

* * *

As the newly-weds departed through another cloud of confetti, a crowd of guests, including Lena and Kirsty driven by Andrew, followed to Waverley Station, where hugs and kisses of farewell were exchanged, and Lena, clutching a box of left-over wedding cake, shed a few tears.

'Ah, come on, Lena,' Reid said, laughing. 'We're only going to Glasgow – no' Timbuktu!'

But you might be going to Timbuktu, Kirsty thought, remembering what Niall had told her – and, as Lena had pointed out, the young couple were going a lot further than Glasgow anyway. Into a new life, leaving their old one for ever.

It all seemed a little flat, when the Glasgow train had pulled out and the final waves had been made, and Kirsty, like Lena, felt the tears coming, thinking that there would be changes for her, too, without Angie and Reid.

'We'll just go home, eh?' Lena murmured, wiping her eyes.

'Aye, we'll all go home,' Vinnie said comfortingly. 'Niall, you coming?'

'Sure, why not?'

'I can take everyone back,' Andrew told them. 'Plenty of room for five.'

Lena glanced at Vinnie, whose eyes had lit up at the prospect of a lift, and said it was very good of him.

'Won't say no, eh, Vinnie?'

'This way, then. The car's at the back.'

At Clover, after the others had made their thanks and gone inside, Andrew and Kirsty exchanged quick kisses.

'I suppose you'll not want to come out this evening?' he asked quietly.

'Think I'd better stay with Lena. Cheer her up.'

'And tomorrow? Sunday, remember.' He hesitated. 'How about if I take you and Lena out to lunch somewhere? Think she'd like that?'

'She'd love it!'

Kirsty kissed him warmly. 'See you tomorrow, then. And Andrew, thanks – for all you did today.'

'My pleasure, sweetheart.'

Back in the flat, she found Lena making tea and Vinnie setting out the board for a game of Monopoly.

'Brought this round,' she told Kirsty, pushing back her thick tangle of hair. 'Nothing like a game to take your mind off things, eh?'

'Have some tea first and a wee bit more wedding cake,' Lena offered glumly. 'Angie's going to come over some time to cut it up for sending away. If she doesn't eat the almond icing first, eh? Always was one for the almond icing.'

'Oh, Lena, Reid's right,' Kirsty laughed. 'You're so sad – anybody would think they'd really gone to Timbuktu!'

'Quick, let's have the tea, then get started,' Vinnie urged. 'I love a game of Monopoly. Next to bingo, it's my favourite.'

'Shake the dice, then,' Niall ordered cheerfully.

He'd changed from his dark suit into sweater and jeans but Kirsty, covertly studying him, wondered ... Was he back to being the Niall she knew? Or still the one she'd glimpsed at the reception? His character was deeper than she'd thought. As deep, as unknowable, perhaps, as those heavy-lidded eyes he seemed to like to turn on her.

'A six – that's great,' he was saying to his mother, but she knew he had caught her gaze and quickly looked away. 'Shake again!' he cried. 'Euston Road, Ma. OK, move the hat – you always take the hat.'

'Euston Road – that's where we stayed in London,' Kirsty murmured. 'Seems so long ago.'

'A lot of water's passed under the bridge since then,' Lena remarked.

'Oceans,' Kirsty said, and the newly-weds came into her mind. Would she ever have thought, only a few short months ago in London, that she'd be sitting here, playing Monopoly, while Reid and Angie were on their way to Glasgow? To their honeymoon?

'Come on, then, Kirsty,' Niall murmured, touching her arm. 'Your turn.'

'She's miles away,' Vinnie commented with a laugh. 'With that nice Mr Macrae, I shouldn't be surprised. What a sweet man, eh?'

'Just what I say,' Lena said. 'Why, Kirsty, you've landed on Pentonville Road. Want to buy it? Niall's banker.'

'Might as well,' Kirsty answered, counting out her money.

Fifty-Seven

On Monday morning, when it was back to work after all the excitement, Lil didn't seem to mind hearing about the wedding. In fact, she took pleasure in being given all the details, and quite understood why she hadn't been invited, the numbers being limited to those who knew Reid or Angie.

'I'm sure they'll be very happy,' she told Kirsty. 'From what you've said, they seem right for each other.' At one time, she'd thought the same of herself and Dermot, but of course did not speak of it. 'Andrew enjoy the wedding?' she asked.

'Said he did, and was very good about driving us around. Aye, even took Lena and me to North Berwick for lunch yesterday – to cheer her up.'

'Bet she was thrilled over that!'

Kirsty smiled reminiscently. 'She was.'

In fact, there had been a bitter sweetness about taking Lena to North Berwick. She'd been so happy, having lunch at the hotel, seeing the sea again and the Bass Rock, the ships on the horizon, the boats close at hand. It had saddened Kirsty to think how rarely they'd done this sort of trip together. Very occasionally, there had been a coach outing for her stepmother with

Vinnie, and she'd enjoyed it, of course. But how long had it been since they'd come out as a family after they'd all grown up? Reid, Angie, herself? And now, Reid and Angie had gone, and it had been left to Andrew to think of taking Lena out, to cheer her up.

I'll do more in the future, Kirsty vowed. *I'll make sure Lena gets to the sea again*. But as her eyes sought Lena's with that message, it was suddenly very clear that Lena's were saying something else.

'Who's brought us here, Kirsty? Who thought of it? Such a kind-hearted man, Andrew is – why aren't you marrying him? He'd give you every-thing you want – what are you waiting for?' And with all these unsaid things so very obvious in Lena's eyes, Kirsty's gaze had fallen.

It was true that she was waiting and wasn't sure what for. 'Canna keep a man dangling,' Lena had told her. Perhaps the time had come – not to wait any longer, not to let Andrew dangle any more.

'Mrs MacNee not in yet?' Kirsty asked casually now, bringing herself away from yesterday and laying out the kilt she was finishing. 'It's nice, just the two of us, eh?'

'Better tell you, before she comes, that she was saying on Saturday that it was funny you and Mr Macrae had taken the same day off.'

'Funny? Why should she think that? I booked the Saturday some time ago, and Andrew can take time off any time he likes.'

'I know. Search me, why she should've said

anything at all. But it's all right, I sidetracked the interest.'

'How?'

Lil laid down her needle, smoothed her work with a slightly shaking hand. 'Told her I was putting in my notice,' she said quietly.

Kirsty's eyes widened, her lips parted, but for a moment she couldn't speak.

'I did say I might,' Lil murmured.

'I ... never thought you would,' Kirsty got out huskily.

'And still don't believe me? You're like Madam, when I told her. She just couldn't take it in. Mind, it was all a big surprise to her.'

'Have you found another job, then?'

'Aye. With Foster's Investments. Firm in St Andrew Square. It's just clerical, but they're going to give me training. I'm going to work for more exams.'

'Oh, Lil!' Kirsty had given up all pretence of working. 'You've no idea what this means to me. Home's changed, now work's going to change. I'm all at sea.'

'Well, thanks for the congratulations,' Lil said dryly. 'Means a lot to me, too, what I'm doing. No' to mention change.'

'Oh, Lil, I'm sorry I'm just thinking of myself, instead of you! And you've done so well. I do congratulate you, honest I do!' Kirsty rose and hugged Lil hard. 'It's just ... well, it's taken me by surprise. Have you written your notice out for Andrew yet?'

'Yes, I've got the letter all ready. I'm going to put it on his desk this morning.'

'He's sure to try to get you to change your mind.'

'Not a chance.'

Kirsty sat down at her table again. 'So, what on earth did Mrs MacNee say? She must have been ready to explode, thinking of having to train somebody again! Oh, she'll be in a state.'

'Told me to take the weekend to think it over.' Lil shrugged. 'I didn't even say I would. I'm looking at a new future – why should I stay stuck where I am, just to suit her?'

'I think she's going to miss you, that's all, Lil. Just like I am.'

'I'm going to miss you, too, Kirsty. But it's the way things are. You know the situation.'

'Morning, girls!' came Mrs MacNee's voice, and in she came, staring from one to the other of the young women without smiling. 'Well, Kirsty, how did the wedding go? Very well? That's nice. And now you'll have heard Lil's news, I take it?'

'Yes, Mrs MacNee.'

'It's pastures new for you, isn't it, Lil? You've finally got tired of fuddy-duddy Macrae's, eh?'

'I wouldn't put it like that,' Lil said in a low voice.

'Well, I'm sure I don't know how else you'd put it. You must've found something wrong, to want to move into the great money-bags world of St Andrew Square!'

'You know what went wrong for me here!' Lil suddenly cried, leaping up with a scarlet face. 'If you'll excuse me, I'll go and give Mr Macrae my letter.'

'He's no' in yet.' Mrs MacNee advanced and put her hand on Lil's arm. 'Look, I do know things haven't gone well – on the personal front, sort of thing – but you were getting through, you were weathering 'em. There's no need to give us all up and go into a new job you mightn't even like!'

Lil stood still, her flush gradually fading. 'Mind if I make a cup of coffee?' she asked wearily.

'I'll make it,' Mrs MacNee declared grandly. 'Coffee all round is what we need.'

As she swept out, Kirsty stared across at Lil. 'See anything different about her?' she asked. 'No, what?'

'She's taken off her hat.'

While Mrs NacNee tried to remember how to make the coffee – she hadn't done it for years – Lil slipped into Andrew's office and laid her letter on his desk, while Kirsty hovered around, waiting for him to arrive.

He was leaving that afternoon, she knew, to take his mother for a holiday with relatives in the Borders, and would be staying there a couple of days himself. How would he be, though, when they met, unusually, at lunchtime as they'd arranged? In as much of a state over Lil's notice as Mrs MacNee, was Kirsty's guess. No owner of a kilt makers' business ever wanted to lose good staff.

Meantime, Meriel was watching with amazement as Mrs MacNee finally came staggering along with a tray of coffee, and Dermot's eyes on Lil, who was still outside Andrew's office, had sharpened.

'What's up?' he whispered, striding across to Kirsty, but she only shrugged.

'Better ask Lil.'

'She's just been into Mr Macrae's office – what for?'

'I told you, speak to her.'

'Here comes Mr Macrae, anyway,' Dermot muttered, turning away.

'And you've got customers,' Kirsty called after him, but he made no reply, leaving Meriel to step forward to give her sweet smile to the man and woman who'd just come in.

'Morning, morning,' Andrew called cheerfully. 'Not too bad, either. Is that coffee I smell already?'

'Early today, Mr Macrae,' Mrs MacNee told him. 'I'll bring yours in now, shall I?'

'Oh, hell,' Lil said to Kirsty, 'Madam's going to be there when he opens my notice. Then they'll talk about me.'

'Only to be expected,' Kirsty answered. 'Quick, let's drink this coffee before the balloon goes up.'

It was terrible coffee, but scarcely mattered, as they'd hardly begun to drink it before Mrs Mac-Nee was out of Andrew's office and calling for Lil to go in to see him at once.

'Won't do much good,' Kirsty murmured, as Lil, rather pale, set down her cup and hurried to obey the summons. 'She's made up her mind to go, and I don't blame her.'

'After all her training,' Mrs MacNee moaned. 'All her experience! Now we'll have to try to find someone new. It'll affect you as well as me, Kirsty. And you'll have lost a friend, as well as a work mate.'

'Don't need to tell me that, Mrs MacNee.'

'Och, I feel sometimes I could strangle Dermot! If it hadn't been for him falling for Meriel, we wouldn't be losing Lil now.'

'Some people might blame Meriel?' Kirsty suggested, but Mrs MacNee shook her head.

'No, it's Dermot's fault. I always blame the man, being so stupid as to be taken in by some silly girl. It'll all end in tears for him, too. Mark my words.'

It was not long before Lil returned to the workroom, now red in the face again, but Andrew came with her. His eyes went to Kirsty, then Mrs MacNee, and he gave a brief smile.

'Looks like Lil here is definitely going to leave us,' he said lightly. 'My words were to no avail.'

'I'm sorry,' Lil muttered, staring at her feet. 'I just feel I've got to move on.'

'It's your life, Lil, you must do what you think is best. But I'm not going to say I'm happy about it. You'll be a great loss.'

'That's right,' Mrs MacNee declared. 'And how we're going to manage, I don't know. We're going to have to find an experienced kilt maker. No point trying to train somebody up when we'll be so short-handed.'

'We've got contacts; we'll have to do what we can.' Andrew glanced at Lil. 'In the meantime, could you give us more than a week's notice,

Lil? When do your new employers want you to start?'

'Middle of September, but I could ask them to make it the end, if that would help.'

'It would indeed. All right, we'll leave that with you. But could you get on with drafting an advertisement for the local paper, Mrs MacNee? Stressing that we need someone with experience?'

'Certainly, Mr Macrae, I'll do that now.'

Andrew, with one last look at Kirsty, had returned to his office, and Mrs MacNee was busy writing out the advertisement, when the uneasy peace of the workroom was broken by Dermot's sudden appearance. He went directly to Lil.

'Lil, can I speak to you for a minute?'

'I'm busy, Dermot.'

'Dermot, leave Lil alone!' Mrs MacNee called. 'She has work to do.'

'Meriel says she thinks you've put in your notice,' Dermot said, keeping his eyes on Lil, refusing even to look Mrs MacNee's way. 'Is it true?'

'Aye, it is.' Lil's voice was a little high, but she was succeeding in keeping calm. 'I'm moving to a firm in St Andrew Square. I'm going to be making a complete change and I don't want to discuss it with you. OK?'

'Look, Lil, you mustn't do this. It'd be stupid, right? How will you get on in an office, after working here? You'll regret it the minute you start. And if it's just to get back at me—'

'It is not to get back at you!' she flared. 'I

333

wanted to do the bookkeeping course, didn't I? And I stuck at it, I did well, and I'm going to do well at Foster's, too. So will you just get back to the front shop and leave me alone?'

'Lil, please!'

'Dermot!' Mrs MacNee thundered. 'Do you want me to call Mr Macrae? Please return to your work now!'

As Lil kept her eyes steadfastly down, Dermot reluctantly moved to the door, from where he turned to look back, only moving away when Meriel's voice was heard calling, 'Mr Sinclair, can you come? There are people waiting.'

After he'd gone, no one spoke. Mrs MacNee took her advertisement through to show Andrew, while Lil rose and put on the iron for pressing. Kirsty worked on for a little while, then looked across at Lil.

'He doesn't want you to go,' she said softly.

'Too bad. I'm going.'

'I think things might be falling apart between him and Meriel.'

Lil set up the ironing board and said nothing.

'Mrs MacNee just said this morning that it would all end in tears.'

'No' mine,' Lil said, damping a cloth. 'My tears are over. I'm starting afresh, and that's all there is to it.'

'That's all right, then.'

'Want to meet for lunch?' Lil asked, after a pause.

'Sorry, for once I am meeting Andrew. How about tomorrow?'

'Fine.' Lil smiled. 'You see, you made it,

didn't you? You changed your life?'

'I'm still here, Lil.'

'You know what I mean. And I say, good luck to both of us, eh?'

'Good luck to both of us,' Kirsty echoed.

But it seemed to her that it didn't do to rely on good luck to be happy. You had to be sure what you really wanted, and maybe Lil no longer knew. Her face, for instance, as she tested the pressing iron, was showing a sadness her brave words denied.

Fifty-Eight

It was a lovely evening. As Kirsty walked down the Mound, the air was so soft and warm, she fancied herself abroad somewhere – the South of France, maybe, or, Spain, where people went on holiday these days and where, of course, she'd never been. Without the usual Edinburgh wind, and surrounded by Festival visitors from every sort of place, it was easy to imagine she might be somewhere different, and just then, she rather wished she was.

The day had been so tiring. So hot, so stressful. With Lil grimly working away, as though to make the point that Mrs MacNee needn't think she was slacking off, just because she was working her notice. And Dermot serving in the front shop with such a look of misery, Meriel was so exasperated that she couldn't even put on her smile for customers. And Mrs MacNee had expressed herself worn out with the strain of it all, and wished that Mr Macrae had not chosen this particular time to go on holiday, leaving her to cope.

As though Andrew had wanted to go away! As he'd said over their snatched little lunch, it was the last thing he wanted, to be away from Kirsty, to be away from work, now that they had to start looking for Lil's replacement. But what could he do? He'd promised his mother, he couldn't let her down.

'Of course not,' Kirsty had agreed.

Besides, there was no immediate need to worry. Lil would be staying on for a while yet, so there'd be plenty of time to find another kilt maker.

'Another kilt maker!' Andrew had groaned. 'As though they grow on trees! You know how difficult it is to find someone good who's looking for a job. If they're good, they'll have a job already.' He had looked at her with hopeless eyes. 'You don't know anyone, do you?'

She'd thought for a moment, but had had to admit that all the experienced kilt makers she knew were already happily employed.

'There you are then. Oh Lord, Kirsty, I've got to go! Got to collect my mother and throw some stuff into a bag.'

'You'll only be away a few days,' she'd told him as they parted at the door of the café. 'Back in no time.'

'See you soon, then, darling.' He'd kissed her

336

quickly. 'Take care.'

'And you.'

'Of course.' He gave a smile and a wave, but as he hurried away to his car, she could tell his thoughts were again with Lil and her notice to quit that was so ruining the pleasant status quo at Macrae's.

Looking down at the visitors strolling round the West Princes Street gardens, Kirsty thought she might take a little walk there too. She was in no hurry to get home, having warned Lena that she might be working late, but Mrs MacNee had surprised them all by deciding to close at the winter time of five.

They'd all had a difficult day, she declared, with a cold glance in Lil's direction, and she was sure Mr Macrae would not have objected if they wanted to close up.

'Too right!' Meriel had whispered, and had immediately telephoned a friend to arrange a meeting, while Dermot stalked out and Lil said she had to dash to the shops while they were still open. Which had left Kirsty free to enjoy walking on her own down the Mound, to smell the flowers from the gardens, to enjoy the evening.

'Kirsty?' a voice said close by, and she stood still.

'Kirsty,' the voice said again, and because she had to, she slowly turned her head. Yes, he was there, beside her, vivid blue eyes smiling, his hand on her bare arm. Jake MacIver had been following her down the Mound.

For some moments, they did not speak. Tourists passed them, some exclaiming at the floral clock they could see at the foot of the Mound, some more interested in the castle above, wrapped in heat-haze mist. All probably wondering why these two people were stuck to the pavement, not moving on with the job of sightseeing, just getting in everyone's way.

'I was waiting for you when you left the shop,' Jake said, quietly. 'Felt sure you'd have someone with you, but you seemed to be on your own.'

'So, you followed me.' Kirsty, trying to appear calm, could hear her voice shaking. 'Why? What are you doing here?'

'I just came back from Germany yesterday. Wanted to speak to you.'

She put her hand to her damp brow and turned away. 'There's no point, Jake. We have nothing to say.'

'I have. I have a lot to say. Ever since I saw you at King's Cross, I've been thinking out just what it would be when we met again. And here we are, meeting again.'

'We aren't meeting, I'm going. I'm going for the bus.'

'No, no.' He slid his hand to hers. 'We're going for a drink. You can't refuse me that.'

'I am not going for a drink with you.' She pulled her hand free. 'Why don't you just walk away and leave me to go home?'

'Because things have changed. I've changed, Kirsty.' His eyes on her face were very serious. 'You have to hear me out.'

338

'No. No, I don't.'

'Yes.' He took her arm, made her walk beside him. 'Look, it's a beautiful evening. If you won't come for a drink, let's just walk in the gardens. Join all those folk down there. What harm could that do?'

In spite of herself, she let him lead her down past the floral clock and into the gardens, once the site of the old Nor' Loch, long since drained, where now the trees were still in full luxuriant leaf and the scent of the flowers filled the air. How pleasant it would have been – without this man, walking at her side.

He was still holding her arm, but she wrenched it away.

'You needn't hold me, Jake. I'm no' a prisoner on the run.'

'You might run away from me, though.' His far-sighted eyes were searching for a bench, but all were, of course, taken. 'Shall we sit on the grass? It's dry enough.'

'I don't need to sit down, I shan't be staying long. Let's keep walking.'

'All right. As long as you stay long enough to listen to me.'

'Looks like I've no choice.'

But she knew, and he would have known, too, that she did have a choice. She could have run away from him when he'd first appeared. Taken off for her bus stop, where he could hardly have followed, unless he'd wanted the queue to hear what he'd had to say. No, he'd have given up. He'd have seen she was serious about not want-ing to let him talk to her, and that would have been the end of it.

Instead, she'd somehow, she didn't know how, allowed him to bring her here. She'd given him the power he'd always had. Or seemed to have done. Now she must show him it wasn't true. He had no power over her. All that was over.

'Say what you have to say,' she told him quickly. 'Then I can go.'

He looked down at her with a considering air.

'You've changed, too, Kirsty, haven't you? Grown up. Become more confident.'

'About time,' she murmured.

'Just as beautiful, though. Perhaps more so.'

He stopped suddenly in the middle of the path, and for a moment held her shoulders.

'Oh, Kirsty, what the hell was I doing, letting you go? I've been over and over it, in my mind. Asked myself, and asked myself – and got nowhere.'

'I seem to remember you said you didn't want commitment.'

'I know. I thought it was true. Always had been before.' His smile was rueful. 'But after I'd been in America a while, I came to see that it wasn't true any longer. I knew I'd made a mistake.'

At the look in her eyes, he let his hands fall.

'You don't believe me? Why d'you think I sent you those postcards? I gave an address. I thought you'd reply.'

'As though I would!' she cried hotly. 'After what had happened!'

He winced and shook his head. 'That's me, you see, Kirsty. Never think things through. Of course you didn't want to reply, after what had

340

happened, but it took time for me to see that. When I did, I suppose it sank in ... that I'd lost you.'

'Let's go,' Kirsty said abruptly. 'I don't want to listen to any more of this.'

'No, there's a bench free – someone's just got up. Please, Kirsty, let's sit down for a moment. Give me that, at least, won't you?'

Once more, against her better judgement, she let him lead her where she didn't want to go, and together they sat down on the empty bench.

Fifty-Nine

He took her hand in his and gently smoothed it.

'For a long time, I pretty well resigned myself to thinking I'd just have to accept things. I'd made a mistake and I had to live with it. Then I saw you at King's Cross.'

When she said nothing, he gave a short laugh.

'I couldn't believe it. You, in London. My Edinburgh girl! It seemed like a message.'

'A message?' She stared at him.

'Sounds ridiculous, but it seemed to me that seeing you again was a sign that I shouldn't give up. At least, not without finding out if there was any hope of a second chance. But I was going to Europe. I couldn't get out of it, without letting everybody down.'

'You said I'd changed,' Kirsty said slowly.

'You couldn't tell that at King's Cross?'

'Because you brushed me off the way you did? It was only what I expected. You'd no reason to think I might have changed myself.' His mouth twisted a little as he let her hand go. 'All you could see was a guy who'd let you down. A womanizer, "one for the lassies". Somebody you couldn't trust. But what I have to try to make you see, Kirsty, is that that's not true. You can trust me.'

'Can I, Jake?'

'Yes. Because I love you.'

She was silent for so long, he bent his head to look into her face.

'Doesn't that mean anything to you?'

'Not now.'

'How can you say that?'

'It's come too late. One time, it would have meant everything. But I've moved on.'

'Not from me. No, I don't think so.'

'I'm sorry, Jake.' She raised her eyes bravely. 'I should've told you before. The fact is, I'm engaged.'

In spite of the awkwardness and pain of her meeting with him, she couldn't help feeling sweet triumph at the look of astonishment in his eyes. Had he believed she'd still be pining for him? Just waiting for him to come back and pick up her shattered pieces?

'Engaged?' he repeated, recovering himself. 'I don't see any ring.'

'Unofficially engaged, I should've said. We've no' announced it yet.'

'Who's the lucky man, then?' His tone was curt. 'Do I know him?'

'Oh, yes. It's Andrew Macrae.'

'Andrew Macrae?' Again, there was the look of astonishment, mixed now with something else. Amusement? As Jake put his hand to his mouth, perhaps to hide an actual smile, Kirsty felt a flush rising to her brow.

'The one we used to call the Grey Man?' he asked. 'No, that's impossible. He's far too old for you, for a start.'

'He's your age. And he's no' grey at all.'

'My age? He looks a hell of a lot older, then.' Jake's amusement, if it had been amusement, had faded. 'You're serious, though, aren't you? You're actually going to marry him?'

'Why not?'

'Because you don't love him.'

'I do love him! He's kind and loyal; he's somebody I'd always trust!'

'Yes, and I suppose he's not badly off, he'll make you nice and comfortable, but you don't love him the way you loved me. The way you still love me, in fact. Come on, Kirsty, admit it. In spite of all that's happened, it's there, isn't it? That feeling for me? In your heart?'

Very smoothly, he drew her into his arms – oblivious, as she was, too, to passers by – and kissed her gently, the way he'd first kissed her all those months ago outside the flats. There was nothing threatening about the kiss, nothing in fact passionate. Just a reminder of how things used to be for them, in the early days of their affair, before love and its problems had over-

343

taken them. And when he let her go, he was smiling as he'd smiled then, though Kirsty was still as a statue, reliving a time she thought she'd put from her mind.

'"Ae fond kiss and then we sever,"' he whispered, close to her face. 'To quote dear old Rabbie Burns. Is that what you want, Kirsty? One kiss before we sever? But why need we sever at all? That's my question. Give in to what you really want, my darling. Forget the kind Grey Man. He can never make you happy – not like I can.'

Then he kissed her again. A different kind of kiss. Strong, passionate, a demonstration of what he was offering; intended to make Kirsty remember and compare, to realize what she would be missing if she chose Andrew instead of him.

And it should have worked. She should by now have been so won over that there was no more need for him to fight. Only, when he let her go, he was smiling again, his blue eyes dancing, and she knew the smile was meaningless, that there was nothing there behind it, nothing for her, never would be again. A Cheshire cat's smile, as in the story, with nothing real about it. Nothing, in fact to love.

And the blue eyes that could mesmerize audiences all over the world? She closed her own eyes against their power, seeing other eyes – grey eyes, then, strangely, dark ones. Fine dark eyes that she had come to know so well. The image vanished as quickly as it had come.

'I have to go, Jake,' she said, rising quickly. 'Don't come with me. It'd be best just to part

344

here. I'll go for my bus.'

'Are you joking?' he cried, leaping to his feet. 'I'm not letting you go now we've found each other again! Kirsty, wait!'

In spite of all her efforts, he caught her, easily, as she went zigzagging through the strolling tourists to her bus stop in Princes Street, and though her face was set and turned away, his hand was on her arm again, and she could sense that he was smiling.

'Kirsty, there's no point in running away.' He stood close, keeping his voice down so that the people in the queue couldn't hear. 'You're not running from me, you're running from yourself. What good will that do?'

She opened her mouth to speak, to tell him again he was wasting his time with her, when the screaming siren of an ambulance hurtling along Princes Street, followed by two police cars and a fire engine, made her stop and turn pale. Such sounds, such sightings, always made her nervous, and in that, of course, she was not alone. Nearby people were looking worried and exchanging glances, and even Jake was wincing.

'Ouch,' he murmured, 'where are they going?'

'They're no' the first,' someone murmured. 'There's been a whole fleet o' ambulances and fire engines tearing along here.'

'Must be a big fire somewhere,' a woman whispered. 'Och, makes you shiver, eh? Canna wait to get home to see if it's still there!'

'Shouldn't think they'd be going to Pleasant Hill,' Kirsty said, almost to herself. 'Probably a

345

warehouse, or something.'

'I'm sure you're right.' Jake took her hand. 'But look, my car's not far away – let me take you home quickly. Put your mind at rest.'

'There's no need for that, thanks. The bus'll be along in a minute.'

'No strings, I promise you. It'd just be one last thing I could do for you.'

As she raised her eyes to his, she saw that his smile had vanished and that he seemed genuinely concerned.

'Just straight to the flats, then,' she said slowly.

'Of course. Didn't I say, no strings?'

Back again in his Lotus Elan, driving out of the city almost as fast as the ambulances, Kirsty could scarcely believe what was happening. How had she let him persuade her to take her seat again in his splendid car? To be close to him, as in the old days, when the closeness had given her pleasure, but now only reminded her of how those days had gone and of how she didn't want them back?

Because the evening was still so warm, the top of the Lotus was down, and the breeze rushing through her hair made her feel a little better. At least, they couldn't talk, and Jake, concentrating on his driving in his best serious manner, made no effort to do so.

Stealing a glance at his profile, she toyed with the idea that if it was true he had really come to care for her, this last drive might be a painful experience for him. The tables would have been turned then, all right, wouldn't they? And she would be having the last laugh. But she couldn't imagine Jake suffering over her, whatever he had told her, and she didn't feel like laughing anyway.

Just let him get me home, she prayed. *Just let him say goodbye to me, and drive away. Then I'll be happy.*

But as they came to Pleasant Hill and tried to drive round to Clover, it was plain that Kirsty was not going to get home that evening and was not going to be happy.

She'd not been right about the emergency service vehicles making for some warehouse instead of her home. For there they were, the police cars, fire engines, ambulances, and Gas Board vans, too, with their crews already out, milling around, carrying people on stretchers, or digging in rubble, or calling to doctors, as clouds of smoke hovered and a sickening smell of gas filled the air.

And Clover? Kirsty's home? Could that be it? That building split down its side as though opened by a mighty tin opener, with all its in-nards of chairs and beds and baths exposed to view? Where was the rest of it – their flats, their homes? Where were the people? Oh, God, where was Lena, and all who'd lived there?

'What's happened?' Kirsty whispered, staggering from the car. 'Oh, no, no! What can have happened?'

'There's been an explosion,' Jake said, tight lipped, his face deathly white. 'Gas, from the smell of it, and see, there are the Gas Board vans. Quick, we have to get out of here! Kirsty, get in the car, now!'

But she was already away, running towards her ruined home, avoiding the watching crowds being held back by police, calling and calling Lena's name. Filled with dread.

Sixty

Of course, they wouldn't let her through, wouldn't let her get close.

'Sorry, miss, you can't come here, it's not safe,' a policeman told her. 'Stand back with the others, eh?'

'I live here!' she cried. 'I have to find my stepmother! She'd have been inside, she'd be there—'

'We're doing everything possible to find folk. Just go back with the others, eh? Come on, I'll take you—'

'No,' she was sobbing. 'No, no, I have to find her, I have to find everybody, I have to see they're all right...'

'Look, don't worry, we'll find 'em for you. This way now...'

'It's OK, I'll look after her,' said a voice Kirsty knew, and she swung round to find Niall, covered in dust, standing beside her, his eyes large on her face, his hands, scratched and sore, taking hers.

'Kirsty, let's go back,' he said gently. 'We

348

shouldn't be here.'

'I'm looking for Lena!' she cried.

'Lena's OK, so's Ma. But I'm looking for Cormack.'

'You should both o' you be out o' this area,' the policeman told them. 'Anybody you're looking for, we'll find, so come on now, move back and take care.'

'It's like a nightmare,' Kirsty whispered, as they joined the silent, watching crowds. 'Look, the sky's dark when it should be light, and there's all this stuff – this rubble – and the terrible smell – are you sure Lena's safe? Where is she, then? And where's your ma?'

'They've both been taken to the Royal Infirmary. Ma's got concussion and cuts and bruises. Lena's shoulder is dislocated and she's badly shocked. They'll both be all right, though, there's no need to worry.'

'Thank God, thank God. But what happened, Niall, what happened? Was it a gas explosion?'

'Don't know for sure. I just heard some of the gas engineers talking when I was trying to look through the rubble. Seemed to think it was a gas leak.'

'Where?'

'Too early to say. Maybe the basement where the boiler is.'

Kirsty had begun to shiver, and to rub her arms, up and down, up and down, as though she couldn't stop.

'Must've been casualties, Niall, with such a powerful explosion?

349

He nodded gravely. 'Nesta Harvie, for one – she was taken to the Western General. And Dick Murdoch's missing, and so's Cormack. Look, I'd better get back to looking for him – they'll let me help search the rubble if I tell 'em I've lost my brother.'

'I'll come with you, Niall!'

'No, no, look at you, you're shivering like you've got the flu. Here, take my jacket...'

She stood quietly, as he wrapped it round her shoulders, and as his eyes met hers, she was reminded of something, but didn't know what. Had she been thinking of dark eyes? Or, grey? Didn't matter now, whichever it was. All she could think of was getting to the infirmary to see Lena, but that would have to wait till they found out what had happened to Cormack.

'I should be helping,' she murmured. 'Niall, I want to help. Where's Dick's wife, then? And the girls? Where's everybody?'

'I wish to God I knew!' He suddenly put his arms around her and held her close, as though to comfort her, or perhaps himself. 'Will you stay here, then, Kirsty, and I'll come back as soon as I can? Somebody said folk from Harebell and Heather were making tea, and the WVS are coming, with blankets and stuff.'

Folk from Harebell and Heather, and probably Briar, too. Lucky, lucky people, she thought, whose homes were still standing – wrapped in smoke, peppered by flying rubble, but safe, so safe.

'Oh, God, why Clover?' she murmured, and then felt ashamed, for why should it have been any of them?

'Yes, I'll wait here, Niall. I'll see if I can find anyone we know. They might be watching – if they're all right.'

'I won't be long.' He waved a battered hand.

She tried to smile, longing for him not to leave her, knowing he must, and she must go searching herself, see what she could do. All these faces around her, some must be from Clover – she must just keep on looking. Oh, but she was so cold, so weary. She would have given her soul just to slide to the floor and lie and close her eyes to the terror around her...

'Kirsty!' a voice voice shouted. 'Thank God I've found you!'

Oh, God, Jake. Come to take her away.

'Kirsty, Kirsty, what the hell have you been doing? I've been looking for you everywhere.'

As he reached her, she saw that his face had picked up the flying dust and his hair seemed dark and strange, but he was the same old Jake, exerting his will, even in a situation such as this, never experienced before.

'Don't you realize we've got to get out of here?' he cried, grasping her arm, knocking Niall's jacket to the ground. 'There may be another explosion – you never know with these things – quick, come with me to the car!'

Very firmly, she shook off his arm and stooped to pick up Niall's jacket.

'No, Jake, I'm staying here. I have to see to my family, I've got to help. I'm going nowhere.'

'Kirsty, I've waited for you, I've been looking for you. I tell you, it's not safe!' He tried to take her hand, but she snatched it away, gaining strength with every moment that she looked into his handsome, frightened face.

'Oh, go on, Jake! Drive away. Drive away, before it's too late. Don't wait for me, I shan't be coming. Don't you understand? I'm never coming with you again.'

Poised to move, he stood for some moments staring at her, his famous blue eyes dimmed. Then he turned and walked swiftly away, through the crowds and the rescuers, the rubble and the dust, and she could no longer see him. Only Niall, who was suddenly back at her side, smiling with relief and holding the arm of an awestruck Cormack, who, considering his surroundings, seemed amazingly free from dust.

'Look who's here!' Niall cried. 'It's Cormack. He's only just come back from work – never was in the flats at all!'

'I was doing overtime,' Cormack said hoarsely. 'Then me and some other guys went to the pub and folk were talking – saying there'd been an explosion and – oh, God, I thought everybody would be dead!'

Tears suddenly squeezed from his eyes and ran down his cheeks, and he put up his hand to wipe them away.

'Look at me, eh? Greeting like a babby!'

'We all feel like that,' Niall told him, hugging him. 'Kirsty, shall we try to get to the Royal?'

'Oh, I want to, I want to – but I haven't found anybody here yet.'

'Still, I think we should go. See how our folks are.'

'Aye, let's go now,' chimed Cormack.

But Kirsty was standing with her hand to her head.

'There's Reid!' she cried. 'And Angie! They'll be sure to come over from Glasgow. They'll be looking for us.'

'The police know who's been taken to hospital – they'll tell 'em where to go.' Niall put his hand on Kirsty's arm. 'I bet they'll follow us there. First, though, let's see if the WVS ladies have arrived yet. You need to borrow a coat, Kirsty, or a cardigan, or something.'

She stared at him, transfixed.

'Why, that's true, Niall. And I've just realized – all we've got in the world now, is what we stand up in. Doesn't that give you a funny feeling?'

'An expensive feeling,' he said with an attempt at a grin. 'Come on, then, let's get going!'

It was only when they were on the bus on their way to the Royal Infirmary that Kirsty remembered Andrew. All formalities had been completed. The police had taken note of their names to tick them off their lists, and they had been given the address of a hostel in the Canonmills area where they would be temporarily put up. Clothes had been lent to them and as they'd been able to wash at a neighbour's in Harebell, they might almost be said to be feeling a little better. Except that they still didn't know exactly who was safe and who was not.

And then for Kirsty, there was Andrew, away in the Borders. She should have phoned him, told him what had happened. He'd be so worried, wouldn't he? Perhaps she could ring him from the Royal? Yes, she'd do that.

'Still worrying?' Niall asked quietly. 'I'm sure Lena will be fine. Ma, too. Or, are you thinking of the others?'

She shook her head, and leaned back against her seat, closing her eyes. Somehow, it seemed easier not to speak of Andrew at that time. He was in her thoughts, though.

Sixty-One

As soon as she saw Lena, lying in her hospital bed in a long Nightingale ward, wearing a hospital nightgown and with her injured shoulder strapped up, Kirsty burst into tears.

'It's just the relief,' she murmured, wiping her eyes, at which Lena managed something of a smile.

'That's good, eh?' she asked weakly. 'Thought it must be the way I look.'

'You look wonderful!'

Which was not, of course, true, for Lena's face was yellowish white and there were violet shadows lining her eyes, but considering all things, she looked well enough to be reassuring. The doctors had replaced her dislocated shoulder joint to its normal position, and having treated her for pain and the symptoms of shock, said she might soon be free to be discharged.

'And go where?' Lena asked. 'Tell me that.'

'We've all been given hostel accommodation till we can be rehoused,' Kirsty told her. 'And we're being loaned anything we need. No need to worry that we'll be homeless.'

'Och, I'm just thankful to be alive.' Lena moved her head on her pillow. 'Thank God you and the laddies weren't home, eh? Thank God there was just Vinnie and me.'

'Can you say what happened, Lena? You're no' too tired?'

'I can tell you, we were in Vinnie's flat – just having a cup o' tea, you ken, before we went to bingo – and then ... oh, God, it was deafening – a terrible noise, like a bomb going off – and a great rushing and rushing of air – until me and Vinnie went sailing across the room. Aye, just sailing, like fairies in the panto, and I remember looking down at the floor, and then hitting it.' Lena's eyes closed, then opened wide with fear. 'And that was it. I never knew a thing till I woke up in the ambulance, with this shoulder giving me stick.'

'Oh, Lena,' Kirsty sobbed. 'To think you might have...'

'Died? Well, I didn't, and neither did Vinnie. She looked so bad when we got here, I thought she'd never make it, but then she opened her eyes and said, "Hi, Lena, hen, you OK?" You know they've put her in a side ward, when she'd sooner be near me?'

Lena sighed, and looked round at the other patients in her ward, most dozing for it was late, and Kirsty had only been allowed in as a special favour. Even now, the ward sister was approaching, probably wanting her to go, but Niall and Cormack, who'd been with Vinnie, were following, and would be anxious, Kirsty knew, to see Lena.

'No, no,' the ward sister said firmly, 'Mrs Muir must sleep now.' But then she looked down the ward at a man and a woman hurrying up and shook her head.

'Are these *more* visitors, then, hoping to see Mrs Muir?'

'It's Reid!' cried Kirsty, leaping up. 'And Angie! Oh, it's so good to see you. Lena, here's Angie, and Reid!'

After the sister's heart had softened enough to let the new arrivals stay, she pulled the curtains round Lena's bed so as not to disturb the other patients and pointed to her watch.

'Ten minutes only, now is that understood?'

'It is,' Reid solemnly agreed, 'and we're very grateful.'

'They've just got in from Glasgow,' Niall put in. 'Though how, I don't know. Reid, did you borrow an aeroplane?'

'Borrowed a company car – drove like the clappers.'

When the sister had departed, Reid stooped over Lena's bed and kissed her cheek, while Angie tearfully pressed her hand.

'I'll no' try to hug you, with your poor shoulder, Auntie Lena,' she whispered. 'But oh it's so grand that you're all right. When we heard the news of the explosion ... Och, we were in such a state ... We thought you'd all ... we thought there'd be nobody left...'

'Me too,' Cormack said. 'I thought the same. When I saw Niall in all the dust, and he told me Ma was OK, I couldn't believe it!'

'And she is going to be all right,' Niall murmured. 'There is the concussion, so they'll be keeping her in for observation, but she should be out soon.' He glanced at Kirsty. 'Maybe we should go, and let Reid and Angie have their time with Lena?'

She nodded and, putting her face close to Lena's, whispered that she'd be back next day. Then she and Niall, with Cormack following, crept from the ward.

'Feeling all right?' Niall asked, as they made for the lift.

'Sort of light headed.'

'Maybe we can get coffee or something downstairs? Or will the refreshment place be closed by now?'

'There's a machine in the waiting room for Casualty,' Cormack told them. 'Saw it when we came in. I suppose I canna smoke a cigarette?'

'You can not!' cried Niall, pointing to a huge notice strictly forbidding smoking. 'But let's see what they've got in this machine you saw.'

Tea, coffee, and hot chocolate were provided by the vending machine in the crowded Casualty waiting room, and they chose the hot chocolate.

'Next stop, this hostel we've to go to,' Niall remarked. 'Don't know about you folks, but it's

357

all just beginning to hit me now. I think I could fall asleep at this table right now.'

'Me, too,' Cormack muttered.

'Should have had the coffee,' Kirsty said. 'To keep us awake till we get to the hostel.'

'This chocolate tastes like coffee, anyway,' Niall said with grin. 'Or could be tea. I think the drinks are all the same in that machine.'

They were smiling with him, when his expression changed and he lightly touched Kirsty's arm.

'There's someone just come in,' he whispered. 'He's looking around. I think it's Mr Macrae.'

Sixty-Two

Hollow-eyed and pale, Andrew sank down next to them on their bench, drinking tea in a paper cup from the vending machine, while describing how he'd driven like a madman from the Borders the minute he'd seen the news of the explosion on the television.

'It was just a small item, but it gave the name of the flats – oh, God, Pleasant Hill, outside Edinburgh. Can you imagine how I felt?'

'Yes,' Niall said quietly. 'We know how you felt.'

'All I could think of was Kirsty,' Andrew murmured, his gaze fixed on her face. 'I didn't even know if it was Clover that had been damaged. I just had to drive and drive, not knowing, and when I got to the site and saw it was Clover, I ... well ... I thought, this is it, this is the end, there's no hope.'

He set down his paper cup and swept his hand over his brow, while Kirsty lowered her eyes.

'I should've phoned you, Andrew. I'm sorry, I did mean to.'

'Who'd have expected you to phone? Anyway, I'd have already left – there was no way you could have contacted me.' He gave a faltering smile and felt for her hand. 'But I've found you, haven't I? Thanks to the police.'

'They'd have had my name,' Kirsty agreed. 'We all had to give our names before we left, so that they could account for us. Did they tell you I'd gone to the Royal to see my stepmother?'

'They did. God, I was so grateful, when they said you were safe.' For some time, Andrew looked down at her hand without speaking. Finally, he looked up, to ask after Lena.

'I hope she wasn't badly hurt? They said your brother was with her in the ward, but wouldn't be staying long.'

Kirsty explained about Lena's shoulder and that they expected her to be released soon, though where she would be going wasn't certain. Perhaps back to Glasgow with Reid and Angie, or perhaps to the hostel.

'What hostel?' Andrew asked.

'The one in Canonmills where we've been offered accommodation. They say it's OK. Nothing special, but clean and well mananged. Vinnie, Niall's mother, will probably have to go there, too, when she's better. She's suffering from concussion.'

'They're just keeping her in for observation,' Niall said quickly. 'She's going to be fine.'

'Thank God you're all OK,' Andrew said fervently. 'But what's this about a hostel? I can't let you go somewhere like that. You must all come to me, in the Grange. My mother'll be only too glad to have you, and tomorrow, we'll set about getting you what you need.'

There was a stunned silence, then Kirsty said, 'Andrew, that's so kind, but we couldn't accept. I couldn't accept. We couldn't impose on your mother that way, could we, boys?'

'Oh, no, couldn't do that,' Niall replied. 'It's very, very kind of you to offer, Mr Macrae – I mean, Andrew – but we really should go to the hostel.'

'Aye, we'd best do that,' Cormack put in.

'They'll be expecting us, you see,' Niall went on. 'And folk from the Council will want to see us, to try to find us what we need – mebbe somewhere else to stay.'

Andrew's eyes went to Kirsty's. 'At least,' he said slowly, 'let me drive you there. It'll be no trouble.'

'Here come Reid and Angie!' Cormack called, with a certain relief in his voice. 'Daresay they'll take us, thanks all the same, eh?'

In the end, though, it was Niall and Cormack who went with Reid and Angie, and Kirsty who went with Andrew.

'You could still come to my mother's,' he said

360

quietly. 'For heaven's sake, why not? You won't be seeing anyone from the Council tonight, anyway. It takes time to organize these things.'

'I know, but I couldn't stay with your mother, Andrew. It just isn't possible.'

'Why? Tell me why?'

She twisted in her seat, as they drove through the darkening streets. 'I'm really tired, you know. If you don't mind, I'd rather no' talk now.'

He drew up, however, some distance away from the hostel, and looked at her in the dusk of his car.

'What is it, Kirsty? Something's changed, hasn't it? I know you're tired – must be exhausted – but please don't make me wait till tomorrow to hear what it is. Please.'

'This isn't the time,' she said huskily. 'Can I see you tomorrow? I won't be going in to work, though.'

'Of course you won't be going into work, but I want you to talk to me now. I want to know – what's changed?'

'Nothing's changed,' she said after a long silence. 'I see that now. What I felt – it's always been the same. But I tried to make it something else.' She swung round to look at him, her brown eyes seeming almost black in her white face, and as he read their message, his own face that had taken on a little colour grew pale again.

'Just say it, Kirsty, say it straight out. You don't love me.'

'I do, Andrew. I do care for you. But if I married you, it'd be for all the wrong reasons, and it

361

wouldn't be fair. You should have somebody who's...' She stumbled a little. 'Someone who's got the right reasons. That's what I can see now.'

'There was a time, Kirsty, when we had a discussion like this before, and I told you then that love would come. I said you didn't have to love me, the way I love you, that marriages are often best when love comes slowly. I said we'd end up being very happy, and I still believe that. Especially after what happened today, when I knew I might have lost you.'

'Andrew,' she said, half crying, 'it was what happened today that made me realize I shouldn't marry you. It's so terrible to think that some folk I know might still be under that rubble. Might be dead. But we're alive and we've only got one life.' She began to cry in earnest. 'We should try to do the right thing. I mean, *I* should.'

'And the right thing is giving me up?'

'For the right person,' she sobbed. 'It isn't me, Andrew. I wish it was!'

'Oh, Kirsty...' He took her in his arms and kissed her with painful sweetness. 'You're very tired, you said so yourself. Maybe you'll feel better in the morning...'

'No,' she said definitely. 'I see now that I've been wanting to tell you this for a long time. I should've done. I was a coward.'

'There's no one else?' he asked wearily.

'No one else.'

She thought of Jake MacIver, who'd told her she didn't love Andrew, and she'd denied it. In her heart, she'd known he was right, but not about the return of her love for him. Oh, no, that would never return. So, there was no one else. Only a pair of dark eyes moving into her mind again, and vanishing like melting mist.

'No one else,' she said again, and kissed Andrew, long and sadly, for the last time.

'"Ae fond kiss, and then we sever,"' he said bleakly, but she put her fingers across his mouth.

'Don't say that, don't quote Burns.'

'He knew about love, though.' Andrew sank back against his seat. 'Ah, Kirsty, I suppose if I'm honest, I've seen this coming. Would never let myself believe it, but deep down, I think I knew. You would never set a date, would you? Never let me buy you a ring. Even when I came into Casualty just now, you didn't run to me, as I wanted to run to you.' He touched her damp face as she turned it from him. 'Don't cry any more, Kirsty. You're not to blame.'

But later, when he had left her at the hostel, saying he'd come back next day to see what he could do, she felt that there should have been blame, and that she should cry.

Sixty-Three

It was quite astonishing to her, when she finally returned to work, to find she was being treated like some kind of hero returning from war, even though, as she pointed out, she hadn't been injured at all.

'I was lucky,' she declared. 'And my step-mother and my friends – we were all lucky.'

Not like poor Mrs Farnes, who'd lived over the basement – she had died. So had a man in one of the top flats, who'd fallen several floors, and another, on the seventh floor, who'd had a heart attack when he'd been thrown across the room. Dick Murdoch had finally been dug out from rubble with serious head injuries, but he was recovering in hospital, while Nesta Harvie had had a miscarriage, and George, her husband, had been badly cut by flying glass.

Oh, yes, Kirsty had been lucky, all right. Lucky to be back at work, too, for she'd tentatively suggested to Andrew when he came to the hostel, that he might prefer her to find another job.

'Another job? Good God, no!' he'd cried. 'We can't afford to lose you, Kirsty.'

'I just thought...'

'It might be difficult for me?' His tone had hardened a little. 'Yes, you can say that. But I'll

364

get by. Just don't bring me my coffee.'

Seemingly, that was as far as his reproaches were going to go – which didn't help her to stop feeling terrible. Never before had it occurred to her that being the one who didn't love might be almost as bad as being the one who loved. How she wished now that Andrew could find someone right for him, someone who'd want what he could give, as she had not. But she couldn't find that person for him.

'Ah, but there's other ways of being injured, eh?' Mrs MacNee reminded her, when she'd spoken of her luck in not being hurt. 'I mean, what you went through, finding your home gone and your poor stepmother away to hospital, what a shock that must have been!'

'Could've been you hurt, if you'd gone home sooner,' Dermot muttered. 'Or worse. We were that worried when we heard about the explosion, weren't we, Lil?'

What was this? Kirsty's eyes widened as her personal antennae fluttered. Dermot and Lil standing together in the workroom? Lil not objecting? What had been going on in the week she'd been away?

'I was so happy when I came round to the hostel and found you OK,' Lil was saying. 'Oh, the relief!'

'We had a drink on it when she told me,' Dermot said with a grin, as Meriel, watching, gave a smile of her own.

'Hope you find somewhere to live soon, Kirsty.'

'As soon as Lena gets back from Glasgow, we're going to look for a flat of our own, back in town. Lena's had enough of blocks of flats, even if the boilers don't blow up.'

'Was that what it was? The boiler?'

'So they're thinking, but there'll have to be a full enquiry.'

'Back to work everybody!' cried Mrs MacNee. 'We'll have a celebratory coffee in a minute, eh? And do I hear Mr Macrae's door? You'll take him his coffee, eh, Kirsty?'

'I thought Meriel might do that. I've a lot to do, now I'm back,' Kirsty said quietly.

As soon as they could manage it, she and Lil had a private word in the washroom.

'So?' Kirsty asked. 'Are you going to tell me about it?'

'What?'

'Come on. Dermot.'

Lil coloured and gave a shamefaced smile.

'Oh, Dermot. Well, it was when we first heard about you, we sort of ... well, came together again. For sort of comfort, you see. Because we were so upset. And then he told me.'

'Told you?'

'About him and Meriel. It's all over, that's the thing.'

'She gave him the push?'

'No! Well, to be honest, I don't think she was ever that keen, but he ... well he always said he was under her spell. Then, one morning, he woke up and it was gone.'

'Gone?'

366

'Yes. The spell. It was broken. He said he didn't feel anything for her any more.' Under Kirsty's scrutiny, Lil was smiling nervously. 'Couldn't understand it. I mean, how had it happened?'

'Just died,' Kirsty said. 'They say it can.'

'Well, she didn't seem to care when he told her. Sort of laughed, and said it saved her the trouble of breaking it to him that it was over for her, too. She'd other fish to fry.'

'Other fish to fry ... What sort of fish would they be, then?'

Lil shrugged. 'I expect she's got her eye on somebody.'

'I expect she has. But is it true, then, Lil, that you and Dermot are together again? I thought you'd never take him back.'

'So did I. But then I never thought he'd want to come.' Lil's eyes fell before Kirsty's. 'You think I'm weak?'

'I think, if you're sure he's the one and he's no' going to change again, you should give him another chance.'

'He says there'll never be anybody but me now. And I believe him. He looks like a chap who's just got better from something.'

'Meriel Fever?' Kirsty laughed. 'But what are you going to do about your new job? Are you going to stay here now?'

'No, I'm still leaving. I've worked hard for that job and I want to give it a go. Dermot agrees. In fact, he's going to re-do the book-keeping course. He was the one who wanted to leave for something different in the first place.'

'Is everybody leaving, except me and Mrs MacNee?' Kirsty cried, and Lil sympathetically touched her arm.

'You haven't actually said what's happened between you and Mr Macrae,' she said softly. 'But I can tell something has. Is that all over, too?'

Kirsty nodded. 'Had to be. We were never right for each other.'

'Oh, Kirsty! And he'd have been such a wonderful husband!'

'I'm no' looking for a husband at the moment. Come on, let's put the coffee on, eh?'

'And let Meriel take in Mr Macrae's?' Lil asked, with a lift of her eyebrows. 'You don't think he's the fish she wants to fry?'

Sixty-Four

The days went by and Kirsty, carrying her own special burden, was relieved when Lena decided to return from Glasgow so that the two of them could begin looking for a place to live. It gave her something else to think about, other than Andrew's misery.

'Angie and Reid were that kind,' Lena told her, 'and wanted me to stay on, because I'm no' right yet, but – poor things – it's their honeymoon, eh? I just wanted to come back and get settled again. Somewhere safe.'

Somewhere safe. Well, everybody wanted that. All the survivors of the explosion, at present still in the hostel, wearing their borrowed clothes, felt vulnerable and feared returning to high-rise blocks. But rents being what they were, they knew that that was where they'd probably end up.

'Thing is, we've looked into the abyss,' Niall said to Kirsty, when they'd walked out one evening after their hostel supper. 'Makes us different. Once you've looked into the abyss, you know it's always there. That's why folk are desperate to feel safe again.'

'You can never be really safe,' Kirsty murmured. 'In this world.'

'Just have to do what you can.' Niall shrugged. 'Pick up the pieces, try to be happy.'

'I've given up on that for the time being. Being happy, I mean.'

For some moments, he was silent, glancing at her and then away. 'It's over with Andrew?' he asked at last.

'Yes, it's over.' As he said nothing, she added, 'For the best.'

'I should say I'm sorry.'

'No, I told you, it was for the best. I wasn't right for him.'

Niall cleared his throat. 'So, how's he taking it?'

'Just as you'd expect.' She shook her head. 'Making it easy for me.'

'He's a nice guy, Andrew.'

'Yes. But I feel bad. All I want is for him to

find someone else.'

As long as it wasn't Meriel, thought Kirsty. She'd been looking very pleased with herself lately, hadn't she? Could it be true she was setting her sights on Andrew? He did think her a very pretty girl. Who wouldn't?

'Better go back,' she sighed.

'Suppose so. Och, we should be grateful, eh, to have a roof over our heads? But I don't mind telling you, I'll be glad to move on. Ma wants to look for something in town, like Lena.'

'Maybe we'll be neighbours again?'

'I'd give a lot for that.'

As he took her arm and they began to stroll back to the hostel, she felt how pleasant it was to be with him, how his presence had always soothed her and helped her in a way she couldn't explain. Yet, at the door where they paused and she looked up into his face, his eyes seeking hers were suddenly not soothing at all. Not soothing ... What, then? She felt a tremor pass through her as their arms tightened and she was suddenly conscious of his body close to hers.

Oh, not soothing. Exciting. Passionate. That was how his look seemed now; that was how she found his nearness, and his breathing that was, like hers, coming fast, as though they'd both been running. Exciting. Passionate.

'Lena's thinking of Stockbridge,' she gasped.

'Good idea,' he whispered.

'She's heard of a flat near a photographer's we know.'

'Is that right?'

He was bringing his face close to hers – surely,

they must kiss – when Cormack's voice sounded and his tall, thin figure, complete with cigarette drooping from one hand, was inserting itself between them.

'Look out, you two, I want in!' he cried cheerfully. 'Cocoa time, you ken.'

The moment had gone, and with it the magic. Had she imagined the whole thing, Kirsty wondered, as they stood for a moment in the hallway that smelled of floor polish, humanity and food cooked long ago.

'See you tomorrow,' she said at last.

'No, thing is, I'm away to London.' His gaze on her was tender, but he had lost his smile. 'Got to go on a course.'

'Oh. How long for?'

'Two weeks.'

'I expect it's important?'

'Aye, I need it. Think I'll look OK in someone else's suit?'

'You'll look fine.' She managed a smile herself. 'See you when you come back, then. If we haven't moved. Lena's very keen to take this flat Mrs Moffat's found.'

'Think she could find one for Ma next door?'

'And how long will you be able to stay with your ma?' Kirsty touched his cheek lightly. 'In the future, when you get your qualifications, I bet you'll have to move away.'

'Who knows about the future?' he asked quietly. 'Kirsty, folk like us have to live for today.'

That night, in the Spartan dormitory she shared with Lena, Vinnie and other women, she lay awake for some time, reliving those moments with Niall that had so confused yet thrilled her. It seemed so strange; she'd known him for so long as Reid's friend, and maybe Angie's admirer, and he'd always been in the background. Just a friend – a good friend, sympathetic, encouraging – but not more.

But then there had been those mysterious flashes through her mind of dark eyes fixed on her, and she had known they were special. Dark eyes. Niall's eyes. And it was with Niall that evening, at the hostel door, that her world had turned upside down.

Had she really imagined what had passed between them? Or had it been as real for him as for her? That sudden excitement – passion – it had been something she'd never felt with Andrew. And if it had been part of Jake MacIver's spell, it had only been based on shifting sands. Not real. Not like those fleeting moments of intense feeling with Niall had been real.

And as she turned against her pillow, and listened to Lena's steady breathing and Vinnie's spluttering little snores, she knew that there had been nothing imagined about that little encounter at the hostel door. It had been just as real for Niall as for her. Which meant – what? That she wished he wasn't going to London in the morning.

She looked for him at their self-service breakfast, but as she set down her tray of bowls of porridge, Vinnie, whose face was still an artist's palette of colours from old bruising and healing

372

cuts, told her that Niall was already away.

'Aye, gone for the early train to London. Very pleased, too – shows they think well of him, eh? To send him on that course?'

'He'll do well, just like Reid,' Lena told her, adjusting the sling on her shoulder and beginning to spoon up porridge with her free hand. 'Two clever laddies, they are.'

'And I'll tell you something else,' Vinnie said, accepting a cup of tea from Kirsty. 'Our Cormack's turned over a new leaf since what happened to Clover. Aye, it's true. He told me he's taking up his piping again – going to earn more money – and he's giving up thae awful guys from Briar. There's more to life than them, he says. Would you credit it?'

'Where's he now?' asked Lena.

'Gone to work. Nice and early. Just shows, eh? You never can tell what good'll come out of something bad. Kirsty, pet, will you pass me the sugar?'

'Next thing is to get us moved,' Lena declared. 'I'm definitely going to take that flat over the post office that Junie Moffat told me about. It's dear, but it'll be worth it, eh?'

'Definitely. I feel the same. No more council blocks for me. When can I come and see this place with you, Lena?'

They began to discuss details as Kirsty gathered up dishes to stack at the end of the table.

'I've to get to work,' she told them. 'See you this evening, Lena. Mrs MacFall, you try to get something in Stockbridge, eh? Then we can be neighbours again.'

'What a thoughtful girl she is, then!' Vinnie exclaimed when Kirsty had left them. 'Fancy her wanting me and the boys to be neighbours again. Some I know would've had enough of us!'

Sixty-Five

'Closing time!' cried Mrs MacNee one evening in late September, and Lil, looking across at Kirsty in the workroom, burst into tears.

'My last day,' she whispered. 'Last time I'll see Dermot lock the door.'

'Might be Prue who locks the door.' Kirsty was smiling sympathetically. 'He's training her.'

'Nice, having Prue,' Lil sighed. 'And no Meriel. Strange, the way it's all happened.'

Strange, indeed. For in only two weeks, there had been many changes at Macrae's. First, Flora Lawson, an experienced kilt maker whose children were now at school, had been appointed to Lil's job and was already working under Mrs MacNee's supervision. And so nice she seemed, and so capable, that everyone had heaved a sigh of relief.

But the really interesting development had been the sudden departure of Meriel and the appointment of Prue White in her place. Kirsty's idea, actually, for she'd always remembered Prue, the sweet girl with a cold at the original interviews, and when Meriel had left them in the lurch without a day's notice, it had been Kirsty who'd thought of asking Prue if she was still interested.

'Am I not!' had been her answer, for she'd just been made redundant at the china shop where she'd been employed, and had been willing to come to Macrae's almost immediately. But, whatever had happened to Meriel, she wanted to know, and who could answer that?

All anybody knew was that she'd come out of Mr Macrae's office one day, after serving him coffee, with a face like thunder, and the next morning had phoned in to say that she wouldn't be coming back. Stunned, everyone had looked to Mr Macrae for an explanation, but, keeping his face totally impassive, he had maintained that he knew no more than they, and they'd been left to their own speculations.

'I'll tell you what,' Dermot had said to Lil and Kirsty, 'I bet she tried something on with Mr Macrae and he told her to get lost. She was like that, you know, always making up to men, smiling and giving the come-hither look, or whatever.'

'We know what she was like,' Lil had told him coldly.

'Well, I think you're right,' Kirsty said thoughtfully. 'I think he was the one she had her eye on.'

'Sure he was!' cried Dermot. 'She was green with envy of you, hooking a big fish like him. Couldn't believe her luck when you let him go.'

'Dermot, have a bit of tact!' Lil cried hurriedly.

'Kirsty doesn't want you discussing her private affairs!'

'That's OK,' Kirsty murmured. 'Just hope Andrew – I mean, Mr Macrae – wasn't upset.'

'If it had been any other guy, folk might have thought he was the one to be trying something on,' Dermot remarked. 'But no' Mr Macrae. Too much the gentleman, eh?'

'That's right,' Lil agreed. 'And I'll tell you something hopeful – for him, I mean.'

'Hopeful?' Kirsty repeated.

'If you want him to find consolation. The other evening I saw him going towards the New Club with that old flame of his. You know the one I mean?'

'Mildred Grier?' Kirsty asked, staring.

'Aye. The one his mother likes. She looked really happy – stars in her eyes, no less.'

'And what did he look like?' asked Dermot.

'Same as usual. Bit down in the mouth. But it's a start, eh? Maybe they'll make a go of it.'

'I hope so,' Kirsty said, and meant it.

But now it was closing time, on Lil's last day. Mr Macrae had already presented her with the fine handbag everyone had chipped in to buy, as well as a farewell card they'd all signed, and now Dermot was ushering out the last of the customers and locking the old door.

'Got you!' he cried, waving the key with a flourish. 'Lil, you'll have to stay.'

'Now, now, Dermot, enough of that,' Mrs MacNee ordered. 'We want to say goodbye to Lil properly.'

'Oh, don't,' Lil groaned, the tears welling in her eyes again. 'I hate saying goodbye.'

'You'll be coming in to see us,' Dermot said swiftly. 'Hi, maybe buy one of our kilts?' He laughed. 'Kirsty can make it, and I'll sell it.'

'Lil will always be able to make her own kilts,' Mr Macrae said kindly, as Lil gave another sob. 'And we'll always be grateful for the excellent work she did for us. Lil, we wish you all the very best in your new post, and hope you will come in and see us. As often as you like.'

'Aye, we'll be here,' Mrs MacNee murmured, dabbing at her own eyes. 'Just canna believe we'll no' be seeing you for work again, Lil. Don't forget us, eh?'

'As though I would!' Lil cried.

'Coats on, then. And we'll shut up shop.'

One by one, everyone shook Lil's hand and wished her luck, but when it came to Kirsty's turn, the two friends hugged each other with sniffs and smiles, remembering all the years they'd worked together, until Dermot took Lil's arm and she really had to go. Mrs MacNee open-ed the door, and after a last look round and a wave, Lil Buchanan finally left Macrae's, to move to a new life. Though still with Dermot, who was walking her up the High Street, smiling as though Meriel had never been.

As the two newcomers, Flora and Prue, left together, Mrs MacNee went around switching off lights and Andrew Macrae stood looking at Kirsty.

'You're going to miss Lil,' he observed.

377

'I am. We'd worked together for a long time.'

'Might have been nice if we'd all gone for a drink with her. But she and Dermot seemed to want to go off together.'

'Yes, I think Dermot was treating her to a nice meal somewhere.'

'I'm glad they've made things up.'

'Yes, it's good.'

He hesitated. 'Everything all right with you, is it, Kirsty?'

'Oh, yes, fine, thanks.' It was her turn to hesitate. 'And with you?'

'You could say, keeping busy.' He cleared his throat and looked at his watch. 'Must go, I suppose. I'm meeting someone. Expect you are, too?'

'I might be.' Why had she said that? Kirsty wondered.

'Goodnight, then.'

'Goodnight, Andrew.'

'All set?' asked Mrs MacNee, bustling back. 'Let's away, then. I'm meeting my Donald. We're going to the pictures.'

'Everyone's meeting somebody,' Andrew remarked, relocking the door when they had left the shop.

Except me, Kirsty thought, watching him walk away, with Mrs MacNee tapping alongside. Why had she pretended otherwise? Because it might be true.

A fortnight had passed. He was due back that day, which was why it might be true that she would be meeting someone. And it was true. For

378

there he was, moving towards her, wearing the casual clothes that had been found for him, the intense gaze searching her face.

'Hello, Kirsty,' he said, stretching out his hands to take hers.

'Hello, Niall.'

'Did you think I'd come?'

'I thought you might. How was the course?'

'Fine. Went very well. Did you get my postcard of Trafalgar Square?'

'Thanks very much, I did.' She could hear herself sounding formal, stilted, and suddenly squeezed his hands in hers and cried, 'Oh, Niall, it's so grand to see you! I've missed you so much!'

'I got the earliest possible train home,' he said quickly. 'Went to the hostel to change and told Lena you might be late back.'

'Oh, my.' Kirsty was laughing shakily. 'That'll have given her something to think about. You and me, meeting up.'

'Why not? I told Ma as well. Seemed pleased, as a matter of fact.'

'Both of 'em?'

'Both of 'em.'

They looked at each other and smiled, then Niall took Kirsty's arm and they joined the tourists strolling up the High Street. 'Shall we go for something to eat?'

'That'd be nice.'

'Where'd you fancy?'

'Anywhere at all.'

'There's a café in Victoria Street.'

'Perfect!'

* * *

Over the meal of chicken and chips, they didn't talk much, only looked at each other a lot, brown eyes meeting dark eyes, and smiled a lot, too, until the waitress brought coffee. Then Niall said quietly, 'It was always you, you know, Kirsty. Always you for me.'

Her glance was startled. 'I thought it was Angie for you, Niall. I thought you were having to hide your feelings when she married Reid.'

'No.' He shook his head. 'Angie's a lovely girl, but she wasn't the one I hid my feelings over.'

'Well, Angie said once she thought you were interested in someone from work.'

'Someone from work?' He laughed. 'How on earth did she get that idea?'

'Saw you once, talking to a girl in George Street. Someone smart, she said, with red hair.'

'Someone smart ... with red hair?' Niall's brow wrinkled, then cleared. 'Pat Webster! Ah, come on – she was just a colleague I must've met one day. She's married to one of the designers, and very happily, as far as I know.' He laughed again, then grew serious. 'No, I mean what I say, Kirsty, you were the only one for me.'

'You never dropped even a hint.'

'Wanted to. Thought I hadn't much to offer, but I was just plucking up courage to speak, when ... well, you know what happened.'

'Jake?'

'Jake, followed by Mr Macrae.' Niall laughed softly. 'Then I was sure I hadn't much to offer.'

'Oh, you had, though,' Kirsty whispered. 'You

380

had. You'd yourself, Niall. Only I wasn't bright enough to see it.'

Their eyes met again, then Niall, taking money from his wallet for the bill, asked huskily, 'Shall we go?'

Out into the darkening evening, they moved slowly, savouring their togetherness, walking arm in arm, as close as they could manage, so wonderfully in tune with each other, that Kirsty could only marvel again that she had been so very slow to recognize what Niall could mean to her.

'Back to Canonmills?' he asked, his eyes never leaving her face. 'Might have gone to a film.'

But by common consent, they decided, on this first special evening, just to walk through the streets they knew, never losing contact, never having eyes for anyone or anything, except each other.

'No need to wait for a bus now,' Kirsty murmured.

'True, but did you know I'm planning to buy a car? Second-hand, of course. I'm going to ask Reid's advice what to get.'

'That's wonderful, Niall.'

Kirsty, reminded of Reid, was wondering what he and Angie would say about her and Niall. Not that there was anything to say yet. But there would be. Oh, yes, there would be.

'I've had a pay rise,' Niall was continuing. 'I'm no' doing too badly these days.'

'That's wonderful, too.'

'Are you listening?' he asked, stopping and cupping her face in his hands. 'Here's me trying to tell you how I'm placed and you're some-where far away.'

'I'm remembering you said we had to live for the day, Niall. Angie said that once, but she didn't mean it. Because you have to think of the future, don't you? What would life be like if you could never look forward to anything?'

Standing in the quiet New Town side street they had taken, Niall slowly drew her into his arms.

'I've changed my mind,' he said softly. 'I want a future, too. Oh, God, I do.'

For a long time, they leaned together, revelling in their nearness, before kissing, sweetly, pas-sionately, for the first time, but not the last. And looking into the dark eyes that held hers, Kirsty knew there would be no 'severing' after this 'fond kiss', no need ever to say goodbye to Niall.

Time passed, and then they walked on, as close as before, through the fading light of the Sep-tember evening, ready for love, ready for the future. Whatever it held.